THE DREAM OF SHILOH

An Arkansas Love Story

The Shiloh Saga, Volume 2

Written by
Patricia Clark Blake

Cover Photograph
Satori. 123rf.com.

Other Titles by *Patricia Clark Blake*
In Search of Shiloh: A Journey Home Through Arkansas© 2017
ISBN 0999841602
ISBN 13: 9780999841600
Library of Congress Control Number: 2018931979
Patricia Clark Blake, Jonesboro, AR

DEDICATION

The scepter shall not depart from Judah, nor a
lawgiver from between his feet, until Shiloh come;
and unto Him shall the gathering of the people be.

Genesis 49:10

The second volume of the Shiloh Saga is dedicated to the Holy Trinity, the source of all creation, inspiration, and grace. I continue to be inspired by the pioneer spirit of early Arkansans as I learn more of the struggles they endured to create the state I now call home, so I dedicate this book to those pioneers of my state who embodied the faith, industry, determination and pride that has built the Land of Opportunity.

I will be forever indebted to the editors who helped me take the manuscript and bring it to the finished novel, The Dream of Shiloh: An Arkansas Love Story. Each of these ladies brought a unique eye and talent to my completed book. Thank you, Beverly Thompson, Brenda Thakkar, Mary Lee Cunningham, and Martha Rodriquez. The book is still not perfect, but without you, it would not have been.

Finally, I dedicate this second book to friends and family who read and loved the first book in the saga. Thank you for your encouragement and requests for more. With love, I dedicate all I write to Tara, Kinley, Kennedy, and Noah. I thrive in your love and support.

CHAPTER ONE

If a man speaks a vow unto the Lord or swears
an oath to bind his soul with a bond;
he shall not break his word. He shall do according
to all that proceedeth out of his mouth.

Numbers 30:2 [KJV c1850]

A marriage of convenience. What fool coined that expression? Patrick MacLayne had experienced neither a marriage nor convenience in the last few weeks. And he could blame only himself for the confusion, frustration, fatigue, and doubt he was feeling.

A solitary two-foot tall stake with a green ribbon fluttering across the meadow of wild flowers and grass captured Mac's eye that April morning in 1857. He rose from the wagon seat where he'd sat next to his wife of seven weeks, raised his hand to shield his eyes from the rising sun, and surveyed the site of his future cabin. He saw neither the beauty of the purple cone flowers nor the delicately swaying Queen Anne's lace dancing in the morning sunlight. He hardly noticed he wasn't alone. The meadow was glorious with black-eyed Susan, scarlet flax, and lupine scattered among the clover and grass, but Mac saw only a green ribbon whipping in the wind. He rubbed his palms against the welt of his dungarees. He ached to sink his pick into the earth beneath that ribbon which marked the place for the cornerstone of his cabin. This late in the growing season, a garden must come first.

Driving that pick deep into the soil of Greene County, Arkansas, would set into motion the last act necessary to meet the pledge he'd made to Laurel's father when he promised Mark Campbell in March she would have a safe, comfortable home. The final obstacle to his hope of a family and home would be eliminated by the construction of a simple cabin, and his own father would no longer be disappointed with him. The MacLayne family line would not end in three short generations in the new land his grandfather had made their home. That cabin was so much more than just a house, but it would have to wait. Homesteaders knew their first obligation was to provide food for the coming winter.

Though married legally four days after meeting, the seven weeks of their marriage proved to be their courtship. True, Laurel slept next to him and at times, nestled on his shoulder in her sleep, but the promise was intact. The vow to Laurel that he'd not take her to wife until he'd earned the right by giving her a home would be met in full. Nothing would stop him from building that cabin before the end of summer. His dream of a home in Shiloh was too near reality. And to date, she'd given no indication she was ready for more.

In his prayers, he wrestled. Was he willing to allow this woman a place in his heart? He swore he'd never give his heart to another woman after the faithless Marsha. Could Laurel be satisfied with a marriage based on a solid friendship and their mutual faith in the Lord? Would his faith allow him to live that way? The day was too beautiful for these bothersome questions.

"Look, Mac. Isn't that yarrow?" Mac jerked his head upward as her words pulled him back. "Do you remember how Shirley Lamb used that plant to take down my fever? How nice to have some medicine on your land."

"Nice you remembered what it looked like. I didn't." Mac barked in reply. *Lord, forgive the tone. She was just making a comment. I didn't have to snap at her.*

"It's almost a shame to have to destroy all these wonderful flowers to build a house here. Your land is so beautiful."

"This is our land, Laurel, and they are only wildflowers. They grow all over the place. We can plant more if you want them, but we've got to build some place." Mac flung the pick and shovel over the side of the wagon. "As much as I want to start the house, we've got to get a garden planted first. Those saplings and vineyard cuttings we brought from Washington County won't survive much longer. You do want your orchard or don't you, Wife? The cabin has to wait."

With the foundation site chosen for the cabin, placement of the orchard and the garden plot was obvious, and planting must take priority, but Mac knew he didn't have to be so curt in his remarks. What was wrong with him? Being late in April, planting season was well underway, so they had days of back breaking labor in this unbroken land to assure a garden would fill their larder with enough to feed them through the winter and up until the next spring. It would be several years before the orchard would bear good fruit, maybe up to ten years, but the grapes would grow enough to produce fruit in about four years. Until that time, the woods would supply ample blackberries and mulberries.

Mac lifted Laurel from the wagon seat, and they began to clean the site for the first orchard in Greene County. They worked until the site was ready to receive the plants. The area was on a slight incline that would drain well in wet weather but near enough the creek where the plants could be watered if the rains failed to provide adequate moisture. Side by side, the MacLaynes, dug out rocks, pulled vines, felled small trees, and removed debris of uncounted years making the soil ready to plow. When it was too dark to see, they headed back to the Widow Parker's cabin, their temporary home, to deal with nightly chores.

Mac and Laurel headed back to the homestead early the next day. The newlyweds toiled on their land for three days. Breaking the virgin soil was difficult work, but by the time the sun reached its zenith on Wednesday, Mac and Laurel finished planting the dozen fruit trees and five grape cuttings that had survived the long trip across the state. Only one peach tree seedling died on that long trek from Washington County to Shiloh.

When the orchard was planted, Mac wanted to hitch the two mules that had pulled the wagon across the state into halters and sink the first plow into the soil for their garden at his homestead. He'd plant potatoes, pole beans, onions, and pumpkins. They'd marked off another section for tomatoes, cabbage, corn, and okra, which he'd put nearest the cabin site. After the garden, many more days of work preparing plots for oats, hay, and wheat would follow. Such was the common lot of an Arkansas homesteader who must feed himself, his family, and his animals. Without question, crops came first. Only then could Mac sink his pick into the ground to start the work on a cabin. That time was still days off.

"Can I help you with the plowing, Mac?"

He picked up her hands and turned them over to look at her palms. "You amaze me, Laurel. We've put in three very hard days, but I don't see one blister."

"I'm no pampered city girl, Mac. I worked hard on my papa's homestead doing these same things. We had gardens, orchards, and fields to tend in the mountains too."

"But your hands aren't hard and rough."

"They are used to hard work. Now can I help?"

"You've done your share these past three days, Wife. I'm thinking, you've got another obligation this afternoon." Mac pulled his hat off his head and wiped his forehead on his shirt sleeve.

"I can seed behind you, as you plow."

"That'll be work for another day. If you remember, school marm, you have a meeting this afternoon. You promised Matthew you'd meet with the school committee after the noon meal today." Why did Laurel always have to be willing to work so hard with him? He didn't ask her for her help.

"I'd forgotten. Will you ride with me?"

"You don't need me there."

"They may want to thank you for bringing me here. If you hadn't come to Washington County to get a teacher for the subscription school, you wouldn't have been married to the Spinster of Hawthorn, you know."

"I thought we'd put that issue to rest several weeks ago." Mac turned his back to her for a minute. Laurel reached out and hesitantly touched his shoulder with her hand, which he brushed away.

"Laurel, I came to pay court to the daughter of my best friend's brother. It was just nice that she is also smart enough to be a good teacher. Now don't get my dander up. Just stay on the road, and you'll end up by the church yard. I'll start gathering stones for the foundation. There's too much work to do here. I'll never get a cabin built if I have to take an afternoon just to ride a mile down the road with you. Anyway, it's the same path you'll take to school every day."

"I'm sorry. I didn't think of the work. I can find my way."

"Sorry, Laurel. I didn't mean to be short. I'll meet you back at the widow's place before nightfall." Mac hoisted her up on to Sassy Lady, her little mare that she'd ridden that morning. Almost smiling at her, he waved good-bye.

Laurel blotted perspiration from her brow and smoothed the front of her skirt a second time as she stood on the porch of the church. Shuffling from one foot to the other, she reached for the door. In Hawthorn, she helped the teacher or filled in for a teacher on leave. She knew she could do what was expected, and she was confident she was a good teacher, but this was the first time she'd be a head teacher. Regardless, she was pleased her Uncle Matthew was a part of the committee who oversaw the school. At the set time, Laurel stood face to face with the school committee of Shiloh subscription school.

"Laurel Grace, good to see you. I think you met Ransom Nolan the other day, and this fellow is Nathaniel Trice. The three of us are responsible for keeping this school going."

After the pleasantries, Mr. Nolan became the spokesman for the group. "Mrs. MacLayne, we were more'n satisfied with your qualifications to teach. What do you plan to teach our children?"

Belying her nerves, Laurel looked directly at Mr. Nolan. "Mostly language, arithmetic, reading, spelling, and penmanship. I won't know exactly until I see what the students can do now and how old they are. I would hope to teach some history and oratory skills, too. I will use the Scriptures to teach whenever I can." The men nodded their approval.

"Can you show me what books we have here for the children to use?" A frown appeared on her face as she examined the few books the school owned. "We'll need to replace these books. I was told nineteen students across all the grade levels are enrolled. We'll need things for all of them."

"Presently, Mrs. MacLayne, we may have to make do. The school fund is low right now."

"Is it all right if I order a few new books?"

Mr. Trice looked away and cleared his throat gruffly.

"You don't understand, Laurel Grace." Her uncle Matthew explained. "Right now, we only have enough tuition money to pay you.

Since you have a place to live, we will pay you ten dollars a month. We usually pay eight dollars and board. We want you to teach through May, June, and July so the students will be free to help with the harvest until mid-November. If the weather permits, we will have a winter term, but that needs to end at Christmas because of the weather and the roads. January and February are often treacherous, and we don't want to put our kids in peril. Of course, spring is the most important time for us when we have to plow and plant. All the families need their older kids at home during planting season."

Determination in her voice, Laurel spoke quietly, "That'll be fine, but I want half my pay now so I can order books." Mr. Trice turned around and looked at Laurel, his mouth agape. The expression on the faces of the school committee showed them somewhat taken aback at Laurel's outspokenness.

"Mrs. MacLayne, do you mean to tell us that you want to be paid in advance?" His face florid, Mr. Trice asked.

"Well, yes...but I am going to use the money to buy things my students need. I want to give them the best schooling I can in the short time they have to learn. I will wait to the end of the term for the rest of my pay, which I will keep."

"Well, Nathaniel, it's not an unreasonable request. Since Laurel Grace is asking for her due, and then to make a generous gift to our school. I think we should say yes."

"Mrs. MacLayne, we may not be able to repay your generosity."

"I was told this is my home now. That being the case, I want to live in a community where students get a good education."

Ransom Nolan offered his hand. "Mrs. MacLayne, we'll talk about your unusual request. You can order a few books from the general store in Greensboro. Tell McCollough to put them on the account, and we'll take care of it when we can."

"Thank you, gentlemen. I am pleased to be the teacher for this school." Mr. Nolan and Mr. Trice paid their respects to the new school marm and left the church.

"Did you have a good morning with Mac?"

"Oh, yes. Uncle Matthew. We got all my trees planted and the grape vines set out. Mac's ready to break ground for the garden. We want to plant our entire garden before the end of the week. Today, Mac's gathering stones for the foundation and fireplaces for his cabin. You won't believe how much progress we have made."

"You two seem happy. Are you?"

"Most days are good. We've been crosswise at times, too. We still have a lot to learn about each other."

"Is Mac the husband you expected, Laurel Grace?"

"I never expected to have a husband, Uncle, so I don't really know how to answer your question."

"You make it hard for a person to understand you, niece. Is Mac living up to his vows?"

"He treats me well. He has taken care of me and defended my name. He wants to live up to the promises he made to my papa."

"Can you love him, Laurel Grace?"

Laurel didn't want to have this conversation with her uncle. She hesitated.

"Will you answer me? I'm not just being your nosey old uncle. I am also your pastor. Mac is my best friend, and I want to help both of you if I can."

"Uncle Matthew, truthfully, I don't know if I can love Mac. I'm not sure I know what that means. When I was a girl, I believed in romance, just like every other girl, but I am not a girl anymore. Right now, I am building a friendship with Mac, and that's enough–for now."

"I sense you're upset with me, niece, but I got one more question, then I'll stop asking for now. Why did you agree to marry Mac?"

"Uncle Matthew...what choice did I have? Papa sold our land because he knew the law would not let me inherit it. No one in Hawthorn would ever ask me to marry. I was the Spinster of

Hawthorn, too plain, too smart, and too different from the other girls. How would I make a living for myself? I could have come here and lived with you as an old maid dependent, tried to go to Texas and find my brother Daniel and do the same in his household, or marry Patrick MacLayne. I made the only choice I could live with."

"Laurel, I want you to be happy above all else. How much do you know about Mac's past?"

"He's told me about his love for a beautiful woman when he was younger. I think he said he was about twenty-one. He said something about wasting seven years of his life in what he called low living."

"Niece, ask Mac to tell you the details of him leaving Maryland. You deserve to know how he felt about that time of his life, and the limits he placed on himself because of it."

"Why should he tell me about the ugly part of his life? I don't want to tell him about mine. Besides, Mac told me he has no plan to love me. Is that what you are asking?"

Matthew stared back at her. "Laurel Grace, talk to Mac. I know him pretty well. He hasn't told me yet about the circumstances of your marriage, but I was surprised when he brought a bride home and you being my own niece. But I also believe the Lord means good for you, Laurel, and for Mac. Mac is a good man, and he loves the Lord. If he believes that God meant y'all to be together, then it's right. Make sure you really understand. I don't want you to become a victim of his past and end up with a broken heart. Live in God's time, and let Him work out His plan, darlin'."

"Thank you for caring, Uncle. The Lord will take care of me. We believe He planned this marriage so eventually everything will work out for the good." Laurel hugged her uncle and left the church to ride home. As uncomfortable as the topic of the conversation was, Laurel was grateful her family was nearby.

Laurel prepared a filling supper and brewed Mac's evening coffee. She baked corn pone over the coals in the fire place. Baking was a chore in the widow's cabin because she didn't have a hearth oven, but Laurel knew how her grandmother Wilson baked in a kettle over glowing coals. By placing a lid on the kettle and using stones to keep the baking pan from settling directly on the bottom of the kettle, a skilled cook could turn out a decent pone.

At dark, Mac arrived at the widow's cabin, and he took care of his evening chores before going in to supper. He used the water and soap Laurel left for him on the back porch so he could clean up before eating.

"Did you get much done this afternoon?" Laurel asked over her shoulder.

"I did. I stacked two fair-sized piles of rock near the home site. What about you?"

"Good meeting. I asked them to give me half of my pay before school starts."

Mac slung the towel down on the wash table. "Why did you do that? We don't need the money, Laurel."

"The students need new books. I asked for the money to buy them. I'm not sure how many it will buy, but it'll be more than we have now. I hope it is all right with you. I didn't stop to think."

He shrugged. "It's your money, Laurel. You can spend it how you see fit. Anything else happen?"

"Not really. I chatted with Uncle Matthew for a while."

"What'd Matthew have to say?"

"He just wanted to know how we were getting along." Laurel paused for a second. "He asked me if I loved you." Mac turned to face Laurel. "He told me he didn't want me to end up with a broken heart."

"Neither do I, Laurel. I want you to be sure you made the best choice for yourself."

"Matthew suggested there were things about your past that I needed to know. I told him you've already confessed your past life to me, and you never intend to fall in love."

Mac stopped in his tracks and stared at Laurel for a minute. "What did he say about that?"

"He said we need to talk about things."

"He is right about that."

"We have made some good progress, don't you think? Things have been good since we moved here to the Widow's cabin. Perhaps this place is charmed."

"We have just been avoiding the serious issues because they cause us to get crosswise with each other."

"I like the charmed idea better."

Mac took her by the shoulders and looked into her gray eyes. "I like the truth. Seems to last longer. We get upset for a little while, but things seem better afterwards. Laurel, on our trip across the state, I told you my story. I don't think I left any of the horrible details out, but we haven't talked about your story much."

"I don't have a story. I was born plain. My cousin Susan got all the beauty in the Campbell family. Well, maybe not all. Little Mary is going to be a beauty when she grows up too. You can already see it in her."

"That's not the truth, Laurel. It's an excuse. Day before yesterday, you told me your glasses were part of your mask. Why do you need a mask?"

"Mac, I don't want to talk about it. Today's been good. Don't spoil it, please." Laurel pulled away and walked toward the hearth.

Mac followed and turned her to face him. "Laurel, how can your story be any worse than mine? I told you I broke or considered breaking every commandment. I spoke the truth to you. Can you give me less?"

"Masks hide what we don't want other people to see."

"So, you are telling me you hide behind a mask to hide the fact that you are beautiful?"

"Don't be ridiculous. You've got two good eyes."

"Then I don't understand your need for a mask. If you have no beauty to hide, why make an ugly mask to hide behind?"

"I don't know."

"Yes, you do. You began to remember when we were attacked by those thieves outside Jasper."

"Yes, I was scared by what those men tried to do. I was afraid for you, and I didn't know what they would do to me. I don't remember anything else." Her voice trembled as she spoke.

"Laurel, tell me about the nightmare last night."

"I don't remember anything else. I don't. Please stop asking me."

Mac's face reddened, and his breath grew shallow. "Laurel, I don't know what else I can do to earn your trust. I've already given you mine. You dishonor me when you shut me out. Goodnight. I'm going to the loft to read for a while."

"Mac... Mac I'd tell you if I knew what happened that night, but I don't know. I only remember the sheep shears and the laughter..." A lone tear traced its way down Laurel's cheek.

"I'm tired. I won't argue with you anymore. Come up when you are ready to go to sleep. Goodnight."

CHAPTER TWO

I will seek that which was lost, and bring
again that which was driven away,
and will bind up that which was broken and
will strengthen that which was sick.

Ezekiel 34:16 [KJV c1850].

Laurel knew her fear had brought to an end the special week they'd shared. She was frustrated and more than confused. Why wouldn't she let go of the past and get on with living in the present? God gave her blessings beyond her wildest dreams, and she wouldn't allow herself to claim them. What a fool she was!

She jerked her shawl from the peg by the front door and rushed out of the cabin. Perhaps a walk in the cloudless spring night would clear her mind or at least bolster her courage enough to go back and tell Mac what he wanted to know. The bright moonlight over-powered the glow of the stars, and if Laurel were not so lost in her own thoughts, she'd have enjoyed the wonderful scene laid out before her at Shiloh.

She resided in Shiloh, but she didn't yet claim the peace and joy Shiloh promised. Somehow, the past continued to corrupt the promise of what the present could hold. At that moment, Laurel's path was just too long and hard for her to find the way to Shiloh. She believed she was right when she tried to discourage Mac from his proposal. She didn't have what he needed from a spouse. She continued to cause him unhappiness. She clinched her fists and screamed out of her frustration…. "No. He is too good a man, and he deserves better." The woods around echoed her scream.

Laurel stopped in her tracks. Aware now…but after how long a time? She turned to retrace her tracks to the path leading back to the cabin, but when she looked, the path had vanished. She looked for smoke from the chimney, but the fire from cooking supper burned itself out much earlier. Once bright moonlight was now obscured by clouds, and darkness hid the path back. She stopped for a few minutes, praying that God would help her regain her bearings. The last thing she wanted was to give Mac another problem to solve. What kind of fool gets lost so quickly? Laurel knew if she walked any more she would get further into the woods. Common sense told her to just sit down and wait for sunrise.

She pulled her shawl around her and looked in all directions. She never spent much time walking in the woods or exploring places unfamiliar to her. She scolded herself…Stop feeling so helpless. You are a sensible person. Let your reason take control. She walked around the area until she found a fallen tree. She crouched down and wrapped her skirt around her legs and feet. She pulled her shawl higher around her neck and shoulders to keep warm, and then she leaned back against the fallen tree and waited. She startled when something screeched in the distance. How long was she gone from the cabin? Was dawn near? Every noise from the forest startled her. She was not one who could recognize the sounds made by the birds and insects. She also knew that black bears and occasional wolf still inhabited this country. Her body ached from crouching on the ground next to the fallen tree. Into the night, Laurel leaped onto the log as a vine blew across her leg in the dark and a leaf brushed the scar where a cottonmouth once sunk its fang into her ankle. When she realized what happened, she laughed at herself, but she pulled her feet inside her skirt and tucked the hem around to cover both her shoes anyway. Sleep certainly would not come this night.

An eternity later, the sun began to edge above the eastern horizon. Laurel rose and looked again for the path home. Even in the light, the path was no more discernible. To make things worse, Laurel didn't know how long she walked the previous day or even what direction she was from the cabin. Her thoughts were top priority last night, and the walk just happened. Laurel was lost. She knew little about the ways of the woods, and she certainly didn't know anything about this part of the state. Yet, neither of those things bothered her as much as the thought that Mac might not want to find her after their fight. She certainly wouldn't blame him. Perhaps he would be relieved she was no longer on his hands.

"Stop and think, Laurel," she talked aloud. "You're not feeble-minded." What did she know about the southern part of Greene County? The ridge was the dividing line for the area. She knew Shiloh was on the western side of the ridge. If she didn't go over the ridge, she would find a community or a homestead where she could ask for help. She should follow the ridgeline. Surely, she would find her way home, so she started walking.

⇌┼⇋

Mac awoke with the light, and he knew immediately things weren't right. The cabin was cool and there was no smell of brewing coffee or frying bacon. He knew Laurel was upset when they parted the previous night, but she wouldn't pout and refuse to do her

15

duty. She would prepare breakfast, just because she should. He rushed from the bed, dressed quickly, and pulled on his jacket. He skipped every other rung on the loft ladder and hurried to the barn. The stock waited to be fed, the cow was ready to be milked, and the eggs remained in the nests. Over in her stall, he found Sassy Lady. If Laurel ran away from Shiloh, she'd not leave her much loved mare behind. Laurel must be in the yard, somewhere.

Again, remorse and shame reared their ugly heads in Mac's mind. They'd enjoyed such a pleasant time since moving to the widow's cabin—until yesterday. He'd been so short with her all day. What possessed him to push Laurel farther than she was willing to go? Actually, he was surprised he slept through the night without her beside him in the tall bed. He walked to the well at the back door. "Laurel, where are you?" He went back into the kitchen to look for some hint of her leaving. He found no sign that food was gone, and except for her shawl missing by the door, nothing else was different than when he climbed to the loft.

Picking up his belt, rifle, and knife, he fastened the ammunition belt around his waist and went to get Midnight. Instead of planting a garden today, he would spend his time looking for his bride. When he found her, what would he do? At that moment, it didn't matter. He would search until he found her. He led Midnight from the barn, and with the reins across his shoulder, he walked slowly around the yard, hoping to find Laurel's footprints. "Lord, please show me how to find her and what to do with her when I do."

With his whispered prayer, he began a long morning search. First, he rode a short distance down the path toward Greensboro, but he found no sign that Laurel went in that direction. He went back along a wooded path that led to Shiloh church. Mac knew this wooded area was very dense, and someone not familiar with the woods may very easily lose the way. Three years ago, two nine-year-old boys died in these same woods. Mac's level of concern rose when he lost the trail himself. Recent rain storms broke trees and blew large limbs across the path in many places. Mac realized that with the new damage to the path he would need some help to find his wayward wife.

He returned to the road and rode as quickly as he could to Matthew Campbell's cabin. As he reached the homestead, he called out, "Matthew, Matthew Campbell. I need your help. Laurel is lost."

Matthew came from his barn, carrying two pails of fresh milk. "What's wrong, Mac?"

"Laurel left the cabin sometime during the night. I can't find any trace of her."

"Did she leave you?"

"I don't know. She didn't take her horse or any of her personal things. The only thing I missed this morning was her shawl. I think she just went for a walk and got lost."

"Why would she go out alone in the night?"

"I don't know that either. Does it matter? She's lost."

"Let me tell Ellie. She can rustle us up some help. I'll saddle my horse, and we'll head out."

Matthew went into his cabin and within two minutes returned with his shotgun and coat under his arm. He threw a saddle on his horse, and the two men rode back toward the widow's cabin. When they got to the property, Mac showed Matthew the footprints that he looked at earlier. Matthew got down to look more carefully. He followed the tracks that made a meandering path around the cabin, across the road, back toward the well, and back to the front porch. A second set of prints lead back to the road and ended at the path leading to the woods.

"Mac, Laurel wasn't headed anywhere. She was just out walking. Doesn't look like she was paying much attention to where she was headed either. Look at this print. She passed here more than once. What could she have wanted out here in the dark?"

"She just wanted to get away from me. We started the evening fine after a pleasant week here at the cabin. We'd been working on our homestead, planting the orchard, and breaking ground for the garden. A spell after supper, we read and talked. Laurel even worked on some lessons for school. We'd talked about some of the problems we knew we were facing. Everything was good, until.... Well, she refused to talk to me about those nightmares she's having all the time. We spoke a few harsh words. I went to bed to end the fight. Laurel never came up. I should've noticed sooner than I did, but I didn't realize she was gone until dawn.

"Sorry you are still at odds. I didn't see y'all in several days, so I thought everything was good. Let's follow the path and see if we can't locate my wayward niece." They rode into the woods along the path as far as they could make it out.

⚔ ⚔

In the meantime, Laurel continued to walk along a path that she thought followed the ridge. By noon, she was tired and more than hungry. She needed water, and there were no streams running along the top of the ridge. Knowing the creek was at the foot of the ridge, she began to make her way slowly down the hillside. There was no hint of a path, but the brush was not so dense. Returning to the valley was the right thing to do. At least she could find water to drink at the bottom. The brambles and briars tugged at her skirt and the fringe of her shawl. In two places, blood stained the sleeve of her blouse where briars dug into her arm. Determined, she trudged on, stumbling and falling over rough areas. After a while, Laurel saw the stream below. In her eagerness to reach the water, she stumbled over a fallen tree and fell several yards down into the ravine. When she was stopped by a large boulder near the bottom of the slope, she didn't get up.

⚔ ⚔

About two in the afternoon, Mac and Matthew caught up with a large group of fellow church members who came to join in the search. After Ellie Campbell raised the alarm, they met at the church and started their search coming from that direction. They saw no sign Laurel passed in that way. The group searched on. They stopped at the log where Laurel spent the night. Matthew found a piece of ecru cloth torn from Laurel's sleeve.

"Men, we have to split up. We only have about five more hours before the sun goes down and we lose our light."

"Yes, sir, Brother Matthew. Don't worry Mac. We'll find your missus before then."

"Don't worry, just keep praying, Mac. I'll go along the ridge back toward the church. You go along the valley. Laurel's smart. She'd think of a way to find help." Matthew tried to reassure his friend.

"She's smart, I know, but a stranger to these parts. Matthew, if I lose her now... I promised her pa that I'd keep her safe. Since we met, three times she's been in real danger. I didn't stop any of it."

"Don't lose your faith now, Mac. You've never put Laurel in harm's way on purpose. She'll be all right. Let's just get busy and cover the ground."

The party of nine men continued to look until dusk threw shadows so deep over the rocky terrain that spotting anyone was next to impossible. If clouds covered the light from the moon and the stars, they may very well lose more people in the woods. At sundown, Mac and Matthew joined up again, having no luck in finding a lead. The other members of the search party all headed back to the road before dark hid their ways home. No one could search this wilderness without light.

"Mac, let's ride down toward the stream on our way back to the road. Laurel knows water is there in the valley. If we don't find her, we'll start at the stream again at first light."

"Matthew, I can't leave her out here alone for another night. She doesn't know how to take care of herself out here."

"Let's just keep looking and riding as long as we can see." They began their ride down from the ridge. The sun dipped just below the horizon, and a rim of crimson edged the ridgeline. The wind picked up, and the air cooled considerably. They rode on. As they neared the creek, something fluttering in the breeze caught Mac's eye.

"What's that over there?" Mac dismounted and ran across the short distance as quickly as the brush would allow him to go. Laurel lay unconscious with blood covering part of her face. "Matthew, hurry. She's hurt, looks like she fell from up there."

Mac sat down and pulled Laurel into his lap to get her up from the ground and pushed her blood-soaked hair back from her face. He saw she'd hit her head, and there was a deep cut just at her hair line near her left ear. The bleeding ended, but he was not able to rouse her.

"Hurry, Matthew. I need some water. Please bring your canteen. Lord, please let her be all right." Mac used his kerchief to wash Laurel's face. "Laurel. Can you hear me? Please, please hear me." He saw her rouse up when he touched the wound. She cried out from the pain. Fresh blood appeared, and Mac stopped cleaning the wound.

Laurel opened her eyes. "Mac..."

"Oh, dear Lord! Thank you. Don't try to talk now, Laurel. You are safe, and your uncle Matthew is here."

"Mac, I didn't mean to cause problems. I just went out for a walk." Her head wavered in a near swoon. Mac pulled her closer into his shoulder.

"I know, Laurel. Let's just get you home." Mac gently lifted her and silently offered a prayer of gratitude.

"Thank the Lord, you are safe, Laurel. The whole community was out here looking for you." Laurel's uncle spoke.

"I'm sorry to be a bother."

"We'll talk about it later, niece."

Mac carried her to his horse. "Can you ride, Laurel?" She nodded, and he placed her in the saddle, and then took the reins and began the walk home. Well after dark, they reached the widow's cabin, and Mac carried her to the small cot beside the hearth in the main room of the cabin.

"Matthew, please stay with her while I take care of the horses and the livestock I've neglected all day. I'll be back as soon as I can." Mac needed a few minutes. How could such intense feelings of relief, anger, hurt, joy, and confusion fill him at the same time? Without a few minutes alone, he'd surely say or do the wrong thing again, just as he had the previous night. Matthew nodded, and Mac rushed from the cabin.

⇥⇥ ⇤⇤

Matthew went to the hearth to get hot water to clean the gash on Laurel's head. The fall down the ravine left Laurel with a number of other cuts, scrapes and bruises, but only the gash on her head seemed serious.

"I should get the doctor to clean this and give you a couple of stitches. You got a pretty good gap in your scalp. Laurel, why did you run away last night?" Matthew gently cleansed the gaping wound.

"I didn't run away, Uncle Matthew. I got lost in the woods while I was walking. I tried to find my way back, but it got too dark when the sun set."

"What were you doing out by yourself after dark? Did Mac mistreat you?"

Shaking her head, Laurel whispered, "No. No...he's good to me. I don't deserve him. I've only caused him disappointment and problems. I tried to tell him before we spoke our vows I wasn't a

21

suitable mate for him. I did try to spare him from being saddled with me."

"Do you want to talk about it, Laurel? I know Mac would be willing to listen to you."

"Oh, my head hurts." Laurel turned over on the pillow with her head in her hands. Matthew took a warm wet cloth and laid it across her forehead.

"Rest now, Laurel. We have lots of time. You're safe now."

"Uncle Matthew, please help me tell Mac I didn't mean to cause problems for him. I just wanted to walk and think. I tried to come back. I mean to live up to our vows. I promised him I would. I will tell him everything I remember about my nightmares."

"That is not necessary tonight. You need to rest. There is time to work out the rest."

Mac returned from the barn and took a few minutes to wash. Before he could go to Laurel's side, Matthew approached him. "She's got a bad gash on her scalp and several cuts and bruises. None seem very serious except that head wound. The doctor may need to put a couple of stitches in her head."

"Should I go to Greensboro to get Dr. Gibson tonight?"

"Not tonight. She's resting now. Tomorrow will be soon enough. Mac, why did Laurel go out alone last night?"

"I pushed her too far. I asked her to talk to me about her nightmares, like I told you. She shut down and wouldn't talk to me. I lost my temper and told her I was frustrated trying to get her to trust me. I went to bed and left her down here alone. At the time, it seemed better than fighting with her."

"She's not upset with you, Mac. She told me you're too good for her and that she tried to talk you out of marrying her in the first place. She thinks you've saddled yourself with her."

"She told you all that?"

"Just now."

"Did she say anything else?"

"She apologized for causing problems."

"Sounds like her. I thought she was starting to see herself differently than she did in Washington County, but I guess not. I am afraid she is going to do something to hurt herself bad one of these days. Did she tell you what I did to drive her away this time?"

"Said she only wanted to walk a while and got lost in the dark."

"Wish I could believe that was true. Do you believe her, Matthew?"

"No reason not to, but I don't hear much trust coming from you. Do we need to end this whole thing before you both get seriously hurt?"

"There will be an end when God ends it."

"Maybe He never started it, Brother. Mac, you asked me once if God frowned on a physical union outside love. I didn't have an answer then. Now I only have a question. I know you can take her to you, but you asked me about making love. How can you make love to a woman when you feel none? Just pray about that, Mac."

Matthew set about making a fire and fixing an evening meal as Mac helped Laurel up and supported her as she climbed up to the loft. He came back to get fresh water to give her. He took a cloth and washed the blood from her face and forehead. Blood matted the curls on the left side of her head. Fresh blood seeped from the wound. Mac tried to remove the blood from her hair. He didn't speak until she asked him to stop. He replied with what he thought would be a witty comeback.

"Maybe I need to go get the sheep shears and cut this matted mess of hair off. Then we can start over. That's the only way I'll be able to get this all out. Would that be okay with you, Wife?"

For a moment, she said nothing. When Laurel did speak, her tone was flat. "You wouldn't be the first one to do so."

He sat motionless for a few minutes, aware his words brought up an event from Laurel's past. Yet, he dared not ask, not after the previous night. "Laurel...I was teasing. Of course, I will help you wash the blood out of the matted places. I love your curls. I'd never want to cut them."

"Mac, I was coming back to tell ..."

"Laurel, let's don't talk about anything that will cause an argument tonight."

"I didn't mean to get lost. I was foolish to leave the cabin so near dark. I caused a lot of trouble."

"Laurel, everyone makes mistakes. I made one yesterday when I tried to make you confide in me."

"Mac, please listen. I never wanted to talk about it, but I need..."

"Laurel. No more talk tonight. You're tired. We'll talk later."

"Mac, I want..."

"Goodnight, Laurel. I'm going back to get Matthew bedded down for the night. Sleep well." He pulled the yellow coverlet over her and left the loft.

Mac returned to eat supper with Matthew. He was exhausted. Mac's expressionless face and eyes without a single spark of life spoke his defeat. "Get it off your chest, Brother. What did Laurel say to take the wind out of your sails?"

"Nothing...she didn't really say anything, just apologized for causing problems. I'm at a loss. Matthew, do you know anything about Laurel's being attacked when she was a girl?"

"Mark wrote me once and again. I seem to remember that he spoke of an incident a couple of years after they moved to Washington County." Matthew rubbed his hands across his unshaven chin. "He didn't tell me much, but he did say that Laurel decided to leave school. She'd already finished her studies at common school, anyway. From what Mark said, she did more teaching of the little ones, than she did learning anyway. Mark said that some of the older students resented her because she was so much ahead of them. Said she was too smart for her own good. Did she tell you?"

"No, but I stepped on a sore spot when I teased her about cutting her hair with sheep shears to get the matted blood out. I never heard a colder, deader statement from anyone in my life. She said, 'You won't be the first one to do so'."

"I don't know about that. What else did she say?"

"It's her story to tell or not. I hope she will decide to tell me about it, but I'm not asking anymore. There is still much I wish I knew, but I am not going to push her again. She will tell me when she wants to or not. What was she like when you knew her?"

"Back in Carolina, we called her 'sprite with spirit.' She was full of life and as happy as any child reared in love could be. Laurel's hair was a mass of beautiful tawny curls, and Leah, her mother, dressed her in ribbons and ruffles. Always so full of curiosity and questions. She was in adult company all the time. Beautiful little girl. Needless to say, Ellie and me...when we saw her the other day when you brought her into Shiloh, we couldn't believe she was the same girl. She is so quiet and rarely smiles now. Only her curls are the same."

"She'd hide those too if she could have her way. She hates wearing her hair down, but I told her she couldn't put it in a braided coronet."

"Well, it's been a very long, hard day. I'm going to bed down in the hay."

"No need for that, Matthew. Widow's little cot there by the fireplace is right snug. Least I can offer...small thanks for all your help."

"No thanks required. Laurel Grace is family and so are you. Good night, Mac."

Mac climbed the ladder to the loft. Laurel slept peacefully in the tall bed. Mac took a minute to wash his face and brush his hair. Then he dropped to his knees beside the bed and offered a prayer of thanksgiving. His prayer continued for some time...often unspoken. When he rose, much of the anxiety he'd been feeling was gone. He slipped into his place beside Laurel, trying not to disturb her rest, but no sooner was he down than Laurel moved next to him. He turned and drew his sleeping wife into his arms. The warm, firm touch of her cheek begged a tender kiss and then he rested his head against her curls. For the night, things were at ease in the MacLayne household.

CHAPTER THREE

Except the Lord build the house, they
labor in vain that build it.

Psalm 127:1 [KJV c1850].

B y Saturday morning, Laurel was nearly recuperated from
her wilderness adventure. Mac and Matthew took her to
Greensboro to have Dr. Gibson examine her gash. He made a care-
ful check for infection, but not finding any, he made three small
stitches to close the wound. Dr. Gibson sent her away with a stern
warning to avoid midnight walks in the woods.

Greensboro was bustling on this spring Saturday. People
came from the countryside to take care of business, catch up
on the local gossip, and purchase needed supplies. Shiloh didn't
have a local post office, so most of her citizens used the one in
the Greensboro general store of John McCullough. Mac told
Laurel that Greensboro was the business center of the area, and

a constant flow of goods made the way to town through several freighters who brought provisions from Wittsburg in the south and St. Louis in the north. Hub towns served as distribution points for a myriad of goods brought on the riverboats that landed in Jacksonport, Batesville, and even as far away as Little Rock. Even with this description, Laurel didn't expect this village to be a bustling town. She pictured a busy trading post or mercantile, like the one near Hawthorn where she'd grown up. People in the northeast part of the state called Greensboro "the metropolis of Northeast Arkansas." This thriving frontier town included a shoemaker, three blacksmith shops, a saddler, a log hotel, an apothecary, a seamstress, and three mercantile stores. Greensboro was also home to three doctors and a lawyer. A busy gristmill ran six days a week to process corn during harvest season. To the disgust of the local matrons, Greensboro was also home to three saloons with the reputation of providing a rambunctious night of entertainment for anyone who wished to spend their hardearned money inside. Greensboro was convenient to Shiloh. A trip to town and back was an easy afternoon's journey.

Since Laurel seemed well enough, Mac declared, "Wife, I think it's time we visited the mercantile. If you don't get some more clothes, I'm afraid you'll be traipsing around our home in your natural state."

"Patrick MacLayne! What a thing to say. I'd never do that."

"Then let's go find you some more clothes." As they entered the mercantile, they were greeted by John McCullough, storeowner and postmaster. Mac's friendship with this tall, lanky man began at the time he'd first arrived in Greene County to make his home at Shiloh. "John McCullough, I'd like to have you meet my wife, Laurel."

"Morning, Mrs. MacLayne. We heard you got a bit turned around in our woods. Good to see no permanent damage done. Mac, I never thought I'd see the day you'd introduce me to a missus."

McCullough slapped Mac across his shoulder and laughed. "What can I do for y'all today?"

"Laurel is going to teach at the subscription school, and her trunks haven't arrived. She'll be needing a couple nice dresses to wear until we can get her things back to Shiloh."

"Mac, I didn't bring any money with me." Laurel whispered to her husband.

"John, give her anything she takes a fancy to."

"Well, I got a few readymade ones, but most of the women folk around here make their own. Got a sight more yard goods than dresses."

"Just show her what you have."

Laurel looked at the few dresses that were in the store. One of them was a matronly black bombazine dress with long sleeves and a high collar. Mac shook his head in a heartbeat. He did let Laurel chose a white lawn blouse and a grey calico skirt. Then from across the aisle, he spotted a bolt of green gingham, nearly the same shade of green as the Easter dress Laurel made for herself but had given to a bride who lost her wedding gown in a fire. He picked up the bolt of green gingham and handed to the clerk. "Give us a normal dress length of this fabric, John. I also want a dozen pearl buttons and that dainty lace over there. Laurel's a good hand with a needle. She'll have this new dress done in no time. While you're at it, cut us some of that pretty pink and white muslin with those tiny rosebuds on it."

"Mac, it's too much. I told you I didn't bring my money."

"You need the things...the pink one will make a perfect summer dress for the Fourth of July."

Laurel left his side and picked up items to replenish their larder. While she was occupied, a couple of men approached Mac and Matthew.

"Good morning, Mac, Matthew. Good to see you both in town. It's been a spell since we've seen you Mac. Thought you'd left the country."

"Brother Mac here just took himself a little trip to the west side of the state. He found himself a bride over in Washington County."

"Congratulations, Man! We thought you'd end up a confirmed old bachelor before you'd find anyone who'd put up with you."

"Good news for all of us. You'll be more electable as a family man than not."

"What are y'all talking about, Al?"

"Several of us men from Shiloh and a few of us business men from Greensboro think you'd be our best representative in the state legislature come next fall. Too much going on down in Little Rock that we got no say in."

"You know I don't hold much with the politics of the Family. That same group of politicians have controlled our state from the earliest days, even when Arkansas was just a territory. I won't be a very electable candidate."

"That's what we want. We need a man who will speak for us, not just go along with the political nest down there right now. The Johnsons, Seviers, and Conways have been in control in the state since '36, ever since statehood. The Family's been in control long enough. We need some new blood down there."

"I will not vote against my conscience, fellas. You know me. I won't support pro-slavery causes nor vote for secession, if it comes before the house."

"That is how most of us feel. Just give it some serious thought, Mac. We got some time to kick this idea around."

"I'll pray about it." Mac and Matthew Campbell collected the bundles and left the mercantile with Laurel between them.

"You know, Brother, we could really use a good man in the state legislature, someone with some gumption to go along with some values. You'd sure have lots of votes from Shiloh." Matthew said.

"Enough politics, Matthew. I need to get my injured wife home to rest, and I'll bet yours is beginning to wonder if you've deserted your family all together."

"Not much chance she'd think that. She knows I'd never leave the best blessing the good Lord ever gave this old sinner!" Laurel and Mac both laughed as Matthew's smile spread across his face.

"Brother, are you one love sick rascal!"

"You know that's the Lord's truth, and Mac, they ain't no finer feeling on the face of the earth. You ought to try it yourself. You'd like it."

Mac didn't reply. He envied his friend, but he also knew his choice was the right decision for himself...he'd made a good marriage of convenience with a woman who could be a dear friend. Laurel would be a fine help mate for him. He didn't need a sweetheart to complicate his life.

"Get on with it. We'll be home by midafternoon, which should get you home for supper. Just in case you forgot, tomorrow is Sunday. Do sermons write themselves?"

"No, Brother, they don't, but I never run short of things to praise the Lord for. Don't worry. You'll have your sermon tomorrow."

Sunday morning turned out to be a glorious spring day on Crowley's Ridge. Flowering trees were in full bloom. Pink and white dogwoods provided vivid splashes of color throughout the woods, and early crops were poking their green shoots through the recently tilled soil. Matthew Campbell kept his promise and delivered an inspired message he called The Wellspring of Joy Arising from the Circumcision of the Heart. He used a passage from Luke 9:23-24, along with a tract from one of John Wesley's sermons. He stirred his congregation with powerful words when he spoke of the path to stronger faith, love, joy and peace. The music and the company of the worshippers at Shiloh added to the blessing. As the service came to an end, Mac rose to thank the members of the Shiloh congregation who helped search for Laurel and for all the prayers. He also invited all the families to come to the log rolling at their new homestead the following Saturday.

After Matthew dismissed the Shiloh family with the benediction, he and his family joined Laurel and Mac for a picnic at their new homestead. Mac was pleased to be able to show off the progress they'd made. Heaps of stone stood at the four corners of the double pen cabin he was planning. Mac could almost imagine the cabin finished with smoke drifting from the stone chimneys.

⟞⊹ ⊹⟝

Laurel walked with her aunt through the new orchard. All but one of the transported fruit trees had taken root and seemed healthy, ready to grow into the future orchard for the MacLayne family. They enjoyed the packed lunch and the good company. Laurel especially enjoyed the renewed acquaintance with her cousin Susan. Her previous comments about the beautiful blonde cousin were true, but more than that, Susan would be a new friend for Laurel. She was easy to talk with, and they shared many common concerns. Both were young marrieds in the process of building a home at Shiloh. Susan and her husband Randall Martin recently raised a new cabin on the back side of her father's section. Susan was still nursing her newest son, and she spoke openly of the ups and downs of being a parent. She even told Laurel that she hoped their children would grow up together. Laurel smiled at her and nodded. She would like children who would grow up with an extended family someday.

The last week before school started was a time of much progress on the cabin. Mac hired one of Uncle Matthew's sons to help lay the foundation for the double pen. By noon the following Saturday, the entire stone foundation was complete. The smaller chimney that would heat the bedroom in the second pen was nearly three feet tall. The logrolling planned for that weekend was timed perfectly. The weather was glorious, and it was nearly time to start raising walls for the cabin.

The social would be Laurel's first time to serve as a hostess. She fretted that everything be just right. She even used precious sugar to make two large cakes, which she would bake at Ellie's house since there was no oven at the widow's. Matthew and Mac provided meat for the day by making an evening hunt to get a small buck. The venison would be cooked on an open spit, and the aroma would urge the workers on all morning. The deer was of a size that the entire Shiloh congregation would have ample food for the entire day as they snacked off and on as they worked to supply the logs for the new cabin. Laurel had attended many log rollings back in Hawthorn, but never before was she in charge of a social event of this size. Yes, she was nervous.

⊨⊣ ⊢⊨

Mac also felt butterflies in his stomach. He didn't doubt that the day would be a success, but he was anxious to have his home finished. He was grateful it was going up quickly because he'd set a goal of finishing the cabin by the time school was out in July. Eight or nine weeks was a short time to build a cabin of this size, but a completed cabin would fulfill all the promises he'd made to Laurel's father. The surprises he'd planned were still in the making. Mac ordered glass-paned windows for the cabin. Laurel mentioned them first when he'd asked her about her home. The windows must to be shipped from St. Louis, and they were costly, but Mac spared no expense to give Laurel all she'd asked for. The second surprise would be a space dedicated to the real copper bathtub he ordered from Little Rock. The freighters would deliver the copper tub along with Laurel's family things they'd stored in Powhatan. Grand plans they were, and Mac worked from the time the sun rose on Crowley's Ridge until the light faded to purple each night. The orchard and garden were thriving and the building was going up each day. Nothing would deter Mac from having the cabin ready for those special things by the end of the school term. He was determined to begin the life he'd asked the Lord for...a wife and family in a comfortable, safe home. Perhaps the other obstacles would just fade away too.

Every night his prayer time with Laurel was spent mostly in thanksgiving. The Lord poured blessings into their lives every day, and he was aware of the gifts and believed Laurel felt it too. In their study time, they discussed the difficult book of Romans, which was the foundation of their faith, and Mac had never enjoyed having an eager study companion more. As they talked, Laurel sewed, working to finish the green gingham. She told him it was to be her first-day dress for the new school term.

Their day to day life was good. As long as they talked about their homestead, the Bible, the community, Laurel's plans for the school year, the garden, or any other impersonal subject, Mac and Laurel were the best of friends and got along as well as any two people living in Shiloh. Quite naturally, they avoided anything of a personal nature that might break their harmony.

On Thursday, Laurel rode to the building site. She was almost dancing with excitement. When her Uncle came from Greensboro on his way home, he told her he'd ordered the textbooks for her school. She was able to buy fifteen books to use with her students. She'd have three first level McGuffey's readers, two copies of both level two and three of McGuffey's readers, three copies of Ray's Basic Arithmetic, two copies of Mitchell's Geography Text, and three Cobb Spelling Books of various levels. "Mac, look how many new books I'll have. I will be able to do a better job teaching with these books."

"Now, niece, don't get too excited. They still gotta come from St. Louis. Hopefully, they'll get here in time to use this summer. If not, they'll be here in the fall."

"You can't put a cloud on me. I'll just make do until then, but they are coming. How wonderful it will be to have new books to teach from."

"Seems the strangest things bring the spirit back to the sprite. I'm glad to see you so happy."

"Of course, I am. Now I will have a few more books to share with nineteen students who will walk into Shiloh school next Monday. And that sweet Mr. McCullough, he sent me two books from his store. They were dusty and a bit worn, but he sent them. Uncle Matthew said he said they were in his way, taking up shelf space, but I think he just wanted to help with the school." John McCullough sent a copy of Jonathan Swift's Gulliver's Travels, and a copy of Emerson's Essays and Lectures. Laurel knew she and Mac would spend hours in front of the fire reading and discussing them when the weather turned cold.

On Friday morning while Laurel worked on her final dishes for the log rolling, she sang to herself. She reflected on what a perfect week she and Mac spent here in the widow's cabin and at the homestead working. During the whole week only two things brought shadows over Laurel's happiness. More than once she found herself wanting to say 'I love you, Patrick.' Most all of her thoughts were tied in some way to Patrick MacLayne. She compared other men to him whenever a visitor stopped by the cabin. She eagerly awaited suppertime every day because it marked the beginning of their evening together.

That afternoon, Mac felt her forehead. "Do you have a fever?"

"No, I'm fine, why?"

"Your cheeks are a bit flushed. I just wandered."

Laurel realized she was blushing as she'd been thinking about spending the night next to Mac in the tall four-poster. She must get control of her feelings. On some nights Mac teased her, hinting of what might be. Once or twice in the month since they shared the widow's cabin, Mac asked if he could brush her hair. On a few occasions, Mac kissed her, giving her a gentle kiss at bedtime. Truthfully, the kisses could be described as brotherly perhaps, but still he kissed her. The feelings that Laurel experienced were new to her, but she believed she was falling in love with Mac. From the start, Mac told her he would never love her, so Laurel knew her feelings would be a problem in the relationship, a cause for rejection. She needed only to be Mac's friend. That is what he offered, and she didn't want him to leave her. Anyway, she knew she could never meet the standard set by beautiful, lively Marsha, the love of his life.

The second fear was worse than her feelings for him because Mac avoided all personal discussion with her. Since the time she was lost in the woods, Mac seemed different–restrained in his interaction with her. They discussed day-to-day happenings, argued a biblical question, and talked at length about the homestead, yet if the conversation veered toward anything personal, either about herself or Mac, he would find an out. He'd suddenly remember he'd forgotten something in the barn, or he would think to fill the water bucket from the well before bedtime. At times, he suddenly became so tired that he would want to go to bed earlier than usual. Their conversations were pleasant and frequent, but they left a void. Laurel felt as if she were talking to an old acquaintance, not the man she wanted to know and whom she wanted to know her. Laurel shook off the dark thoughts. She plunged her hands back into the dish water. No time for daydreaming. Tomorrow would be here before she realized it.

The MacLayne's homestead filled quickly. Families from all over the area came to help the them provide logs to raise a cabin. Most of them were members of the Shiloh family, yet some were Mac's friends from all over the county. Some came from as far away as Herndon and Lorado, including the entire Lamb family who sheltered them when Laurel encountered the cottonmouth in Cache River Bottoms. The Kimbrells, Mac's adopted family while he worked on their homestead before his trip to the west, came to meet Laurel for the first time. Laurel was pleased to greet her old friends, like the Lambs, and new friends who knew and loved Mac already. Even two of the Crowley men rode over to help gather the logs. Men came prepared with broad axes and handspikes. The women brought food and drink to help prepare a midday feast. Mrs. Dunn, a dear old widow who was raising both her grandchildren, brought a large pot of sweet butter to spread on the bread. Even in her lack, she always provided whatever she could. Laurel admired the generosity of this fine old woman.

The venison roasted on the spit, and a makeshift table stood not far away. It was covered with red gingham, embroidered linen table clothes, and pieces of homespun. Some of the women brought flowers they'd cut from their yards. The daffodils were plentiful so early in the spring and added bright splotches of yellow up and down the plank table. The table bowed with huge amounts of food, including fish, cornpone, vegetables, including some spring lettuce and onions from early gardens. Pies and cakes would make a tasty end to the picnic. The community was in high spirits, but before they would partake of the feast, four good hours of work would take place. The work began following a short blessing for the cabin they would raise in their community.

Teams of six to eight men would go into the area Mac marked to cut the lumber he would need. They would fell a tree and then use their metal spikes to pick up the logs and carry them to the stacks Mac already started.

"Momma, why do they call this thing a log rolling? Seems like they are carrying more logs than they are rolling." Mary at age five took a practical view of life, it seemed. Her words suggested a log rolling should have more logs rolling. Laughter rolled across the valley. Like most children, Mary took everything so literally.

"Well, Mary, my little one, it don't make no difference how they get the logs up here, just as long as they have lots of them to build Mac and Laurel a good house." Truly, that is what happened. Before lunchtime, the men of the community stacked scores of logs into piles on each side of the cabin site.

Laurel found herself enjoying the company of all the ladies who came with their menfolk. Her aunt was planning a surprise for Laurel. That day the ladies of Shiloh and the area would piece a Double Wedding Ring quilt for the MacLaynes. They all brought scraps of cloth from garments they made for their families. The wide array of fabric and colors would create a beautiful quilt top when pieced together at the end of the day. They would finish the project by quilting the top at another community get-together. Laurel loved the friendly chatter and storytelling and sisterly advice these ladies shared while they passed the time waiting for their men to come for lunch.

When noon came, Mac called a halt to the work, and the men came into the yard to eat. "Matthew, ask a blessing for this feast. We're so hungry a riot may erupt if you don't do so pretty fast."

"Hey, Mac. If you want a short prayer, you'd better ask someone else to bless the food. You know how Matthew is when he gets wound up!" Everyone laughed.

"The Lord don't care if the blessing is long or short, as long as the faithful remember to say thanks. 'Lord, the day's been fine, the friends are enjoying the fellowship, and now we plan to enjoy this feast our womenfolk have prepared for us. We ask you to bless it and us. We give you thanks'." Amen echoed among those gathered.

Mac walked up behind Laurel and whispered into her ear. "You are being a gracious hostess. Are you enjoying the day?"

"I am. And Mac, the women are making us a quilt."

"I'm glad you are having a good time. This is a common celebration in our community. I look forward to the MacLayne family attending many more." He bent down and kissed her cheek. Laurel blushed. Except for their wedding day, Mac never publicly kissed her before.

The afternoon was as productive as the morning, and by the time the log rolling was declared finished, there were enough logs stacked nearby to complete the first pen and much of the second one. Mac and Laurel expressed their gratitude to their friends over and over and wished them a safe journey home. As he drove Laurel back to the widow's cabin, his mood spilled over as he sang to his wife.

"Oh, Annie Laurel...Her brow is like a snowdrift. Her neck is like a swan.
Her face is the fairest that ever the sun shone on.
Her face is the fairest that ever the sun shone on.
And the dark green of her e'e. I'd lay me doon and dee.
"Max Welton braes are bonnie where early falls the dew,
And it's there that Annie Laurel gave me her promise true
"Like dew on the gowan is the fa' of her fairy feet.
And like the wind in summer sighing, her voice is low and sweet.
And like the wind in summer sighing, her voice is low and sweet.
She's the world to me and for bonnie Annie Laurel
I'd lay me doon and dee."

"My goodness, Mac. I thought you'd be exhausted after the long hard day you worked. How nice to have a serenade. Uncle Matthew taught you well. Your song's nice."

"Thank you, my bonnie Annie Laurel. I am totally intoxicated with blessings we received today. If things continue as they've gone the past two weeks, we'll be moving into our home the week after the school term ends. Our stay at the widow's has been nice, but I want to be home. I look forward to carrying you over that threshold into your house."

"That will be a glad day. Nice to see you so happy."

And Sunday proved to be another outstanding day for the MacLaynes. Being the last Sunday of the month, dinner on the grounds was followed by afternoon singing. After the benediction, Matthew Campbell announced that Shiloh school would open at 8:00 the next morning. Laurel felt blessed to the core of her being, happier than she remembered being in her entire adult life. She offered a silent prayer of gratitude all the way back to the widow's cabin.

CHAPTER FOUR

*But when thou doest alms, let not thy left hand
know what thy right hand doeth; That thine alms
may be in secret; and thy Father which seeth
in secret himself shall reward thee openly.*

Matthew 6:3-4 [KJV c1850].

"Get up, school marm. You don't want to be late on the first day of school." Laurel awoke to Mac's teasing and the smell of breakfast cooking. She completed her green gingham dress with its tiny pearl buttons and dainty lace down the front panel of the bodice. Laurel pulled her hair back with her green satin ribbon. She sat down on the side of the bed, looked at her ugly brown work shoes, and began to pull them on. Before she laced the first one, Mac appeared at the door.

"Gee, how nice you look this morning. If you only had new shoes to wear with that spritely new dress...I wonder if these will do?" He handed Laurel the new white shoes.

"I was just sitting here fretting about having to wear my old brown work shoes. Mac, you are too good to me." She flung her arms around his neck and kissed him. In an instance, she realized what she had done and stepped back. "Excuse me. I didn't think. But they are white, when black would have been more practical."

"I take it you approve of the gift. The white is fine for the summer, just replacing the ones you gave away at Easter." Mac got down on his knee, put the shoes on her, and laced them. "Now you look like a proper school teacher."

Laurel stood up, smoothed down the front of her skirt, took a deep breath, and they went down to breakfast. When Laurel rose to leave for school, Mac handed her a lunch basket that he packed for her. "My goodness, I don't know when I've been treated so royally in my entire life. Perhaps I should have gone to work much sooner."

"You don't have to go today if you don't want to."

"I do want to. Teaching is the gift the Lord gave me. How could I not use it? Besides, those little ones were so excited at church yesterday. I certainly couldn't disappoint them."

"Well, school marm, ride carefully. I'll be at the homestead until dusk. I hope to get a good part of the floor joists in place for the first pen. I got me a deadline to have a new house...August 11th."

"Take care as you work. I'll see you at supper." Laurel made the two-mile ride to the church in a short time. When she arrived, she opened the building and set about preparing for school. She moved the few hymnals to the table behind the pulpit. She set up another table to serve as her desk, and she moved the preacher's stool behind the table. She went back to her horse and retrieved the few things she'd brought from the Widow's.

Then she went to the slate board on the side wall and printed her name in large block letters...LAUREL CAMPBELL. When she stepped back to look at it, she realized she had written her maiden name. How could she have done that when Mac was so good to her that morning? She took the clean rag, rubbed out the last name, rewrote LAUREL MacLAYNE, and sat down to wait for her students.

Before 8:00, the students gathered in the schoolyard. She stood by the door to greet each boy and girl who entered the building. Twenty young people from very small to those much taller than Laurel came inside. Laurel learned quickly that a new family moved into the Shiloh community during Mac's absence. Three of the little ones were in school for the first time, and the four older ones, three girls and one boy would finish their courses and receive their diplomas for the completion of the eighth grade at the end of the next term around Christmas time. The other thirteen children were unequally divided into the other grades. A challenge lay before her.

"Good morning, students. My name is Mrs. MacLayne. Most of you know my husband, Mac. He has told me that y'all are fine young people, and I look forward to meeting and getting to know each of you. Please take a seat, anywhere for right now. Now starting with you, young man, please tell me your name and something about yourself."

Laurel spent the rest of the morning session getting acquainted and answering questions about the school term. The students were very quiet and seemed nervous. When Laurel would walk up and down the aisles, some of the students would move away from her. Even when she tried to make light conversation to ease the tension, the students would not smile or laugh. She tried for a while to draw them into a discussion about their expectations for the year, but to little avail. At 11:30, she sent them out to lunch and midday recess.

When all the boys and girls left the room, Laurel noticed one shy little girl remaining in her seat. Laurel saw she wore no shoes, and her dress was clearly too small. Regardless, she was clean and her hair was neatly combed and braided. Laurel remembered from her introduction talk that she seemed very bright and eager to be in school. She'd brought no lunch.

"Didn't you tell me your name is Catherine?" The small girl nodded. "Well, I think that is a wonderful name. Catherine, my husband fixed me a nice lunch today, but I'm afraid it is too much for one person to eat. Would you please help me eat this? I really hate for things to go to waste."

Catherine raised her head, and her eyes flashed a moment of surprise.

"I'm not really very hungry, ma'am."

"I'd like to share my lunch with you."

"Thank you, Ma'am. If you are sure you have too much."

Laurel gave Catherine the larger portion of the meal. She knew she'd have supper later, and she didn't know if the child would have a hot supper or not. "Will you tell me about your family, Catherine?"

As they ate, Catherine told Laurel she lived with her widowed grandmother and her brother Roy.

"He ain't at school. He does odd jobs to help granny with our living."

"Where do you live?"

"Oh, a way down toward Big Creek. We got a good road to get home." Laurel was shocked. Big Creek was several miles from the school, at least three and a half or four miles. This slight girl had walked all the way without shoes.

At 12:30, Laurel called the class in from play. She arranged the seats, grouping students by their level. There were no fifth level students. She asked the students to stand and tell her what they wanted to get from the school year.

"Mrs. Mac? Do you want us to call you that or all your name?" One sixth level boy asked.

"I like Mrs. Mac. That will do just fine. What's your name again?"

"I'm Ben. I hope we get to do some more arithmetic. Sums is easy, and I can subtract okay…but them dang multiplying rules is real hard."

"I promise. We will do some math…and we'll work on our English grammar too."

Another girl stood up and asked about homework. "Do we have tons of homework?"

"You're Linda, aren't you? Well, we have homework at times. I hope that won't be a problem."

"Last year, the teacher gave us tons of homework. I didn't get all of it done some days. I have to do chores at home."

"Well, we'll try to leave some play time…I hope you will think the time you spend working at home is interesting, and maybe even some of it will be fun."

"Fun! Ain't nothing fun about school." A large boy from the seventh level spoke up.

"What is your name?"

"I expected you'd not remember me…My name is David."

"Seems you don't like coming to school very much."

"I'm doing it because I don't want to be ignorant like some people I know."

"David, some things about school can be really fun. I hope we get to do some of those things."

"Mrs. Mac, teachers don't like to have fun, do they?" another child asked.

"Of course, I love to have fun. Why do you think teachers don't like to have fun?"

"I've had two other ones, and they didn't never have no fun. The one from last term was just plain mean. He made us stay outside unless he told us to come in, even when it was cold. See that cane… he'd smack our knuckles when we didn't do things right. He was just plain mean!"

"Yeah, the one before him, well, he wasn't mean, but he just sat at this desk and talked to us all day. We couldn't talk or laugh or nothing. I guess you'd say school ain't been much fun."

"I have always loved to learn new things, so I always thought school was fun. I will try to find things you want to learn so school will be fun for you too. Well, it's time to get down to tasks…"

She began the lesson by reading Proverbs 10:14. "Wise men lay up knowledge; but the mouth of the foolish is near destruction." Laurel stopped and laid down her Bible. "Let's talk about what this means, young people."

For the last half hour of school that day, the class carried on a discussion about the adage. Laurel was pleased at the keen observations some of the students made. She even asked the youngest to speak, and while they mostly repeated what older students already said, they knew they were a part of the class. The one gem she garnered from the discussion was that nearly every one of the students in her class wanted to learn. Only two of them were at school because their parents demanded their attendance. It would be a good school year. At 3:30, Laurel dismissed the first day of school, feeling very happy that things went well. She straightened the room and then rode Sassy Lady out to the homestead, anxious to tell Mac what she'd done that day.

When she arrived, Laurel was excited to see so much work finished. The smaller of the two chimneys had capstones, and the floor joists were finished in the main room. Two men from the Shiloh congregation who weren't able to attend the log rolling came to help Mac and John that day. Together the four men were able to accomplish as much as one man would have done in a week. Mac stopped work when he saw Laurel approach. "You look happy, Wife."

"It was wonderful day at school. The students are just as you told me they would be. They are so eager to learn, well most of them. Two new students just moved into the community. I think I am going to have a wonderful term."

"I didn't hear of any new families. Well, it's good to have our community growing. We can stop and call it a day, men. I can't thank y'all enough for all the work we got done today."

"You're welcome, Mac. Milt and me, we just wish we could've come on Saturday. Log rollings are always fun times. Maybe we can do it again when you need a barn."

"Harold, I am beholding to y'all. If we do have another log rolling, I'll be sure to find a time when you fellas can be here. If you need a helping hand, I expect you to call on me. We got us a great congregation at Shiloh. No man has to bear the load alone."

"Mac, I didn't mean for y'all to quit working. I thought I could come and help until dark. The more we do, the closer to moving day."

"I didn't know you were in such a hurry to move."

"Of course, I want your dream to come true."

"All of my dream?" Laurel blushed at Mac's last comment. She knew what he alluded to even though her cousin couldn't follow the conversation. "I think we have worked hard enough for one day. Tomorrow we will be ready to start building a wall."

Laurel continued to share her lunch with Catherine. Little by little, the girl became comfortable with the new teacher. Laurel learned that Catherine was bright, and she did excellent work on all her lessons. However, reading was the thing the little girl loved most. Frequently, she would ask for extra things to read. Sadly though, Laurel found her to be a very lonely child, shunned by nearly all the other students. They didn't tease her or speak ill of her, but they acted as if Catherine were not even there. Laurel felt it was more than just the poverty that caused the barrier between the little girl and her other students. She wanted to learn as much as she could, hoping she could help the youngster.

On Friday of that week, Catherine began to talk about her family. The story was heartbreaking, but Laurel began to understand part of the problem. Catherine said her father was in prison. He was accused of falsifying land deeds and selling property he didn't have title to sell. Laurel also learned Catherine lost her mother two years earlier to a diphtheria epidemic in southeast Missouri where they lived. She came with her brother Roy to live with her widowed grandmother, who had little means to care for the children. Catherine did tell Laurel that her granny fixed them a good breakfast every morning, and often they ate stew or cornpone for supper. "My brother is a fair shot. Sometimes he'll get us a rabbit or some squirrels. We get us a good supper most every night. He's real smart, too. I wished he could come to school, but he says he needs to help grandma."

Catherine's story brought tears to Laurel's eyes. She knew the pain of living without a mother, but she had never known hunger. She was determined to find a way to help this beautiful little girl. Just before the students returned from recess, Laurel asked Catherine if she would let her take her home that afternoon.

"You don't have to do that, Mrs. Mac. It's not too far to walk."

It turned out that 'not too far to walk' proved to be just more than three miles, which Catherine walked every day, rain or shine, in her bare feet. Laurel wanted to meet the grandparent who took the two children to raise, even though it meant hardship and hunger for herself. When they arrived at the one pen cabin, smoke drifted out of the chimney. Inside, Laurel found the extremely clean, neat, but sparsely furnished home of Eleanor Dunn, the sweet lady who embroidered the bread cloth for the pounding the Shiloh community gave her when Mac brought her as a new bride.

The elderly widow sat in a straight-backed cane chair near the fireplace, sewing. In her lap lay the makings of a new dress for her granddaughter, and on the dinner table, Laurel saw a folded piece of material that had been a much larger dress. This dear woman cut up one of her own dresses for material so she could make a new dress for Catherine. Laurel was awed by the generosity and love of this old lady.

"Mrs. Dunn, I am so pleased to know you are Catherine's grandmother. She is such a good student and so willing to learn. I just wanted to meet the person who gave her this love for learning."

"Tain't me, Missy. I ain't able to read nary a word. She just wants to read and write and cipher so bad. Told me she wants to be a school marm, just like you."

"There are many ways to encourage a child. I'm sure Catherine is very aware of all the work and effort you put in to give her a home."

"That's what we had to do after her ma died. I do like having the kids here with me. They are both good children. Bless his heart, Roy walked to Lorado today, near on to five miles, just looking for work. When he finds a job, he always brings me his wages."

"Did he find one today?"

"Got to work half the day…earned twenty cents. Helps to put food on the table for us."

"Roy must be a determined young man. May I see the dress you are making?" Eleanor Dunn smiled a broad grin as she showed her handiwork to the schoolteacher. Laurel saw delicate stitches. The Widow Dunn was an excellent seamstress, and the garment was beautiful, even made of used fabric. A broad smile broke across Laurel's face too. "Mrs. Dunn. This is a beautiful dress. I don't know if you have the time, but I have material for a new dress that I need to have finished before Independence Day. Since school has started, I just don't have time to sew. Would you consider making the dress for me?"

"I'd be pleased to help you out. Least I could do after you been so good to my Cathy."

"Thank you so much. I'll send the muslin home with Catherine on Monday. I am relieved I don't have to make time to finish the dress." A few dollars for sewing could help feed this family. She'd also ask Mac to use Roy to help build their cabin. Walking the three miles would be easier than going to Lorado or Greensboro and perhaps not finding any work. Laurel whispered a word of thanksgiving. She found a way to serve today. How good it felt!

When she arrived at the widow's cabin, Mac was already at back from the homestead. "Laurel, you are very late today. I was about to gather my friends to search the woods for you again."

"I learned my lesson already, Mac. I was just visiting a student's home. I need to do this with all my students so I can get know them better. Do you have work for a fourteen-year-old boy? His family is destitute. The boy has been walking all over the county seeking part time jobs."

"Surely could use some more help if the boy wants to work. I can pay him four bits a day. What's his name?"

"Roy Dunn. He's Eleanor Dunn's grandson."

"Do you know who the Dunns are, Laurel? Their father is a cheat. He took money from several people of our community. Didn't care he was stealing their life savings."

"That has nothing to do with those children or their sweet grandmother who is trying to support them. If that is the way they are treated, like criminals because of their father, no wonder they live in such poverty. Little Catherine doesn't even have shoes to wear to school. Her grandmother took one of her dresses to salvage material to make a new dress for her granddaughter. I thought the church was supposed to care for widows and orphans...Well, they certainly fit the description."

"All right, school marm. I stand shamed. I see your point. I'll give him a trial. If he works hard, I'll keep him around to work on our cabin. Are you happy now?"

"I'm satisfied. You have a good heart, Mac."

"Yes, it's about half the size of yours. I must have a pretty good heart. What's for my supper, Wife?"

⊰⊱

The next week at school was a good one for Laurel. She was keeping a good pace with the students, even though she was dealing with seven grades. She was glad there were no fifth graders to add to the overloaded schedule. She especially enjoyed the little ones, so shy and sweet…so very excited to learn. She often praised the excellent progress they were making. A simple thing like putting a check mark on the reading chart every time they read a sentence correctly made them beam with joy. Laurel loved teaching these small scholars.

Even in the two short weeks since school started, most of the first level students could recognize the letters of the alphabet and write the numbers to ten. Watching their rapid progress was more than a blessing to Laurel. On the other end of the spectrum were her eighth level students, preparing for their common school exam at the end of the fall term. She hoped to see four of them receive their eighth-grade diploma at the Christmas party. If they passed the exam, it would mark the end of their formal education at Shiloh. Although Caleb Crowley was an extremely strong student, Laurel knew he would not go on to higher education. No school of higher learning was anywhere near Greensboro or in Northeast Arkansas. Her students saw little need for more school, but Laurel knew there were students in her class capable of becoming professional people, like doctors or lawyers or teachers, but the best that could be offered to them was an apprenticeship with a practicing professional. Of course, any of them could take the teacher's exam and find a school. Yet because of the low pay, few students wanted that life, knowing they would not be able to support a family on a teacher's pay. They, like their parents, planned to make their living from the land.

51

When her second week ended on Friday, Laurel was proud of her week's progress, but she was happy she would have two days to spend at the widow's cabin and with Mac at the homestead. Time with Mac was pleasant. They never lacked for things to share.

Of late, there was a lot of talk about Greene County being divided into a second county. Of course, that made for much speculation about what would happen to their region of the county, as Shiloh was at its extreme southern end. Well, time would work it all out, but it did provide interesting topics of conversation among the county folk. Nearly every week visitors came to talk politics with him. At times, they brought their wives or lady friends and even their entire families. In her role as lady of the house, Laurel began to make friends with many women in the community. She surprised herself, for within a short time she lost her shyness around new people. She learned that most of them wanted to offer her friendship. Naturally, she attributed their easy acceptance of her to the fact that she was the wife of their favorite son.

Just as she was about to close the schoolhouse door, her Uncle Matthew rode up. "How's my favorite niece, Laurel Grace?"

"I'm not sure I've ever met her. What's her name?"

"You do have a sarcastic streak, don't you, girl?"

"Papa said so. Mac thinks so too. Guess if the shoe fits…"

"Have a good week?"

"I did indeed. I was just thinking about all the progress the children have made in these two short weeks. Is that what you came to find out about, to ask if the school term was going well?"

"To speak true…no. I'm more interested in knowing how my niece is doing being married to my best friend."

"We've been very busy, building the cabin, tending the garden and orchard and me teaching every day during the week. I think Mac's pleased we're making good progress with the homestead."

"I already know all that. I've been out there three times in the past two weeks. Besides John brings home reports every night. I want to know how you are getting along, Laurel Grace. Are you happy, girl?"

"Life is pleasant here at Shiloh. I miss my friends from Hawthorn Chapel, of course. I miss my papa, but Mac is good to me. We have common interests, like church and reading. He's helped me plant the garden and tend my orchard. Things are going well at Mac's homestead."

"You still didn't answer my question, or maybe you did by avoiding the answer, Laurel Grace. Do you see anything Mac is doing as belonging to both of you? I heard you say his homestead and my orchard. I didn't hear you say ours, not once."

"What do you want me to say, Uncle Matthew?"

"I want to know if you are happy with Mac and being here at Shiloh."

"I guess I'm as content as I can be under the circumstances. Uncle, you know Mac and I have a marriage of convenience. Mac told me before I married him we'd have no romance. We are becoming good friends. Has he complained about me?"

"Of course not. Mac would never be disloyal by speaking ill of you behind your back. Don't you know that about him yet? Mac is the most honest man I've ever met. He's always been frank in all his discussions with me. I believe he's that way with you too. That is just his nature."

"I know he is loyal and good."

"Laurel Grace, I was just asking because I am concerned for you. I want you to have a good life. I promised your papa that I'd look after you if he would let you come here to live with us at Shiloh."

"Thank you for caring. I am well and I have no complaints. Mac is doing everything he promised me when we took our marriage vows. What more can I expect?"

"Expect blessings, niece. Blessings! I know they'll come in time."

When Laurel got to the widow's cabin, Mac was not there. Laurel changed from her school clothes to work clothes and went to the barn to milk and gather eggs. She finished the evening chores, even filling the wood box on the porch. She didn't want to go in. The day was so pleasant. Mid May brought more than a hint of summer. The temperature was in the mid 80's, and the cabin was too warm for comfort. Laurel surely didn't like the idea of having to build a fire in the hearth to cook supper. However, she knew it would be unwifely of her to put a cold meal on the table for her husband who worked all day in the heat. Laurel went to the hearth and built a fire to prepare supper. By the time she finished, the cabin was sweltering. Oh, how she missed the springhouse from her papa's land! Yet, that was just another part of her past now lost to her. By the time Mac arrived home at dusk, Laurel's mood was quite low. She was wiping perspiration from her face. She was puzzled by the nature of her uncle's comments at the church, and memories brought her grief back to the surface. Together these things all but overshadowed the good feelings she'd felt at the end of the school day.

Laurel could not stand the thought of eating a meal in the heat. She knew if Mac found her in the hot cabin in her present mood, the evening would not turn out to be the pleasant end of the day she planned that morning. Perhaps a picnic under the trees would be a better way to share the evening meal. She carried the yellow coverlet outside and placed the food there, waiting for Mac to return.

"What's this, a picnic under the stars? What a nice surprise."

"More of a necessity, I'm afraid. I don't remember the evenings being this hot last summer."

"Laurel, we aren't on top of a mountain now. This little ridge won't keep the temperature mild like the mountains did."

"I guess I didn't realized there would be such a difference."

"You seem a little down tonight. Is something wrong at school?"

"No, the week went well. I know the students by name now, and most are doing well."

"Is something else bothering you?"

"It's just the heat. Did you get much done today, working in this heat?"

"I'm used to the climate here, Wife, and we did accomplish a lot of work this week. Two fireplaces totally done and a well dug and ready to have the stonework laid. Next week, we'll get those walls up." Laurel could tell Mac was pleased the progress of his homestead. His eyes lit up when he talked about it. She wanted to feel happy for him, but she felt sad. She wished her uncle hadn't come by school that afternoon. She was in such a good mood until he brought other things to mind, all the things Laurel tried so hard not to think about. "Laurel, you seem a hundred miles away tonight. Tell me what's bothering you."

"I have been thinking about home and missing my papa. I thought about the springhouse and how good a cold glass of water or milk would be. I wondered how Elizabeth is doing and Rachel. It's been more than a month since I have heard anything from Hawthorn. Only one letter's come from anyone back home. Just a little homesick, I guess."

"It's natural to miss your father and your friends, Laurel. I am surprised though. You've seemed pretty content these last couple of weeks. Did something happen to bring all this up for you today?"

"My uncle Matthew came to see me today after school. He asked me if I was happy here at Shiloh. I didn't know what he wanted me to say."

"Knowing Matthew, I'd say he just wanted you to tell him the truth. What did you say to him?"

"I said we were great friends, and I am content here."

"Oh, and what did he say?"

"Just said he was looking out for me, like he'd promised my papa."

"Does he think you are unhappy?"

"He didn't say that. I told him you are kind to me and you are keeping every one of your vows. He told me you are the most honest man he knows. I agreed with him."

"Thank you for those kind words, Ma'am. That being said, why does all that make you feel low? Makes me feel pretty good."

"Who knows what brings on melancholy? Let's just forget it and finish our supper. I went to all the trouble to make a hot meal so we may as well eat it while it is still warm." They ate in silence until neither of them wanted anything else.

The widow's cabin was still too warm, so Mac knew sleep would not come for a while. "Laurel, it's a moon bright night. Let's go for a swim in the creek. It's not a bad walk across the back pasture, and that water will feel wonderful on a warm night like this."

"Mac, don't be ridiculous. I have nothing to wear swimming."

"Come on. Your chemise will do fine. Only the two of us will be there. Come on."

Mac seemed determined to go. Laurel wasn't much of a swimmer and had never been swimming in the company of a man before. She went along, hoping Mac would swim alone while she sat on the bank to watch.

After the short walk, they reached the creek. When Laurel protested about being a poor swimmer, Mac relented and said, "Just sit on the bank and put your feet in the water. It's cool. You'll change your mind." Laurel knew if she protested, an argument could ensue, so she gave in. She sat down and took off her shoes and stockings. She pulled her skirt up to her knees and dangled her feet and calves into the cool creek water. Mac was right. The water was cool and pure pleasure on her bare legs. The bright night under the full moon and stars should have been a taste of paradise. The night sky looked almost gray-white. She could clearly see Mac swimming a short distance away. Why didn't she just relax and take pleasure in the evening? Her low thoughts continued to run through her consciousness. Mac called to her, taunting and pleading with her to come into the water. She just waved him away and went back to her musing. Her attention turned to the night sky. The moon shone so brightly many of the stars vanished in the spring sky. The scents from the spring flowers wafted across the meadow. She listened to the rustling of the leaves in the trees and bushes surrounding the creek on that warm, humid night. The immense beauty of the night carried her from reality until she felt a strong tug on her legs. The next moment she found herself shoulder deep in the creek with Mac smiling at her.

"I don't know where you were, but I doubt if the place was as nice as this beautiful creek. Don't you think the water feels wonderful? I couldn't let you miss a treat like this."

"Mac—my clothes are all wet now."

"I tried to get you to take them off. You wouldn't listen."

"I told you, I don't swim very well. I told…" Mac captured her lips, just a tiny kiss, before she could register her second complaint.

"Just relax. I won't let you go. Just lay back in my arms. Enjoy the sensation. Lord, thank you for this fine evening and this cool water."

Laurel tried to relax. She may as well try to have fun because she was already drenched from head to toe. She floundered a couple of times when she stepped on slippery rocks.

"I told you if you'd just lean back in my arms, I'll keep you afloat. You don't always have to do everything by yourself."

Laurel leaned back, and Mac encircled her body with his arms. He held her close to his bare chest and kept her afloat, just as he promised. After a few minutes, Laurel pushed the melancholy away and let herself enjoy the present. They drifted for some time, just the two of them, enjoying the cool water and the closeness.

Laurel's low mood totally vanished by the time the swim ended. She was close to Mac. He was holding her. The emotion that came over her was not just the lovely sensation of the cool water on her body. She loved Patrick MacLayne, and she didn't want this feeling to end.

"Better get you home, Wife. Tomorrow will be another busy day. Thanks for coming to swim with me tonight. Maybe next time, you'll take off those bulky outer things. Then you won't have to walk home in wet clothes. Laurel put on her shoes and stockings, and they walked back to the widow's cabin hand in hand.

All the way back, Mac inwardly scolded himself. Why did he pull Laurel into that creek and hold her so closely while they played in the water? For the past two weeks, he was quite aloof with Laurel, a peck on the cheek for a goodbye kiss in the morning and a quick kiss before he turned his back to her at night. He knew much more would bring back strong feelings that arose too often since they shared a bed. He never felt more drawn to her than he did that night. Why did he make that promise to her? Laurel would never feel safe until she gave herself to him, just as he waited for her to take his hand at their wedding. He only hoped he could be patient enough for her to want to be his wife completely. Mac shook his head and took a deep breath. He needed to step up two projects... faster cabin building and more courting. August 11th was only ten short weeks away.

CHAPTER FIVE

A soft answer turneth away wrath:...
The fear of the Lord is the instruction of
wisdom; and before honor is humility.

Proverbs 15:1,33 [KJV, c1850].

For the first few weeks of school, Laurel's days were consumed with preparing lessons, meeting the parents of her students, and learning about Shiloh community. In many ways, the community was much like the one she left in March. Like Hawthorn, Shiloh was made of several "clans" of people who had settled the area to find a better life than the one they left in their native states. It seemed that nearly everyone in the area was related in one way or another to the rest of the citizens. Most of them were devoted to their church. Many came as Methodists together, and they continued to center their community life around their church. Most of the things Laurel found so alien about this community dealt with the nearly flat landscape, the heat, and the heritage of its people. In Hawthorn, a good number of those families claimed their roots in Germany and the northern countries of Europe. If asked, the people of Shiloh said they were Americans. Most of those who knew about their families could trace ancestors to times before there was a United States.

Laurel often remained at school long after her students returned home for the day, and she arrived home near dark many days a week. She was tired, but it was a good kind of tired coming from living out a purpose. On afternoons when she found no school work to do, she would ride out to the homestead to work beside Mac, John Campbell, and Roy Dunn. All the long hours and strong effort were quickly raising the MacLayne house. The foundation for both pens was finished, four tiers of logs, level and straight, lay on all sides of the main pen. The logs, planed on three sides, fit together uniformly, and Mac's attention to detail insured the house would be warm and comfortable for years to come. On three of the walls, openings for doors and windows were beginning to take form. The opening for the back door was only steps away from the newly stoned well Mac and John rocked the previous week. Mac told Laurel that the porch would touch the well so Laurel could draw water under the cover of the porch roof.

Near the cabin, her garden was growing quickly. Within a couple of weeks, they would have fresh vegetables for their table. Meals would be ever so much better when she served fresh greens, carrots, and early pole beans along with the meat and bread. Laurel realized she'd have to make time to can the extra harvest as it ripened. One of the most important roles of any pioneer wife was to assure the larder would hold adequate food to see her family through the winter and early spring of the coming year, and Laurel looked forward to watching the root cellar and smokehouse fill with food to feed her family until spring brought another bounty of victuals. A full larder was the least she could provide for her friend who vowed to take care of her. Another thought dawned on Laurel... there were no canning supplies. The few jars she brought from

Hawthorn were in the wagon in Black Rock. On their next trip to Greensboro, she would need to purchase the paraffin and canning jars she would need to store the harvest from the garden. Laurel also wished she'd asked Elizabeth for her recipe for creamed corn. Her papa loved it so. Just as quickly, Laurel's happy mood ended as she remembered that her papa would not sit at the table and eat the creamed corn that he loved. A tear ran down her cheek. If she could just have her papa back for a little while…Just as quickly, she wiped the tear away with the back of her hand and scolded herself. How could she be so selfish as to want her father back in pain and suffering when he was living in paradise with his beloved Leah? A scolding came inaudibly to her…. Laurel Grace Campbell, quit thinking of the past and get busy building your new life.

"You're lost in thought, Laurel. What's pulled you away from your gardening?"

"Just some memories of my papa…Mac, are you going to Greensboro soon?"

Her need for canning jars provided the perfect opportunity to change the subject. She did not want to get into a serious discussion with Mac that afternoon.

"I thought we might drive over on Saturday if you want. There's going to be a debate on the square, if the weather permits. Have you ever been to a debating contest before?"

"Not that I recall. What is a debating contest?"

"In the afternoon, two men will put on a public debate and be judged to find out who won. We'll go over in the morning to get supplies I need for the cabin and have a nice lunch in the hotel dining room. After that, we'll go to the debate."

"Sounds like an interesting way to spend a Saturday. Who's going to debate?"

"I think John J. Armstrong who lives in Greensboro will be one of the debaters. He usually puts up a good argument and often wins. He's a well-respected member of the town."

"Who will be his opponent?"

"Just an average homesteader from Shiloh—Patrick MacLayne. Interested in seeing a debate?"

"You know I am. I can hardly wait 'til Saturday."

"Well, it's nearly dusk. Boys, you've earned your pay today." Mac took his coin pouch and handed a day's pay to John and Roy. "Best get along home before dark. See y'all back in the morning." When the boys walked out of the yard toward the road, Mac went to Laurel and took her hand. "I have an image of a shy young woman who would flinch every time I touched her. You don't know what ever happened to her, do you? I've gotten used to having her around."

"Oh, you! Are you going tease me forever?"

"Good Lord willing." Mac pulled Laurel into his arms. "Are you pleased with the progress of the cabin, Laurel?"

"Of course, I'm very pleased your dream is getting closer. So nice to see the walls go up…a little more every day."

"I'd be a sight more pleased when you understand this is not just my dream. This is our house, Laurel. The whole reason I came to Hawthorn was to bring you back here to our land so we can build a home.

"Mac, I have contributed practically nothing to this homestead."

"Enough for now. When I've finished the cabin, I will have earned the right to be your husband. I will have met nearly every condition set out by your father. Will you be ready to become the mistress of this home, Laurel?" Mac looked at Laurel's face, but she couldn't look at him. She knew if she did, Mac would see the love she felt for him. She did not respond to his question. "Laurel, this cabin can be our house or it can be our home. You'll have to determine how we live together."

"Mac, with the Lord's help, I will try to be the best helpmate I can be. For now, that is the only answer I have for you."

"For now, that is enough." Mac tilted Laurel's head up to meet his gaze. He pushed a curl away from her face and lowered his lips to hers. The kiss he gave her was the most passionate kiss he'd ever dared share with Laurel. Within a few seconds, Laurel returned the kiss without reservation. He looked up and smiled at Laurel, and then he brought her hand to his lips and kissed her wide wedding band. "Just like the first time, eh Laurel? So nice, but I'm thinking I like this way better." For a second time, he kissed Laurel with a passion that left them both a bit shaken.

"Laurel, we need to get back to the Widow's. The evening chores won't do themselves. It'll be dark before we get back now."

"A nice swim in the creek would be a fine close to this hot day."

"I don't think that's a good idea tonight, Wife. I'm expecting a visitor after supper. John told me his pa and Albert Stuart are planning to visit."

After supper, Matthew Campbell arrived with the Greensboro attorney. Laurel had seen him around the area, but she didn't recall that she ever met Albert Stuart. Mac made introductions, "Albert Stuart, I'd like to introduce you to my wife, Laurel."

"So nice to see Mac get settled. You are a lucky man, Mac!" Laurel was glad she still wore her school dress. What would he have said to Mac to see her in her dungarees, her favorite state of dress?

"Thanks, Al. I know I've been blessed with the best helpmate possible."

"If you'll excuse me, I've some sewing to do tonight. I'll leave while y'all talk."

"No need, Laurel. You probably have a thing or two to add to the conversation."

"No, Uncle Matthew. I'll just sit here in my rocking chair and finish this skirt hem. I am afraid I started it several weeks ago and just haven't gotten it finished."

<hr/>

The men pulled chairs around the table and began a serious discussion.

"Mac, we need you to commit to the representative race for the next election. I know it's near a year away, but we got a lot of territory to cover so the most voters of Greene County will get to know you. Your folks here at Shiloh know you'd be the best man for the job, but there are a lot of voters north of us that hardly know your name."

"We've heard there has been some talk up around Gainesville that a stranger has moved up there, and he is putting pressure on folks to send him to work with the 'Family' in Little Rock. I'm sure someone sent him here to keep us in tow."

Mac looked at Al Stuart with a frown on his face. "Mac, you'll be so much more electable now that you're married and building your own homestead. You are stable, an ideal candidate for our region. Everyone around here likes and respects you. We need a voice in Little Rock and not an ingrained political puppet who keeps Arkansas under the yoke of the Family."

"Al, I'm flattered to be considered, but I haven't discussed this with Laurel at all. You know we got a lot going on right now...newlywed, in the middle of building a cabin, Laurel's teaching... we need to talk about this before I can answer."

"Mac, our congregation wants you to run. We want a say in some of the issues coming around. You know they are talking about splitting up Greene County. What'll become of us? As much as it pains me, the secession talk is growing...and even here in our area, there are people who moved from the states further south that want Arkansas to leave the union."

"Matthew, I know these are serious issues we're facing, and they have been debated in the state legislature for more than one session. They will be talked out again. I need some time to see how Laurel feels about a decision like this. Just this afternoon, we were talking about our workload right now. Give us a couple of days to make a decision."

"We'll ask again on Saturday at the debate. Keep in mind, duty comes before convenience." The talk about politics went on for a good part of an hour. Finally, Al Stuart rose to leave. "I'll bid you good evening, Mrs. MacLayne. Been a pleasure to meet you."

"Thank you, Mr. Stuart." Laurel rose to see her guest to the door of the widow's cabin.

"Mac, will you walk out with me? I need to get back to Ellie and the kids shortly. Good night, Laurel. See you at the debate on Saturday. Ellie is looking forward to a good gossip session with you."

"Good night, Uncle Matthew. Ride carefully." Mac and Matthew walked out toward the barn where Matthew tied his horse. They were silent as they walked the short distance. Matthew pointed to an upturned keg for Mac to sit on, and he leaned his six-foot-four-inch-frame against the fence.

"I know you didn't ask me out here to look at your horse. What's on your mind, brother?"

"You are and Laurel."

"I know. She told me you visited her at school a few days ago. She said you wanted to know if she was happy with me."

"That's true. I asked, but she didn't answer. She talked around the question, but she wouldn't look me in the eye or tell me yes or no."

"Has she said or done anything to make you think she's unhappy?"

"Not in any outward way. She respects you too much to say or do anything to embarrass you."

"I'm aware of her nature. She made that vow to me at our marriage ceremony. She wouldn't knowingly break the vow."

"She looked real content...happy tonight. Sitting there sewing and listening to the political discussion, don't you think?"

"Laurel is pretty content, I think. She loves the kids at school, and she told me she feels a real call to teaching. She said the other day that most of the ladies seem to accept her. I know she felt really isolated at her father's homestead. I think she's glad to be here."

"At times, she seems pretty moody. One moment, she'll be cheerful, and the next time the expression on her face seems sad to me. Have you noticed?"

"Yes, this afternoon she cried a little while. She told me she'd been thinking about her papa. You know, that loss is still new, but tonight, she was happy and busy…"

"Did something happen to bring her out of her melancholy?"

"Matthew…well, I don't know if …I'm not sure…"

"Stop stuttering and tell me what's on your mind."

"We talked about moving into our cabin and whether we'd have a house or a home. I kissed her a couple of times."

"Well, I'm hoping you've done that on several occasions."

"No. I really kissed her – not a brotherly peck on the cheek."

"I see."

"Matthew, did you think about that question I asked you a while back? If I never learn to love Laurel, well, like you love Ellie…do you think I should…"

"Mac…first you have to stop comparing your relationship with others. You two are not like anyone else in the world. You never find one couple who loves like another one. I know you compare your feelings for Laurel to that stormy relationship with Marsha. You are a different man now, and Laurel is certainly no Marsha, from what you've told me. Think about that…you weren't quite 21 when that romance ended. You aren't a moon struck kid anymore. Besides, do you want that kind of relationship now?"

"Would it be a sin if I took Laurel to my bed knowing I don't love her?"

"All I know, it would be a sin to hurt her again. I'm not sure I ever should have set this whole affair up! I am sure that she is way too good for you. Treat her well, brother. I don't want my niece to live with a broken heart. She's already known too much sorrow and tragedy. Don't add to her scars, Mac."

"I'll work to make sure she gets a stable, contented life."

"I hope that is enough. Just keep praying about it Mac. The Lord will answer in His time. See y'all Saturday."

Mac returned to the widow's cabin to find Laurel in the loft. He blew out the oil lamp she'd left burning on the table and climbed to the loft. He found Laurel dressed in a new lawn nightdress. She turned down his side of the covers, plumped his feather-stuffed pillow, and brought the novel Ivanhoe with her.

"Laurel, thank you for being the ideal hostess to my friends tonight."

"You're welcome." Mac put away the clothes he removed and went over to the bed. He sat next to Laurel and read from the book of Proverbs that night.

> *"Who can find a virtuous woman? For her price is far above rubies.*
> *The heart of her husband doth safely trust in her, so that he shall have no need of spoil.*
> *She will do him good and not evil all the days of her life.*
> *She layeth her hands to the spindle and her hand holdeth the distaff.*
> *She stretcheth out her hands to the poor; yea she reaches out to the needy.*
> *She maketh herself coverings of tapestry; her clothing is silk and purple.*
> *Her husband is known in the gates when he sitteth among the elders of the land.*
> *Strength and honor are her clothing; and she shall rejoice in time to come.*
> *She openeth her mouth with wisdom; and in her tongue is kindness.*
> *She looketh well to the ways of her household, and eateth not the bread of idleness.*
> *Her children arise up, and called her blessed; her husband also, and he praiseth her.'*

"The Proverbs writer surely knew you. These words could have been written as a tribute to you, Laurel Grace MacLayne. Good night, friend." Mac rose, bent, and kissed Laurel good night. "I don't know what will be the outcome of our relationship, but whatever does come, you are this virtuous woman, more than worthy to be my wife, worthy to be the wife of any man. You are my gem of uncounted value."

"Goodness, what strong words. What brought that on?"

"Your uncle reminded me of something tonight. That's all." He bent over and kissed her again—not the passionate, sensuous kiss of the afternoon—but a caress of tenderness he hoped would let Laurel know he valued her. "Lord, as we lay our busy life aside for a while to rest, we ask you to look over us and bless our lives together. Amen." Mac beat on his pillow a time or two and made a cradle for his head. "Would you let me hold you tonight, Laurel?"

"I would enjoy being close to you. You make me feel safe and and…worthy. Good night, Mac."

"Before we sleep, Laurel, tell me what are your thoughts about me running for the state legislature to represent Greene County."

"Do you want to run, Mac?"

"I've thought about it often, but that was when I didn't have anyone else to consider. If I do this, it will make demands on you, too. You'd have to entertain strangers at times. You will have to come with me to Little Rock now and again to attend social events. People will come around all the time, wanting my time and attention. I know you are used to a quiet life."

"I wouldn't make a very good hostess for your visitors. You know what I'm like with strangers."

"What I've seen these few weeks since we've been home is a gentile lady who likes people, who works hard to serve her students, and cares for the needy in her community. I couldn't ask for a better partner."

"But Mac, politicians' wives are beautiful, elegant, articulate women who help promote their husbands' campaigns."

"You are more than capable of doing anything I would ask you to do. I told you once to look at yourself through my eyes, remember? Do you see what I see?"

"I don't know what you see, but Mac, I will try to do whatever you need me to do. If you want to serve, then I will support you. If you wouldn't be embarrassed to have me...."

Mac put his finger to her lips as he did many times before. "I am proud to have you on my arm. I will continue to be proud of you."

"I believe you know what answer you will give to Uncle Matthew and Mr. Stuart on Saturday. We'd better get some rest. Fridays are usually hectic days at school. The students are always a little restless thinking about the weekend."

Laurel couldn't have predicted the events of the next day any better. At morning recess, the sixth level girls got into an argument over Caleb Crowley, who wouldn't pay the least attention to either of them. One second grade boy got sick from eating too much at lunch, and he vomited before he could leave the room. The top-level students were working on essays that required them to read several articles from books and a few old newspapers Laurel had salvaged as references to support an argument. They were constantly asking questions of Laurel when she was trying to work with the youngest in the room.

About an hour before she would dismiss school for the day, a seventh-grade boy named David Coffman became belligerent when he thought Laurel was ignoring his request for help. Laurel was forced to deal with her first real discipline issue since school started.

"Mrs. Mac, I done asked you a hundred times to show me how to do them danged arithmetic problems. You're ignoring me."

"David, please don't yell in the classroom. I'll be over there in a minute."

"I'll yell if I want. You just don't like me because I ain't like some of them." David shot out of his chair, and his slate clattered on the floor. Color rose in his face.

"David, sit down please and calm yourself."

"Don't you tell me what to do. Who do you think you are anyway? My ma says you're an outsider and got no business being here anyhow. Everyone knows Mac just married you because he felt sorry for you." Gasps came from several girls.

"Caleb and Suzanna, please help take all the students outside for recess." Laurel walked over and laid her hand on David's shoulder. He jerked away from her touch. "Please do so quickly." She waited as the two students she asked ushered the others out of the church.

"David, let's discuss this matter in private."

Anger clouded his face, but Laurel did not move her gaze from the boy. He could hurt her, if he had a mind to do so. He was certainly big enough, but she wouldn't back down. If she were to maintain her control over her students, she must hold her ground.

"I would like to talk about what made you angry."

"We ain't got nothing to talk about."

"Can you tell me the reason you spoke back to me and attacked me personally? Have I done something to offend you?"

"You do it every day…you mark my tests down. You don't pay me no heed when I ask for help. You play favorites to those high-class kids." Pacing the room, David refused to return to his seat. He was a large boy, standing half a head taller than Laurel. He was fifteen years old and should have been in the top-level class with Caleb and the three girls who would finish this year, but he didn't attend school the last term the previous year.

"I am surprised to hear you say those things. Why didn't you say something before if you felt ignored?"

"I don't talk out until I get mad enough."

"I see. And today I made you that angry. Is that it?"

"Leave it be...I'm quitting school. Who needs to graduate anyway?"

"David, please come sit down and let's talk."

"No. What about them other kids anyway? It ain't recess time."

"I don't want to talk about them right now. They aren't about to make a bad choice."

"What do you care?"

"I care. Please tell me what brought this out today."

"I can't do them danged fractions. I just lost my temper. Don't guess I meant all that stuff I said."

"That doesn't matter. Why would you tell me you're quitting school if you really wanted to quit? Why not just walk away?"

"I can't do that math."

"I don't think that's the reason you're upset. You always understand after I've shown you the mistakes you're making." David was silent, and he sat looking out the window toward the green valley stretching down from the church. Laurel did not speak either.

After several minutes, David looked at her and spoke, "Why didn't you crack my knuckles with that ruler? The last teacher would throw me out of school for sass."

"Is that what you want? Or do you want someone to listen to you?"

"You want to listen to me after I sassed you?"

"People don't usually lose their tempers without a reason."

"Ain't no grown up in my life ever wanted to hear what I say." Again, Laurel was quiet. "Ain't you going to say nothing?"

"I thought you wanted me to listen to you. That is what I am doing."

"Can I tell you anything?"

"Yes, I will listen."

"I like learning, but my pa wants me to quit so I can help out on the farm. I ain't no farmer. I'd like to learn about stuff, the law maybe. I'd like to be a constable or even a lawyer someday, maybe. I can't do that if I quit school."

"Having a dream is a fine thing. How can we keep you in school and still satisfy your pa?"

"Do you think I'm smart enough to have another trade besides farming? Pa thinks I'm dumb."

"David, being smart is more about determination and persistence than it is about how easy it is to learn."

"What do them big words mean?"

"Well, first of all you need to learn those big words. Lawyers must be good spokesmen. Determination just means making up your mind that you are going to do something. Persistence means you won't quit until you get what you want."

"You think I can get a diploma?"

"If you stay in school. Let's think what we need to do to show your parents you want to stay in school. How can you ease the problems at home?"

"Probably can't. My pa's a stern man. He don't like to talk much. He gives orders and expects everyone to do what he says. Maybe if I did my chores before he told me and worked more in the afternoons and on Saturday, he'd be satisfied. Ma wants me to graduate, I know. I guess I could study after sundown."

"That sounds like a plan to try. Is there anything else you need me to hear?"

"No ma'am…except I'm sorry for that ugly thing I said to you. Ain't none of my business anyhow. I'm real sorry…I know I deserve to be kicked out."

"Everyone deserves to be given a second chance, if they ask for it sincerely, but David, never attack me like that in front of the class again. I'll always listen to you if you ask me in the right way."

"Yes ma'am. I'm sorry."

"I accept your apology. There must be a consequence for your outburst. If not, other students may decide to act the same way.

Next week, you will have no recess. Instead, we'll work together on those fractions, understand?"

"Yes ma'am...I deserve lots worse."

Laurel breathed a sigh of relief. Unsure of what would happen when she sent the other students outside, she'd handled the conflict well. She called the students back to finish the day. The last half hour of class, she told the students about some of the things seen on her way across the state. Many of these students were curious, as some of them had never been out of Greene County. She told them about having to cross rivers on ferries and fording streams. They asked questions. Then she told them about the other churches they'd visited along the way, and again they asked questions. She explained to them how easy it is to lose your way on the "roads to nowhere" that lace the state. And finally, she described the mountains she called home before she came to Shiloh. All this led other students, recently new to Shiloh, to share their experiences of how they traveled to Arkansas. When 3:30 came, they hardly noticed the day was finished.

Laurel was exhausted. The day was a good one, but the tension of the confrontation sapped much of her energy. Besides, the unintentional remark about the gossip bothered her. Was she mistaken thinking the community accepted her? Were they only putting up with her because she was Mac's wife and a member of the preacher's family? Did they see her as...Laurel shook her head. She would not let her old self-doubt and feelings of worthlessness return to dominate her new life. She already gave too many years to those demons.

She remained at school until quite late that afternoon. She didn't want to start a new week without being prepared, and there were plans that would more than fill both Saturday and Sunday. The weekend would offer little opportunity to work on school lessons. Before she left school, though, Mac rode up in a rush. He was at the Campbell homestead when their kids arrived home. Of course, the first thing they talked about was the outburst that afternoon. As kids do, they told the story with much more drama than it deserved. Mac rushed through the open doorway.

"Are you all right? Did that Coffman boy attack you?"

"It's all over. David was upset by something else. Everything is fine."

"The kids told us he said some mean things to you."

"Just like everyone does when they are angry or hurt. People always say things they don't mean when they lose their tempers."

"What did he say?"

"Nothing worth repeating, Mac. I handled it. It's part of a teacher's job to maintain discipline in her school. I did my job."

"Did he say in front of all those kids I only married you out of pity?"

"Yes, but he was only repeating what he heard others say. I'm fine. Let's just forget it and get on home. There is much to do if we are going to be gone all day tomorrow."

⚎

Mac hugged Laurel to him. He was upset because he didn't know who spread that gossip among the Shiloh community. He knew Matthew would never say a thing like that. On the other hand, he was amazed Laurel was changing so drastically from the shy, retiring woman he married months ago. This woman was confident, able, and professional. Everything thing about her demeanor showed Mac she was a born teacher. If he could help her transfer the same strength to her personal life, he would have more than fulfilled the fourth promise, the most difficult one, he made to Mark Campbell.

By sunrise the next morning, Mac was out doing his morning chores so he could take Laurel to Greensboro for the day. By 8:00, he was dressed in his suit trousers and the stylish Easter shirt. He tied on his green silk wedding tie. Due to the heat of the day, he left his coat on the peg. Laurel put on her gray calico skirt and white lawn blouse. She tied her hair back with her green ribbon. Mac decided they looked like a couple.... "Well, Wife...let's go to Greensboro."

The little community was buzzing with people. Many were milling around the main street, while others sat outside the livery on bales of hay and on upturned kegs. People came from settlements around the region to do their business, to get their mail, and to listen to the debates. Frequent debate contests were a very popular form of entertainment in the fledgling town. They were not only entertaining, but men would wager on which debater would win the day. Following the day's debate, everyone would stay for square dancing and reels. Some would not return home until the following day. Merchants, innkeepers, and the saloon owners loved debate days. Their businesses profited handsomely with the crowds in town.

Mac, with Laurel in hand, made his way to John McCullough's store to purchase several items they needed at the widow's cabin. Mac also wanted to pick up the mail there, for John was the local postmaster.

"Mac, the prices are really dear at this store. Perhaps we should try another."

"Laurel, don't fret about the prices. You know how hard it is to bring all these supplies by freight. Just get what you need." Mac remembered they had still not really talked about their finances. When they were home, the subject never seemed to come up. He again made a mental note to talk to Laurel soon about their money situation. Married people should know what they could afford to buy or not buy.

⊷⊶

Laurel picked out two spools of thread at ten cents each, four boxes of matches at twenty cents for the lot, a package of three needles costing fifty-eight cents, and five bars of soap that cost sixty-five cents. She hated to pay so much for soap, but what little she brought across the swamp was long gone. To replenish their foodstuffs, she picked up ten pounds of cornmeal, which cost forty cents, a tin of baking soda for fifteen cents, fifty pounds of flour at $1.25, seven pounds of coffee that cost $1.00, and ten pounds of sugar at the outrageous price of $1.25. The sugar was a luxury. When she took her items to the counter where John McCullough stood, she asked for five dozen canning jars and ten pounds of paraffin to store the harvest from the garden. She spent almost $17.00.

"Well done, Laurel. Why don't you add ten yards of muslin to that order, John? I like that one there with the little stripes of blue on white. You like that one, Laurel?"

"Mac, it's too much. I already have three new dresses."

"You do like blue, don't you, Laurel?" Laurel nodded, but she didn't smile. "Add it up, John and make us a neat bundle. We'll pick it up before you close this afternoon."

They left the mercantile together. "Let's see if we can find Matthew and Ellie. They should be here by now."

After walking down the street toward the mill, they found Matthew and Ellie alone. "We left Mary with Susan for the day, knowing we'd return late. Your Uncle Matthew likes to have a romantic day once in a while, when he pretends we are still courting and not an old married couple." Ellie smiled at her niece. "He's always been the romantic sort, you know." Of course, they would have to return home tonight, as the next day was the Sabbath.

The four friends went to the hotel to have lunch together. They'd hardly sat down when Al Stuart approached with two other men that Laurel did not know.

"Tell me, Mac. Can I nominate you to run for the legislature next spring?" asked Stuart.

"Come on, Al. I need to talk to a few more friends."

Laurel smiled broadly as she interrupted the conversation. She stifled a laugh at the surprised look on Mac's face as she spoke up. "Mr. Stuart, my husband is honored at your support. He looks forward to the campaign."

"Well, niece," said Matthew, "I'm surprised you took the lead here. What's come over you?"

"Nothing. I'm the same girl you've always known. Mac wants this, and if that is what he wants, I support him. What is strange about that?"

"Nothing I can think of. What about you, Mac?"

"Gentlemen, I think my opponent better watch out if Laurel is going help me campaign. There is no doubt, I'll win. Thank you, Laurel." She smiled and nodded but did not reply.

"Ellie, are you about ready to start canning? I know your garden is some ahead of mine."

"I have some early…"

The conversation continued throughout lunch. The fellowship and affection shared with her family was real, and Laurel loved the time they spent together. About 2:30, Matthew and Mac left the ladies to go pack their wagon with the supplies they'd bought. Ellie took the opportunity to talk alone with her niece.

"Laurel, the kids told me about that Coffman boy's attack at school. You didn't believe what he said about Mac, did you?"

"He said it was gossip he'd heard, and yes, I believe he heard some people in the community say what he repeated to me."

"I hope you weren't too upset."

"No. I expected some people to be a bit standoffish because they don't know me. Nothing I haven't experienced before. Besides, it's true for the most part. Mac was being kind and compassionate to a dying man. I know that."

"Laurel, dear, are you unhappy?"

"Aunt Ellie, Mac is doing everything he promised he would do. How can I let that upset me?"

"Your Uncle Matthew has been worried about you. We just want you to love our community and be glad to make this your home."

"Aunt Ellie, I am content with my choice, and it was my choice. My papa and Mac both allowed me to choose. I chose to become Mac's wife rather than live as a spinster niece in your home. I am fine. Please don't worry about me. Both Mac and I walked out in faith, so we have to believe this is what we were meant to do."

"What about love, Laurel? Even after more than thirty years I love your Uncle Matthew. I can't fathom a life without him. He is the other half of me."

"And I am happy for you, Aunt. God gave you a wonderful gift. You both deserve the love you share."

"I wish you could have that bond too, Laurel."

"I am grateful for what I have. Don't fret over me. The Lord is watching over me."

"I'll stop prying. Just know, niece, we're your family. If you need anything…"

"You are good to me, Aunt. Oh, look…there are our fellas. Must be nearly time for the debate."

Crowds began to gather at the porch of John McCullough's mercantile. The covered porch would serve as a platform for the judges and the debaters as they competed in two rounds of impromptu debates. At the end of the second round, a winner would be selected. Al Stuart, the town lawyer, would serve as the announcer for the competition. James McNeely, a local apothecary, and Alexander Davis, the owner of the second mercantile in Greensboro, would be the judges. If the two men called a draw to the debate, Lawyer Stuart would cast the final vote to break the tie. Al Stuart announced the rules to the crowd as the event began on that sunny afternoon.

When the crowd found a place to sit, lean, or stand around the porch, Mr. Stuart posed the first topic for the debate. Laurel was excited, and she could hardly believe that her husband was one of the debaters. As he rose at his introduction, Laurel could not take her eyes from this attractive man, handsomely dressed and meticulously groomed with his shoulder length chestnut hair tied back with a leather lace. His too blue eyes were bright with anticipation of the competition. She couldn't believe this man chose to marry her. Her love for him was far beyond the friendship she had promised to give him, and the feelings frightened her. She knew Mac wanted nothing to do with that kind of commitment. Again, she pushed the strong emotion away from her consciousness.

"Friends, listen close. Judge for yourself who's the better communicator here today. Before y'all stand two of our most prominent citizens, Mac MacLayne, who'll be our next state representative after we elect him next year, and Mr. John Armstrong, the man who's won more debates than any other citizen in Greene County. If you are ready, men…here is your first question…John, you will support point A, and Mac you will support point B."

Al took a paper from his sleeve and read, "Is it better to live with a smoking chimney or a nagging wife?" The crowd laughed at the trivial question. They always looked forward to the opening debate, which usually was a topic chosen for its humor. The debaters were expected to use all their wits to make a case when the subject was so silly. Laurel knew this subject was meant to show how quickly a man could think on his feet. "Mr. Armstrong, support your smoking chimney."

John J. Armstrong was a strong orator, and he quickly thought of several good reasons in support of a smoking chimney. He said the faulty chimney provided proof there was heat in a house. People would benefit from the savory flavor it would add to meat roasting at their hearths. Of course, everyone who is fortunate enough to have a smoking chimney can save money by not having to purchase window coverings, since the smoke would naturally coat the oiled paper or glass with a nice opaque color. The most important reason, he stated would be the health benefits brought on with all the fresh air people would breathe in by having to leave their windows and doors open constantly. The clean air from outside would also eliminate the smell that comes from musty homesteads. When his five minutes were over, Mr. Armstrong said he could speak much longer to support the benefit of the smoking chimney. The crowd applauded his efforts.

Mac rose and walked slowly to the front of the porch. He wore a very serious look on his face as he began to explain why a nagging wife was preferable to a smoking chimney. "Well, folks, being recently married to a quiet, well-bred Christian lady, I can't speak from experience."

"Oh, come on, Mac. Save your sweet talk for your own time." Again, the crowd laughed at the heckler seated in a nearby wagon.

"I'll just have to share what all y'all husbands out there have told me about your wives." Again, laughter erupted, but several women looked at their husbands as if they didn't think the remark was amusing. "The best thing about a nagging wife is the prosperity she brings to her family. You know her husband will work from before sun up to well after sun down every day, just to stay away from the house." Laughter filled the street. "A nagging wife also keeps her man happier as she keeps his mind off his own aches and pains because she's always complaining about her own. Moreover, the man with a harping woman in his house can always find his way home in the dark due to the constant yakking he hears."

"You must've heard my woman!" Again, laughter erupted.

Mac continued to make point after point to support his side of the debate. When he was just about out of time, he closed, "Most important, that nagging wife puts her husband's feet on the path to heaven. She keeps him on the straight and narrow. She assures he won't do any sinning because he knows the consequences. He knows after a life of haranguing, fussing, and bossing, he will receive his reward of peace and solace once he reaches the pearly gates."

When the applause and laughter subsided, each of the debaters was allotted three minutes to poke holes in the other man's arguments. Both men found plenty of faults with the other man's reasoning. Then the contestants were given a minute and a half to make a closing statement. Mr. Armstrong spoke, "Friends, everyone prefers a smoking chimney over a nagging wife because even with the smoke, the chimney is a valuable thing to the well-being of a family. A nagging wife is a disagreeable creature that causes nothing but discord and unhappiness to all who live in the house." The crowd clapped and cheered when he finished his closing statement.

Then Mac had his chance to make his last pleas. "Folks, that nagging wife is not the problem. She only speaks up to remind her husband of his obligations. No real man wants to live with a nagging wife, so he should take heed of scolding words so he can get back in line with the vows he made when he married in the first place. No woman nags when she is honored, cherished and..." Mac hesitated for a few seconds, longer than he intended and an unplanned frown arose to replace the smile he displayed during most of his presentation. The frown was short-lived. Shortly he continued, "...cherished and provided for. She won't have a cause to nag if we live up to the promises we made to her." Again, the crowd applauded. Mac looked out over the people and caught Laurel's eye. She smiled at him. He returned her smile. Mac had been true to himself. He told her he didn't want to love again, so he wouldn't use that as a point, even to win a debate.

During a brief recess from the contest, Mac came down to speak with Laurel, Matthew, and Ellie as they sat together on the wagon seat. "How did you like the debate?"

"You did very well. Your argument was much more logical than Mr. Armstrong's. Thank you for the nice compliment you made to me." Laurel gave him a coy smile.

"Only spoke the truth. Anyway, I will do much better in the second round."

"Well, brother, you might make that closing statement a little smoother next time. That was one long pause at the end! Made me think you'd lost sight of your point." Matthew, too, noticed Mac's long pause.

The second round was a serious topic. This part of the debate gave people a chance to see where a man's opinions lay in the political spectrum. Laurel knew Mac would have no difficulty with this part of the contest for they frequently talked about the current state political issues.

Al Stuart came to the front of the porch. "Gentlemen, we will extend the debate time by double. Opening presentations will be ten minutes, the rebuttal will be five minutes, and the closing remarks will be limited to three minutes. The judges have decided the opening round is very close so this debate will determine the outcome of the contest. The topic is…" Al stopped and pulled another piece of paper from his sleeve, "…Should Arkansas support or reject the abolition of slavery? This time we ask you to speak to your own opinions, whatever they may be. Mac, you will go first."

Mac spoke eloquently in support of abolition. He cited economic reasons, moral issues, and social benefits. When his ten minutes ended, he still wanted to make several more points. Mr. Armstrong was an anti-abolitionist, and his feelings were as strongly pro-slavery as Mac's were against slavery. Strong feelings emanated from the bystanders, some supporting Mac and others supporting Mr. Armstrong. Laurel became edgy as she sensed the hostility arising as the debate continued. The five-minute rebuttals were specific attacks on the opening arguments of the opponent. The atmosphere became even tenser, and strong emotions surfaced several times from both sides of the debate. When time came for closing remarks, Laurel was sitting at the edge of the wagon seat, her back straight, her head high, and her shoulders so tense they ached.

The atmosphere was ominous. Neither laughter nor idle chatter broke the tension. Everyone was waiting to see how these men would close the cases they were making.

Mr. Armstrong closed with a statement about people's property rights and strong need for labor if prosperity was to continue in the South. He spoke of the tradition of the South and the benefits of slavery to the Negro population. He concluded with a familiar argument of slave owning members of the community. "We treat our people well and care for them. They would be lost if they were left to fend for themselves without the support and guidance of their owners."

About half the audience applauded strongly at his conclusion, and the other half applauded politely, as this was the expected etiquette for the event.

Then Mac rose to finish the debate. "Friends, this is not a statement to simply end a debate. I want to state here and now, if you decide to vote for me come election day, this is the position I will take in the legislature. I do not now, nor will I ever support the growth of slavery in our country. Given the opportunity to free the black man, I would vote yes. As a God-fearing man and a practicing Christian, I cannot accept any law that allows one person to own another. We have no right to earn our prosperity on the back of another man. The institution makes us less than the Lord intends us to be. With the help and guidance of the Lord, I will strive to end slavery in our state." Some of the men in the crowd booed loudly while others applauded. Mac did not receive polite applause from his opponent, and it was apparent that the crowd was as divided on the question of slavery as the two debaters were.

When Laurel noticed her uncle wore a scowl on his usually smiling face, she voiced her concern, "Uncle Matthew, is something wrong?"

"Mac should have tempered his words. I hope brawling don't break out. Some of the ruffians in this crowd would enjoy the opportunity to make Mac eat his words."

Her voice trembled. "Is he in any danger?"

"This is just a very touchy subject, that's all." Mac approached his family again to wait with them for the results. The judges were taking a long time with the decision. The crowd became restless and began moving into small cliques where a great deal of murmuring began, and the talk grew louder. Some of the men started jostling and pushing each other around. Matthew Campbell believed a fight was on the brink if something didn't quell the emotions that were growing. A woman screamed when a man near her accidentally stumbled into her, and she fell down. A couple of little girls began to cry as the tension grew worse. Some of the mothers began to pull their children away from the crowd, fearing a brawl was in the making. Matthew Campbell walked to the front of the crowd and climbed to the top step of the McCullough's porch. In his best sermon voice, he spoke.

"Friends, please join me in a brief prayer of thanksgiving for the excellent debate we have just witnessed. Please bow your heads with me. 'Lord, we are so grateful that we live in a land where every man can speak his conscience and know he has that God-given right. We are grateful to have in our midst two such strong debaters whose skills allowed us to see the different sides of this difficult issue our country faces. And Lord, we ask patience and tolerance to see us through these times of trial. Show us Your way. Amen." Matthew's prayer coupled with the high esteem most of the people in the crowd felt for him as a man and as a pastor soothed the tension. The noise ebbed, and even some laughter was heard. Laurel relaxed a bit and then realized how tense she was. Her shoulders ached.

Mac put his arm around her when he sensed that a brawl was about to break out. He noticed Laurel allowed herself to relax.

"Are you all right?" Mac said.

"I'm relieved."

"Laurel, this is just the start of this. If you don't want me to get involved in this campaign, you need to tell me. Remember I told you that it would affect your life as much as mine."

She grew quiet for some time. She hated the ugly side of politics. Her thoughts were of fulfilling Mac's hopes for service and for making a positive change to their state. She never stopped to think that some people would disagree with their vision of what Arkansas life could and should be. Fear began to raise its hateful head.

Al Stuart came to the porch. "Ladies and Gents, this one is a close debate. We haven't seen one this tight in a long time. The judges call the debate a draw, just being too close to call. As the tie breaker, I declare that Mac MacLayne has taken the day by one point. That comment about the nagging wife putting her husband's feet on the path to Heaven was just too powerful to ignore."

Al Stuart, being the astute man he was, knew he needed to close the debate with some humor to steer the attention away from the emotional topic of slavery. Thankfully, the crowd dispersed.

At 7:00, the dancing began. The tiny band was composed of a fiddler, a guitar player, and a short plump lady who was also the local seamstress. Her accordion playing was known far and wide. People from four counties would ask her to play at a variety of social events, anything from a christening party to an Irish wake. They performed a number of reels and square dances. On a rare occasion, they would drop in a waltz. The crowd was familiar with the program of music, and John McCullough, whose porch also served as a band stand, was a very able square dance caller.

Laurel enjoyed the music and watching the couples dance. Her uncle and aunt danced nearly every dance together, looking at each other as if they were the only couple on the street. Laurel's wistful hope was that someday Mac would look at her that way. Of course, her great fear was that when Mac found a woman to love, he would realize he made a dire mistake in taking her to be his wife. He wouldn't discard her, for he would maintain his vows, but being an obstacle to his happiness was not a role Laurel wished to play.

Mac was called aside by William Little and Al Stuart to talk about the official kick off of the political race they planned for Independence Day. People of the area always used Independence Day to announce candidates and stir up political discussion. Mac wouldn't be able to back away from his decision to run for the state legislature after that day.

Shortly, Laurel's uncle came to ask her to dance a reel with him, but she shook her head. She continued to sit on the upturned flour barrel, one of many that was placed around the area in lieu of chairs. The spring evening was beautiful. The temperature was just cool enough to keep the dancers comfortable as they circled, bowed, turned, dipped, and snuggled to the music. The star-lit skies and a bright full moon made for a perfect backdrop to the swirling hues of the ladies' brightly colored skirts. Laurel was enjoying the atmosphere of the town's party. Even from the sidelines, Laurel was pleased to be here. Anyway, she didn't really know how to dance.

Sometime later, Mac returned to the street party to claim his wife. He looked through the crowd. He walked around the outside of the three or four groups dancing reels, but he was unable to find Laurel among the dancers. Then, he saw her sitting in the shadow, almost behind the band. He yanked her to her feet, swirled her in a circle, and pulled her to his chest.

"There you are, Mrs. MacLayne. Why are you hiding here instead of enjoying the dance?"

"Hello, Mac. The local band is good. They know a large variety of dance music, don't they?"

"You are avoiding my question, Laurel. Why aren't you up, having a good time?"

"I'm enjoying the music, the sights, and the nice breeze blowing across the square. Besides, I don't dance very well. I'm afraid I didn't go to dances at Hawthorn Chapel, not since I was fourteen."

"Not a good excuse. Come with me, woman. Anyone can dance." Mac brought her to the street, and he put his arms around her and began to waltz...one, two, three...one, two, three...one, two, three. Within a few minutes, Laurel was smiling, enjoying the sensation of floating around the streets of Greensboro in the arms of the man she loved.

CHAPTER SIX

He that spareth his rod hateth his son; but he
that loveth him chasteneth him quickly.
The angry man stirreth up strife, and a
furious man aboundeth in transgression.

Proverbs 13:24[KJV c1850];
Proverbs 29:22 [KJV c1850].

The first week of summer held such promise as Laurel mounted Sassy Lady to ride the two miles to school. Laurel's students were making excellent progress. Even the youngest had
mastered their ABC's and were working on the common word
list. At lunch that Monday morning, sweet little Catherine walked
to her desk and waited for Laurel to speak to her. Laurel was a
bit surprised to see her. She had made friends with some of the
girls and didn't seek the refuge of her teacher as often. With
small fees for sewing, Mrs. Dunn now provided a small lunch

for Cathy so she was not so hesitant to join the other students. "Hello, Cathy. Can I help you?"

"No ma'am. My granny just wanted me to say your dress is ready for fitting. When can you come over our way?"

Laurel smiled at the little girl she'd grown quite fond of. She knew life was easier for her since her brother was working and her grandmother's reputation for stitchery had found her several jobs about the Shiloh community. Catherine's skills improved daily. Laurel was pleased with all her students, but especially with Cathy Dunn.

"Cathy, that is such a welcome message. I was hoping to have that pretty pink dress with the daisies ready to wear to Shiloh's Fourth of July celebration. That is Mr. Mac's favorite holiday."

"We do have lots of fun on Independence Day. Can you come this week?" Cathy smiled as she turned to go.

"Yes. I'll come tomorrow. Tell your grandmother thank you for me." Laurel knew it was more than thinking of wearing the new dress that made her happy. Independence Day would be another time of dancing with Mac in the starry night. He would use a good part of the day politicking, but not all the time. He would spend much of the night dancing with her. When Cathy went back to finish her recess, Laurel returned to her lovely daydream for too short a time. All too soon she was abruptly brought back to her role as a teacher by a piercing cry from the school yard.

She ran to the front door where she saw Adam, a second level student, lying at the foot of the tree under the rope swing. She lifted her skirts to her knees and covered the yard faster than she knew she could move. When she reached the seven-year-old, she saw he broke his leg in the fall from the swing. Blood was covering his pant leg, so Laurel knew the fracture was more than a simple break. She picked the little boy up and carried him to the porch.

"Caleb, please run to get me some help. Go to my Uncle Matthew's... it's the closest place. We will need to get a doctor to help Adam. We'll need a wagon to take him to Greensboro. Hurry.

Take my horse." She ripped the pant leg to see where the blood came from, knowing she must stop it. When she opened the pant leg, she not only found the protruding tibia, but the entire length of Adam's leg was covered with red, nasty welts. Laurel couldn't believe the extent of the bruising. She tried to calm the frightened boy. She tore a length of her petticoat to make a bandage attempting to halt the flow of blood. She held him in her lap and rocked him gently, back and forth. The other students stood in quiet groups at the base of the stairs. They were concerned for their friend and in awe of their teacher who was covered in the little boy's blood, trying so hard to comfort the frightened child.

"Children, we will have to wait for help to come. I think you should return to your seats. Anna, please choose a story from the level three reader and share it with the entire class, or get that book from my desk instead. Read the first chapter of David Copperfield to them. I know they will enjoy that story."

"Yes, ma'am." The children quietly followed Laurel's directions, and Anna began the story. Laurel was relieved that she wouldn't have to try to keep an eye on the other seventeen students at play while she tried to tend the scared boy in her lap.

Before the hour was over, Matthew Campbell rode up with his team and wagon. In the back, he prepared a pallet with several blankets atop a layer of hay so Adam could lie down during the trip to Greensboro.

"Laurel, I'll take the boy to Dr. Edwards. Looks like you stopped the bleeding for now."

"You'll need some help getting him there. Do you know where his parents may be?"

"His pa is a mill worker over at Wiley's. Mac knows him. They worked together for a spell."

"Find someone to stay with these other students, and I'll go with you." Laurel said.

"It's only an hour 'til school would be out. Send 'em home early today." Matthew was part of the school committee, so

Laurel felt justified in letting school out early. Within minutes, they were headed to town. They didn't cover the four plus miles as quickly as Laurel wanted, but thankfully, Dr. Edwards was in his office late. Matthew picked up the little boy and carried him inside.

"He's got a bad break, Doctor Edwards. He fell from the swing at Shiloh school. The bone broke through the skin, and what's more I think he's been badly beaten." Laurel clasped her hands over her mouth when she heard her words.

Indeed, the exam proved exactly what Laurel reported. He removed Adam's torn bloody pants and shirt only to find more welts on both legs, his buttock, and across his back. There were even a few scars across his thin arms.

"Oh, my dear Lord! Adam, tell me how you got these bruises on your legs, arms and back."

"Mrs. Mac, it ain't nothin'. My leg really hurts. Am I gonna die, Mrs. Mac?"

"No, Adam. Dr. Edwards is going to fix your leg. He'll help you go to sleep and when you wake up, it'll be fixed."

"I won't cry. Papa says big boys never cry, but if it hurts too bad, maybe some tears might get loose from my eye. Don't tell the kids at school I cried."

"It's all right to cry, Adam. Everybody cries sometimes." Laurel was appalled at the sight of the welts, but she waited until Dr. Edwards put Adam to sleep with a noxious smelling concoction from a bottle labeled chloroform. "That stuff is terrible."

"Well, don't breathe too deep." Dr. Gibson told her. This is a new sedative I just recently ordered from Chicago. Getting new things in medicine every day it seems."

"Dr. Edwards, this youngster has been beaten and often. Look at the old scars on his body."

"I've seen the likes of them often. Nothin' I can do. Parents have the right to discipline their kids. Even the Bible says 'spare the rod; spoil the child'."

"This boy hasn't been disciplined. These marks didn't come from a spanking. We have to do something to help him."

"Mrs. Mac…don't get into another family's business. It'll only open a can of worms. Let things be." The doctor's answer to this disgusting sight infuriated Laurel. She could not believe an educated Christian would even suggest the treatment of little Adam was acceptable. Adam needed someone to stand up for him. She left the doctor's office and went to the square to find her Uncle Matthew.

"Uncle Matthew, do you know that poor little boy has been badly beaten? He has welts all over his legs, buttock, and back. He looks as if he has been severely whipped with a belt. The bruises are all different colors, which tell me he gets whipped nearly every day."

"Calm down, Laurel. His pa probably whips him with a razor strop when he is disobedient. Common practice in these parts."

"Do you beat your children with a razor strop?"

"Well, of course not. Have little occasion to scold my young'uns. But many of the other people in the settlement still keep to the old ways."

"How could this be allowed in our congregation? We preach love and acceptance. Forgiveness is the key to our faith. How could a child learn these priceless lessons when he lives with such beatings?"

"Laurel, calm yourself. I'm sure it's not that bad. You are just upset with the accident happenin' at school."

"I am not exaggerating. I saw all those welts, just as I described to you. Come see for yourself!" Matthew followed his niece across the square to Dr. Edward's office. When he arrived, the doctor was setting the fractured leg. He pulled the sheet from the sleeping boy.

"Precious Jesus! Please bless this boy. I would not have believed that Lem would hurt his own child like that."

"Brother Matt, I don't know much about this family or the people in your congregation, but here…well, we'd have a real issue with people getting into the midst of family business."

"Doc, this is a serious matter. My niece is right to be outraged. My church elders will certainly look into this child's treatment. That boy has an older brother and two younger sisters. We have no choice. We have to protect these children."

"Uncle, what are we going to do?"

"Just what scripture tells us to do. Two or three of the elders will go talk with his pa to see if we can solve the problem. That is the first step."

"I want to tell him…"

"No, Laurel. This is men's business. I'll do the talkin', and I'll take Mac with me."

"But you need two witnesses and none of…"

"Laurel, I said let it be. I'll handle this now." Laurel lowered her eyes and walked back to the table where Adam was beginning to awaken. She took his hand and whispered to the frightened boy. Just as she bent down, a large, broad-shouldered millhand walked into the outer office with his wife at his side. She wore an old dress and a dull, faded poke bonnet that in some years past may have been red.

"What done happened to our boy, preacher?"

"Lem and Ruth, you know my niece is the teacher at the school. Lem, have you met her yet?"

"Got no time for visitin' school. Got more work to do than a man can handle in a short day. What I wanna know is how come my boy got hurt at school?"

Laurel walked into the entry room.

"I'm Laurel MacLayne. Adam fell from the tree swing at afternoon recess."

"Why ain't you watchin' all them kids better?"

"I do my best to watch twenty children all at the same time. I could have been standing under that swing, and Adam still could have fallen."

"Iffen ya was doin'…"

"Calm down, Lem. Adam is gonna be fine. Dr. Edwards set his broken leg and stitched up the wound. See for yourself, Ruth. He's just in there."

Adam's parents started to the backroom where their son was awake now. "Missy, ya ain't heared the last of this yet." They closed the door behind them.

"Uncle, why didn't you say something about the welts?"

"It's not the time nor place. Didn't ya see how upset and frightened they are? There'd been a fight. We'll get to it in the right way when the time is better."

"But Uncle Matthew...the little boy will go home with them."

"Laurel. You are the teacher, not the parent or guardian angel. Let me handle things."

Laurel's chin was beyond set. Her eyes flashed green without one hint of their normal gray. She stomped her foot and stormed out of the front door of the doctor's office. Shortly, Matthew followed across the street to the wagon. He offered his hand to help Laurel into the seat, which she totally ignored as she climbed up. They headed down the Greensboro road toward Shiloh. When he drove into the churchyard, Laurel was still upset.

"If I send ya home to Mac in this state, he'll be sleeping on a pallet by the fireplace."

"Uncle Matthew, we've endangered that child. He should not have to live in a house where he is beaten."

"I believe that no child deserves that kind of whipping, but if this ain't done right, those other kids could get hurt, too."

"Or maybe they are already. We don't know."

"Whoa...take a breath and settle yourself. I will meet with a couple of elders, and we will look out for those kids. Now, will you just trust me to take care of things and go on home? Mac's gonna fret not knowing where ya are."

"I'll wait to hear from you for a day or two."

Laurel mounted Sassy Lady and began her two-mile ride back to the widow's cabin. She kicked Sassy into a trot.

⊶⊷

At dark, Mac rode into the yard, the scowl on his face told the story of his day.

"You don't seem yourself tonight, Mac. Is something wrong?"

"Just another delay at the cabin. Sometimes it's so frustrating."

"Mac, it will be fine. We've only been here nine weeks."

"Rode over to Greensboro this morning to McCullough's store. I'd ordered our windows out of St. Louis. They should've been here last week. Now the freighters are saying they won't get here 'til July 10. That is when the next freighter from Missouri's due here."

"Well, we aren't ready for them yet, are we?"

"Near to. We finished the rafters on the second pen today. Putting the shakes on the roofs on Saturday. Matthew and the Campbell boys are coming to help me."

"That's good news. We'll make a picnic of the whole day."'

"Can't lay those walnut planks for the floors down until the cabin is water tight. Sometimes I don't know if I'll ever get you a house of your own."

"I'm safe and comfortable here at the widow's cabin, Mac."

"That's the other thing. I got word today from Al... His wife is a niece to the widow... Mrs. Parker is coming home before the Fourth of July. We may have to find us another place to stay. We could live in our cabin if it was in the dry."

"Mac, don't worry about it. It doesn't matter to me. This time of year, we could even camp out if we need to."

"Laurel, I promised your pa I'd build you a house of your own. I didn't tell him I'd pitch you a tent. What if something happens to me? What would become of you without a home?"

95

"What are you saying...if something happens to you?"

"Things happen, Laurel. I can't rest until you've got your house."

"Wash up, Mac. Supper is ready." Laurel brushed her hand against Mac's cheek as she turned to the kitchen to dish up the supper. Mac's voice was tense, almost angry. Every movement was restless, marked with anxiousness. Laurel turned to get the ewer of water, and she did not see him follow her across the room with his eyes nor hear the sigh of regret that escaped. He turned toward the back door and walked out to the well. He drew a bucket of cool, clean water and poured it over his head. How wonderful a swim in the creek would be now, but he knew that would only make matters worse. Laurel dressed in her school marm clothes with her hair rolled into the chignon she'd adopted when he'd forbade the braids he could resist, but Laurel Grace in her wet chemise and that gorgeous hair in wild array around her face and shoulders was another thing. Not tonight, he resolved to himself. I will keep my pledge to Mark Campbell. These were the thoughts that ran through his mind, but where his will was strong, his flesh was getting weaker by the day. The news from Greensboro today meant at least another two-week delay in getting the cabin finished. As the water dripped from his face and hair, Mac whispered a prayer, "Lord, please...let me be patient. Please send me an angel or two to help me get that cabin finished."

He returned to the table to share his supper with Laurel. She prepared a good meal, including the surprise of fresh cornbread. She also made butter from the cream that she'd skimmed off the milk yesterday. Mac was always amazed at amount of work Laurel did after school every day. Their cabin was always clean and tidy, never did she fail to get a meal on the table, and she took care of the animals before he returned to the widow's most afternoons. Laurel worked tirelessly to help him build the homestead into a fine home. In fact, she had many excellent qualities. She was generous, almost to a fault. He'd never met anyone with a stronger work ethic. He truly admired her intellect and quick wit, so much so that he never found conversations with her boring or tedious. She could talk about so many things that were important to him. Laurel's beautiful skin and hair were sensuous beyond belief... Mac shook himself out of his reverie. That was not what he wanted to think about at that moment.

Why didn't Laurel come into his life before Marsha put such a blot on his soul? Why weren't all those fine qualities enough to burn out the passion he felt for Marsha? He wanted to love Laurel, didn't he? No. He never wanted to love anyone again. No woman would control him like that, not ever. He wouldn't love again. Yet, as quickly as he resolved to keep his emotions under control, again the guilt arose. Laurel wasn't to blame for the pain and brokenness he lived with. He cheated her of the life she deserved. His mood grew worse.

"Let's eat."

Laurel sat next to Mac. He took her hand and offered a brief blessing for the food. Instead of their usual pleasant evening chat about the day, they shared a silent meal.

"I'm going out for a while. Don't wait up for me."

Mac picked up his hat and left the cabin. Mac's walk to the creek only added to his low mood. Thoughts of the last evening they'd spent swimming came back to him. How much they both enjoyed that time together! When he got to the swimming hole, he threw off every stitch and dove into the deepest place. The cool water did feel wonderful on his skin. He felt good to be rid of the dirt and grime from the long hot day's work, but while the outside was clean, inside Mac felt dirty...consumed with anger, guilt, and confusion. He swam for a long time, pulling hard against the current, pulling his lean, muscled frame through the water as if he were in a race. He didn't stop until he was gasping, and his heart was pounding in his chest.

"What demon are you fleeing, Patrick?" That thought rang loud and strong in his head. He didn't know where it came from. He never thought of himself as Patrick. He never considered he was running from a demon. He just left the cabin to get some air and clean up. That was a lie. He ran from having to spend the evening with Laurel. Mac knew this internal battle could not be washed away in the creek.

He needed to talk to someone. He needed to find some time to spend with Matthew. Their time together was limited since he'd returned from Washington County. He invested nearly all his time building the homestead and meeting with the small group of men who wanted him to seek the state house seat. He was losing his anchor. Matthew would help him put things back on the right path. When he married Laurel...how long ago was that? ....more than two and a half months... Mac told himself he was doing God's will. He felt so strongly God intended their match then, but now, he didn't know how he got to this place. He wanted to talk with his brother in faith, but even that wouldn't be easy because his best friend was also Laurel's uncle.

"Lord, help me. You did plan this, didn't you? Or was I just playing good Samaritan out of my own pride and desire? Lord, help me." Mac got out of the water and dressed himself. He could tell from the moon set, it was after midnight. He hoped Laurel was asleep. The last thing he needed right now was a scene where he would be forced to explain himself. That prayer, the Lord answered. Laurel lay with her back to the right side of the bed, and she slept. Mac removed his outer clothes and slipped beside her. Unfortunately, sleep did not come to him.

⚜

The following morning, a contrite Mac teased Laurel awake by drawing a curl of her hair under her nose until she brushed his hand away. "What are you doing?

"Just flirting with my wife before the day begins. Okay with you?"

"I suppose, but you woke me up from a fine dream."

"Was I in it?"

"Never mind…I need to get ready for school."

"Will you be home early today? I thought we could go for a swim in the creek."

"No. I've got to ride out to the Dunn's after school. Sorry. A swim would've been nice in this heat."

"Maybe tomorrow."

Adam was the only student absent that hot July morning, and the students were curious about what happened to the seven-year-old. Laurel told them briefly about how the doctor had set his leg and that he would be well enough to return to school in the fall. She told them nothing about the confrontation with his parents. After a short time, the day fell into its normal routine, and before they noticed the school day ended.

Then, Laurel rode to the Dunn homestead with Catherine riding behind her. She was excited to try on the new dress she would wear to the Fourth of July celebration. The thought of dancing the night away dressed in such finery was intoxicating. Mac would be pleased as he chose the fabric and the pattern himself. After setting Cathy down from her little mare, Laurel hurried into the little one pen cabin, fairly dancing across the yard. When Mrs. Dunn slid the dress over her petticoats, Laurel felt the perfect fit. The dress made her feel so feminine. She saw herself in a small peering glass and gasped. Her shoulders and upper torso were exposed, and a hint of her cleavage was clearly visible in the tiny mirror.

"Mrs. Dunn, is something wrong with this pattern? The bodice fits so nicely, but look how low this neckline is."

"Well, Missy, that's how the pattern is cut. What a beautiful gown! Your mister will be speechless when he sees you in this dress. I don't see one thing that needs to be altered, just a hem, and it's finished."

"It's beautiful, but I don't know if I have the courage to wear it in public. I've never owned such a dress before."

"It's a dress for a woman, Mrs. Mac. All the things you brought with you, except maybe that blue calico are dresses for girls. This here dress is for evenings, to wear to parties and such. I am sure Mac wants to see you dressed like a woman. He'll love you in that dress."

Laurel thought to herself…I'd wear it every day if Mac would learn to love me. She shook her head to remove the hopeless thought. "When can I get the dress?"

"I'll have it to you on Friday. I'll send it to school with my Cathy."

"Thank you for your beautiful work, Mrs. Dunn. I'll feel so pretty in this dress every time I wear it." Laurel took three dollars from her pocket, part of her dowry. She took it that morning, anticipating her dress would be ready. "Here is for your work. I have two more pretty fabrics I'd like you to make up for me, when I get my wagon here from Powhatan. One of the patterns is for a ball gown, but I can't image how anything could be nicer than this one you just made. I'll be so happy to get it from Cathy on Friday."

After a brief good-bye, Laurel mounted Sassy and rode at a quick trot all the way to the homestead, thinking to catch Mac there. When she arrived, he was not working on the cabin and neither were his two helpers. Laurel wondered why no work was being done that afternoon. To keep from wasting the trip, she took the hoe and went to her garden. Most of the vegetables were growing toward maturity. Today, she spent the last hour of daylight weeding.

Mac used the afternoon to ride to Greensboro with Matthew. He'd wanted to talk with him in private, and it seemed the best opportunity. They were a short distance from the church when Mac asked, "Matthew, can we stop and talk a spell?"

"We got a bit of time. Mac, what's on your heart?"

"What makes you think something's on my heart? Maybe I just need to speak my mind."

"Know you better than that. We'd ride on while we talked if it was something on your mind."

"Guess that is so. Got a lot on my mind and on my heart too right now. Didn't sleep much last night, just needed to talk with you. You always seem to help me find my path when I get to wandering."

"Have you been wandering?"

"I don't even know how to start. Matthew, I feel guilty and even ashamed, I guess. I am not sure I should have married Laurel. What if it was my own arrogance and selfish wants that led me to that decision and not God's hand leading me?"

"Thought you believed you were doing God's will. What changed your mind?"

"She is so good. She works hard every day to be a helpmate. She loves people and is always helping someone who's in need. She's an excellent cook. We have great conversations. She supports the things I want to do. Laurel is sweet and fun to be with."

"I can certainly see why you think you've made a bad choice."

"Be serious, Matthew. I'm trying to get my head around all this. When I talked to you about the time we moved to the widow's, you told me to pray about it. Well, I have and the more I try to think about this and pray about it...the worse I feel."

"I hate to see you wrestle with this, Mac. I wish I knew how to help. I'll be glad to listen."

"Cabin's near to finished. I could have finished by July 10th if those windows were here. I told Laurel that when I got her a home

I'd have met all my promises to her father, and I would expect her to be my wife… truly."

"Well, I'd say it's about time."

"Matthew, I'm not sure I can do this."

"You telling me you're not attracted to her at all?"

"No. No. At times, I've left her alone not to have to deal with wanting her. I did last night."

"Did she refuse you, Mac?"

"No. I never gave her the chance."

"Patrick MacLayne. You are a saint or a fool or maybe some of both. She's your wife, man."

"She deserves a husband who is in love with her, Matthew. You know how I feel about that. If I use her out of my need for a woman or just to be a mother to my children and can't give her the love she deserves…what kind of man does that make me? I can't use her like that. She's too good a person. She is my friend. I can't use her."

"Have you told her?"

"She knows how I feel about falling in love. I told her about Marsha. I told her before we spoke our vows. I thought a marriage of convenience would be best for both of us, but Laurel doesn't need it. She is beautiful when she wants to be, and she's a tremendous help mate. If she'd waited, she would have wed a worthy husband, some man who would love her as she deserves.

"I'll not deny that point. She is a worthy woman. I don't agree she'd ever gotten that chance if she'd stayed in Washington County. My brother told me she chose to be a spinster. So, what are you going to do?"

"That's what I came to you for. I feel like I've lost my anchor, and I'm drifting with no control in my life right now. Matthew, I don't want to hurt Laurel, not ever again. She has dealt with so much unhappiness already. Tell me what I should do."

"Not my role, brother. Give it some time. What makes you think you don't already love her? You've done nothing but praise her for the past ten minutes."

"Matthew, I don't have feelings for Laurel that I had for Marsha. I never want to feel like that again."

"Pray about it and finish her house. Those are the only things you can do right now. Wait on the Lord, and He will show you what He intends."

"I hope he speaks in a loud voice."

"It'll be loud enough."

"I need to get back to the widow's place."

"Before you go, did Laurel tell you about the accident at school yesterday?"

"No. I was in a surly mood yesterday, and I didn't give her much of a chance I'm afraid. What happened?"

"A second level kid fell from the tree swing and broke his leg. Bone came through the skin. We carried him over to Doc Edwards. When we took his clothes off, we found welt marks all over him. Laurel was right mad and was gonna handle it with his pa. I told her it was a church matter. You and me and another brother will have to go over and talk with that family in a day or two."

"She never said a word."

"She saw your mood. She's smart like that. You better talk to her about that too, when you get home."

"Too?"

"You know what I'm talking about, Brother."

CHAPTER SEVEN

*Moreover, if thy brother shall trespass against thee, go
and tell him his fault between thee and him alone:
if he shall hear thee, thou hast gained thy brother.
But if he will not hear, take with thee one or
two more that in the mouth of two or three
witnesses every word may be established.*

Matthew 18:15-16 [KJV c1850].

Mac jumped from Midnight's back and all but ran across the
yard to the back door of the widow's cabin intending to do
just what Matthew not too shyly hinted at as he left the churchyard.
He pushed open the door to find an empty cabin. Yanking his hat
from his head, he slammed it to the floor, remembering hours too
late Laurel told him as she left for school she planned to go to the
homestead to work in the garden that afternoon. He missed the

perfect opportunity to do just what he needed and wanted to do. "Tarnation. Am I ever gonna get things right with that woman?"

Then, life placed scores of things in front of Mac's need to talk to Laurel. The next afternoon, Matthew called on Mac to go with him and another brother of the church to talk with the family of the young boy who was hurt in the accident at school. Matthew told Mac that if he waited much longer, he feared Laurel would intervene herself. About sunset, Mac waited atop Crowley's Ridge. Matthew told him he dreaded the discussion with the parents and even with the support of Mac and an elder in the church, the confrontation would be difficult, but it was the part of his job as a preacher he hated the most.

Together the three rode on to the Smith family's homestead. Lemuel and Ruth were basically good people, but life had made Lem a very stern, stubborn man, who did not see that his form of discipline for his children to be excessive or harsh. It was the same way he'd been raised. Matthew was right. Speaking to them about the welts on Adam's back, legs, and arms was a thoroughly ugly encounter. The red splotches on Lem's face reflected rising anger as the preacher confronted him.

He interrupted. "Dag nab it, preacher. I always respected you… but what right ya got to tell me how to raise my own young'uns? You may call yerself a preacher, but you got no more schoolin' than me. Don't go actin' all high and mighty on me, Matthew Campbell."

"Yer right, Lem. I parted ways with school in eighth grade. The only learnin' I have is what I've got in studyin' the good Book and from goin' to conference every year…but I'm not tryin' to tell ya about book learnin'. But I treasure learnin' and try to learn more about my callin' any chance I get. But it ain't education that sent me here today. I'm a pastor because of grace. God called me to preach. Kids learn about God's love from their parents. How are your kids gonna know that if you are too harsh with 'em? Please think about it, Lem. Ruth, I know y'all work hard to care for them, but they need to learn about forgiveness and affection from y'all too, not just right and wrong. Look to the examples of our Lord. Think about it."

Lem turned his anger toward Mac. "I know yer wife's got a hand in this. Well, tell her we don't need her meddlin' in our kids' upbringin'. My wife and me take good care of 'em, so we don't need her help. If you'se a man, you'd give 'er a couple of babies of yer own so she'd keep her nose out of other's business."

"I didn't come here to condemn you nor to defend my wife. I'll treasure any children the Lord sees fit to send my way. That is the Lord's decision, not mine nor yours."

Matthew listened patiently to the tirade, and Mac's calm response. Then he took a step back. Pulling himself to his full height, he spoke in his most commanding, yet compassionate voice, "Brother Lem and Sister Ruth, the Lord loans us our offspring. He expects us to love 'em and teach 'em the way Jesus loves and teaches us. I'm thinkin' Adam and perhaps his brother and sisters don't have a very clear view of our Lord right now. Please just pray about it and think about what I said. We only want all our people to be well and happy and safe in God's grace. We'll be lookin' in on y'all from time to time. I hope after ya have some time to think on what I said, we'll see y'all in church on Sunday."

They rode away from the sturdy log double pen cabin, the Smith family home for more than thirty years. "Joe, you and Mac come on over to the homestead with me and let Ellie fix us a good supper. After that, we deserve a nice meal."

"Thank you, Brother Matthew, but I'll be headed on back home. I've got more than enough work to keep me occupied, and Margie Ruth will be waiting for me. Actually, it wasn't as bad as I feared it would be."

"We did it the way the Good Book says. Confronting a brother, even in love, ain't easy. Don't say it'll be easy, but if we can help then we did what we ought to do. I appreciate ya going with me, Joe. Mac, you hungry?"

"I think I'll just go on back to the widow's place. Maybe Laurel will be home, and we may have a chance to talk tonight."

"What did Laurel say when you talked to her the other night?"

"Still trying to find the opportunity."

"How hard is it to say, 'Laurel, we need to talk.'?"

"She wasn't home."

"In two days…"

"See ya, Matthew." Mac kicked Midnight into a run back toward his homestead. Matthew was right. Every day he let pass put more distance between him and Laurel. Once again, he resigned himself to open the conversation that evening, even if it meant they got into a huge argument.

Even before Mac rode into the yard of the widow Parker's homestead, he saw two fires burning not far from the back porch. What could Laurel be doing so late? While it wasn't pitch black outside, it was dark enough to need a lantern. The black wash kettle sat over one of the fires and a smaller pot sat perched on a stone ledge over the second blaze. Laurel stood over the larger kettle blanching a large mess of pole beans. She harvested the green beans from her garden that afternoon in large enough number to can. She filled six jars, which Mac saw sitting on the back porch, and she was melting paraffin to seal the jars. Those beans would be the first of stores for their winter larder. The two fires added to the ninety degrees plus temperature making the nighttime as unbearable as the heat of the day.

"Hello, Wife. You've picked a hot job for the day."

"You have to can the harvest when it's ready. Just happened to be ready today. They are nice beans though. We'll enjoy them this winter."

"I know we will." Mac went on into the barn to unsaddle his horse. Maybe tomorrow would offer a better opportunity to talk seriously with Laurel.

The opportunity didn't seem to arise. The next week was crowded with one incident after another. Visitors dropped in unexpectedly to talk about the upcoming Fourth of July celebration, asking

Mac to debate again. A neighbor needed help with a downed fence. Laurel was late from school when she made a home visit to one of her students. As the week ended, Mac had not brought up a personal topic of conversation with Laurel even once. Truthfully, the air between the couple became very polite, very calm, much like the eye of a storm. Mac felt the tension. He saw the unease in Laurel's every move. He tried to do whatever he could to placate her. He did chores so she wouldn't have added work after school. He avoided small talk because he knew she disliked it. He tried not to touch her when she didn't expect it. Mac saw his relationship with Laurel was as estranged as it had been the day he married her in March.

⊫ ⊨

On Friday afternoon, Mac came to the widow's cabin early, seemingly more at ease than he had been in more than two weeks. "Laurel, I've done all I can do on your cabin until the windows come. I figure when they get here, I'll have them set and trimmed out within a week, and another week will see your walnut plank floors finished. You'll have a house by the time school's out if all goes well. I guess I'll start the barn tomorrow. No need wasting the time."

"That is good to hear. You seem pleased with the progress. Will you take me over there tomorrow to see?"

"Perhaps we can make a family picnic of the day. I'll ride over to see if Matthew and Ellie and the kids can come."

"I'd enjoy a ride this afternoon. Would it be all right with you if I ride along with you?"

"The company would be nice, but I won't be coming straight back. A few men who are working with me on the campaign have asked me to meet them. I don't want you riding home alone after dark. We'll ride later. Besides, you still have chores to do before night fall. I think you need to stay here at the widow's place tonight."

The aloof tone of his voice and his rejection of her request to ride along spoke more loudly than the words he'd spoken. "If that is your wish, I'll remain here." He felt the ice in her reply.

"Laurel, I'm sorry. That didn't come out the way I intended. I should have told you earlier I made plans for tonight."

"No apology needed. You have important things to take care of. You are right. I have several things I need to do here. I shouldn't have intruded."

"You..." Before Mac could finish his comment, Laurel turned and left the cabin through the rear door. He called after her, "Laurel, please...." She did not acknowledge his words, nor did she return.

He would give her time to calm down. He went to saddle Midnight and walked the big stallion into the yard, hoping he would see Laurel so he could tell her good-bye, but she wasn't outside. Mac, angry with his lack of tact and the humiliation he caused Laurel, shrugged his shoulders and shook his head. He flung himself into his saddle and raced toward Shiloh Station. He'd cut short his meeting to spend the evening with her. At least, that is what he told himself. When he reached Matthew's place, he found his friend was out making a house call to an older couple in the congregation who lost a grandson the evening before. Ellie also told him their family was headed to Susan's new homestead the next day to help with the barn raising. She invited Laurel and Mac to join them.

"I'll ask Laurel when I get home, Ellie." Mac then rode to the church where a few men from Shiloh and a couple more from Greensboro awaited him. The planning of the campaign and debate on some of the issues Arkansas was facing—a new land fraud scandal—began and then went on and on. When he arrived home, it was just past ten and no lantern lit the cabin.

When he realized Laurel was already in bed, he rode into the barn, unsaddled Midnight, and fed and watered his horse.

Mac walked to the porch, sat on the top step and removed his boots. He'd try not to disturb her. When he climbed to the loft, he saw the empty four-poster. Mac turned to search. Had Laurel gone out and lost her way again? He pulled his boots back on and climbed back down to the main floor. He looked around the room to see if anything was out of place. When he walked passed the hearth, he found Laurel on the tiny cot next to the wall. She could not be asleep with all the commotion he'd made as he looked for her.

"Laurel, I know you are awake. What are you doing down here?"

"Please go away and leave me be. It's well past working hours."

"I asked you a question. What are you doing down here on this cot?"

"Stop shouting at me. I do not intend to argue with you."

"What do you intend?"

"I intend to get a good night's sleep so I can get up tomorrow and get my work done."

"Laurel Grace…" Mac spoke too loudly. "Laurel, please come over to the table, sit down with me, and let's talk this out. We haven't talked much lately."

"We talk all the time. I can't see another pleasant conversation worth giving up a night's sleep. Go to bed, Mr. MacLayne. Tomorrow, there will be more chores to do, more people to talk to, more barns to build, more campaigns to plan, and more obligations to meet. I am tired. I am sure you must be too." Laurel turned her back and laid her head back on the pillow.

Mac brushed past the chair at the table, causing it to fall over. He made the three steps to the hearth and dropped to his knee by the cot. He took Laurel by the shoulders and pulled her up to look at him. Only the light from the full moon lit the small room, yet he saw her jaw square in resistance. At the same time, he also saw tears run down her cheeks.

"Please leave me be. I'll be up in plenty of time to get your breakfast and do morning chores."

"Laurel, what are you saying?"

"I finally understand the last few weeks--all this time when we talked but didn't really talk. Each day you seemed to get a little farther away from me, and I didn't know what I did to push you away. I wanted to ask what I did to make you angry, but I knew I didn't do anything. I decided to let you get over your snit by yourself. Then I remembered you told me once before you expected me to do for you what I did at my father's homestead. This afternoon, you refused my company and reminded me that I didn't finish the chores. I know I'm slow, but I always catch on after a while."

"Laurel, what are you talking about? I know how hard you work. You are the best life mate a man could ever hope to find."

"Leave me be!" Laurel tried to jerk her shoulders free from Mac's grip.

"No." He pulled Laurel to her feet. "We are going to have this out tonight. I don't care if we fight all night. For weeks, I've been trying to find an opportunity to talk to you, but you were late from school or canning, or I was busy with visitors from Greensboro or helpers working at the homestead. Tonight, no one is here but you and me."

"You are angry. We can't have a serious discussion when you're angry. I don't want to fight anymore."

"We are having it out tonight."

"Mac..."

"Laurel Grace. I said tonight."

Mac put Laurel in the arm chair next to the hearth and sat on the hearth and placed his hands on the chair arms, preventing her from leaving. "Laurel, I would like to light a lantern so I can see you while we talk, but if I leave, will you run away?"

"Did I say I was going to run away?"

"No, but you didn't tell me the last time either."

"I'm not stupid, Mac. I learned my lesson."

Mac rose and lit a lantern on the table so the room was no longer in total darkness. He returned to the hearth, but did not replace his hands on the chair arms.

"All right, Laurel. Let's talk. Why did you leave the four-poster?"

"I told you. I finally understood our arrangement. You even told me before we were married you wanted me to do what I did for my father at his homestead. I worked hard to make a home for my pa...but I didn't share his bed."

"What does that mean?"

"The help doesn't share a bed with the lord of the manor."

"Laurel, that's not fair. You know I never once thought of you as a bond servant."

"That is what you said. Even today, you told me I didn't do the chores you needed done. You didn't want my company. I will do what you expect, and I will ask no more from you. Now let me be. I have a lot of work to do this weekend."

"Let's just fight this out, here and now. I am frustrated to my limits with this constant up and down between us." Laurel didn't respond. "What can I do or say to get back into your good graces?" Silence was the only response. "Laurel, come up to the loft with me and let's do our Scripture reading and pray. Again, she did not answer his command. "All right. You still refuse to speak to me. I told you to come to bed and finish the night as we vowed to do. I won't let you break that promise."

<hr/>

As meekly as the bond servant she'd declared herself to be, Laurel followed Mac up the ladder. As she climbed the steps, light from the lantern on the night stand and the moon light cast a gold-orange aura around her. Dressed as she was in her thin nightdress skimming over the curves of her slender body and the golden highlights from her curls, Mac saw a glimpse of the angel he'd first seen the night they'd finally arrived at Shiloh. This time, the glistening of tears on her cheeks marred the vision he saw. No wonder he felt so guilty and sensed that he failed Laurel time and again. No wonder he failed to make her feel honored and wanted. Laurel kept every vow she'd made...washing his clothes, cooking two meals a day, working at the homestead, tending the garden, supporting his ambition to hold public office, and keeping their house while she taught school every day. What did he do in return? He'd made her feel like a bond servant. He silently pleaded with the Lord. "Please, help me know what to say!"

When he opened his Bible, the scripture on that page was what he needed. "Therefore, if any man be in Christ, he is a new creature, old things are passed away; behold all things are become new. And all things are of God, who hath reconciled us to Himself by Jesus Christ and hath given to us the ministry of reconciliation." The passage from Second Corinthians 5 spoke to his need and to the lesson Laurel had not learned. He closed his Bible and laid it back on the chest at the foot of the bed. He spoke a silent prayer asking forgiveness for his poor showing as a husband. In his heart, he wanted to show Laurel her value. He still wanted the dream that took him to Washington County, but in his humanness, he didn't know how to reach Laurel.

"Laurel, forgive me." Those were the only words that came to him. "Please let me start over. Let's begin one more time. I believe we can build a good life together."

"It's too late to talk about this tonight." She rose to return to the cot by the hearth. Mac took her hand and pulled her back.

"If it takes all night, so be it."

"We've tried so many times to build a friendship together. I'm just not the woman you want. You can't help how you feel. I served my father out of love and respect. I owe you no such debt."

"The scripture says if we build on a foundation of the Lord, all things are new. Laurel, I have been the weak link here. My moodiness has nothing to do with you. You've kept every vow you made to me. Let me start again. I will never make you feel like a servant again. I know I don't deserve your forgiveness, but I'm asking for it."

"There is no purpose in trying to put something back together that never existed. This whole idea was ridiculous from the time you knocked on my papa's cabin door." She walked away from Mac's embrace.

"Laurel, I want your forgiveness. I want one more chance to build a life with you…. Please."

"There's nothing to forgive. If it makes you easy, Mac, I accept your apology, but I want no conditions, no expectations, and no recrimination from you."

"What do you want, Laurel? What can I do?"

"I don't know, Patrick. I don't want to be the source of your anger and moodiness. I'm caught in the storm as much as you are, and if I cut you free, I'll flounder, too, for you have become my anchor. I know no other path except to try once again to build a life with you… my friend."

Mac breathed for what seemed to be the first time since the conversation started. He asked for Laurel's hand, and he bowed beside her on the floor.

"Lord, forgive my stubborn pride and poor treatment of this good woman. Please keep me ever mindful that she is a prize of great worth and that I have one task–to let her know it. Thank you for the promise of reconciliation. I thank you for Laurel's forgiving spirit. Amen."

Mac got up from his knees and stood above Laurel. He took her hands and pulled her to her feet. He wrapped his arms around her, feeling the warmth of her back and shoulders. He held her so closely the buttons on his shirt were biting into her flesh. He lowered his lips to hers. Laurel savored the sensation for the briefest moment but then turned away.

"Goodnight, Mac. We'll put our faith in the Lord, and we'll forget the ugly words that passed between us tonight. Work hard to finish the cabin, and let's see what comes. I am sorry I accused you of treating me as a bond servant. You don't deserve that." Laurel returned to her place on the left side of the four-poster.

Mac began to undress for bed. He lowered the wick of the lantern. He lay down, propped himself up on his elbow, and looked down at Laurel. "I should have been honest. I've avoided you these past two weeks because I've wanted you too much. I can hardly wait to carry you across the threshold of our house. I will have kept my word to your father then, and I will have earned the right to be your husband. And Laurel, on that day, I will be your husband in every sense of the word."

"I never asked for any conditions."

"I know, but I swore to you…I'll wait for these next couple of weeks, but that cabin is going to be finished one way or another. Good night, Wife. I hope you sleep well. I'll sleep much better with you by my side."

CHAPTER EIGHT

Whoso findeth a wife findeth a good thing,
and obtaineth favor of the Lord.

Proverbs 18:22. [KJV c1850].

The following morning, Laurel woke as the sun broke over the crest of the ridge. She went to the kitchen to prepare breakfast, a normal day's activity, feeling hopeful. The angry words with Mac cleared the tension between them, much like a fierce thunderstorm will refresh the hot summer climate. That morning Laurel believed she was a wife who was important to her husband and a value in his life. While he did not speak of love, at least she now understood his recent aloofness. Thinking of his words from the night before brought color to her cheeks.

When Mac appeared a few minutes later, he drew Laurel into his arms and kissed her. "Good morning, Wife. What would you like to do today?"

"I thought we were going to the homestead to work."

So, they did. When Mac stopped the mule, he jumped from the wagon and helped Laurel down.

"Let me show you how much we finished this last week." He took her hand and led her up the steps, which were missing the last time she was there. The stairs were wide with railings that continued the length of the porch. Laurel loved the broad porch that ran the length of their double pen cabin. Since there were no doors or windows, five openings faced the covered porch. One was a full-length opening where the front door would go and four were waist height where real glass paned windows would sit, if ever they arrived from St. Louis. These windows would face the west where Mac and Laurel would watch the sunset at the close of day, even on the coldest evenings. Two windows were on the east side, one over the dry sink, but there were no windows on the north side of the cabin. Windows there would not serve well in the winter.

The front door opened into the larger first pen. Here was a room with a large hearth and fireplace. Mac built two hearth ovens into the massive stone structure, very much like the ones in Campbell's cabin in Washington County. Mac also built several cupboards onto the wall in Laurel's kitchen. The back door opened directly across the covered porch from the well.

On the other side of the large fireplace was their sitting room. Laurel imagined soon her papa's armchair and her Grandma Wilson's rocker would be there along with a desk and side table with lamps, making this the perfect place for them to read and talk in the evenings. A half loft ran across the kitchen area, but Mac built the walls quite tall so the room did not feel cramped or cave-like. Plenty of light came from the well-placed window. The loft was not huge, but it would allow the MacLaynes to have an extra sleeping space if they hosted overnight visitors.

The area just in front of the stairs held a door leading to the second, smaller pen. Here would be a real bedroom in the MacLayne's cabin, a very nice-sized room with two windows. How beautiful the room would be when they furnished it! In the back of the second pen was a much smaller room. Mac's plan for the smaller space was not known to Laurel. She assumed it would be a nursery. Laurel wanted to tell him it was too small, but they were having such a good time talking about their future home, she didn't want to spoil it with a complaint.

"Mac, shouldn't we have built a bigger loft? If you'd continued it into this room, we'd would have so much more room."

"If we need more room, I'll add on to the cabin. This is our private sanctuary. I don't plan to share this space with anyone else."

"Well, this room is lovely, and a fireplace here will make the room warm in the winter."

"Not to mention the romance of a nice fire blazing across from our bed."

"Mac, I didn't realize you were such a romantic. Thank you for this beautiful home."

"It's your job to make us a beautiful home. I just built the house, and truthfully, I can hardly wait to see it finished. The day I carry you over that threshold, I'll feel we're married. When we're truly a family, this place will be home and not just a house." Mac moved toward Laurel, and he put his arm across her shoulder. "Look, Laurel, see how fine the valley looks from our bedroom window. There's no more beautiful view in all Shiloh Station, except Eden. See, over there's the creek and if you're still, you can hear the water move, rippling across the rocks. Can't you imagine what a wonderful lullaby that'll be for our babies? I don't know why I waited so long to claim my land. I have wanted this all of my life."

Laurel turned so she could see Mac's face. His thoughts seemed to take him out of the real world. Laurel never heard her husband speak so wistfully, hope wringing from every word. Mac was not talking about the homestead or the land, but he appeared to speak of the dream he carried in his heart. At that moment, Laurel felt she knew her husband better than she ever had as he shared his most intimate thoughts with her in their nearly completed cabin. Then he spoke words that brought her to tears.

"I guess it just took meeting the Spinster of Hawthorn to plant my roots. I thank the Lord for it every day." Laurel turned and laid her palm on Mac's cheek. He pulled her into his embrace. "Wife, I don't know when I've been so content. Hallelujah! Thank you, Lord!" He held her face between his hands and softly kissed her lips.

Laurel was happy. Who needed love when a friendship so true grew between two people? Mac did not have to declare he loved her. She would keep her vows to him because he wanted her in his life. She too offered God a prayer of thanksgiving.

⟞⟝ ⟞⟝

Mac was the most attentive partner all day on Sunday. As they attended worship in the morning, the potluck dinner on the grounds, and the afternoon singing, Laurel was never out of his sight. Even when his political supporters came by to pull him away to talk, he took Laurel's arm and brought her into the discussion. At supper, just before evening worship, Mac spent a pleasant hour with his head resting in Laurel's lap, where she fed him pieces of bread, fried chicken, and even some oatmeal cookies a bite at a time.

Matthew and Ellie smiled at the flirtatious behavior carried on between Mac and Laurel. Matthew leaned over to his wife and whispered, "See, I told you. Mac is in love with our niece. Silly man, he just doesn't know it!"

"Hush, Matthew. They'll hear you."

"So? I was thinking I'd announce it from the pulpit tonight myself."

"Not unless you want to sleep in the barn 'til winter. How embarrassed Laurel Grace would be!"

"Relax, Wife. I'm teasing. He'll figure it out in time."

The next morning Laurel hated to leave for school. She wanted to teach and be with her students, but the weekend was too wonderful, and she didn't want to leave Mac. Yet, at 7:00, she opened the door to the barn and walked to Sassy's stall. There, Mac was waiting for her. He already saddled the mare and attached Laurel's school satchel. When she opened the gate to the stall, Mac approached her with a bouquet of daisies. "I think I remember these are your favorite flower. They are blooming all over the banks of the creek near our cabin. I brought home a few bunches with their roots. I wanted to give them to you to carry to school today. I also brought some to plant here at the widow's cabin. It'll make a nice surprise for her when she comes home."

"These are so pretty. I'll put them on my desk and when I see them, I'll remember the weekend we just spent together. Thank you, Mac."

"Thank you, Laurel. Before you, I'd never paid much attention to these spritely little flowers." Mac pulled her closer and kissed her for some time. "Laurel, this weekend was way too short. Just a taste of the life I'm dreaming about. I really don't want to let you go. We could just stop time…"

"Work time, friend."

"Not 'til you tell me…no, I don't want to hear you say good-bye. Just kiss me again and say, 'I'll see you later'."

"I'll see you later…today." Laurel mounted Sassy and then bent down to plant a farewell kiss on Mac's cheek.

"Not good enough, woman." Mac pulled her back into his arms so he could kiss her lips. "Meet me at the homestead about 4:30. We'll spend some time together before dark."

Laurel reluctantly rode to the Shiloh school to do her job. The day was a productive one, and before she realized the time came to dismiss school. At 4:00, she gathered her school satchel and her bonnet and headed to the door. Then she returned to her desk and laid her satchel down. She would do no school work tonight, for she promised to spend the evening with her husband. That was her only thought as she went through the door.

When Laurel arrived at the homestead, she found Mac sitting on the broad front porch. He'd already sent his helpers home for the day. Truthfully, there was not much they could do until the windows came anyway. The walnut floor planks would be the last job, but they would not be laid until the cabin was dry. Fine wood could be ruined by an unexpected rainstorm. Windows, two doors and floors—that was all that remained to be finished. Mac was not very patient waiting for the freighters.

Thanks to the nearly endless stream of neighbors dropping by to help Mac, the hired help he was able to get from time to time and his two constant hands, John and Roy, the work at the homestead went very quickly. The barn was nearly finished and the well was providing plenty of good tasting water. Mac even built a replica of the springhouse at Hawthorn Chapel. The walk was a bit farther, but the shade, swift running creek and the insulated rock structure would help keep their food fresh, even in the hottest summer. Laurel's orchard was growing well. The apple saplings had taken root and grown several inches. The grape vines were doing even better. If they continued as they were growing, they would have grapes within three years, four at the most. Apples would be ready to harvest before their tenth anniversary, not a terribly long time to wait in the span of their entire lives. The garden was blooming. New onions, early string beans, and some leafy greens would be ready to use for the Fourth of July picnic at the end of the week. God was indeed providing a bounty to feed them all winter.

"You look mighty content this afternoon. What's happened to-day?" Laurel asked pertly.

"Nothing really. Just nice to have some time to play this afternoon."

"Well, this weekend is the Fourth of July. That will be a fun day if the celebration is all you've told me it will be."

"You'll see...visits with neighbors, speeches, reading the Declaration of Independence, picnics and dancing. We do the Fourth up right here at Shiloh."

"I am looking forward to it. My beautiful pink party dress will be ready to wear. Mrs. Dunn did such a fine job of making it."

"My lady will be the belle of the ball." Mac lifted Laurel off Sassy and pretended to dance to the unheard orchestra. He swung Laurel around until she was laughing aloud.

"Ain't that 'bout the prettiest sound you ever heard?"

"What are you talking about?"

"Your laughter. I don't think I ever heard a nicer sound. I've heard you giggle a time or two, seen you smile a few times, but real laughter? I do believe, Mrs. MacLayne, that is the sound of happiness."

"You know Ecclesiastes says there is a time for every purpose under heaven. A time to weep, a time to laugh, a time to mourn, a time to dance, a time.... Oh well, you know how it goes."

"And the time to laugh has finally come for you, Laurel." Mac took Laurel to him and held her close for a short while. Then he took her hand and started pulling Laurel toward the creek.

"Where are you taking me?"

"To Eden. I just remembered that next line says a time to swim, doesn't it?"

"No, it doesn't."

"Well, it should. Hot day, so I know we'll enjoy a swim."

Laurel didn't hesitate. After a leisurely swim, Mac pulled Laurel out of the water and carried her over to an old quilt he brought. They lay under the shady bower, the breeze and sun drying their clothes. And they talked for more than an hour, sharing just every day simple conversation. No problem came up and no hurt feelings arose. The MacLaynes napped in Eden. Later, Mac roused

Laurel by pulling a tress of her hair under her nose. The wisp on her lips startled her briefly, but the tickle was quickly replaced with several gentle, playful kisses.

"Hey, school marm, it's time to get dressed and get on home. What would the good people of Shiloh say if they saw you, half-dressed and lying in the arms of a near bare man?"

"They'd say, 'Ain't that a lucky woman to be so close to such a good-looking fellow?"

"Golly, ma'am. You shouldn't be so bold. I am a married man."

"You'd better say that to all the rest of the females who decide to get bold with you." Laughter again sounded across the valley.

"Laurel, this is Eden. Let's keep it this way. I am happier than I've any right to be. You've taken away my restlessness. I can think of nothing else I want or need, just my best friend and our home together."

"I wish I could keep the day from ending. Can't you hold back the night?"

"Only once in history I know of when time stopped, and the walls of Jericho fell. Maybe it'll stop once more when the walls of Hawthorn crumble totally to the ground. Come on, Wife. Let's go back to the widow's. Chores don't do themselves."

⊷⊱ ⊰⊶

Tuesday morning brought a welcomed summer rain. Laurel was up at dawn, preparing breakfast, singing Annie Laurie, the old Irish ballad Mac had sung to her first on the trail and then many times since getting to Shiloh. She especially enjoyed the ballad because Mac called his lass, Annie Laurel. She danced her way across the floor as she put the coffee on the hook to make.

"You're in mighty fine spirits this rainy morning." Laurel commented as Mac came in from the barn.

"Yes, I am."

"Are you hungry?" Laurel asked.

"Indeed I am." He pulled her next to him and soaked her gown and wrapper from his wet work clothes.

"Mac, You're wet!"

"Sorry, I just wanted to ease my hunger." He kissed her and picked her up and danced around the room while he picked up the melody of Annie Laurel. She laughed and he laughed and repeated the kiss.

"Such a nice way to start the day. Now how about putting me down so I can feed you."

With such a special beginning of the day, Laurel wanted to pinch herself to assure that she wasn't under the spell of a lovely dream. Five days in a row, she was happy and life was wonderful. Mac had told her the freighter was due the next week, and he planned to move well before the end of July. He'd said that his dream of Shiloh was so close he could touch it, and then he'd hugged her. She remembered how she giggled as he tickled and teased her.

"Laurel, you're blushing. What's going on?"

"I've got to get dressed for school. You're going to make me late." She pulled her hair back from her face, pushed his hands away, and turned toward the loft. Mac pulled her back into his arms.

"You were blushing. Aren't you going to tell me what you were thinking about?"

"I was thinking about our afternoon swim yesterday, Mac. Now let me go. I've got to get dressed for school." Her cheeks continued to glow, but she would certainly not tell her husband that she was trying to imagine their first night in their new home.

Ellie Campbell found Laurel nearly as pink cheeked at the noon break the same day. "Laurel, are you running a fever, darlin'?"

Laurel drew her hands to her cheeks. "Aunt Ellie! No. I'm fine. Is something wrong? You don't usually come to school in the middle of the day."

"Maybe it's a good thing I did. You don't look so good. I stood there at the door for a good spell and then when I got your attention and was close enough to see you I find your face all flushed." Ellie Campbell laid her palm on Laurel's forehead. "Well, you don't have a fever, but those cheeks are red."

"I suppose it's the heat. I can't seem to get used to this flat land climate." Laurel lied to her aunt. "Did you need to see me?"

"No, Laurel Grace. I was just missing my baby. We stirred up a batch of cookies while we cooked supper. I thought she'd like to share them with her friends. Besides, the house seems so empty now with her off at school. You know I didn't have a baby in the house for all those years after John, and then the good Lord sent Mary nearly six years ago. She brought me such joy. I'd kept her home another year, but Matthew sets such a store by learning. He said now that we got us a good teacher, we'd take every advantage of you."

"Aunt Ellie, Mary is a bright girl. She is learning very quickly."

"And what about those pink cheeks, Laurel Grace?"

"School is not a place to talk about it. Maybe later. I wish I could talk to my mother."

"I'd love a walk by the creek after school. Will you go with me?"

"If you have the time, I would love it." Laurel hugged her Aunt Ellie and then stood and smoothed her hair. "Goodness. It's past time to call the children back in from noon recess. Where has the time gone?"

━━┿ ┿━━

"Mac and I call this place Eden."

Ellie smiled and replied, "I can see why. This valley is the most beautiful in the county."

125

"When Mac first brought me here, he talked about building our cabin there near that great oak tree. I told him it would be sacrilege to destroy Eden."

"You were right. Besides your place is more practical and nearly as nice, but is that what you wanted to talk about this afternoon at school, the site of your cabin?"

"Mac thinks we will be leaving the widow's place when school is over for the summer."

"That sounds fine. Aren't you pleased?"

"Of course, Aunt Ellie. Mac's so excited. He's talked about his homestead as long as I've known him...as long as I've known him." Laurel laughed nervously. "Aunt Ellie, I've known Mac exactly thirteen weeks. We've been married more than twelve of those weeks." Laurel sat on a fallen log and removed her shoes and stockings and tucked up her skirt. She walked to the edge of the creek with her back to her aunt and spoke in a barely audible voice. "Aunt Ellie, I've never been a true wife to Mac."

Ellie Campbell approached Laurel and drew her niece into her arms and held her for some time. "I suspected you'd tell me that, Laurel Grace."

"Oh, goodness. Is it obvious we are so unsuited? Does the community know?"

"No, darlin'. I expect I'm the only one who thinks so. It is just so precious to see you two together, like a couple of courtin' kids."

"Aunt Ellie, I'm no kid. I'm twenty-eight years old. Mac is a man, not a boy sparking a barely grown girl on her papa's front porch."

"Tell me why you are so upset."

"People make comments about having babies and oh...oh... never mind. I can't talk about this with you."

"Who can you talk with?

"I've never had anyone to talk to about personal things. I've missed my mama so many times when I was growing up. I don't know anything about being a wife, Aunt Ellie."

"It's hard to lose your mother when you are just becoming a woman yourself, Laurel. There were only men in your household so I can see how hard it was for you when things came up you needed answers for,"

"Pa called them 'womanly ways.' An older friend named Elizabeth Wilson tried to tell me about some of the 'womanly ways' that we females face, but she didn't tell me about getting married. Frankly, neither of us thought I'd ever get married. She stood with me at my wedding. She told me that Mac would be a gentleman. He always has been."

"Aunt Ellie, my mama and papa loved each other so much. Until the day mama died trying to give papa another baby, he adored her. They shared a great passion. I believe you share that kind of love with Uncle Matthew. When I see you two together, I remember seeing mama and papa looking at each other. I wish I could have that kind of marriage, but Mac and I made a marriage of convenience. I know Uncle Matthew told you that. My papa was dying of consumption, and he asked Mac to marry me so I'd be cared for. Mac wanted a wife and a family so he agreed. He's a good man. I'm grateful he accepted me, but we don't share the passion you and Uncle Matthew have or that Papa and Mama shared with each other. Please don't repeat what I just told you to another living soul. I'm sure Mac has told it to Uncle Matthew, but I couldn't bear to have it repeated to anyone else."

"Laurel, your words are safe. I am not sure they are all true, but they will never be repeated."

A single tear traced a path down Laurel's cheek. "I really should head to the widow's. Mac will be home soon."

"Is there more?"

"I'm falling in love with Mac, Aunt Ellie. I can't let it happen. He told me very plainly our marriage was to be a friendship. He wants no romance or declarations of love on his part. I don't want to drive him away."

"Laurel Grace, the heart wants what the heart wants. You can't help who you love any more than the dew can help where it falls or the daisy can choose who plucks it from its bed. Trust the Lord to take care of that dilemma in His time." Ellie Campbell waded a bit closer to her niece and hugged her again. "I'm so happy you love Mac. When Mac decides to make you his wife, darlin', just relax and let it happen. The Lord already took care of that part too. Making love is a natural reaction of a man wanting his wife and her wanting him back. Mac will know what to do when the time comes. Just remember, 'Whoso findeth a wife findeth a good thing and obtaineth favor of the Lord.' That's a saying I quote to Matthew all the time. Mac's no fool. He'll understand much faster than you think."

CHAPTER NINE

*Honor thy father and thy mother that thy days may be
long upon the land which the Lord thy God giveth thee.*

Exodus 20:12 [KJV c1850].

Laurel arrived at the widow's only minutes ahead of Mac. The
hem of her skirt was still wet from wading in the creek with
her aunt. She met him on the porch, a smile across her face. She
handed him a glass of cool well water and offered him the rocking
chair on the porch. When he sat down, she moved behind him and
began massaging his shoulders.

"What did I do to deserve such fine treatment today, Wife?"

"Nothing special. I just assumed you'd worked today and were
tired."

"Well, you worked today, too, didn't you?"

"Most of it."

"Most of it? What did you do with the rest of it?"

"Spent a little time with Aunt Ellie. Nice pastime after a long day at school."

"Good girl. You did something nice for yourself without someone telling you to so."

"Did the windows come today?"

"No. We started putting up some fence for cattle pens. Just passing time, waiting on those freighters. So, what did you and Ellie talk about while you waded around in the creek?"

"Who said we waded in the creek?"

"Your skirt got wet somehow."

"Oh, just girl talk...plans for the Fourth of July. My students are going to participate this year...." Mac interrupted Laurel's monologue by grabbing her arm and pulling her into his lap.

"Did you talk about me?"

"Of all the conceited...why would we talk about you?"

"You said girl talk.... do girls talk about their fellows?"

"Mac!" She stood up, smoothed her skirt, lowered the pitch of her voice and started again, "Mac, some things need to stay between ladies."

"Is that so?"

"Yes. I made Aunt Ellie promise she'd never repeat what we spoke of."

"Well, I guess some things are like that between husbands and wives, too."

"What are you talking about, Mac?"

"Things like this." Mac pulled Laurel back into his arms and began kissing the nape of her neck beneath the carefully coiled chignon.

"Mac! What are you doing? It's broad daylight, and we're on the front porch."

"That's right." Mac laughed.

"Stop." Laurel futilely pushed against Mac's shoulder to get her feet to the floor, but he wrapped his arm tighter around her shoulder and began pulling the pins, one at a time from her hair. Tress by tress, the curls began to fall down her back and across her face. Laughter rang across the widow's yard, both Laurel's and Mac's.

⊶⊰⊷

July broke hot and humid, so typical of Arkansas. Even as Laurel prepared to leave for school, the day seemed so much warmer than normal. Heavy black storm clouds lay to the east and north.

The time she'd spent with Mac the past several days was the happiest of her life, and as she began to saddled Sassy Lady, she relived the precious time in the beautiful old four-poster in the widow's loft the previous night. The banter and play continued after Mac picked her up and dropped her into the tall carved bed and refused to extinguish the lantern after they'd read their scripture for the night. He'd chosen to read part of the Song of Songs, "*Let him kiss me with the kisses of his mouth, for thy love is better than wine...His left hand is under my head, and his right hand doth embrace me...By night on my bed I sought him whom my soul loveth: I sought him, but I found him not.*" Pink rose in Laurel's cheeks again as she remembered Mac stopping to act out the words as he read them to her. She bent to pick up the bridle to get her mind off the memories.

Touching the smooth leather of the bridle brought back the sensuous feel of Mac's back on her palm. The night before when Mac had laid her palm on his bare back that same sensation permeated her hand and ran through her arm. The sensation of Mac's lifeforce. Laurel stood in reverie for the moment, making no move to put the bit in Sassy's mouth.

Finally, Laurel shook her head, threw back her shoulders, and screamed, "Snap out of it, Laurel Grace. Get yourself ready for school." The words were no sooner out of her mouth than she reached up to touch her lips to brush away the ghost of the kisses that were playing on her lips. Those memories would be the hardest to dispel, for Laurel was not a passive partner in that part of their night's playfulness. Once Mac began the less than brotherly kisses, Laurel found herself willing and eager to allow herself to be carried away by the joy and emotion she felt. Mac's embraces were thrilling, and she'd longed for those feelings often during the weeks they'd been married. And he'd asked, "Laurel, will you let me look at you?"

Shyly, she'd removed her lawn night dress.

"How beautiful you are, Laurel."

"No different than any other woman."

"Laurel, your body is beautiful and strong. Thank the Lord. What a life mate He has given me."

"Thank you, Mac. I am happy you are pleased with me."

"I am more than pleased with you, Wife."

Mac and Laurel continued to hold each other and their playful, passion-evoking teasing continued until Mac stood up and told Laurel to stop.

"Laurel Grace. Understand what I'm telling you. Don't think I don't want you. I do. I want you too much. That's why I'm going outside for a spell. Don't come with me and don't get upset because I'm leaving you here alone. Just remember what I told you. The windows will be here next week, and I won't leave our bed after that. I've told you before...not everything is about you. I hope you sleep well." Mac climbed down the ladder to the main room and left the cabin. Laurel smiled, curled up, and fell asleep on her side of the beautiful old four-poster. When she awoke the next morning, Mac lay next to her, both were covered with their yellow crocheted wedding gift from the ladies of Hawthorn Chapel and little else. As long as she'd live, she would never forget that scene. The rose color in Laurel's cheeks attested to that fact.

"Laurel, are you ready to leave for school?"

"Nearly so."

"Thank you for last night, Wife."

"I was thinking about that just now."

"I wish you didn't have to go to school today. This past week we have been the family I've wanted us to be since we met in Washington County in March. We've talked, and we've worked together, and we've gotten so much done. Not one cross word's passed our lips. I know the Lord has finally blessed our marriage, and we are going to make it together. I'll bet those windows will be in Greensboro when I go over there today. I'll just bet there will be some news waiting for me. Our cabin will be finished, and we'll be home. Every promise met just like I told your pa."

"I hope so, Mac. Last night was special for me, too." Laurel was almost afraid to acknowledge her blessings for fear they'd prove to be a dream. For some reason, Laurel carried a nagging sense of foreboding with her on her way to school. At noon that day, the bliss would come to an abrupt end.

At the students' noon recess, Mac rode up to the Shiloh church. He dismounted and walked to the front door with his hat in his hand. His usual so blue eyes were the color of the open lake during a storm. Mac wore no smile on his face. Laurel knew before he spoke that something was terribly wrong.

"Can we talk?"

"Yes, of course. David, you can spend the rest of the recess outside with the other students. You've worked enough of the problems now to understand how to do your homework." Laurel walked him to the door and then closed it behind the boy who had become her protector. "What's the matter, Mac? You've never come to visit me at school."

"Bad news has just reached me from home. I received a letter in the mail this morning when I was in Greensboro. I recognized my father's script right off. He never writes himself, just includes messages in my mother's letters."

"The letter came from Maryland?"

"Yes. Laurel, my mother has asked for me. She has a cancer."

"Oh, Mac, I am so sorry. Of course, we must go. How can you get there the fastest? It took us nearly three weeks just to come across the state."

"Luckily, the railroad is finished to Memphis. It'll take me a good two or three days to get to Memphis, but then the rest of the trip will go much faster."

"When can we go?"

"I will go tomorrow at sunrise."

"Do you want me to go with you?"

"Yes. I want it, but I don't see how we can both be away. The supplies to finish our house are due any day, and the garden is near ready to harvest. I don't have anyone to look after the livestock."

"Yes, besides you'll travel faster alone. Anyway, my students are in the last few days of study for their exam. I can't leave them right now. I am glad you want me with you, but we both know it's better for you to go alone."

"I don't want to leave you. It seems like we just got things together." Mac walked to Laurel and put his arms around her and sank his face into her shoulder. Laurel could feel the weight of his concern. "Mac, I am sorry about your mother. I'll be fine here while you're back in Maryland. My friends and family will see to my welfare. You just go be with your mother."

"Laurel, I haven't seen my parents in more than four years. I told my mother I'd come home as soon as I got my life straightened out. That didn't happen until four days ago. Now I'm walking away when the dream is so near."

"Nothing will change here, except the season. Just go and care for your family. Your papa will need you if something happens to your mother. As long as I know you are coming back, I'll be fine."

"Wife, I am coming back. Shiloh is my home now that you're here."

"Go on now. Start putting your plans together. You have people to see and things to do. I'll be home by 4:00."

They walked arm in arm to the front door. Mac rubbed his hand across her cheek. He raised her wedding ring to his lips and kissed it, just as he did on their wedding day.

"Don't be late today, Laurel. Please."

Laurel watched as he rode down the hillside toward her uncle's house. She knew it would be his first stop. He would exact a promise from Matthew Campbell to watch out for her. The gaiety of her mood was gone. She would put on a good front for Mac until he left, and then she would deal with the sorrow...but not just yet.

Before Laurel arrived from school, Mac returned from his visit to Matthew and Ellie. He'd also packed a single carpetbag with a few of his necessities, including his Easter shirt, the first gift he received from Laurel. He should head toward Memphis, but he wanted one more night with Laurel.

"Mac, you've already done your packing. I'd have done that for you. Some of your things may need attention."

"I'm the only thing in this cabin that needs your attention, Wife. Let's go out to the creek so we can talk a while. It's too hot in this house to be comfortable right now."

They walked hand in hand to the creek that meandered its way along the boundary of the widow's property. When Mac found a small grove of trees that gave the best shade and some semblance of privacy, he spread the Double Wedding Ring quilt that the ladies of Shiloh Church made for them at the log rolling. That symbol of a happy marriage finally meant something to Mac, for he had been happy with his wife for five special days. He helped Laurel sit, and he joined her. He sat with her back cradled to his chest and his arms wrapped tightly around her. He nestled his face in her curls and smelled deeply of the scent he found so familiar.

"Laurel, I don't want to leave you. I wish I could think of some way to keep us together. I don't know how to be a loyal son and not go when my mother has asked for me. I'm sorry…I am sorry."

"Mac, I want no apology from you. I've never known a man with more integrity, more loyalty than you. If you could even think of ignoring your parents' summons, I don't think I'd know you. We all have to make hard choices at times, but we do the right thing. You have to go."

"I know I do. I told Matthew you would feel that way, but because you are so unselfish and care so much, going is even harder."

"Well, it's settled. Let's just enjoy the afternoon. Won't you tell me about your family back in Ann Arundel County?"

"So little left. My mother and father still live on our family farm. My older brother Sean died in the Mexican War at the siege of Puebla. He joined the military at seventeen, and he died so young, but he'd always wanted to be a soldier. He never intended to become head of our family holdings. The year after Sean was born, Mother delivered a baby girl who was stillborn. They named her Kathleen, Irish and Scottish to the bone. Mama said her hair was the color of copper. I was born a few years later. My father's name is Thomas MacLayne, first American in our family. My grandfather Patrick fought in the Revolution after he came to Maryland from Scotland around 1770. The old family story says he fought because he hated the Brits more than he felt akin to the colonies."

Mac continued, "My mother is beautiful, has always been as I remember. Her name is Ann, and her family name is Hays. Her family has been in America for several generations. She is a devout Catholic. She tried to raise both Sean and me up as faithful to the church, but we didn't take to it back then."

"Telling me about them makes me feel closer to you. I guess I know you a bit more."

"My family are good people, but the man you know was only born about three and a half years ago, back there in that very place where you teach five days a week. I wouldn't want you to know that old Mac. You'd never have married me."

"You'd never have come to ask."

"Probably right. Grace didn't mean anything to me when I was that other man."

They sat without talking for a while. The gentle east breeze felt cool in the heat of the first day of July. The sounds of the woods interrupted occasionally.

"Listen, Laurel. Hear that dove?"

"Yes. What do you think he is saying?"

"He's calling to his mate...wait for me...wait for me. Don't you hear him?"

"So now you are a bird translator!"

"No. I just know the dove won't be happy until he is back with his mate." Mac pulled Laurel down to the quilt. He took all the pins and ribbons that held her hair in restraint, and he placed his hands on both sides of her face. Tears glistened in his eye lashes. "Laurel, you are so beautiful. I want no argument from you. Do you see in my eyes that you are a beautiful woman?"

"Yes, Mac. You have taught me to see myself through your eyes. When you hold me, I feel pretty and valued. You've taught me that I am worthy. Your friendship has been a gift I'll never be able to repay."

"God bless you, dear friend, and keep you safe while I'm gone." Mac kissed Laurel with such ferocity and yet tenderness, she ached for the caress to continue. She felt a sense of wholeness in the embrace, but at the same time a terrible sense of loss.

"Mac, how long will it take to get to your parents' home?"

"With God's speed, two days to Memphis where the train line is finished back to the East. After that, I'm not sure. I'll write from Memphis with details when I get to the train depot. They can surely tell me about the routes east, the layovers between trains, and connecting lines. I need your promise you'll write to me often. Post letters in care of Thomas MacLayne in Ann Arundel County, Maryland. Baltimore is not far from the farm, and everyone there knows my father. I'll write often to tell you what's happening."

They continued to talk and hold each other and kiss and laugh and cry until the dusk threatened to fade completely. Mac lifted Laurel from their quilt, and arm in arm, they returned to the widow's cabin to spend one final night in the beautiful tall bed they borrowed some two months earlier.

"You know, Laurel. I'll miss this wonderful old bed. Our house will be finished when I get back, so we won't get to spend another night together in this fine old bed."

"That is almost sad. I'd probably be heartbroken if I didn't know that a wonderful life waits for us in our own home, just as soon as you can get back to Arkansas."

"Please come and pray with me one last time." Together they knelt beside the tall bed as they did every night since they'd arrived at the widow's cabin. They offered up thanksgiving and praise for the peace and joy they'd found together. Laurel interceded asking safe passage for her husband and asking for healing and ease for his mother. They prayed for their church and its congregation and the courage Thomas MacLayne would need. And in an unspoken plea, Laurel thought, *please bring Mac home to me.* After some time, Mac spoke, "Amen."

"Laurel, my obedience in going to Hawthorn has been a blessing. You have slain my restlessness and helped me sink my roots here at Shiloh as I wasn't able to do in the four years I lived here without you. Because you walked out in faith with me, I want to return home. I cherish your friendship."

"You have honored me. I'm indebted to you." Mac embraced Laurel and kissed her again. He lifted her to her side of the tall bed and then went to the right side and lay down. "Please hold me tonight, Mac. It will comfort me all the time you are away."

"I'd have it no other way."

━╪ ╪━

The next morning dawned gray and threatened rain. The gloom outside mirrored the sadness in the cabin. They arose as the sun did and Laurel went down to fix Mac a hearty breakfast so he would be well-fed before he would make do with two days of trail food. She placed griddle cakes, molasses, eggs, biscuits with butter, and bacon on the table. Laurel also stuffed a saddle bag with things to sustain Mac on the trail, including several oatmeal cookies she baked Monday after school.

Mac came down dressed in his buckskins and blue chambray shirt, his hair tied back with a leather cord and his beard trimmed. He went to the table near the hearth where he'd laid his money pouch, his hunting knife, and rifle. He picked up the things he needed and walked to the table where Laurel stood, waiting for him.

"Breakfast smells wonderful. I'm glad you went to so much trouble."

"Just wanted to give you something to remember me by."

"I'd rather have this." Mac again pulled his wife into a strong embrace, kissing her until they were both breathless.

"Mac, please carry this cross in your pocket all the time. The Lord will keep you safe." Mac looked at the finely carved cross tied on a rawhide cord. He looked at Laurel and smiled.

"Laurel, this is your papa's cross. You told me he always kept it by his bed. Are you sure you want me to take this?"

"I need you to carry it."

"Thank you." Mac turned to pick up his money pouch, but Laurel pulled out his chair for him to sit and eat his breakfast. He sat, took her hand, and offered the blessing, and Laurel went to the hearth to bring back his coffee. They ate a very quiet breakfast. Laurel poured him a second cup of coffee. Finally, Mac rose to leave. He again picked up his money pouch, his knife, and rifle. He placed the cross Laurel had given him in his pocket, rubbing his thumb across the satin of the wood as he knew his father-in-law had done thousands of time in prayer. The touch brought him some solace. He picked up his hat and pulled out Laurel's chair. They walked to the door.

"Patrick, I can't let you leave without speaking the truth to you." She lowered her eyes, and the words broke as she spoke. "I love you, Patrick. I am happy to be your friend, but I have to tell you, I love you." Laurel's eyes were filled with tears, and the green lightning that so fascinated Mac, flashed. Every thought of how he would tell her good bye and last-minute details he'd planned to give her vanished from his mind. He stood for what seemed hours and looked at the woman as she spoke her heart to him. Mac could find no words to reply.

Laurel wiped her hand across her face to prevent the tears from spoiling their farewell. Laurel turned and opened the door for him. With a final kiss, he stammered, "Thank you... for the fine breakfast. And Laurel, I will be back." Patrick MacLayne walked out of the door of his temporary home for what he believed to be the last time. Laurel stood on the porch and waved good-bye to him as long as she could see him riding down the road toward Greensboro. She then closed the door. She climbed to the loft to dress for the beginning of another day at Shiloh school.

When Laurel reached the right side of the tall bed, she picked up the pillow which recently cradled Mac's head. She put it to her face and breathed deeply to capture the last scent of Mac's presence in their bed. She lay for a time in his place on the left side of the bed wanting to cry, partly in regret for her spoken words and partly in relief that she'd told him. She remembered her time was short, so she pulled the muslin sheet and light weight yellow coverlet over the bed. When she finished, she turned to her bureau to begin dressing for the day at school. As she reached to pick up her hairbrush, she touched a small wooden box that lay next to her brush. Beneath the box, she found a single folded sheet of paper that Mac left for her to find after he was gone. The note was brief, clearly written in Mac's strong hand. It said simply, *"I'm sorry to miss the Fourth of July dance. I know you were looking forward to the celebration. Please enjoy this small trinket I got to complete your outfit. Your blessed husband."*

Laurel laid the note aside and opened the small box. Lying on a piece of lace, she found a gold filigree broach in the shape of a cluster of daisies. Among the ornate gold stems and jade leaves were tiny flowers made of mother of pearl and gold quartz. The delicate petals of the flowers were perfectly shaped, yet so tiny that the entire cluster of flowers was hardly larger than a twenty-dollar gold coin. He remembered, for on the day he picked the fabric and the pattern for the dress, he'd commented on the need for a piece of jewelry to complete the outfit for the party. Laurel never dreamed Mac would give her gemstones.

She placed the broach, a beautiful yet now unneeded gift, along with the note in her bureau drawer for safekeeping. She sighed. The gift brought no real joy. She'd rather have the gray homespun with Mac at her side than all the finery which would now hang on the peg in the upstairs loft. At that moment, she felt no reason to celebrate.

The next two days at school were busy ones, and Laurel was relieved the activities kept her busy, and her mind off Mac's absence. When she was helping a second grader learn to read or an eighth level student rephrase a poor sentence, she didn't have to think about returning to the empty cabin. Two nights in the quiet house were scary and sad. She knew the next day, the Fourth of July, would offer her no such diversion, and Laurel dreaded facing the long empty weekend alone. She pulled her thoughts back to the tasks at hand. She helped two of the eighth level girls make final changes to essays they would read after the picnic at the Independence Day celebration. She put all her focus into working with any student who asked, until finally at 3:45, Caleb Crawley raised his hand.

"Mrs. Mac? Is school going long today for some reason? I got my chores at home. Can we go yet?"

"Say may we go. I am sorry I kept you late. Yes, you all may go. Enjoy your holiday, and I will see you on Monday."

"Ain't you coming tomorrow?" Laurel looked up to see her uncle standing at the door. He let the students pass, and then he came to meet Laurel at her desk. He noticed the dark circles under her eyes and the fatigue which was evident in her slumped shoulders and downcast face. "You look tired, niece. You all right?"

"I'm okay. I haven't slept well the past couple of nights. I'm not used to being by myself."

"The widow is supposed to be home tomorrow. I'm sure she'd like you to stay on until Mac gets back. She'll be company for you, or you can stay with Ellie, the kids, and me."

"You got a houseful already. Besides, it wouldn't change anything. I miss Mac."

"He'll come back as soon as he can."

"I hope that is so."

"He told you he'd come home, Laurel. Mac is a man of his word."

"I know he will try."

"So, are you coming to the celebration tomorrow?"

"I'm not much in the mood to celebrate right now, Uncle Matthew."

"So, you're going home and pout the weekend away?"

"I'm not pouting."

"What do you call it?"

"All right. I'll come to the picnic and listen to the speeches of my students. Is that enough celebration to suit you?"

"It's a start. We'll see about the rest later."

The following day Laurel arose and dressed to do the morning chores. The work didn't stop just because the calendar marked a holiday. After milking, gathering eggs, cleaning stalls, and feeding the livestock, Laurel rode to the homestead. Her garden did not disappoint her. She gathered green beans, tomatoes, and a few cucumbers ready to share at the Shiloh church grounds. Her picking of green beans was huge, and she'd have enough beans to can at least two quart jars for her winter stores in addition to the large bowl she'd carry to the community potluck. By Monday, cucumbers would be ready to pick in large enough numbers to pickle. She needed to remember to ask her Aunt Ellie for her recipe. Mac always bragged on Ellie's pickles after every meal they shared with the Campbells. As much as thinking about Mac put a cloud over her mood, Laurel took a great deal of satisfaction from the idea of having a full larder ready by the time her husband returned from Maryland. As she stood and looked from her thriving garden to the other parts of the homestead, she realized that many other provisions for fall and winter must to be made in Mac's absence. Wood must be cut, split and stacked under the shed roof. Hay was still green and growing, but soon it would have to be cut and stored for their animals. Laurel suddenly realized how grateful she was that Mac hadn't yet bought cattle. She wouldn't have enough food to sustain a herd of twenty or more animals this winter. Then she laughed, loud and strong. She remembered that she told her father that she could take care of herself, manage a homestead, and provide a livelihood on her own. Now she was doing exactly that... Imagine that...Laurel Grace Campbell a self-sufficient adult. Her papa would have been so proud.

She looked at the house, nearly done. Mac had already hung the doors and mounted the shutters so the house could be closed up. The windows were due on Friday, and the walnut floor planks were in the loft of the barn. After her inspection of the homestead, she began to scold herself for sulking and pouting. She must step up and do the things Mac couldn't do right now. She was determined to get the homestead ready to be their home before Mac returned from Maryland. She would hire John Campbell and Roy Dunn to come back to work for her. They could lay in the firewood, and when it was ready, cut and store the hay. When her windows came, she would ask her uncle to come over and supervise their installation and the laying of the walnut plank floors. She'd pass the time by working toward Mac's dream. She skipped from the garden back to where her horse was tied under a nearby tree. Her mood was light, and she looked forward to the day.

Instead of the daisy print party dress, Laurel put on her gray calico skirt and white lawn blouse. She tied a bow at her neck with her green wedding ribbon. In high spirits, she rode Sassy to the churchyard to join the Shiloh community in celebrating the Fourth of July. When she listened to her students' speeches, she was very glad she was there to hear the presentations. Both girls were proud of their essays, and their oratory was good, too. Laurel decided to score the presentations for school and exempt them from the next assignment. Afterwards, parents and grandparents came to thank her for the good schooling their kids were receiving. The lunch was a feast. So many fresh vegetables and berries and fruit from the summer's harvest along with roast pork and fried chicken provided a fine meal. As much as she enjoyed the holiday with her family and church friends, Laurel did not want to play the wallflower at the dance. At four o'clock that afternoon, she made her excuses to Matthew and Ellie Campbell and turned to return to the widow's cabin.

"Laurel Grace, please stay for the dance. We always have a high ole time."

"Aunt Ellie, I want to go home and write a letter to Mac." Laurel stood firm, hugged her aunt, and mounted Sassy Lady to make the ride home. She wanted to do only one thing for the rest of the day...to write a long happy letter to Mac and to have it ready to post the next morning. She wanted Mac to have a letter soon after he arrived at Ann Arundel County.

Laurel picked up her writing paper and a pen and ink bottle. She went to the front porch to sit in the afternoon breeze as she wrote her letter.

Dearest Mac,

I have so much to tell you this Fourth of July afternoon. I went to your homestead this morning and was so excited to find all going so well. The garden is simply growing leaps and bounds. I took a very large bowl of green beans and a large platter of sliced tomatoes and cucumbers to share at the pot luck. I have enough fresh vegetables to start canning tomorrow morning. On Monday, I am going to harvest cucumbers and pack them away to pickle. Ellie gave me her recipe, so you will have lots of your favorite pickles to add to your supper all winter.

I decided to ask your 'crew' to stay on while you're away. I want them to lay up several cords of wood for winter. I have noticed a few broken limbs and a dead tree or two on the hillside not far from 'Eden.' I'll have them cut those first. I also want them to harvest the hay in early fall, although I hope you will be home long before then. We will need to store the hay to feed our animals this winter. I have plenty of money from my salary at school to cover their pay.

I hope the trip has gone well for you. Since you have been gone four days now, I assume you've gotten to Memphis and have been able to catch a train east. I hope for a letter soon, telling me the news.

I pray nightly for your mother and your father, too. I hope her suffering is not too difficult. I pray too for you, Mac. How I wish I could be with you to share this heartbreaking time and to help...just as you were there for me when my papa passed. I would not have coped without you there to hold me, to listen to me, and to care.

My dearest husband, please know my words at your parting were true. I do love you, and I ache for you to return to me when you are able. God keep you, my dearest friend.

Your loving wife,
Laurel Grace.

She laid down her pen, realizing she wrote both her names. She rarely used her middle name, but then she'd been with her family all day. They always called her Laurel Grace.

⇥ ⇤

The same four days were a challenge for Mac. The low lands around the St. Francis River were a boggy nightmare. The roads were nearly impassible in many places. He was so grateful that Midnight was such a strong animal, for a weaker horse would not have made the trip even in the three days they needed to ride to Memphis. Even crossing the Mississippi proved a delay as Mac missed the morning ferry across 'Old Muddy', and he waited several hours to get the afternoon ferry to leave Arkansas and get to Tennessee.

On the first evening, though, when he stopped a few miles north of Bolivar, Mac found the oatmeal cookies Laurel stored in his saddlebags. His thoughts were not far from her the entire day, but her gesture of making him cookies and then taking pains to pack them so they would survive the trip made him wish she were there – or that he was at Shiloh. He knew he'd find the rough, hard ground a far cry from the comfort of the tall bed he'd left that morning. "Lord, please keep her safe and comfort her during these days we're apart. Thank you for the good woman you gave me. Amen."

Mac did not sleep quickly. There was little light except for a small fire he'd built to make coffee and warm his supper. The fire was too dim to read by. He tried to make mental notes of things he wanted to do at the homestead when he got back, but even that did little to push back the memory of Laurel, still in her nightdress, hair tumbling down her back, looking at him with her gray-green eyes, sparkling from unshed tears as she shared her heart with him. "Mac, I have to speak the truth. I love you." Those words were almost audible to him twenty-seven miles from Shiloh.

What courage she possessed. Mac told her how he felt about falling in love, yet she still spoke her heart to say those words to him. Yes, that is what he saw in her admission. She spoke the truth to him. How extraordinary she was! Yet, he was in turmoil at the same time. He couldn't reply when she spoke those priceless words to him. He'd just stood there looking at her. What would she think? Even more, he wondered how HE felt. Did he want Laurel to love him? He would search for answers to many questions in the time they were apart. At least, he'd have lots of time to ponder the dilemma as he would spend at least four and maybe five days on a train.

On the next leg of the trip, while Mac crossed the sunken lands to the east and then waited to cross the Mississippi, he began to make a list of what he would write in a letter to Laurel, a letter he planned to post before he started east on the train. He was worried about the slow pace of the trip because his father wouldn't have written for him to come if his mother's illness weren't serious. He knew the train trip would take only slightly longer than the three and a half days that he used to ride the seventy-five miles from Greene County. He feared he would arrive too late to see his mother. His fatigue and the thoughts of his mother's death left Mac in a very low mood. Nevertheless, he was determined to write an upbeat, cheerful letter to Laurel because he didn't want to add to her burden of dealing with the homestead alone. As he sat on the log bench at the ferry dock, he thought of so many things he should and could have done to help her, but he didn't think of them in time. The only help he'd asked for was that Matthew keep Laurel safe and that he visit her from time to time. He'd neglected to make arrangements for work on the cabin, for cutting wood for winter heat, for feeding the livestock, and for putting up forage the animals for winter feed. He didn't even asked Matthew to get Laurel's things from the freighter in Powhatan.

He shook his head in exasperation. As he waited at Bradley's ferry landing, he pulled his money pouch from his inside coat pocket to get the passage fee. When he did, he saw the roll of bills he'd planned to give Laurel to cover expenses while he was gone. He stood up and slammed his fist against the log pylon at the dock and swore under his breath. He forgot to give Laurel one cent to take care of routine expenses for several weeks. Some provider he was! He must get a message back to her and to Al Stuart as soon as he was able. When Laurel spoke her truth to him.... No, this was not Laurel's doing. He was to blame for leaving her unprepared. After all, she even remembered cookies, and he hadn't provided for her at all.

As soon as he got across the Mississippi, he headed up the bluff to find a hotel or inn where he could stay for the night and where he could ask directions to the train depot. The newly completed Memphis-Charleston Railroad Line made a trip to the east coast possible, but Mac hoped to make a connection north and east so he wouldn't have to make the trip back from Charleston to Baltimore.

He knew there was a connecting line from North Carolina, but he hoped he could save the time.

When he bought the ticket for the first part of his trip to Maryland, he returned to the waterfront hotel and took his carpet bag and saddlebags up to his room. He ordered a tub with hot water so he could rid himself of the mud and grit from the St. Francis River bottoms. When he opened the door, the first thing he saw was the copper tub. Immediately, memories of the night he asked Laurel to wash his back and shoulders flooded back. He remembered her tentative touch, and the shyness showing on her face. He also remembered her loose curls and shapely body barely covered by her well-worn nightdress. He remembered the desire he felt and fought back.

During the four months since they'd met on her father's porch in Washington County, Laurel had woven herself into his life. He lingered for a while in the lukewarm water. When he finally decided to get out of the bath, he dried with a rough towel and dressed in his clean underclothes from his bag. When looking for his clean clothes, he removed his favorite shirt, the soft, white lawn shirt that Laurel made for him at Easter. Again, precious memories came to him: Her generous gift of her own Easter dress to Lonnie Thomison's sister, the serene joy that she displayed at worship on Easter Sunday as she sat dressed in her blue calico, and the sensuous touch of her hand on his chest as she checked the fit of his new shirt. All of these memories flooded back to fill Mac with a longing for home. The want was almost painful. He shook away the low thoughts. He must face his obligations. He loved his parents, and Laurel would be waiting for him when he returned.

He sat at a small table in the room and found a sheet of paper in his saddlebag to write the letter to Laurel. He would write an upbeat, positive message to his life mate. Maybe it would ease his longing to be with her.

Dear Laurel,

I am sending you this letter from Memphis, as I am staying overnight here awaiting the train going east tomorrow. The Memphis Charleston Railroad goes to the Atlantic in about three and a half days. That is how long it took me to ride Midnight across the St. Francis wetlands. I hope to get a connecting line as I go since Charleston is considerably south of Baltimore. I am going to board Midnight here in Memphis and hope he'll still be here when I get back.

I am so beholding to you for packing me ample food for my trek across the bottomlands. I had plenty to eat. I certainly loved every crumb of those cookies you packed. I only wish I provided as well for you. Yesterday, I realized I left you with a huge amount of work to do and not one cent to use to cover expenses. As soon as I get to my father's home, I will arrange to send you funds you'll need to cover costs while I am away. Your papa would not like the thought of me leaving you penniless. What was I thinking? Please forgive my thoughtlessness.

I have had some interesting experiences on my trip east. I stopped at a rowdy little village called something like Esperanza Camp. The local folks called it Hopefield. That is where the ferry crosses the river. Men were brawling and shooting off guns, the taverns were filled to overflowing, and I saw a variety of female companions, if you know what I mean. In Hopefield, there was lots of talk about a train coming across the river to Little Rock. That should make some interesting talk in the Arkansas legislature next year. That place was so full of noise, bad smells, and rowdy behavior, I was happy to get on that ferry at 2:00. With all the rain of late, the Mississippi lived up to its name of 'Old Muddy' and seemed to be miles across,

but the ferry man said it's just less than a mile. The water there is very swift and deep.

Well, I'll stop now and get this letter to the post office. Dear friend, I am praying you are well and content. I ask the Lord nightly to keep you until we are together again. Remember your Uncle Matthew is nearby if you need anything. I will try to write soon and often. Until I am back in Shiloh, I remain,

Your faithful husband

The next morning, Mac posted the letter to Laurel just before he boarded a train to Maryland. He knew the mail was slow and unreliable, but he hoped Laurel would get the letter shortly after he reached his father's home. He resolved to write often so she would know he was thinking of home and her. Truly, he was. Until now, Mac had never known homesickness. All the wondering, exploring, and drifting he did after leaving the MacLayne home in 1845-- the spring Marsha betrayed him -- until he brought Laurel to Shiloh in late April of this year was one long period of searching. He never missed home because he had never built a home. Now his dearest dream was waiting for him at Shiloh. Mac felt almost a physical pain from the separation. He vowed he'd return to Laurel, as soon as God would allow.

>=+ +=<

Several days later, Laurel received two letters at the end of the long school week. On July 17, her uncle brought her mail from Greensboro. The temperature reached nearly 100 degrees, and the church was stifling with only an occasional breeze blowing through the open windows and doors. Laurel finished closing the building at 4:00 and went to sit beneath the shade of a tall hickory tree outside the church. The dense covering of leaves provided a welcome shelter from the afternoon sun while Laurel read her letters. The first one from Mac was a blessing. He had been gone long enough to be at his parents' home now. She re-read the letter and smiled a second time at the compliments Mac wrote her about his travel food. He loved the cookies since they'd become his favorite dessert, and he rarely got them in the heat of the summer. She also smiled when she read about his forgetting to leave her money. They never talked about money, so she was not surprised. In fact, she'd not given it a thought either.

Her second letter was more of a surprise. Since Laurel moved to Shiloh, she received only one letter from Hawthorn. Elizabeth wrote in early May and sent a long, newsy letter from Washington County, but Laurel received no other news from her former home. This new letter was from Rachel. She wanted to savor the news so she tucked it in her satchel and mounted Sassy to ride to the widow's cabin where a third surprise awaited her.

When Laurel arrived, she found the Widow Parker sitting in the rocking chair on the front porch. The dear old lady was smiling and wiping tears at the same time. Laurel wasn't sure she should intrude on this scene, for it was clear that Mrs. Parker was glad to be back in her home.

"Dearie me. What a nice job you did taking care of my little place, here. Don't remember when it's ever been so spruced up! You even got daisies growing by my front porch. Thank you, Mrs. Mac, for loving this dear old cabin for me."

"You're so welcome and thank you for allowing us to stay here while Mac is building our own place."

"You've been a godsend for me while I been gone taking care of my daughter and her family. She suffered a long while, bringing this new granddaughter into the world, but all's well now."

"Praise the Lord. It's nice to have you home, Mrs. Parker. Can I help you move your things back to where they were?"

"No need to put things away. I'll only be here three days. I'm going west with the daughter and son-in-law. They're heading out to Oregon. Just wanted to come for one last look. Would you mind if I stay until they come for me?"

"This is your home. Of course, you will stay as long as you want."

"You know, Mrs. Mac, my husband brought me here more than thirty years ago. He's buried at Shiloh. I'd always thought to rest next to Harold some time later, but it's not to be. My family needs me, and I don't want to be so far separated from my grandbabies."

"Family is important. I'm sure Mr. Parker understands."

"Speaking of family, where is Mac?"

"Like you, he is answering the call of family. His father wrote in June that his ma is sick and asked for him. He should be in Maryland by now."

"Bless that man. He's got such a fine heart."

"Let's go in and fix us a bite of supper before time to do evening chores. With you leaving in a few days, I know you will want to start packing soon."

"We'll take that chore on later." The widow replied as Laurel helped her from the rocking chair.

They entered the tiny cabin that the widow called home since 1823. She walked around the room, running her hand over each piece of furniture and the window ledges and the hearthstones, as if she were storing memories. Tears ran down her wrinkled face. Laurel sensed she was saying good-bye to her dearest friend. Laurel left the cabin to give the old lady some small privacy to make her parting. She sat a few minutes in a rocking chair on the porch with no desire to start a fire to cook a meal anyway, for Mother Nature already supplied plenty of heat for one day.

After some time passed, Mrs. Parker came to the porch. "I fixed us a cold supper. I hope it's all right. Seemed so hot in there, I didn't build a fire."

Laurel joined the widow at the table. "Won't you ask the blessing, Mrs. Parker?" The widow smiled at the younger woman. They ate together for a few minutes, and then the widow looked directly into Laurel's gaze.

"I'm really sorry Mac's not here. Once a few years back, he asked me to sell him my place, and I said I'd never leave my cabin. 'Course we never know what the Lord has in store for us. It'll be hard giving my land up to someone else. I know Mac'd take care of it right."

"You are going to sell your homestead? Are you sure?"

"I know when I go to Oregon with my kids that I'll never see Arkansas again. I have a few things I can take, but most of it'll have to stay with the land."

"I know how difficult it is to transport your treasures across the wilderness. I left much of my family's keepsakes behind in Hawthorn."

"So many memories, but I'll just have to carry them in my heart and in my head. Conestoga wagons just ain't got enough room to carry a life to Oregon."

"Well, if Mac wanted this land, he surely still does. What would be fair value, Mrs. Parker? I will try to give you what you ask."

"Oh, Missy, I ain't got no inkling of land value or cost to build cabins or barns. Why don't we talk to Brother Matthew? I know he will be straight with me."

"We'll go see Uncle Matthew tomorrow." Laurel got up and started to clean up the table when the widow stopped her.

"Let this be my house for just a few more days. I'll do the house-work." Laurel hesitated, but then she saw the expression on the Widow Parker's face. She agreed to relinquish the chores inside, and she went out to the barn.

That night, Laurel slept on the cot tucked into the nook near the fireplace. The widow would spend the remaining nights in her beautiful tall bed. As Laurel undressed for bed, she remembered Rachel's letter. She retrieved it from her satchel.

"My dear friend, Laurel,

What a pair we turned out to be. By the time you get this letter that I am posting from the trail to Beller's Stand, I'll be somewhere out west. I can't believe how quickly everything has changed for us both. Almost the day after you left heading east, Joshua came home and asked me to move with him and his Baker family out to California. Josh has always had himself an itchy foot, and he's talked so much about the good life out west. I just never said yes before. You know how I love Hawthorn Chapel, and all my family is there. But he wanted it so bad I told him we'd go.

The Monday after Easter, we left Hawthorn to meet up with a wagon train at Beller's Stand. Josh's mother's family, the Bakers, were heading out with another family named Fancher. They're planning to set up a new community there like Mac explained about Shiloh...mostly Methodist families heading out together. The kids are sure excited about the trip.

I'm not sure excited is how I feel...I think I'm just nervous. Imagine a wagon, six mules, a cow, four kids, one being just a baby, and my adventurous husband out there together for four long months! Lord, help me make it through. My ma and pa ain't real keen on the idea, and Elizabeth thinks I lost my mind, but I have to let Josh live his dream. I know it's the right thing for us. We have never been so happy. Please pray for us, Laurel."

Rachel wrote more about her family, the church family at Hawthorn and about preparing for the long journey across Missouri, Kansas, Colorado, and Utah. Rachel told Laurel of their dreams of rich farmland in California and seeing the ocean. Laurel read on, but her thoughts returned more than once to Rachel's words..." Let Josh live his dream." Laurel was awed by her friend's sacrifice for her husband's dream. Laurel realized she understood what Rachel was feeling. In that brief moment, Laurel grasped the true meaning of love. Love is sacrifice. When you love someone, you allow their will--and not yours--to prevail. Love is not about receiving, but about giving. Love is pouring out self to allow those we love to be what they are meant to be. She never felt so close to Rachel, or Mac, or Jesus Christ. In that moment, His wisdom flooded her. Laurel felt joy. God taught her that freeing lesson. Mac had shown her part of the lesson; Rachel had shown her a part of the lesson; and Christ had been the example. Finally, she understood. If Mac never loved her, he didn't have to. He didn't promise he would. She knew her loving him was enough. Christ gave his life for a people who showed Him no love, yet he made no conditions. He loved.

Laurel got up from the table and finished closing the cabin for the night. She picked up her Bible and read for some time, trying to remember some of the passages she read with Mac, especially the last few days before he'd left for Maryland. She read Matthew 20:28, Ephesians 1:7-11, and 1 John 3:16-20. Every passage confirmed what she finally understood that night. She couldn't express what she felt, but she didn't feel alone or plain or unworthy. She was a new person, a whole person. She laid her Bible back on the mantle, took paper and pen, and sat at the widow's table near the oil lamp. Laurel was compelled to talk to Mac the only way available to her. She wrote page after page pouring out her joy to him.

CHAPTER TEN

Raise up a child in a way he should go: and
when he is old, he will not depart from it.

Proverbs 22:6 [KJV c1850].

Mac arrived in Ann Arundel County on his fourth day out of Memphis. He was tired, dirty, and very ready to get up and walk. Being cooped up on a train twenty-four hours a day for more than four days nearly drove him to distraction. As annoyed as he was at the forced inactivity, he still marveled at the speed at which he'd covered the distance. The entire trip took only about one-fifth of the time it took to cross Arkansas with Laurel. He made a mental note that transportation would be a central concern if ...when he served in the state legislature. Northeast Arkansas must build better roads if the area were to prosper. Why shouldn't a train line link Greensboro with Memphis? How the entire area would grow with a connection to a major trade center! So many thoughts ran through his mind. He'd write to Laurel to tell her about his revelation and to tell her he'd arrived safely at his father's home.

As soon as the train stopped in Baltimore, he took his bag and nearly ran to the livery stable to hire a horse for the last few miles to his childhood home. Mac enjoyed the ride, even after the long trip, and he was curious to see how much changed since he'd left home. Immediately, parts of the countryside brought back memories of his childhood and youth, but strangely, he didn't feel at home. Each furlong seemed to take him farther from where he wanted to be.

Mac prodded the strong roan to hurry his pace. He wanted to see his mother and renew his ties with his father. He knew his father would be proud of the changes he'd made in his life since they'd parted. Mac was no longer the disappointment he'd been. Thomas MacLayne would see the son he'd always wanted. Mac was well on his way to building his home with his life companion on the land grant from his grandfather. He intended to restore the future of the MacLayne family in America. The MacLayne line would not end in only two short generations.

Early afternoon, Mac found himself knocking on the front door of MacLayne Manor, the large, clapboard house where he had been born and raised. The beautiful old Greek-revival manor was two stories tall with a wide veranda on three sides of the house. The large porch was supported by a dozen double story columns. Dark blue shutters framed the triple windows. Mac smiled to see how little changed since his father sent him to find his way. When the door opened, Mac's jaw dropped, as two russet-colored sateen covered arms closed around his neck. Lydia Golden, Marsha's mother, was the person who opened the door to his parents' home.

"Patrick, dear boy! How wonderful you have come. Your mother will be overjoyed you've made it home."

Mac disengaged himself and stepped away. "Mrs. Golden." He removed his hat. "Yes, I do want to see my mother and father as soon as I can. Are you visiting with my parents?"

"Actually, I come every day to help with Ann's care. She's been bed ridden for more than six weeks now. You know we have been dear friends since our pioneering days."

"Yes, you and your husband have been good neighbors to us. Where is Father?"

"He rode into Baltimore to get some medicine from the apothecary and to look for a letter from you."

"I see. And Mother? Can I see her now?"

"She's sleeping. The doctor keeps her sedated much of the time because of the pain. Of course, you can go up and sit with us if you would like."

"Yes. I will, but first I'll go up to my old room and clean up a bit. I need a change of clothes after nearly five days on a train. Please excuse me."

Mac took the stairs two at a time. He found his room the same as he'd left it. Using the tepid water from the pitcher, he washed his face and hands. He took his Easter shirt and black trousers from the bag and shook the wrinkles from them. As soon as he was dressed, he picked up his Bible and several sheets of paper, ink and a pen, and went to his mother's room.

Mac barely recognized the woman who lay in his parents' bed. Ann MacLayne, a vibrant, energetic woman when he left Baltimore four years ago, remained now a frail, emaciated shell of his mother. He picked up her small hand and kissed it gently. "Mother, I am sorry I have been gone from you all this time. Please forgive me." Ann's eyelashes fluttered briefly, but the strong sleep medicine kept its hold on her. Mac dropped to his knees beside her bed and prayed. "Lord, I give you praise and thanks for getting me back to see my mother, even as ill as she is. Please Lord, don't let her suffer, and if it is your will, take her from this world and welcome her to You. Please keep my father strong, for they have been life mates and best friends for nearly half a century. Lord, please watch after Laurel until we can be together again. Amen."

Within the hour, Mac's father returned from the apothecary's shop with the laudanum. Mrs. Golden met him at the front door.

"Thomas, your son has arrived, and he's with Ann."

"Thank you, Lydia, for staying with Ann while I went to Baltimore."

"It's been my blessing to care for my dearest friend. I'll be going home now. I hope your reunion with Patrick is good. He seemed none too glad to see me."

"Good afternoon, Lydia. I need to see about Ann." Lydia Golden turned and walked toward the door and then stopped.

"Thomas, I hope there is no problem between our families because of the broken engagement of our children. That was such a long time ago."

"We are neighbors and friends. Marsha and Patrick are adults and more than capable of dealing with their own personal lives." Thomas MacLayne left her to see her way out, and he hurried upstairs.

"Patrick, son. how happy I am to see you home again. I feared I'd never see you again." Thomas pulled Mac into a strong embrace and clapped him on his shoulder several times.

"Pa. How blessed I am to be with you." The senior MacLayne was an older version of his son. He looked younger than his age with only a few streaks of gray in his collar length chestnut-colored hair.

"Ma looks feeble. Pa, what does the doctor say?"

"Dr. Murray says your mother has an advanced cancer in her stomach. She's gotten gradually weaker because she eats very little. Bless her, she has stayed cheerful and trusting all these months."

"All these months? Why didn't you write earlier? I would've come back."

"What good could you have done? We can only wait now. I wrote when your mother asked for you, but son, I need you here with me, too."

"Well, I am here, and I'll stay as long as you need me here. How often does Mother wake up?"

"The laudanum wears off about every six hours. I expect she'll be able to speak with you in about an hour. Come over here and let's sit by the window. It'll be cooler…nice breeze coming from the bay today."

Mac brought the chair from his mother's bedside and sat facing his father. He noticed the fatigue and sadness around his father's eyes. Mac knew his mother's death would take a terrible toll on his father. Ann and Thomas MacLayne had lived a true marriage for forty-nine years.

"She's been the best of wives, Patrick. Your mother has been the best part of me since the day we met. If you were not home to help me through this, I'm not sure I could stand it. Ann has always been the strength in this family. She kept me going when we lost Kathleen and Sean, and even when I sent you away. Bless her. She has been my mainstay through all the worst parts of our lives."

"I know. She has always been strong."

"How was the trip from Arkansas, son? You made very good time, it seems."

"Took me three and a half days to ride from Greensboro to Memphis, and about five days to ride the train from there."

"You must be very tired then, over a week without a hot meal or a decent bed. You want to rest awhile before dinner, son?"

"No, Pa. I want to visit with you and Ma for every minute we have. I have missed you."

"We hoped you'd get tired of roaming and come home to us, you know. We've prayed that selfish wish since the day you left."

"I was trying to do what you told me. You said I needed to find my passion in life and build myself a home. I just decided what I needed to do with my life a few weeks ago, and things are beginning to fall into place. I'd have come home to visit next summer, even if Ma wasn't sick."

"I am anxious to hear about your new life in the west, Patrick."

A weak, barely audible whisper came from across the room. "Patrick, is it your voice I hear?" Mac hurried across the room to embrace his mother.

"Yes, Ma. I am here."

"Let me look at you." For more than a minute, Ann MacLayne looked up into the face of her son. Tears rolled unrestrained down her face. "How handsome you are, Son. What a blessed vision, so like your father."

"You are just biased because I am your son, but it is nice to hear those words from you again. I've never forgotten all those times you said those exact words."

"Ann, dear, are you in pain now?"

"No, Thomas, I am fine and so happy to have our family back together. Patrick, sit here by me and tell me about your life in the wilderness."

"Mother, dearest, Arkansas isn't a wilderness anymore. We've been a state for more than twenty years. I live in a thriving community called Shiloh. We have about thirty families, mostly from my church. I live only four miles from a town called Greensboro. Why we have doctors, a lawyer, three or four churches, a hotel, and several stores where we buy anything we can't make at home."

"I'm glad that there is civilization there." Thomas MacLayne remarked. "You know we hear awful stories of that area...how backward and primitive it is."

"No, Pa. It's not true. My wife is even a teacher."

"You have a wife, son? You didn't write to tell us."

"Yes, Ma. We were wed recently. She is a fine woman and much too good for me. I know you'll love her when you meet her."

"Well, Patrick, why didn't you bring her home with you? I know we would love her, if you do."

"She wanted to come with me, but she knew travel would be slower, and she feels an obligation to her students. Four of them are about to take their first commons exam for graduation." Ann

MacLayne was clinching her fists and biting her lips. Mac saw she was enduring extreme pain so she could visit with him. He looked at his father, and Thomas saw the same thing. Mac stood up and kissed his mother and hugged her a short while. "Ma, I love being here with you, but I need a bath and some clean clothes. I've not been clean in a week. Will you excuse me?" Mac made the first excuse he could think of. "When you rest awhile, I'll come back and tell you and Pa about life on my homestead."

"You always were aware of everything around you, Patrick. I'll look forward to our talk later."

Mac left the room and his father followed a few minutes later. Together they ate in the family dining room, waited on by the MacLayne's household staff. Mac nearly forgot the ease he'd grown up with. He was no longer used to be being served. Nevertheless, he wondered what Laurel would have put on their table back in Shiloh. He needed to write to her as soon as his parents retired for the night.

About midnight, Ann MacLayne woke from her drug-induced sleep. Laudanum kept the pain at a tolerable level but also robbed her of precious time. The only sound in the room were the murmured words of a prayer.

"Father, give my mother ease. Please don't let her suffer. If it is your will that she leaves this world, please, Lord welcome her into paradise to live with You and her children. Please, Jesus, give her all the grace she needs. Cover her with Your endless love as she always loved me. As ever, I give You praise and thanks for the gifts You have given to me. Amen."

"Patrick, it's beautiful to hear you pray for me."

"Ma, I didn't know you were awake. Do you need something for the pain?"

"No, son. I need only your company right now."

"I'd best call Pa. He'll want to be with you too."

"Not just now, Son. Your prayer warmed my heart. Have you found the Savior, Patrick?"

"Yes, Mother. Nearly four years ago, I met Jesus, that real person you tried to show me so long ago. When I was a kid, He never seemed real to me, but now, well…He is the most real thing in my life. Bless you, mother, for trying to raise me right. Finally, I found my way."

"I am happy, Patrick. It won't be so hard to leave you when I know we will be together again."

"I want you to beat this terrible disease. I want you to know Laurel and be around to love your grandbabies. I want you to see my home in Arkansas."

"It's in the Master's hands, son. I'm not afraid because all things work for good for those who love the Lord. I can rest easy now because I know you do."

"Annie. I thought I heard you."

"My dear Tom, please come sit here on my bed and hold me while I sit and listen to Patrick tell us about our new daughter."

Thomas MacLayne helped his wife sit up and lean back in his arms. Mac pulled her blanket around her to keep her comfortable.

"Well, Son, you heard your mother. Tell us about your wife."

"Where do I start? We got married in March this year. She is special…smart, faithful to the Lord, cooks like an angel, and has the best wit. I never get bored listening to her. Her heart is good. She loves people. Can you believe she likes to hear me sing? She gave me this fine shirt she made me for Easter. Laurel teaches at our subscription school at Shiloh. The young'uns are learning quickly from her. I would give anything if she were here with me now. I know you'd both welcome her to the family."

"Well, son, you've praised this woman highly, but we've no inkling of her family name or what she looks like or how she won your heart."

Mac didn't realize his description was so generic. He didn't want to share the entire story yet, but he knew they wouldn't be satisfied until he'd made her more real to them.

"Well, ma, she's a lot like you. Laurel Grace Campbell was her name before she accepted MacLayne as her own. She's middle wise tall, just a bit taller than you are, and she's a bit on the slight side. She's got the most glorious golden-brown hair, just full of curls, almost to her waist. The most striking thing about her appearance is the color of her eyes. They are mostly gray, but the least bit of emotion sends streaks of green through the gray. To tell you the truth, I don't know when I find her most comely. She's quite handsome dressed in her Sunday best, but she's just as comfortable at home in her work clothes. She is the best helpmate any man could ever ask for. The Lord blessed me when he sent me to meet her in the northwest part of the state."

"How did you manage to win the heart of such a prize? You've been such a wanderer, Patrick. Seems obvious to me that you love her very much. She's made a change in you already."

Mac lowered his eyes at his father's comment. He couldn't tell his parents he made a marriage of convenience so he could have children, and he wanted to ease a dying man's worry. "Pa, that is a long, complicated story. We best save it for another evening so Mother can rest a while. I think she's been brave long enough for one sitting. We'll have more time to talk tomorrow."

"All right, son, but don't think we don't still have a lot of questions."

"I'm sure you do. Shall we read some scripture together and have our evening prayer so Mother can rest?" Mac picked up his Bible and read Psalms 27 for his parents. Kneeling by his mother's side, Mac thought of his family while both his mother and father laid their hands on his shoulders. Mac was nearly overcome with emotion, as he realized how much he missed them and their support all the time he was looking for his dream. In his heart, he called out, *Laurel Grace, I need you here with me. I want you to know my mother and for her to know you.* Thomas MacLayne offered the evening prayer, giving special thanks for his son's safe arrival and the addition of a new daughter.

"Goodnight, Ma, Pa. Sleep well. I'll look forward to more time to visit tomorrow." Mac picked up his Bible and walked down the hall to his room. He spent the next two hours filling several pages of news to mail to Laurel. At the close of the letter, he paused. He wanted to write 'your loving husband' to show Laurel he wasn't unmoved by her last statement to him. Yet, he couldn't write the words. He'd sworn to always be truthful with Laurel. That was their first rule. Finally, he simply wrote **Mac**. He melted the sealing wax and wrote 'Mrs. Patrick MacLayne, c/o McCollum's General Store, Greensboro, Arkansas.' He'd post the letter first thing in the morning.

Mrs. Golden arrived shortly after breakfast as was her custom. She kept Ann company in the morning and helped her bathe and brush her hair. Mrs. Golden was an endless source of local gossip, but the past two weeks, Ann showed little interest in the stories about the members of the local Catholic Church or other people of Ann Arundel that her friend decided to make the target of the day's gossip. Mac and his father wondered why she bothered to come so often. Mac resented her daily intrusions, but he said nothing the first week. Her presence made him uncomfortable, but he knew his strong negative feelings were directed more at her daughter than they were toward their neighbor. Lydia was especially accommodating to Mac, as she brought things to add to their lunch, delivered invitations from neighbors asking to see Mac, and posted mail from the MacLaynes and brought any items from the post office. Since Mac and Thomas did not have to go to Baltimore for supplies or mail, they spent the extra time with Ann and with each other. Mac looked hopefully each day for a letter from Laurel or Matthew telling him about the progress of the homestead, news from the community, or just a short note to help ease his homesickness. By the time ten days passed, Mac was concerned about things at home because he did not receive even one letter posted in Greensboro.

On Friday of that week, Ann noticed a faraway look on her son's face. "Son, what's got you worried? Have you gotten bad news from Arkansas?"

"No, I guess that's the problem. Ma, I've had no news at all. Not like my church family not to keep in touch. At home, several weeks without mail is not a concern, but here we have good mail delivery with the trains coming regularly."

"I'm sure everyone is just busy. Harvest time is in their midst, along with canning season, and the beginning preparation for the winter. Takes lots of time to cut wood and to fill winter larders, son. I'm sure you'll hear any day. Mac, will you tell me about your homestead?"

"Beautiful place to live, mother. You and pa gave me a part of Eden to build on. That first 240 acres has good water, valleys, rolling green hills and fine soil that'll grow anything you can plant. I have acres and acres of wonderful pasture. I'm planning to raise beef starting next spring. I bought another 120 acres when the government sold off the land in our county. Along with those 360 acres, we are homesteading another section. Our cabin site is only about a mile from Shiloh church, where Laurel teaches. All together, we got 420 acres and an almost complete cabin. More than enough to make us a good living."

"I wish I could see your place, Patrick. I would have loved your Laurel. She sounds like a lovely person. I have many things I want to give her and you for your home. You will take them back to her, won't you? Do you love her very much, son?"

Mac knew one of his parents would bring up that issue. His parents had loved each other all those years. Thomas was twenty-three, and Ann was seventeen when they married. Their love was passionate from the day they met and grew only stronger as they lived, worked, played, laughed, and cried together all the years since. They would not understand his marriage of convenience to the Spinster of Hawthorn. He dreaded trying to make them understand his match, but neither did he want to lie to his mother.

"Mother, Laurel is a woman worth more affection than any man could pay. I believe God brought us together. I will try to be a worthy husband to her." Mac hoped his evasive answer would satisfy his mother's curiosity. "Did I tell you about our cabin yet, Ma?"

"Cabin…Patrick, you don't have to live in a cabin. You know your father and I will help you build a real home in Arkansas, if you want to stay there."

"No, mother, we want to build a home that suits our community. Everyone in the settlement builds cabins for each other and raises barns for their neighbors. Our house is nearly finished. I am waiting for windows coming from St. Louis, and I will put down plank floors. It'll be a fine comfortable cabin with two stone fireplaces."

"You seem pleased."

"More than I can tell you. Making a place with my two hands with God's help has brought me more pleasure than any work I ever did, Ma. I'll bet you and pa felt that way when you came here to build this place."

"Does Laurel share your strong faith, son? Is there a large Catholic congregation at Shiloh?"

"Yes, it was the first thing that drew me to her." Mac knew he could honestly say that to his mother. He'd never have gone to Washington County had Matthew Campbell not told him Laurel was a faithful Methodist. "Not many Catholic families in our area. In our part of the state we have a few different denominations: Baptists, Disciples of Christ and Methodists…" Mac took a deep breath…. "Laurel and I belong to Shiloh, a Methodist community."

Ann MacLayne didn't answer for several moments, but then she replied. "Well, if you found the Lord, I don't suppose it matters which name the church carries, does it?"

"Thank you, Ma, for understanding. Your blessing is very important to me."

"Mac, to know that you found the Lord brought me the peace I needed. Son, however the spirit worked to bring you to grace, I'll not question. To Him goes the praise. Now will you please get me the laudanum. I need to rest. I love you, son."

CHAPTER ELEVEN

Therefore, if any man be in Christ, he is a new
creature: Old things are passed away:
behold all things are become new. And all
things are of God who hath reconciled us
to Himself by Jesus Christ and hath given
to us the ministry of reconciliation.

2 Corinthians 5:17-18. [KJV c1850].

For the next two weeks, little changed in the MacLayne's house-hold. Ann seemed a bit stronger and was able to spend longer periods of time without the laudanum. Mac and his father spent every waking moment with her, often carrying her out to the porch in the evening to talk in the cool breeze coming from the bay. When Ann slept, Mac and his father would ride around the MacLayne land, walk in the woods, or make short trips into Baltimore. Mac treasured the opportunity to reconnect with his father.

During the trips to town, Mac always stopped at the post office to ask for mail. The postmaster told him a member of the Golden staff or a family member picked up the mail regularly. The following day when Lydia came to visit, she would bring whatever mail was addressed to the family. Mac was disappointed once again. He'd been home for a month, and he'd not received a single letter from Arkansas. He continued to write to Laurel and Matthew every couple of days. He'd even written two letters to Albert Stuart, his attorney in Greensboro, asking Al to supply Laurel with any funds she would need. He felt sure that Al would write soon to assure him all was well. Yet, he received no word.

One afternoon after sharing a light lunch with his mother, Mac left the room while Thomas gave pain medicine to his wife. He paced the wide, shaded porch. *His Shiloh family would not have forgotten him so soon! Why did no one bothered to write to him, even if just to ask about his mother? His church family wouldn't abandon him to face this loss alone.*

Thomas found him pacing back and forth, and he clapped his son on the shoulder and said, "Patrick, she's all right. Don't be anxious. You can return home if you need to go. Your mother will understand. You've made her very happy. All she wanted was to see you one last time."

"What? No, Pa. I can't leave you. I'm sure Laurel's all right. Surely, she's just tied up at school. On top of that, she's doing all the work on the homestead, getting the place ready for fall and winter."

"Let's go for a ride, son. I need some fresh air and exercise." They rode for some time before Thomas broke the silence. "I don't know what I will do here when your ma leaves me. This farm has been a joint dream for all our years together, a place for our family to grow up. Now it just seems an empty place. Your brother and sister aren't here, and you've found your place a long way from home. Your ma is the only thing that has kept me going since you left for Arkansas four years ago. We made it all right through those the first seven years you wondered through Tennessee and Kentucky because we thought eventually you would make this your home. Now we know that wasn't the Lord's plan. This farm is built and it's no longer a challenge. With Annie gone...well, I got no reason to stay."

"Pa, you still have family. I'm only a few days away by rail, and Laurel and I will have children one day."

"So far away."

"Pa, you are just lost, thinking about Mother. She may lick this disease yet. She has seemed stronger these past few days."

"No, Patrick. Your mother won't see the month out. The doctors told me cancer leaves a person with a short period when the pain ebbs before the end. We have to lay it in God's hands."

"I can't imagine the world without Mother. Did I tell you? Laurel is an orphan. She lost her mother when she was young, and her father died two days after our wedding. I guess I didn't realize how blessed I've been to have both of you as long as I have."

"Yes, it's hard to lose people you love, but how much better we are because they loved us. I can't imagine my life here after Annie is gone. I just don't have the heart to keep the place going.

"Pa, let's just deal with it one day at a time."

"We'd best head back. I don't like being away for too long at a time." When they arrived at their doorstep, they found a carriage and two horses parked in the drive. "Tarnation, what is Lydia Golden doing here again?"

Mac and his father entered the foyer to find Lydia and her daughter Marsha picking up their reticules from the table. Ugly memories of a dueling field flashed into Mac's consciousness. He remembered the spreading red stain on the white shirt of his friend, Louis Rawlins, as he bled to death from the single gunshot wound Mac delivered on that cold November morning in '53. His face flushed and his breathing raced. He couldn't believe Marsha Golden Rawlins had come to his parents' home.

"Good afternoon, Thomas and Patrick. We've just finished a lovely visit with Ann. She seems to be feeling so much stronger this afternoon." Marsha drawled.

"Hello Lydia, Marsha. Yes, Ann does seem to be hurting less," Thomas responded.

"Hello, Patrick. I'm sorry your mother isn't well, but it's good to have you back again."

"Good afternoon, Mrs. Rawlins. Please excuse me. I need to see my mother before she goes to sleep again." Mac abruptly left the foyer and climbed the stairs without any further acknowledgement of Marsha's presence.

"I apologize for making Patrick uncomfortable, Mr. MacLayne. We stayed longer than we intended. Please make my apology to him."

"Lydia, I don't intend to be unchivalrous to you or your daughter, but please do not return to our home as long as my son is here."

"Thomas, you can't mean you don't want me to visit with Ann anymore. She is my dearest friend." Lydia cried out.

"I'm sorry, Lydia, but that is exactly what I do mean. Patrick came a long way to spend this time with us. Your bringing Marsha to our home is inexcusable. Good day to you both." Thomas MacLayne opened the door to show them out, and he closed it immediately as they stepped out to the porch, not waiting to see them off.

Thomas found his son sitting at the side of Ann's bed, holding his head in his hands. "Son, I asked them not to return."

"I guess it was inevitable that I would meet her while I was here. I assume she moved back to her parents after I murdered Louis."

"Patrick, you did not murder anyone. Louis provoked the duel. You tried on three occasions to get him to stop the fight."

"I knew Louis was no match for me in a duel. I should have left the territory again when he started prodding me to fight."

"How could you do that? You did nothing wrong, son, unless you believe you should have died instead."

"To this day, I don't have the least notion of why Louis called me out. I didn't make a scene when their engagement was announced at the governor's ball. Of course, the announcement was a total shock to me since I thought Marsha was pledged to me. I'd already been out of the picture for more than six years when I came home, and he challenged me."

"Patrick, she was and is a beautiful woman, but not the woman you needed. If her father sought a marriage between you two, I'd have allowed it because you were so smitten with her, but I'd have been worried that she wouldn't be faithful."

"I know that now, but I wish I'd learned her nature before she led me down the primrose path and before I was forced to kill my best friend."

"Some of our learning comes from very hard lessons, son."

"I tried not to kill him, even as I shot. I put his shoulder clearly in my sights…but just as I shot he moved…."

"Patrick, it's over."

"Why do you think she'd come here? Surely she knows how I despise her after what she did."

"Her life has been a disappointment since she betrayed you. She never bore children with Louis and when he died, his family excluded her from their social circle. First, they claimed her widowhood was the reason, and then Mr. Rawlins brought her back to the Goldens' home to live. Her dream of social standing and prestige was gone. I'm sure she wants to renew her relationship with you,"

"I'd never get involved with her again. What a fool I was to have ever thought she'd make a good wife."

"Tis a narrow line that separates love from hate, Patrick. If you carry strong feelings against her after all these years, you must have born strong feelings back then, too."

"What should I do about it?"

"I'd say forgive her."

"Forgive her? Not likely...she nearly destroyed me."

"No, son. She didn't. You have to accept the responsibility for those reckless years. She did betray you, but you chose the way you dealt with the hurt. You made those bad choices. No one else."

At first, Mac felt betrayed. He'd never heard his father speak such harsh words to him. He turned his back and walked to the balcony outside his mother's windows. For a while, he was angry. He'd never thought his father would condemn him so harshly. After he took a while to let his anger pass, he began to think about his father's hard words. Mac began to recall all the individual incidents which brought the problems in his life, hoping to find what came between them. He remembered the times he'd pleaded with Marsha for her kisses and more, the fellowship he'd shared with Louis, the hurt and disappointment of that Governor's ball more than ten years past. He cringed as he recalled many incidents from his seven wasted years: traveling aimlessly through Tennessee and Kentucky, using and abusing alcohol and people, wasting his money and time and effort in pleasure seeking, and never building anything or helping anyone. Then he remembered the wife he'd left in Arkansas. After a period of reflection, he realized how that wasted period of his life impacted Laurel, too. She was a victim of his past as much as the people he'd tossed aside during his travels. Mac missed Laurel at that moment more than at any time since he left Arkansas. If only he could talk to her or Matthew... or perhaps his own pa. He walked back into the room where his father sat next to his sleeping mother.

"Pa, I don't understand how...why...if...I don't understand how anyone can betray someone they love."

"That is a hard lesson we have to accept, not understanding. You need to forgive Marsha, not for her, but for yourself. How can you truly love Laurel or anyone else if you carry around all the pain and resentment you've kept for all this time?"

Again, Mac could not answer his father. He certainly saw Thomas MacLayne in a different light. He'd always admired his father, but at this moment, he was amazed by the wisdom he spoke.

"Son, take some time to think and pray about this old wound. Then I'd advise you to go talk with her and end it. You have better things to do than spend even one more day letting old wounds impact the rest of your life."

Mac spent that afternoon wrestling with his memories and resentment so that by the time supper was called, he was exhausted from his struggle. He knew all the time he hated Marsha, the only one punished was himself...now Laurel. Mac remembered that last morning when Laurel stared into his eyes and declared her love for him, he hadn't acknowledged the greatest gift he'd ever been given. What he wanted from life couldn't come to pass because he denied himself the option of loving. He wanted a home and a family, but he would have to allow the possibility of being hurt again. He would have to open himself up to feel the love Laurel so freely gave. He didn't know if he could, but perhaps his father was right. Maybe he couldn't love because he allowed hatred to fill the place where the love should grow. Fear is a powerful barrier. He'd seen it in Laurel. Why couldn't he recognize it in himself?

When his father remained upstairs feeding his wife and encouraging her to eat more, Mac ate in silence, alone in the dining hall. Just as well, Mac didn't want to face his father in his present state of confusion. He returned to his room where he spent some time writing another letter to Laurel, the fifth or sixth one, and a third letter to Matthew Campbell, pleading with both to write to him.

After a fitful night, Mac got up, dressed casually, and went in to visit with his mother while she ate breakfast. Ann MacLayne rallied a bit more and felt like sitting up during Mac's visit. They spent nearly an hour recalling memories of Mac and Sean's childhood. Ann managed weak laughter a time or two. Undoubtedly, she was basking in the attention from her son. She asked for her rosary, and Ann spoke the Apostle's Creed and her Hail Marys as her son sat reverently during her prayer time. At the end, she spoke heartfelt thanks for the time she'd been given to become reacquainted with the adult her child had grown to be.

Mac decided to do as his father recommended. He was going to talk with Marsha and put the past behind him for good. When he returned to Shiloh, he wanted to go back without the burden he'd carried all those years. His father was telling him the truth, and the stupid mistakes he'd made were not anyone else's to claim. He had made those decisions. He also knew that Laurel was not the only Arkansas MacLayne who lived inside a self-made fortress. *Oh, Laurel. I so wish you were here. I never wanted to talk to you more than I do this minute.*

As Mac rode to the Golden farm, he thought of what he would say to Marsha. Strangely, he didn't feel angry with her. He just wanted some questions answered. He prayed God would help him keep his wits and not let the old wounds fester with more hateful words. He reached into the pocket of his vest and felt for the cross Laurel pressed into his palm as she took the last embrace that early July morning. He whispered, "Lord Jesus, thank you. She is more than I deserve."

Lydia Golden met Mac at the door of her home. "Has something happened to your mother, Patrick?"

"No, ma'am. She was sleeping comfortably when I left. May I speak with Marsha, please?"

"I'm not sure any good could come from that."

"Please, Mrs. Golden. I mean no harm. I'd just like to have a few minutes to speak with her."

"Well, she may be in the stable. She likes to ride in the mornings before it gets too hot."

"Thank you. I'll look for her there."

Mac walked toward the whitewashed stable, which was some distance behind the house. He opened the door and saw Marsha currying a golden-maned mare. When he looked at her, he saw an older version of the woman he once worshipped. Somehow, she looked harder. Lines on her face and around her eyes were tense and unforgiving. Her hair and her clothes were impeccable, but they seemed to be a part of a molded façade that Marsha showed to all around her. She looked up.

"Well, Patrick. You remembered your manners finally. I guess you've come to give me another chance to renew our friendship. I was sure you would when you knew I was nearby." Her demeanor and tone of voice indicated she planned to play the vixen.

"Hello, Marsha. Can we talk for a few minutes?"

"Well, that is certainly one of the things I have missed about you."

"Is this place private? Some of the things I want to speak about are not for others to hear."

"No one is here, darlin', just you and me. You can say or do whatever you want."

Mac hesitated. He didn't like anything about the way Marsha was acting. He felt uncomfortable. Marsha walked over to him and traced a path down the lapel of his jacket with her finger. "You are still the best-looking man I've ever known, Patrick MacLayne."

Mac took a deliberate step back and gently removed her hand from his jacket. "Marsha, I don't want to give you the wrong idea. I want to talk about our past so I can come to some peace about Louis. Ten years has been plenty of time to waste wondering about a past event that I can't change."

"But you can change it. I love you, Patrick. I always have. Even on our wedding night when Louis took me to his bed, it was you I wanted."

"Marsha, I am married. I don't love you anymore. Truthfully, I'm not sure I ever did. I wanted you. I almost worshipped you, or maybe I did, but love is something different. Neither of us even knew what love meant then."

"I'd be happy to teach you what it means, if you'll let me."

"Marsha, I bedded more than my share of women who showed me that kind of love, sometimes for a reward afterwards. Cheap, ugly, carnal feelings that made me feel worse afterwards."

"Patrick Liam MacLayne. I'm still that same woman you want-ed...begged to love, remember?"

"I hate to admit I do remember, and you are that same woman. Thank God, Marsha, I'm not that same man."

"So... you're too good for me now."

"Nothing about me is good. I've only been forgiven, Marsha.... What happened between you and Louis to push him into the stu-pid duel? I've been able to put everything else behind me, except for that."

"I don't have a hint of what you are talking about."

"Louis and I were boyhood friends. He, my brother Sean, and I were always together, up until you came between us. He didn't have any reason to challenge me to that duel."

Marsha took a step forward and linked her arms around Mac's neck. "All water under a bridge, Patrick. Let's just forget about the past. I know you love me. You've always loved me." Marsha pulled Mac's face to meet hers and kissed him fully on the mouth. "We can have a wonderful life together. Your pa is ready to give you the MacLayne estate. You can be an important man here with our money and political ties. I'm young enough to have your chil-dren. You know you still want me! Don't you think I am beautiful still?" She tightened her embrace and started to renew the kiss when Mac pulled away and walked toward the door.

"Marsha, I am leaving. Coming here was a mistake." She ran to him and tried to put her arms around his neck a second time. "Stop it, Marsha. Don't make this scene any worse than it is."

"Please, Patrick. Just give us a chance. I will make you a good wife, I promise."

"Marsha, I already have a good wife. I'm never returning to Maryland to live. My life is in Arkansas. You could never be my life mate. You couldn't have done it ten years ago. You can't do it now. Laurel is my God-given mate. She is everything I want." Mac's own words struck him like a blow. At that moment, he was stunned by what he'd said, but then he felt as if a light filled the dark places he where lived all those years. He knew he spoke the truth--to himself--for the first time.

He turned his back to Marsha. This ugly confrontation with her led him to know he was in love with his wife! At that moment, every fiber of his being ached for Laurel. The knowing lifted the burden of guilt and shame from his shoulders. He straightened his shoulders, turned and spoke to Marsha Golden Rawlins. His voice was calm and resolute.

"Marsha, I am sorry you've been disappointed in your plans. Perhaps you can lay the past behind you and start a new life. I forgive you. Please forgive me for treating you with such disrespect when we were young. I am laying it all down. I don't intend to think of it ever again."

"You self-righteous fool! You can't dismiss me. You murdered Louis and destroyed my life. "

"No, Marsha, I didn't do either of those things. I was a foolish, brash kid. I didn't know what I wanted or needed. I just thank the Lord that He made a better plan for me. Good-bye, Marsha." He put his hand out to open the stable door when Marsha screamed at him.

"I told Louis I killed your baby because I didn't want to give him a bastard child." Mac turned and looked at her. He felt a rush of compassion and grief for his friend Louis who died for a lie.

"Marsha, I pray God will forgive you. We never lay together but not for my lack of trying. I hope the rest of it was a lie too.

Good-bye." Mac pushed through the stable door and walked away. He didn't look back. He mounted his horse and rode back to his parents' home. He felt liberated, no longer carrying the guilt of Louis's death. He rode toward home, not hearing Marsha's final screams...though they echoed in the air at the Golden farm.

"I hate you, Patrick MacLayne. You'll regret this day. Do you hear me! No one will take my place. I hate you."

CHAPTER TWELVE

*Sarah lived to be a hundred and twenty-seven
years old. She died in the...land of Canaan
and Abraham went to mourn for
Sarah and to weep over her.*

Genesis 23:1-2 [KJV c1850].

A pleasant surprise awaited Mac when he returned home. His
mood on the trip back from the confrontation was as undu-
lating as the terrain between the MacLayne estate and the Golden
property. His emotions ran from anger to almost joy and from de-
spair to hope unbounded. He didn't know if he experienced defeat
or a resounding victory from his encounter with Marsha. Perhaps
the purpose of settling old issues with Marsha was vain, but what
he'd learned about himself was priceless.

In this confused state, Mac walked into the MacLayne dining
room to find his mother sitting at her place at the right of his

father at the dinner table. She wore a rose brocade dressing gown and was propped up with several pillows, but she sat there as the lady of her house that night. Mac rushed to her side, dropped to his knees and buried his face in the lace of her collar.

"Mother, what a wonderful surprise to see you up."

"You're late for supper, son. You must be starving. Let's eat."

"Yes, Ma'am."

The three MacLaynes shared a true family supper with late summer vegetables, ham, and yeast rolls, a feast made to honor the lady of the house who reigned at the family table. They finished the meal with a small glass of wine and freshly baked peach pie. Mac and Thomas ate with zeal, but it did not go beyond their notice that Ann ate little. Regardless, the time they shared that evening was indeed food for their spirits.

Ann MacLayne never left her bed again after that final evening in July. Her strength ebbed every day, and she was unable to eat anything more than weakened broth or the blandest of soups. Thomas tried every day to coax her to take one more spoon of broth or one more sip of tea. Mac and his father took turns sitting by her bedside, talking to her, reading, praying, recalling pleasant stories of the past, and sharing plans for Mac's future.

Ann suffered great pain and took laudanum several times each day. Both men knew they were sitting deathwatch. As the sun rose on August 6, 1857, Ann Hays MacLayne died peacefully in her sleep, held by her beloved husband and attended by her only surviving child. Before evening passed, several of the families who lived nearest came to pay their respect. Thomas and his son received their friends and neighbors for several hours as Ann lay in state in the front parlor. Finally, about nine o'clock they found themselves alone eating supper, supplied by those who came to visit. The generosity of the local people provided a huge feast, but Thomas drank only a cup of coffee, and Mac picked at the plate of food left for him. Thomas spoke little since he'd finished the funeral arrangements. He'd sent word to the parish priest to come for the burial rites. He asked his stablemen to prepare a grave in the family cemetery. He planned to lay his wife to rest on Saturday. Now he needed time to mourn.

"Patrick, son, I am riding out first thing in the morning to look over our home. I'd appreciate you being here for me, but I need to say good-bye to your mother in my own way. I know you'll welcome other visitors who drop by, making my apologies."

"Yes, sir. Is there anything else I can do?"

"No, not that I can think of. I'll return early on Saturday. If you will help me deal with the funeral… well, I'll face the rest of it, one day at a time."

"I'll wait, Pa."

"Patrick, I don't know if I can live here in this place alone."

"Pa, you just said it…We don't have to think about anything else right now. We'll make decisions later. Let's finish our supper and try to get some rest."

After penning a letter to tell Laurel of his mother's passing, he lay down in his bed and he slept. The past week since their final family supper in the dining room had been a long and difficult one. Mac realized that he'd not felt alone during the hardships, because of the mental conversations with Laurel and with Matthew Campbell during his hardest times. He found comfort in these imagined conversations, right along with constant unspoken prayer for both his father and his mother. The following day was harried, a blur of visitors coming through the MacLayne house to pay respect to a lady who graced their community for so many years. Mac served as the host for his father, but fatigue, yearning for home, and grief at the loss of his mother took its toll. He was cold to the Goldens when they arrived to pay their respect. Mac was sure that Lydia's grief was sincere, but he could find no warmth for her. His flaw was not forgiving those who trespassed against him. Perhaps later, he could forgive, but not that day.

On Saturday, Thomas and Mac laid Ann to rest next to her daughter and the marble marker over the empty grave of his brother whose body had not been returned from the Battle of Pueblo. The parish priest spoke of the goodness and piety of Ann MacLayne and allowed Thomas time to eulogize his wife of forty plus years. Mac remembered so little of that service, but he did recall almost verbatim the last sentence his father spoke to honor his wife. "Friends, what I am as a man is due to only two things: my best friend Ann and the gracious Father who saw in his wisdom my need for a strong life mate." Thomas MacLayne then laid a pink rose from Ann's own garden on the casket and grief overcame him. Mac walked to his father and embraced him. Both men stood at the head of the grave as Father Rafferty commended Ann MacLayne to Heaven. Neither seemed aware of the dozens of people attending that morning, including Lydia and Arnold Golden who stood some distance away. Mac wanted the day to end. He saw his father go through the expected motions, but behind the controlled façade, he saw grief and fatigue. As soon as Mac could get his father headed away without seeming too uncaring or rude, he drove Thomas the short distance home. At the house, Mac left his father at the door and took the carriage to the stable. By the time he returned, Thomas MacLayne had gone to his room. When Mac looked in, he found his father asleep. He could only assume that his father had not slept since losing his wife. Mac returned to the parlor to serve as host in the MacLayne house.

When the last guest left, Mac went to the parlor and lit a lamp on his mother's mahogany desk. He slumped in the armchair near the unlit fireplace. Even late into the evening, the heat was intense. He walked to the window and opened it as wide as it would go. Wind blustered around the room, whipping the heavy draperies from side to side. He crossed over to the second window and repeated his actions. The hot humid air off the bay felt hot to his skin and signaled a coming storm. Lightening flashed across the sky, and thunder was so heavy Mac felt it more than heard it as it rolled across the Chesapeake Valley. Mac slumped in the arm chair, but no sooner was he down than he would rise to his feet to pace across the rust and gold braided carpet on the floor. *If he could only talk to Laurel, he could withstand the loss and the difficulty of dealing with his grief and concern for his father. Why didn't he bring her with him? Was he going to be a fool the rest of his days?* He threw himself onto the sofa finally, clutching his head in his hands. "Laurel, I need you. Lord, I want my wife here with me." Again, he rose, went out to the veranda and paced in the rain.

The rain came in sheets at times, and shortly, rivulets of rainwater dripped from his hair, his beard, and his clothes. Mac felt cleansed by the intermittent bursts of wind and water that poured from the Maryland skies that night. His mind cleared, and he focused on the task at hand. The first order of business was to help his father come to grips with his loss and return to the routine of managing his holdings. The second task was to return to Shiloh, as soon as he could feasibly get there. The third and most important task would be to claim his wife. Early the next morning, Mac would make that short ride into Baltimore to get the mail. Surely… this time… a letter from Shiloh would be waiting. If he knew Laurel was well, he wouldn't feel so pressed to get home, and he'd do a better job of attending his father.

Mac picked up his mother's Bible from the small table where she always kept it. He thought back to the many times he'd seen her sit there in her favorite chair, studying from the well-worn scripture book. He flipped through the pages, and he found a lace cross marking the fourth chapter of Philippians. Curious, he read to see why his mother marked that passage.

7And the peace of God which passeth all understanding shall keep your hearts and minds through Christ Jesus. 8Finally, brethren, whatsoever things are true, whatsoever things are honest, whatsoever is just, whatsoever is pure and lovely, whatsoever things are of good report, 9if there be any virtue and any praise, think of these things. And God's peace shall be with you.

Immediately, the image of his mother came to Mac's mind. He felt her love all around him, and the guilt he'd felt for being gone from her so long melted away. Her beautiful smile lit the room where he'd last kissed her warm face only two days earlier. No sooner did her image fade from his mind than it was replaced with the face of his wife. The same pure lovely smile that he'd seen the day he'd left her as she spoke her love to him continued to light the space where he sat in his mother's room, but the image he saw before him was not the Laurel from Eden or the playful Laurel from their four-poster bed with her tawny curls strewn down her back and across her shoulders. Here was Laurel standing in her father's orchard reading him the riot act and telling him that he owned her no obligation of marriage. This was the woman whom he had fallen in love with all those weeks ago, complete with braided coronet, dungarees, and lovely to the core of her soul. Mac knew peace.

"Thank you, Mother, for these words. Thank you, Lord. Thank you for Laurel Grace." Mac knew his mother purposely left her cross there for him to find, and he felt solace in the reading of those words. He went to his room, and beside his bed, he knelt to pray. "Lord, Your word always gives me what I need. Thank You for Your peace. The day has been a hard one for my pa and me, but we will go on trying to live in Your grace. I praise You for taking care of us, and I am grateful I can rest in the truth that Mother is in Your care. You are merciful. Father, Lord. I need Laurel, so please help me return to her. And Lord, take care of her. Amen."

Mac rose and went to sit in his grandfather's old leather armchair near the window overlooking the bay. He stretched his legs and cradled his head in the cushion and inhaled the leathery scent of the aged chair and slept.

≈ ≈

The next two days were dismal. Rain fell almost constantly, and the wind blew in heavy gusts until the late evening on Monday. Neither Mac nor his father ventured farther than the stables on either day. Due to the well-trained staff on the estate, though, life continued as when Ann MacLayne oversaw life at the MacLayne holdings. Stock was tended, meals were prepared, and the status quo continued. Mac was beginning to feel like a caged animal, and even though he tried to hold onto the promise of Philippian 4:5-9, it seemed patience was another virtue he couldn't master, right along with forgiveness. He did little but keep his father company. After that first long quiet day, Thomas remained silent no longer.

"Son, when are you going home to Arkansas?" Mac was not ready to answer that question just yet. He wanted to shout 'yesterday', but he wasn't sure his father was ready to deal with an empty house.

"Soon, I guess."

"You are as fidgety as a six-year-old on a church pew. You worried about something?"

"Cabin fever is all."

"I doubt that is the whole truth, but I'm feeling a bit shut in right now. Tomorrow, we are getting out…rain or no."

"I'd be glad to get out. Pa, are you all right?"

"This house is empty, Patrick. Your mother and I built this place over these forty years. We hired farmhands, grew our crops, raised our animals, and raised you two boys—now…well, she took the home with her."

"Pa, I know your loss. A few months ago, if you'd said those words to me, I wouldn't have understood. Because I have Laurel, I think I know why you feel you lost your home."

"Nothing is here for me anymore. The place is built, only needs maintaining. Neither son to take it over, and my life mate is gone to paradise. Home has no pull for me anymore, except to lay beside your ma, when it's my time."

"Pa, please don't say that. I can't deal with the thought of being orphaned." Mac remembered how Laurel cried for that very reason when Mark Campbell died. He was awed at the strength she must have to live with such a loss. "What do you want to do, Pa? Do you need me to come back here with you?" Mac was almost paralyzed with the thought his father would say yes. He loved his father, but he knew Maryland would never be his home again.

"No, Patrick. I want you to go home to Arkansas and to Laurel. I haven't been totally blind to your situation."

"I didn't mean..."

"You don't need to explain. You miss that young woman you left behind on your homestead. How many letters have you sent west? Five...six."

"Pa, I need to tell you about Laurel...about our marriage. I couldn't tell Ma with her pain, but you need to know the entire story."

"I know you love her."

"I didn't know it...not until that day Ma ate her last dinner with us at the dinner table." Thomas looked at his son, almost as if he were looking at a stranger. Mac surely was a good actor, for he could have sworn that every word Mac spoke of Laurel was filled with affection and desire.

"Is that part of the heaviness I have sensed in you, son?"

"You've noticed that? Part of the unease was just the idea of losing Mother, but you're right. I have been very confused about Laurel since the day we met back in March."

"Well, we have the rest of the afternoon to talk it out. The rain hasn't stopped in three days and from the look of those clouds, it'll go on a while longer. Talk to me, boy."

189

"Let's go sit on the veranda, Pa. This room's stifling." They found themselves in the rocking chairs on the south side of the house where they were sheltered from the occasional gusts of wind that brought with it torrents of rain. There they sat for more than three hours while Mac poured out his story.

"Pa, Laurel is a good woman. I don't want you to think she is anything but the finest lady I've ever known, but Pa…when we wed, ours was a marriage of convenience, not a true marriage like yours and Ma's. Her pa was dying of consumption, and he wanted to make sure that Laurel would not face life as a spinster."

"I can understand his wanting to see his child cared for. Every father wants the best for his children. I seem to remember sending you away for that very purpose, as hard as it was for your mother and me. I don't see what that has to do with you, son."

"Last winter, I was real low, Pa. I went to my pastor and told him I was going to give up my homestead and leave Arkansas. In those four years, I didn't do one thing to build a house or raise a garden or find a wife. The only good move I made was to find my faith and learn to care for a church community, but even that wasn't enough to make me want to stay at Shiloh. Pa, I felt empty and …well, like I was just passing time and not living at all. Matthew scolded me pretty good, him being the person who helped me start my new life. He knew I wanted a home. We'd talked about that many times. He arranged for me to go to the western side of the state to meet his niece. He thought a change of routine and being away from Shiloh would help me realize where my home was. Matthew had no thought that I'd marry his niece. Really, it was a way to get us a school teacher and a safe way to bring her across the state.

"Sounds pretty cold hearted, son."

"Yeah, it does when the words are out, but when I got to Washington County, Pa, Mr. Campbell was sick. He was down real bad with consumption, and he had told Laurel that I came there to ask for her hand. Things just got more tangled from there. Four days later, her preacher from Hawthorn Chapel spoke the wedding ceremony for us."

"You made vows with a woman you didn't know. Those are sacred words, son, to love, honor and cherish...."

"No, Pa. We wrote our own vows, things we could promise each other. I haven't told Laurel I love her to this day."

"I guess I understand why you didn't bring her home to meet your ma. It won't be difficult to have this marriage annulled. You didn't speak the vows in the parish church."

"Pa, that's the last thing I want. Laurel is a part of me now. I didn't know I loved her, not until I confronted Marsha the other day in her stable. I'd made an arrogant, ignorant vow that I'd never love again after I killed Louis. I spent all those years running away from the guilt. I finally understood that I never loved Marsha. I've thought about this constantly since I felt that weight fall off my shoulders. I couldn't love anyone as long as I was the center of my world. Laurel is a fine example. She is always giving and taking care of everyone but herself. I made it impossible for her to make a commitment to me, because I told her before I married her that I would never fall in love again. Pa, just before I left home, Laurel pressed this cross into my hand. It was her pa's. She told me I ought to carry it so I would be safe, and then she told me she loved me."

"I see."

"I just left, Pa."

"I think we need to get you home."

"I will have to return soon. I have been worried. Not one letter from Shiloh has come. I have written dozens of letters, some to Laurel and some to Matthew. I even sent two letters to a local lawyer that has done some work for me. I just wish I knew everything is all right."

"Mail is slow on the frontier, Patrick. I'm sure you'll hear something any day."

"Pa, I don't want to leave you here on the home place by yourself."

"Truthfully, son, I'd always thought you'd take over here because I knew Sean was born with a rambling heart. He wanted the military life since he was a small boy, but you've been the stable one, and I thought you loved life here on the bay, caring for our land. You always did until that miserable summer when...well, you know."

"Pa, I have to ask you to forgive me for those wasted years. I know you and Ma were sick about my worthless behavior. I know I hurt y'all."

"It was forgiven a long time ago. I hate the pain you lived with during those years. Marsha hurt you, I know. I've talked with Arnold Golden about that summer on more than one occasion. He regretted losing you as his son-in-law."

"I was too young. I was blind to who she was. I know now, I could never love her. If we'd wed back then, we would have made each other miserable. She isn't honest or faithful. We don't want the same things. No, Pa, the Lord gave me the right mate, even though it cost me nearly ten years of my life to know it."

"That's the important thing, son. You know now and have a chance to build a good life. You're still a young man, and the building years are the best days of a man's life."

"Pa, I didn't know until this trip home just how wise you are. Have you always been so wise?"

"Wisdom comes with age, son. Life experience gives us insight and grey hair."

"Have you given any thought to selling your property and moving west? There are so many opportunities back in Arkansas to help build a new community and a new state."

Thomas was quiet for some time. "Getting pretty dark out here. Let's go in and get us a bite of supper."

"I'd love to have you around to know your grandbabies."

"Laurel is in the family way? I wish your ma knew..."

"No, Pa. Honestly, we haven't … I didn't…"

"You don't have to speak the words. I understand. Not in your nature is it, son?"

"She is different, Pa. What I wanted to say is that you'll like Shiloh, and someday in the not distant future, a year or so, I intend adding a new generation to the MacLayne family."

The next day was clear, hot, and humid. Mac and his father rode down the side of the bay toward Baltimore. As they rode, he savored the memories of the good times in the rural areas outside the city. He and his brother Sean enjoyed hundreds of hours swimming in the bay, roaming the emerald valleys, and hunting in the woods between the family estate and the town of Baltimore. His older brother spent his days teaching Mac how to take care of himself in the wild. Sean was the one who taught him how to handle firearms, horses, and ruffians who wanted a good fight. Sean and Mac spent no small time wrestling themselves. Sean was the person who taught Patrick how to be the "beau" all the bells wanted to be seen with. Sean was his best friend and constant companion until he left to join the army. Because his brother spent a couple of years at Annapolis, Sean was welcomed as a recruit. Then Mac and Louis became inseparable friends.

Riding along this familiar road made Mac acutely aware of the loss of both Sean and Louis.

"Pa, why did you let Sean join the army?"

"That's an unexpected question. What brought that up?"

"Just remembering the times we'd spent here when we were boys."

"Everyone has to find his own path, Patrick. I let him go because he wanted a different path than I could give him here at home."

"Is that why you sent me to Arkansas?"

"Yes, son. After the duel, I knew any chance of your wanting to take over the estate was gone. Your ma and I – well, we just wanted you to find some peace and have a good life. That wouldn't happen here where all the memories would confront you every day."

"Except for missing you and Ma, Arkansas has been good for me. I got me an anchor now. When I get back to Laurel, I think we will enjoy life at Shiloh."

"Then our separation has been worthwhile. It's time you bought yourself a train ticket."

"Pa, are you sure you are ready to be here by yourself?"

"Patrick, you have done your duty as a son. You made your ma happy. I won't lie to you. I don't want to let you leave, but I'll be all right. Laurel is your family now. As a matter of fact, I have given some thought to moving. I've not made a decision yet, but I may surprise you and come for a visit soon."

"I hope so, Pa." They stopped at the train depot and asked about a direct route to Memphis, only to find there wasn't one, but with the station master, Mac plotted a trip back home. He paid his fare and set his departure date for the last Friday of the month. Another ten days or so would help assure Mac that his father would be all right alone. He would board the train back home that very minute if he felt no obligation to his father. Mac believed that if weather held he would be home the first week of September. He tucked the tickets into his pocket and walked with Thomas into the commercial area of the city.

The thought of going back to Laurel was the foremost thing on his mind. What could he take back for her? What things from the emporium would she love in their house? Inside Forester's Emporium, Mac bought several small gifts to take in his saddlebags and other things he would have shipped back. One gift he bought was a flowing white silk nightdress and wrapper. He also found a stylish emerald green hat and wool coat that would keep Laurel warm in the winter when she rode to church and then back to school when the harvest season was over. He bought several other things to use in their new home. While he usually hated shopping, the morning brought him more joy than any time since he lost his mother. He realized it was because Laurel had not been out of his thoughts all morning.

As father and son left the emporium, they saw Marsha Rawlins across the street, coming from the newspaper office. Mac didn't acknowledge seeing her. The last thing he wanted was a confrontation on the streets of Baltimore, so he and his father walked the opposite direction to the inn at the town square. He'd remembered the family that owned the inn always served good meals. Following a filling meal of beef stew and fresh baked bread, they made their way to the last stop, the post office.

Mac went to the counter to ask for mail for the MacLayne household. The post master handed Mac several letters for his father, but not one letter from Arkansas. Mac was disappointed, and it showed on his face. Doubt, fear, anger, and frustration mounted. He wouldn't believe that no one sent him a letter in all this time. Laurel's last words were that she would write often to keep him up to date on things at Shiloh. She wouldn't lie to him.

"Excuse me, Mr. Walton. Are you certain that no letter has come for me?"

"Well, Patrick MacLayne...I almost didn't recognize you after so long a time. Nice to have you home again. I'm sorry to hear about your mother."

"Thank you. Have you not seen any letters for me in the last six weeks?"

"Yes, I have been sending your mail along with your father's ever since your ma has been so sick. I believe the Goldens picked it up regular...at least twice a week."

"Thanks, Mr. Walton. I'll go by their place on our way back."

Mac was irate! He knew why he received no mail from home. Marsha and her mother chose not to bring mail to Mac when they brought the mail for his parents. Mac felt in his gut that none of his outgoing mail back to Shiloh was posted either. What would Laurel and Matthew think of him by this time?

"Excuse me, Mr. Walton. Have you posted any letters to Arkansas from me in the past month?"

"Not that I recall, Patrick. Did you send some I was supposed to post?"

A cloud of dread washed over Mac. He must get home. He made a silent plea... *Laurel, keep the faith. Please keep your faith. I am coming home.*

He stomped from the post office. "Pa, I want to wring her neck. Marsha has kept my mail from me. I can't believe she'd stoop so low. What good did she think would come of it?"

"Calm down, Patrick. She didn't think at all. She's jealous, and she is lonely and bitter. She needs your pity."

"If I was a bigger man and a better Christian, I'd try to forgive her. Right now, I just have to get back to Shiloh and straighten things out."

"Let's go try to change your ticket. Tomorrow, we'll get your things packed and ready for you to take them back home."

"What things, Pa. I brought very little, and I only bought Laurel a few things to take home."

"Son, we have to go through the things your mother left for you to take back to Arkansas. Heirlooms from her family, pieces of her jewelry she wanted to give Laurel, and at least a wagon load more she said you'd want."

"I wasn't thinking. We'll arrange to ship them later. I've got to make a fast trip. I got no time to pull a wagon across the St. Francis low lands. Not right now."

"We'll not know how soon you can leave 'til we check the train schedule. Let's head back to the depot. Surely, you can get an earlier train. I know we have a westbound that goes out midweek."

"You go, Pa. Get a ticket soon as you can. I'm going over to have it out with Marsha. I am going to get my mail."

"No, Patrick. You should avoid her. You go get the ticket changed, and I'll go by the Goldens' place. I'll bring your letters, if she has them."

The men separated to complete the business at hand. Mac did find a train headed west in two days. That would cut his packing time short, but he was determined to meet the deadline. When Thomas MacLayne returned home from the Goldens' farm later that afternoon, Mac had already begun to crate some of the things his mother left for him.

"Pa, did Marsha have any letters from Greensboro?"

"When her pa confronted her, she denied seeing any. Arnold asked Lydia about the outgoing mail you'd given her. She swore she'd posted everything you'd given her. I doubt that was true. Marsha said nothing. When I told them what the postmaster told us about the letters addressed to you, Marsha pretended she knew nothing about any letters, but Lydia did hand me this one envelope addressed to you. She said it came last Friday."

Mac looked at the script on the envelope, hoping to see Laurel's feminine hand; however, it took only a glance to see Matthew Campbell wrote the letter. As disappointed as he was, he whispered thanks to the Lord, for at this late date, any news from home would be a blessing.

"Excuse me for a few minutes, Pa. I want to read this letter from my pastor. Matthew is Laurel's uncle, so I know he'll have news of her, too."

"Take your time, son. I've a few things to do before supper time."

Mac went to the parlor and sat near the window in his mother's large damask armchair. He ripped open the end of the envelope and read.

Dear Brother,

I am sending a third letter because all here are worried for your safety., I've just visited with Al Stuart and Dr. Gibson. No one here has heard a word from you since Laurel got your letter posted from Memphis. We know mail is slow, but we believed we'd hear from you long before now.

All is well here in Shiloh. The windows for your cabin arrived on the Monday after July 4. They look mighty fine in your cabin. The boys did a fine job laying that pretty walnut planking on your floors. That was a low-down trick, Mac. Now all our female folks will be a wanting new floors. Ellie has already been hinting. The cabin is ready to move in whenever you are free to come back to Shiloh.

All here are praying things aren't going too hard with your ma. We hope she's better so you can come home soon. As for Laurel, I know you've heard from her often as she mails you letters at least every three days and has since you left on July 2. Write to her, Mac. She is worried to distraction.

Your brother in Christ,
Matthew Campbell

Mac re-read the brief letter twice more. Laurel wrote often, just as she'd said. Yet he didn't receive one word. Matthew didn't know that, of course. Mac wanted to know if Laurel needed money since he'd not left any for her, if the property taxes had been paid on time, and if she were well. He wondered how she'd managed to do all the work on the homestead and pay the boys their wages to help. She must have used all her teaching pay, but that would not have been enough. He was hungry to have any news of his wife. Matthew's letter made his early return home even more imperative.

When he finished fuming, he went to the stables to see his father. He wanted to talk...to anyone. He needed to vent his frustration and anger…and even some fear that arose after reading Matthew's letter.

"Pa, Matthew's letter was brief. He pleaded with me to write to Laurel. He said she wrote to me at least a dozen times and received only the letter I sent from Memphis. I don't even know if she ever got the funds I asked my lawyer to give her, or if Albert got that letter asking him to get Laurel money to take care of the homestead."

"Patrick, there is no need wasting energy fretting…Don't lose your faith. I'm sure if something was bad wrong, Brother Campbell would've written about it. Let's just get busy and get you on that train Wednesday. If you are west bound then, you'll be home in a week."

"Pa, I just have a feeling something is not right. I hate the distance to Arkansas. As much as I want to be there, I don't want to be away from you."

"One thing at a time, son. Let's finish your packing."

The task of gathering and packing his mother's things was bittersweet for Mac and Thomas. Some of the things she'd given him were connected to special memories, and Mac hadn't thought of some of those old stories in years. When he double wrapped the mantle clock that came from the frontier cabin of his grandfather Hays, he remembered the tales his mother told him about her father's exploits in the American revolution, and how he'd fought the Indians during his earliest days in Virginia. Mac would proudly display the lovely old clock on the mantel of his home in Shiloh. He remembered his mother sitting near the cut ruby glass lamp. The lamp belonged to his grandmother and was a gift to his mother on her wedding day. Mac's earliest memories of his mother reading to him were connected with that beautiful antique lamp. He stored his mother's wedding china and silver serving pieces. Mac couldn't imagine how they would use these things in their fledgling community, but he would take them to honor his mother's memory. He also set aside the cradle used by both Sean and himself and the small chest that matched the cradle. He knew his own father built those pieces of furniture when he learned he'd be a father. Ann MacLayne had made a special point that those two pieces had to go to their son as the first bed for the next generation of their family.

The only things that Mac added to his bundle to carry home were several pieces of his mother's jewelry. He stored the emerald band his father gave his mother the night Sean was born. She wore it as her wedding ring but called it her family ring. She'd not taken it from her hand until the time of her passing. Thomas replaced it with a wide gold band the day he'd laid her in the family cemetery because Ann asked him to give the ring to Laurel when she gave birth to her first child. Mac thought as he tucked the ring into his pack that his mother intended his father to come to Arkansas and become a part of Mac's world. He smiled.

Mac also took his mother's rosary. Although neither he nor his family were Catholic, he knew his mother spent hours running those jade beads through her fingers as she prayed for him and his father. Mac intended to keep those beads and the gold crucifix in his Bible always. Mac realized when he was finished the chest contained several thousand dollars of jewelry, and he would carry it back personally because of its value. And the dollar value was small indeed compared to the emotional worth they held for him. He would take no chance of losing things his mother treasured. One day his wife and his daughters would wear them and treasure them too. Mac would tell them stories of the beautiful Ann MacLayne so they would come to love and treasure her and the heirlooms that they too would someday pass down to their own children. The MacLaynes had always passed down their heritage, even if they needed to steal it as his grandfather did so many years ago in Scotland when he left MacLayne castle with the family crest.

CHAPTER THIRTEEN

But it shall not be so among you, let whosoever
will be great among you, let him be
to you a minister. And whosoever will be chief
among you, let him be your servant.

Matthew 20:26-27 [KJV c1850].

The second Saturday following Mac's departure for Maryland, Laurel took on the role of head of household. She took the necessary steps to buy the widow's land and pay the property taxes on Mac's holdings. She, along with her Uncle Matthew and Widow Parker, traveled to Greensboro to speak with Albert Stuart about the transfer of the deed. Matthew assured Laurel that the $125 she paid for the thirty acres and personal property that Widow Parker was leaving behind was a generous price, but Laurel insisted on adding another ten dollars when the widow told her she would have to leave the tall four-poster behind. Laurel knew it was heartbreaking for her, but she promised to take care of the beautiful tall bed and move it to the new cabin. Widow Parker smiled. "Love her well, and she will safeguard your love. My Howard made it out of his great love for me. I'm happy it'll bless you and Mac, too."

The widow was able to take so few things with her, only the cedar chest from the foot of the bed, the cradle she'd stored in the barn loft, and the china and pewter wedding gifts from her long dead parents. Al Stuart promised to file the deed to the homestead on the next court day in Gainesville. Laurel took the $135 dollars from her dowry and paid the cash directly to the widow. She was sure she was acting as Mac would have done if he were home. Laurel stood on the porch of Al Stuart's office and waved goodbye to the widow as her family drove their overly stuffed covered wagon out of Greensboro.

The MacLayne homestead now encompassed 450 acres, some cleared as pasture and much of it wooded with a large variety of hardwoods and fir trees. Ample water crisscrossed the acres. The promise of a good life lay in her grasp. The new cabin was nearly completed. Mac would be able to move into his home as soon as he could come back to her.

Time took on the pace of a whirlwind. Laurel was so busy those last three weeks of July that she could barely account for her time. She didn't know taking care of the work at the homestead, maintaining the widow's cabin and the animals she kept there, and doing her job at school would take every waking moment of her day. She rarely had time to sit and read, her attempt to build a suitable wardrobe had come to a complete halt, and visits with her family and friends at Shiloh were limited to the time she spent at church on Sunday. She couldn't have covered the responsibilities without the help of John and Roy. Even then, she added an hour a day to their hire to assure all the work was done.

Her students demanded every minute of the school day preparing for their end of term exams. The last year students were especially diligent, knowing that these exams would determine if they were ready to sit for their final exams in December. School completion could be delayed a whole year if they fell short on the mid-year tests. The little ones were happy to be reading finally, and they wanted Laurel to listen to them read aloud every day. Laurel also borrowed or bought every book she could find in the area to have a summer reading project for each one of the nineteen students in the Shiloh school. She didn't lose one student the entire term.

The heat of the summer added another dimension to the long workday. With temperatures hovering in the mid 90's by the time school was dismissed every day, Laurel sensed the call of the cool water at the creek, but she never went. She felt it would be inappropriate for her to swim alone, and besides her garden required attention, canning waited to be done, and routine nightly chores all required her attention before night fell. In midsummer, the garden was taking up the bulk of her free time. She despised having to stoke a fire in the fireplace on the hot days of July, but the fresh vegetables from the garden must be preserved for winter, so that meant canning when her bountiful garden gave her produce in such abundance. God blessed her with a large harvest that year, and the overabundance of vegetables assured there would be no hunger in the MacLayne house even in the worst of winter. Laurel found herself canning nearly every day, even after she knew she put up more than she needed. Melting paraffin to seal the jars and blanching vegetables was hot work, and as tiring and hot as the chore proved to be, Laurel was delighted at the growing number of jars she'd already placed on the shelves of the larder at the new cabin. Besides the green beans, tomatoes, berries, hominy, and squash she'd already put up, Laurel made soup with many of the vegetables, made creamed corn from Elizabeth Wilson's recipe, and put away several jars of Ellie Campbell's pickles that Mac so enjoyed. She tried to give away much of her excess, but nearly everyone in the community experienced bumper crops. Even the Dunn children's grandmother accepted a basket of the harvest only once.

Laurel saw that the small plot of wheat she'd grown was nearly ready to harvest, and her potatoes were nearly ready to dig and store in the root cellar for the winter. She needed to ask Matthew who would need potatoes, for her hills would provide far more than she and Mac would use in one winter. For her first year of homesteading, she was so glad her labors would let her share the bounty of Arkansas' rich soil. They would have ample winter provisions when she took their corn to be milled and wheat for grinding. She needed to make arrangements to have a hog slaughtered for meat. One animal could provide them with hams, bacon, and sausage, but not unless she found a good butcher. Uncle Matthew would help with that too. Then it dawned on her that she would have to store her meat here in the widow's small smoke house, because Mac's trip to Maryland prevented him from building one on his homestead. That would be an inconvenience. She'd need to mention it in the next letter to Mac. Get home soon, husband, because you need a place to store your meat.

She missed not having apples and peaches to can. Those things were bountiful in western Arkansas, but in this part of the state, fruit was rare. Perhaps she would be able to purchase a bushel or two. Her orchards were growing well, but fruit was still years away. Desserts would be made from eggs, berries, and cocoa for a few years unless the mercantile ordered apples and peaches. No real tragedy there, because blackberries and mulberries grew throughout the hills and valleys, along fence rows and near streams and creeks. But that put one more chore on Laurel's list of things to do. Berries must be picked if they were to be preserved.

The boys were making good progress on the wood. Of course, cutting season for hay was still a few weeks off. They prepared the loft, purchased twine, and oiled the wagon wheels. When they were prepared for hay cutting time, they continued to put back cords of wood beneath the lean-to roof. Preparation for their first winter in Mac's homestead was nearly finished. Laurel stood back and looked at all she accomplished that summer, and she felt a great sense of achievement. She thought, 'See, Papa, I can take care of myself....' Laurel knew she succeeded in her new role as head of household.

Being well ahead of schedule, Laurel decided to spend some time and money to make Mac's homestead comfortable and homey. She wanted curtains for the glass paned windows, and new rag rugs for the wood floors. All the best homes in Washington County and many of the cabins of the Hawthorn congregation were adorned with brightly colored curtains, even at their greased paper windows. The following Saturday, Laurel traveled to Greensboro to Davis's mercantile for the sole purpose of getting fabric to have her curtains made. She'd hire Mrs. Dunn to make them, knowing she would not have time to finish them before the windows were installed. She would also spend a few minutes each evening twisting cloth scraps to begin the rag rugs.

At the mercantile, she chose white lawn for the curtains in the main room. Even though it was quite costly, she also bought several yards of lace to edge the floor length curtains, which would go on all four windows in the sitting area of the main room. For the two windows in the second pen, she picked a blue print cotton to make long curtains. They would look very pretty with the Double Wedding Ring quilt the ladies of the Shiloh congregation pieced for her at the log rolling party last spring. She added a length of the same fabric to cover the small window in the tiny room attached to the bedroom. For her kitchen, Laurel bought a length of sunny yellow gingham to go over the window above her dry sink. She was happy with her choices, knowing the curtains would look very pretty in her kitchen. Besides, she knew the payment for the sewing would allow Mrs.

Dunn to purchase winter shoes for Catherine and Roy before the fall weather set in.

Laurel became attached to the Dunn family and always felt good when she could find a way to help them earn money to supply basic needs. She'd never known want like that because her father always took care of her. She knew they were proud people and did not want the charity of the Shiloh community, but they were always willing to earn their keep. Laurel smiled to herself. She wanted curtains, and they needed shoes. Wasn't it wonderful how God cared for all his children?

The next Sunday at the dinner on the grounds at church, Laurel asked Mrs. Dunn if she could share lunch with them. Laurel brought much more than she alone could eat, and it was a great opportunity to ask Mrs. Dunn to make her curtains. Laurel always enjoyed a visit with the dear old lady, because she always shared stories about the early days of the state and the Shiloh community. She had even told Laurel about the first Sunday Matthew Campbell had preached at the church.

"He was a mighty powerful preacher to be so young, but we'd of kept him if he hadn't known a word to preach. He sang to us that Sunday, and we thought we'd gone to Heaven and heard an angel of the Lord. Besides we fell in love with those young'uns. Ellie already had two babies by then and a third near its time."

"Do you remember Mac when he first came to Shiloh, Mrs. Dunn?'

"I remember meeting him, but Missy, he wasn't the same man we know now. He stayed alone out there on his property...once and again, he came to church but not often. Didn't pay much heed to how he looked and never smiled. But I remember right off, he took to Brother Matthew. They spent quite a bit of time together, hunting and fishing. That October we got us a circuit rider come through and hold us a revival, down in the meadow on Mac's homestead. We were still building our church then. At that camp meeting, Mac met the Lord for real. I know Matthew paved the road, but the circuit rider spoke the words that took Mac to his knees. The man that got up was the Mac you married. Sort of like he wasn't broke anymore. Glory be to the Lord, we surely got us a fine addition to Shiloh." Laurel already knew part of that story, but the hearing was a blessing all the same. "He's a mighty good man now, Mrs. Mac. We all esteem that fine man, and the part he has become in our community. After all he was smart enough to bring us you."

Laurel blushed a bit. She treasured all the history of the settlement, especially pieces that helped her know more about her family and her husband. Her curiosity led her to ask, "How did you and your husband come to settle here, Mrs. Eleanor?"

"Like lots of this community, even Mac, we got us a land grant in Tennessee for service in the War of 1812. My man traded it for this parcel here in Arkansas a few years later. We got us a really good section, too."

"Your husband fought in the revolution?"

"Indeed he did, and again in 1812 when Madison was our president. You saw his papers over the mantle at our cabin. He was so proud of his papers. Papa loved to tell us those stories about saving our independence."

"I'm so glad then that you have his pension to help you support yourself and your grandchildren."

"What pension? My grandson Roy and me, we have always worked to save for our property taxes all these six years since the old Colonel has been gone and to buy what we can't do for ourselves. I don't know about no pension."

"Mrs. Eleanor, all the soldiers of the Revolution and the War in 1812 who were honorably discharged from the military earned a pension to help them if they couldn't work and to help support their widows and children. We need to file yours to help you raise

207

Roy and Catherine. Maybe Roy could even stop working and come to school for a couple of years."

"I don't have any idea how to do that. Besides, I can't read nor write."

"I can help you. I wrote a request for one of our widows back at Hawthorn. It'll take a few weeks, but you deserve that pension. Maybe we can even get the letter off within a couple of days and get your pension started before fall."

"That would be a blessing. I would be able to tithe to our church. Not been able to give much since my husband drowned in the Cache River Flood. Bless you, Mrs. Mac."

"Well, let me earn that first. I'll talk to Al Stuart, and we'll get this process going."

The next Saturday, Laurel took Eleanor Dunn to visit Al Stuart in Greensboro. Al examined the papers Mrs. Dunn brought and knew without a question she should receive the pension. He prepared the letters required and then had them witnessed and set them aside to have them filed in the courthouse. He posted the request that very day. Mrs. Dunn took two dollars from her purse to pay the attorney's fee, an amount that represented more than four days' work for her grandson, but she was proud to be able to pay her own way.

"Thanks to you, Mr. Stuart. If that pension comes to us, it'll let me provide better for my grandbabies. I'm beholdin' for your help."

"My pleasure, ma'am. Laurel, what do you hear from Mac?"

"I got a letter from Memphis, the first week after he left. He said crossing the St. Francis bottom land was slow. Have you heard from him?"

"Not a word. I am a bit concerned because Mac usually pays his property taxes in July. He left in such a hurry that he didn't tell me how to handle this matter. Do you know what he intends me to do?"

"No. We haven't spent much time talking about money. I have some money that came from my father's estate. I'll pay the taxes."

"They can wait a spell."

"No need for that. Can you tell me how much I owe and where I can pay these taxes?"

"Well, actually, I am the tax collector in this part of Greene County. I'll gather the amounts and let you know. Mac's got three separate parcels covered by three different laws, and now you've got the widow's parcel too. I'll let you know next week."

"Fine. Well, Mrs. Eleanor, are you ready to go to the mercantile to see what new things came in on the freighter this week?"

"When you are ready, Mrs. Mac."

Laurel was excited when they reached McCullough's store. He'd brought in apples and peaches. Laurel took money from her reticule and purchased a bushel of each. They would have apple cobbler for dinner on the grounds tomorrow, and Laurel would can the rest. Having apples from time to time would be like having a bit of Hawthorn with her. She knew Mac would be pleasantly surprised the first time she used some of that fruit to prepare a special dinner after his return.

The following day at church, Mrs. Dunn told all her friends of the special thing Laurel did for her. Before the noon meal was finished, half the congregation stopped by to thank her for her writing the request and helping Eleanor Dunn apply for her pension. Laurel was somewhat embarrassed by the attention she got because she didn't think it to be much of a favor. Another lady asked her if she would take time to write a letter to her sister living in the Colorado territory. A third woman wanted Laurel to read two letters she carried in her purse. She received them more than a month earlier, and there was no one to read them to her with her husband and son away working on the roads in the next county. Laurel willingly read the letters for the lady. Her new role as community scribe grew over the next several weeks. Laurel eagerly agreed to help her neighbors. School's ending would leave a large part of each day to fill. She wanted to keep busy. When her mind was occupied, she didn't miss Mac as much, and she was better able to forget the loneliness of being at the widow's cabin alone.

One thing bothered her more. Too many of the women in the Shiloh congregation could neither read nor write. They depended on their better educated husbands, or in some cases, lived in households where no one was literate. She was determined to talk to her Uncle Matthew about this problem. In her view, it was not acceptable when they could do something about it. Later in the week, the opportunity arose when Matthew came by the school to talk with her about storing the school books and other school supplies for the summer break.

"Niece, how are things with you?"

"Busy, mostly. You?"

"We're all well. You seem a bit low today. What's bothering you?"

"I don't know. I've felt edgy all day. Something's not right. Oh, I know that's silly. I think something has happened to Mac. Has he written you at all, Uncle Matthew?"

"No, Laurel. I was about to ask you the same thing."

"Well, it's probably nothing. The mail is just slow."

"Well, niece, it's not four weeks slow. Do you think Mac arrived at his parents' all right?"

"I pray so. He can take care of himself. I know he's all right, but I am aggravated he hasn't kept us up to date. I try to stay positive, Uncle Matthew, but I do worry that we haven't heard a word. Even Al Stuart asked me. He said Mac didn't tell him how to handle the property taxes on his land."

"That's not like Mac. He's a good business man."

"I have enough money to pay the taxes. I'm not concerned about money. I am afraid..." She paused for a moment. "I am afraid Mac doesn't want to come back."

"Laurel, that is ridiculous. Mac didn't want to leave in the first place. He told me that if his mother wasn't so sick, he'd wait until next year when he could take you with him."

"That was before...Never mind...Mac will come back if he can."

"Not if...WHEN he can. Now, let's take care of this school business. Have the kids all taken care of their final assignments and exams?"

"No. All did except one. Ann Browning was ill the afternoon of her final math exam. She wants to teach so she needs that exam. I told her she could take the exam tomorrow after school is dismissed for the term."

"How'd they do?"

"Mostly, they've all done well. If winter term is as good, all will be promoted for next school year. You ought to hear my little ones read. They are just a bright little crew, and so eager to learn."

"You've done us a good job teaching, Laurel Grace. We have been blessed to have you."

"Thank you, Uncle Matthew."

"Tomorrow, Ellie and Susan will come help you put your school stuff away for the summer break. And I want to come out to your homestead on Monday to set your new windows. The rest of the week, John and Roy will lay your new walnut plank floors. When Mac gets back, your house will be ready to move in to."

"Again, thank you. Mac will be glad to have it done. But Uncle, there is something else I want to talk to you about, and also to the rest of the school committee."

"What is that? You know we can't afford a raise."

"I want to start a Sunday school for the women of our church. Most of them can't read or write. They can't tend to their mail or their own legal matters, or even take over their homestead business if their husbands – most of who can't read either—aren't around to do it."

"You want to teach them to read and write on Sundays?"

"Most of them are here anyway."

"Whoa. How do you know they'd come?"

"They will if you tell them it's a good thing if they learn to read. How can they study the Scripture if they can't read? Think what a blessing that would be!"

"Let me think on it and pray about it for a while. Laurel Grace, let me know if you hear from Mac. I sure miss him."

"Don't think and pray too long. I want to start while I've got free time during the school break."

"Yes, Laurel Grace. I'll think quickly."

Matthew Campbell turned and left the building, and Laurel turned back to erase the work from the slate board left by the students that day.

"Can I talk with you a minute, Mrs. Mac?" Laurel did not immediately recognize the woman. Dressed in her Sunday best calico and her hair neatly pulled into a neat chignon at the back of her sun-bronzed face, she lifted her eyes to Laurel's. "Ya don't know me, do ya?"

"You do look somewhat familiar to me, but I'm not sure..."

"I'm Adam's mother. My name is Ruth Smith. I met ya at Doc Gibson's office."

"Yes, I remember now." Laurel was amazed at the change in this woman. She saw her on several occasions at church and a time or two when she brought Adam to school, but she never looked so well kept and neat. Before her hair was disheveled and drab. Laurel looked around and saw her husband Lem sitting in his wagon several yards away. Laurel squared her shoulders and turned to face her. "Can I help you in some way?"

"Ms. Mac...I wanted to ease my mind."

"Ease your mind?"

"Yes ma'am...when Brother Matthew, the elder, and your man came to our cabin and spoke of Adam's welts, well... at first, me and my man was real mad. Lem said it weren't none of yer concern how we raised our kids. We stayed away from church a spell, and 'course Adam couldn't walk to school 'til he healed up. Lem and me we talked on it ever night for two weeks. I told him more'n once he whupped 'em too hard. He's really a good man. He works so hard fer us. That's the way his pa raised him. I ain't sayin' they won't get no more whuppin's now and again, but iffen they need correctin', we'll do it right. We ain't never gonna put no more whelps on our kids."

"Thank you for coming to tell me."

"We owe ya an apology. We's the ones in the wrong. We spoke bad about ya more'n once. Brother Matthew's been out to see us three or four times since he was there with Mac. Lem's always liked and respected Mac, so it embarrassed him to have them face us for our wrong. After a couple of talks, Lem saw his wrong. Brother Matthew explained to us about sparin' the rod. He also told Lem that the punishments were too harsh, just like when the Romans beat Jesus too harsh. He helped us see we needed to let our kids know love. He helped us see."

"I can see how that would happen. Uncle Matthew has a way of helping us see things better."

"Well, Lem and me just wanted to say we're right sorry about our mean words about you, and to thank you for teachin' Adam so good. He's learnin' real fast, and he loves comin' to school."

"He's a bright boy. He is learning very quickly. Thank you for coming to talk with me. I am glad you and your family have returned to church."

"We're happy to be back. Brother Matthew done told us we'd be welcome." Ruth Smith turned to leave the churchyard, but before she left, she turned back to speak to Laurel once again. "Mrs. Mac...I know Adam's done missed a whole bunch of school this year, but will he get put back when he comes in November? He'll get real embarrassed to be back with the younger kids."

"Tell Adam if he will do his summer reading, we'll get caught up in the winter and he'll get promoted with all the other students at his level. He really is very bright and has done well all term. He'll have no problem getting the missed work done before Christmas."

"I thank ya, Mrs. Mac. Ya been kind after we've been bad mouthin' ya to everyone. We won't never do it no more. See ya at church on Sunday."

"Good-bye, Mrs. Smith. Thank you for coming."

Again, Ruth Smith started to leave.

"And Mrs. Smith, please tell your husband I'm proud to teach his smart son, and I look forward to getting to know y'all better."

The visit from Ruth Smith was a high point in Laurel's week. She missed Mac, and her life at the widow's was lonely and even a bit frightening at times. Yet, never in her life had she seen so clearly the working of God's redemptive love. Mr. and Mrs. Smith were learning to parent in a new way so their children could now grow up in a home where they would know both love and discipline. Her uncle's concern for his congregants and his courage in addressing the wrong of a follower in his church delivered the Smith children and restored a family. Christ's love worked its way through her uncle, and she even helped a little.

⊷⊱ ⊰⊷

The next day was the final day of the spring term. Laurel told all the students good-bye and challenged them to read whenever they could. She passed out the books she'd gathered and told them it was a summer assignment, and they would have to make a report on the book when school started again in the fall. A moan arose from the students, but most eagerly took the books Laurel offered. She also praised them for their hard work and announced they would all be promoted if they worked as hard in the winter term. She told them school would reconvene on November 2nd if the harvest went well. At 1:30, Laurel dismissed Shiloh school for the harvest break, and Ann took her math exam. By 3:30, she finished her first term as Shiloh's teacher. She knew she did a good job, and she was proud of the work she'd done. She didn't think she'd ever accomplished so much in her life. She also dealt with her role as head of household more than adequately. More than that, she nearly completed the provisions for winter, and Mac's cabin was all but ready to move in to. She increased the land holdings, and she dealt with the taxes and the deed as well as any property owner in the community. Tomorrow, she would ride to Greensboro, knowing this time she would surely have a letter from her husband. Laurel Grace Campbell MacLayne was feeling very capable and worthy that Friday afternoon.

Even with the disappointment of finding no letter from Mac in Greensboro, Laurel's sense of accomplishment was bolstered again on Sunday. Brother Matthew announced the formation of Shiloh's Sunday school. He explained that the reason was to promote Scripture reading, and he urged all who needed to strengthen their reading skills to attend. Laurel was surprised when the congregation clapped and spoke their amens when he finished. Before she left the church that morning, seven people asked to attend, four women and three men. Laurel never expected any men would want to come. She told them they would begin the next Sunday at 1:30. Her excitement over the first Sunday school helped ease the disappointment she felt from having received no letter from Maryland. She fairly danced her way to Sassy to ride home. As she prepared to mount her mare, she was once again approached by Mrs. Smith.

Peering beneath her poke bonnet, Ruth Smith spoke, "Excuse me again, Mrs. Mac. Would it be all right if I came to Sunday school with my oldest daughter? Don't neither of us read too good. She was sickly when she was school-age, and we just never made her come to school enough for her to learn to read or know her arithmetic. She's near sixteen now and says she's too old to come to school with all the little kids."

"I'd be pleased to have both of you come to Sunday school. I understand. What is her name?"

Ruth looked up with a slight smile on her lips. "I'm glad you'll let us. Her name's Leah Ruth." Laurel smiled briefly at the mention of her mother's name.

"My mother was named Leah. Please tell Leah Ruth I understand her not wanting to come to school with small children. She'll be welcome with us on Sunday. We'll be finished in time for evening services on Sunday.

"I'm beholdin', Ma'am. "

�==⟨+ +⟩==⟩

The following Friday, the MacLayne cabin was finally completed. The walnut floors were laid and waxed to a beautiful sheen. The curtains made by Mrs. Dunn were hanging by every glass-paned window, all eight of them. Laurel's uncle and other members of the school committee planned a surprise to thank Laurel for her work at the school during the last term. They arranged with a freighter from Bolivar who made a circuit from Bolivar to Newport to Smithville to Powhatan to Crowley's plantation to Greensboro to bring Laurel's family treasures across the route to Shiloh. When Laurel went to the homestead to gather food from her garden, she found a small group of church members waiting on her front porch. Laurel turned pale at the sight.

"Uncle Matthew, did you have bad news about Mac?" Her voice trembled, and she felt her knees buckle under her.

Matthew caught her as she fell. "No, Laurel...no bad news. We just thought we'd help you move."

"You scared me! No, Uncle, I'm not moving into the cabin until Mac gets back. I do thank y'all for the kindness to me though." Roy drove the small wagon that brought Laurel across the state around the side of the cabin. "Well, Laurel Grace, then what do you want us to do with all this stuff?"

Laurel was speechless. The sight of her papa's arm chair, and the bureau which had been her mother's wedding present unleashed her tears.

"Well, darling, we wanted this to be a happy surprise," her aunt Ellie said.

"Oh, Aunt Ellie. How wonderful to have my family things after all this time. I am happy."

Laurel's uncle hugged her tightly. "This is an oversight, niece. We should have brought these things to you a long time ago, but on behalf of the entire Shiloh community, we just wanted you to know how much we appreciated having you here. You are so much a part of us already."

"I don't know what to say. Thank you all for making me welcome."

"Where do you want these things?" Roy called out from the wagon seat.

Laurel spent a happy morning placing all the treasures around the cabin. The multicolored rag rug from the Campbell's living room added a touch of bold warmth to the floor of the new sitting room. Her papa's chair and her mother's rocker sat one on either side of a small side table near the fireplace. Her mother's beautiful bureau and Grandmother Wilson's rocking chair found a new home in the second pen bedroom. She unpacked the trunk and was about to put the old clothes into the bureau, but then she remembered how badly they fit her. She decided she wouldn't wear them in Shiloh. They were a part of her old life in Washington. Those with sound fabric she would give to Eleanor Dunn. She knew the excellent seamstress would put the material to good use. Perhaps she could even make herself a new dress, which she'd not done in some time. Next, she unloaded the crate holding the material for her gray sateen ball gown, which Mac bought in Jasper all those months earlier. Laurel didn't know what to do with such luxurious cloth. She certainly didn't need a ball gown in Greene

County. She already owned a beautiful party dress, which she'd never worn. She placed it carefully in the bottom drawer of the bureau. Perhaps it would find its use some time in the future. The last length of fabric was the sunny yellow print, which she hadn't really cared for when Mac picked it out. She didn't need a new dress for school. Five different changes of clothes for school already hung on her clothes pegs. Laurel laid the length of material into the bundle of old clothes she'd set aside for Mrs. Dunn. Perhaps one day soon she'd see Catherine dressed in that sunny material which would make the perfect dress for a young girl. Laurel opened the final crate to find her books and her mother's candlesticks and polished pewter pieces. Those items would remain stored away until shelves could be built to display them. The final task of the day was to add three jars of fruit which survived the trip across the state to her nearly full larder. By noon, Laurel was finished. She looked around and saw the beginnings of the home Mac described to her many times in the last few months.

"Friends, thank you from the depths of my heart. You have no idea what it means to me to have my family's things around me. God bless you for your kindness and love." Happy tears made their way down Laurel's cheeks. Several of the ladies of Shiloh hugged her and spoke soft words to her. Men tipped their hats, uncomfortable with her tears, and made their ways from the porch. Within a very few minutes, only the Matthew Campbell family and Laurel remained at the homestead.

"Welcome home, Laurel Grace. I hope having your things from Washington County will help you feel you have come home."

"Uncle Matthew, Shiloh is good to me. Seeing all these things here in Mac's cabin is wonderful. I thought I'd be sad and think of mama and papa's not being here, but these things are a comfort to me. They just seem to belong here. "

"That's because you belong here, niece." Those were Matthew Campbell's parting words to Laurel. After her kin departed, Laurel spent the next two hours tending her garden and harvesting ripe vegetables. There was so much squash and piles of green beans and black-eyed peas ready to pick. She knew the rest of the day she would spend canning the food, but she didn't mind the chore, as she walked on clouds. For a brief moment, one dark blot appeared for her. She'd still received no letter from Mac.

In mid-August, Shiloh community celebrated another special occasion. Mark Campbell, Laurel's younger cousin, married his longtime sweetheart, Deborah Sanford, the daughter of one of Greensboro's doctors. Their courtship had been a long one, over two years. Mark was very unlike his father or Mac, for that matter. Mark vowed he wouldn't take a bride until he could bring her home to a finished cabin and an established farm. Even though Deborah pleaded with him from time to time, his resolve stood. This year proved a boon to Mark Campbell's farm. He harvested crops above his needs and sold the excess at good prices. The few animals he owned produced healthy offspring. At last, he could take care of a bride. Mark's concern was sincere…his wife-to-be was raised in comfort, as her father was the second best respected doctor in Greensboro.

The Sanford family planned and carried out the most elaborate wedding Laurel ever saw. Although they were members of the Baptist Church in Greensboro, Dr. Sanford allowed his daughter to be married at Shiloh because she would attend the Methodist church with her husband, just as the Scripture directed. Matthew would perform the rites for his son. Both Matthew and Ellie were delighted at Mark's good match. In the more than two years since their son told them of his intentions, Deborah had become a part of their family. They were more than pleased that Mark finally reached the level of financial security he set for himself. At the age of nearly 25, Mark wanted very much to start a family.

The wedding began at 1:00 in the afternoon. Deborah was a stunning bride, dressed in a full-skirted lace wedding gown with a veil that fell in multiple layers into a train. She carried a lovely bouquet of violets and white roses tied up with sunny yellow ribbon. Mark, dressed in his dark blue suit and white shirt, stood smiling broadly as he saw his life mate approach the altar. When he took her hand from her father, the expression on his face told the story of his feelings. They had waited a long time, but the wait wasn't in vain. Laurel could see very clearly the look of a man in love, and she envied Deborah. As she listened to the words of the traditional wedding service between the young couple, and the spoken vows ordained in the Book of Worship of the Methodist Church, she was struck by the simple, yet binding eternal promises of the wedding ceremony. She remembered the almost, business-like commitment she made the previous March. How she wished she had been able to speak those traditional vows with Mac. Of course, at that time, speaking those vows would have been a sin. She didn't loved Mac then, and she knew he didn't feel that way even now.

"Mark, do you promise to love, honor, and cherish Deborah, so long as you both shall live"

"I do."

"In the Lord's Name, I now pronounce you man and wife. Whom God hath joined, let no man put asunder."

Mark helped Deborah kneel at the altar of Shiloh Church, and together they spoke their first prayer together as married people. "Our Father, who art...." Matthew Campbell ended the ceremony by telling his son that he could kiss his new wife. Laurel remembered how her wedding ended. Mac offered his hand to her, and he kissed the wedding band he'd placed on her finger. He did not kiss her as Mark was kissing his bride because he feared her rejection of his touch.

Following the simple, touching ceremony, the parents of the bride provided a grand wedding supper for the entire community. Table upon table was filled with the bounty of Greene County: venison, fried chicken, ham, and bergu, a traditional stew made of a variety of small game. Fresh vegetables were bountiful as the harvest season was nearly finished. The bridal cake was a beautiful white three-tiered desert decorated with fresh flowers, like those in Deborah's bouquet. Nearby sat another table loaded with pies of many flavors, some puddings, and mounds of fresh bread. The Sanfords brought beverages directly from nearby springhouses so the tea, cider, and punches could be served cool.

The Sanfords brought together a small orchestra of local musicians to provide dance music for the party. The couples danced waltzes, reels, and square dances well into the evening. The Shiloh church yard was a place of joy that day, as the people laughed, talked, sung, joked and danced. Laurel was pleased that her cousin enjoyed such a wonderful start to his marriage, just as it should be. The new Campbell family left the party at dusk in a beautifully adorned buggy, trimmed out in every kind of wild flower that Greene County could offer this time of year. They would spend their wedding night in their new home. Laurel caught word that a few of the younger men were planning a chivaree for about midnight. That was a cruel thing to do to the newlyweds, but again a chivaree was one of those old traditions brought with the settlers. No wedding would seem complete without it. She suspected that both Mark and Deborah expected they would be receiving a visit from Mark's friends that night.

Laurel volunteered to help return the church to its usual form. The next day was Sunday, and church services would be held as always. She removed some ribbon and flowers from the pews but decided to leave the lovely vases of flowers that stood by the pulpit.

"You've been quiet today, Laurel Grace. Are you feeling all right?"

"Of course, Aunt Ellie. What a beautiful wedding Mark and Deborah had."

"Yes... Pretty as could be. What about yours? I don't remember hearing anything about it."

"It was nice in its way. A very quiet one compared to this one. My papa was so sick then. He did walk me to the minister, though. I wasn't the beautiful bride that Deborah is… But Mac put a beautiful ring on my hand. I don't know much else to say about it."

"Did the Methodist preacher marry y'all? Did you use the traditional service, too? Mark insisted they speak those vows as they are going to attend this church. He said it only made sense."

"No. We wrote our vows, but the ceremony was legal and sincere. We made our covenant to each other. Did you and Uncle Matthew have a beautiful wedding like this one?"

"Goodness, no. My papa said we were too young. Matthew was barely nineteen, and I was a month past sixteen. We eloped. I guess we didn't have the good sense our son has. We didn't have a thing to start out with…. We just loved each other so much, we didn't want to wait. I guess I missed all the pomp and ceremony, but I wouldn't change one minute of our years together. My life has been good."

"I can see that."

"You seem sad tonight. Can I help?"

"Not unless you can tell me that Mac is all right and coming back. I miss him and not hearing in all these weeks…well, I expected he would write, even if it were a short note to answer some of the questions I have been asking him."

"Don't fret, Laurel Grace. Mac is a man of his word. He will return as soon as he can."

Laurel knew her aunt spoke the truth. Mac was a man of his word. Laurel remembered the words… *I never intend to fall in love again.* She seemed to remember he spoke almost those exact words.

"I hope you are right, Aunt Ellie. Well, I need to get back to the widow's cabin. I still have some work to finish on the first Sunday school lesson for tomorrow."

"That is such a fine gift to our church family. We should've thought of it long ago."

Laurel hardly slept that night. The next day, she would take on a new challenge – teaching adults to read and write. She felt very confident in teaching those skills to children, but she never thought how it would be to conduct classes for grown people. One thing she did know…she would be very cautious so her adult students would never feel ignorant or embarrassed. None of the materials she used at school was suited to adults. The only thing she could do would be to make her own. The first step she would take would be to teach each person to write his own name and to learn the letters of the alphabet. Laurel knew all her adult students wanted to be able to read their Bibles, so she decided that would be a good place to start. Each week they would start memorizing words using Biblical characters and events. Homework between classes would be learning ten words a week.

At 1:30 on Sunday afternoon, Laurel began the first class of the Shiloh Sunday school. She faced seven adults and one teen aged girl who accompanied her mother and her grandmother. Shortly after she started with an introduction, Eleanor Dunn walked in followed by her grandson, Roy. "Mrs. Mac, do you think me and Roy can come to Sunday school?"

"Anyone who wants to be a part of the class is welcome, Mrs. Dunn. Hello, Roy, please take a seat. Thank you for making up the first Sunday school class at Shiloh. I'm very happy y'all came to strengthen your reading so you can read and study scripture better. The work will not be easy, but before Christmas you will all be reading some of the psalms and gospels stories for Brother Matthew on Sunday mornings. Let's get started."

All the older members of the class seemed eager to get started. They were surprised that Mrs. Mac thought they could learn so quickly.

"Let's begin by learning to write your names. Everyone here at Shiloh will be able to sign his signature at the voting polls, on your deeds, and other personal papers. We'll have no more X's here at Shiloh." Laurel passed out the slates she'd purchased in Greensboro so each student could have his own to take home at the end of the lesson. She wrote each name on the top of the slates and asked her learners to copy the letters several times. She walked about the room observing, correcting, and praising the progress. When she came to Roy Dunn, he'd written his name quite well and sat smiling.

"I'd could've done this a long time ago, Mrs. Mac, if I knew how easy it was."

"Nice job, Roy." His grandmother said with doubt in her voice. "Don't think I'll get mine so quick 'cause look how long my name is."

"You will, Mrs. Dunn." Laurel bent down to praise her work. "See, how nice your letters are shaped." The members of the class laughed at her frustration, and they all returned to their practicing until Laurel was sure each could write his name. "Now, let's learn the letters, both sounds and shapes. We will have a list each week for you to learn. At the start of each lesson, we will review before we learn new things that week. Copy these words from the board to your slates. Remember to carry your slates home carefully so you don't wipe away your new words." Laurel stopped and walked to the front of the church to write the alphabet and the words to study. "*A* sounds like its name, *A*, or like *AH* or short *A*, like in cat. Sometimes it will sound differently when there is more than one in a word. This word is ABRAHAM. The first *A* sounds like its name...*A*, but then the second *A* says *AH* and the last one is short, Ham. Repeat it with me." Laurel touched each *A* as she changed the sound for her students. "The two words we will learn for *A* are ABRAHAM and APPLE. You all remember Brother Matthew has told us about the father of the Israelites, Abraham and all of you know the story about the apple in the Garden of Eden."

The lesson progressed until they copied a list of ten words, two for each letter *A* to *E*. She had them repeat the words until the entire class could repeat them even when she pointed to them out of order. Laurel was pleased that her class worked so hard for their first lesson. She dismissed them promptly at 3:30, providing a good break before evening services began at 6:00.

Her uncle walked into the room as she was erasing the lesson from the board. "Well, teacher, how did it go? Are your grown-up students as bright at the little ones you brag on all the time?"

"We'll see. They did well…I think this is a way I can make a real contribution to this community. I hope they will come back."

"Laurel Grace, you have been making a difference since you came here. The school is better, our family is better, and Mac is so much better for having you here."

"I hope what you say is so."

They walked out toward the oak grove where the rest of her Campbell family was resting on quilts and sitting on the tailgate of a wagon. Mark and his new bride were there acting every bit the newlyweds they were. Her uncle sat next to his napping wife on a quilt. Susan and Randal were reading together while their children were playing nearby. John took a walk with the pretty daughter of Ransom Stephenson. Even in the midst of her family, Laurel felt alone. She felt her separation from Mac more than at any time since he'd gone more than seven weeks ago. She decided to take a walk. She didn't want to be a fifth wheel, which she realized would have been her life if she'd not married Mac and instead chosen to become the spinster boarding in her only uncle's home. She hated the feeling of being the extra one, a female without a partner who was an obligation to her family. She vowed she would never become that person, even if Mac never came back to Shiloh. She was not a fifth wheel, and with God's help, she could make a life on her own. Because of the strange mood she found herself in, she decided not to go back to the widow's cabin. She untied Sassy and trotted to the homestead instead.

Once there, Laurel walked through her garden and orchard. She noticed that much of her harvesting was done. Only mounds of potatoes still remained in the ground, nearly ready to dig up and store in the root cellar. She found several tomatoes still growing on the later plants. Beans, corn, and most squash plants already yielded huge amounts of food and were near the point where they would do the most good by being tilled into the soil to enrich the ground for the next growing season. Perhaps the weather would turn cooler in September so this chore would not be so burdensome. Perhaps tomorrow she could start the task that lay ahead of her. She could turn up the potatoes and decide which beans, squash, and other early summer crops were past bearing. She could plant some fall crops when the ground was cleared. Her mother always planted late turnips. She also knew some varieties of wheat did better in the cooler weather. She would have to find out which crops people along Crowley's Ridge grew in the early fall.

Laurel looked at her orchard, too. She knew the eleven apple saplings and three peach saplings put down strong roots and grew enough that summer to survive the upcoming winter unless the temperatures proved too brutal. She prayed that would not be the case, for those trees were so important to keeping her ties with her home in the western part of the state and with her family, now gone. Her grape vines were hearty and triple the size of the starter vines she'd brought across the state. God blessed the first year's work at the homestead. Yet with all the good she saw before her, she felt a heaviness she could not explain. She scolded herself for her lack of gratitude. She tried to rid her mind of the doubt and negative feelings. Today was such a good one, but she knew all of it meant nothing if Mac decided to remain with his family in Maryland.

Laurel sat on the strong fine porch Mac built, and she cried. She was convinced that the long weeks without any word could only mean that Mac couldn't live with her when he didn't share her feelings. She also knew that she pushed him away from her with the rash declaration of love she made on the morning he left. He kept his covenant with her. She was the person who stepped across the well-drawn line Mac set for their relationship. What a fool she had been! She wouldn't settle for enough. After some time, Laurel stood up and wiped her face. *Enough self-pity, Laurel Grace. Get up and take yourself back to the widow's.* Tomorrow would be a new day, and many tasks remained to be done.

Laurel used the next week to come to terms with the reality of her life without a husband. She napped often, walked around the small homestead she'd bought from the widow, and read long hours to pass the time. On Saturday, she returned to Mac's homestead to begin the task of turning under the garden. She spent most of the day digging up her potatoes. By early evening, she stopped. Fatigue was more than obvious, but Laurel enjoyed the hard work. Her mind was occupied, and she didn't think of Mac as much. She managed to get through church on Sunday, and even taught the second Sunday school class.

On Monday, Laurel returned to finish the task of harvesting the last of the potatoes. Like the other crops, she reaped a bumper harvest. About noon, her uncle Matthew rode up to her porch. He tied his horse and walked to find her in the garden. "We missed you at church last night. Were you afraid you'd sleep through my sermon?"

"I never sleep during your sermons. What was it that Eleanor Dunn told me about your preaching? Oh, I remember. She said that you were a mighty powerful preacher to be so young, but they'd hired you even if you didn't know a word to preach because you'd sing to them. She swore you were an angel singing praise to the Lord. Of course, when she said you were an angel, I was sure she'd confused you with someone else."

"Saucy girl. Why did you leave? I was hoping we could talk a bit about the Sunday school. Ellie was curious about it, too."

"When we walked back to the churchyard, everyone was gathered in families and in couples. Aunt Ellie was napping under the tree. I guess I was just feeling a bit envious. I was being silly. Sunday school went well again. I hope they keep coming back."

"Laurel Grace, you're worried about something more than Sunday school. I know you've been fretting about Mac and him not writing. Well, maybe this will help you stop your worrying."

Matthew held out a thin envelope addressed in Mac's strong, clear hand. He brought the letter from Greensboro. Laurel took the envelope and stared at it for a few seconds. She smiled as she recognized Mac's handwriting. "Thank you, Lord."

"Well..."

"I wonder why the letter is so brief. There can't be more than one sheet of paper here."

"Quit guessing and open it. Read what he has to say. I'm sure he is only telling you when he'll be home."

Laurel felt a strong sense of dread wash over her. She knew this message was not what she'd hoped for. "Uncle, this envelope does not hold good news. I am afraid to open it."

"Laurel Grace, you've waited for nearly two months for news. Now it's come. What's come over you?"

She looked again at the envelope. She shook off the dread and carefully ripped one end of the envelope and pulled out a single sheet, but it was not a letter but a broadside of the *Baltimore American and Commercial Advertiser,* dated August 12, 1857. Laurel unfolded the paper and at the top she found an article about the passing of Ann MacLayne, wife of the prominent land owner, Thomas MacLayne. Laurel turned the sheet over and at the bottom of the broadsheet she saw an article announcing the engagement and upcoming marriage of Mrs. Marsha Rawlins and Patrick Liam MacLayne. She stared at the names on the paper. For what seemed a lifetime, she couldn't breathe. The unfolded broadside fell from her hands.

Matthew bent to pick the paper up. As he did, Laurel returned to her work of turning up the last three hills of potatoes. "Laurel, what does it say? Is there a note from Mac?" She shook her head and dropped to her knees to pick up the newly dug potatoes and place them in the basket she'd brought to the garden earlier in the day. Matthew opened the paper and read the broadside. He saw the obituary for Mac's mother. "Laurel Grace, is this what has upset you so much? You knew Mac didn't expect his mother to recover. This happened back on the 6th of August. Her funeral was on the 8th of the month. Laurel Grace, that's been nearly three weeks. Mac will be home any day now."

Laurel said nothing and continued picking up the mature potatoes and wiping the dirt from them as she placed them in the basket. Matthew turned the paper over and saw the second headline. He could not believe the Mac he knew would have acted so heartlessly as to send this poison broadside to his wife. "Laurel, this can't be. Mac would never hurt anyone like this. Something is very wrong."

Laurel continued. She filled a second basket and carried it to the root cellar and returned with a third basket. "Laurel, stop that and come over here and talk to me."

"I've got to finish this task. I can't waste this excellent harvest of potatoes."

"Hang those potatoes. Did you read this article?"

"No need. I know what it says and why it happened."

Matthew sat on the end of the porch and began to read the article aloud.

Marsha Golden Rawlings/Patrick Liam MacLayne Betrothal Announced

"**Mrs. Marsha Rawlins is announcing with members of her family, Mr. and Mrs. Arnold Golden, her upcoming marriage to Mr. Patrick MacLayne of Ann Arundel**

County. The match is not unexpected as they have been friends since childhood. Mrs. Rawlins, the widow of the late Louis Rawlins, is planning a Christmas wedding. She explained the delay was necessary since Mr. MacLayne is now on a trip to Arkansas to complete the sale of his lands and to finalize some legal issues. The couple will reside at the MacLayne Estate where he will manage the property for his recently widowed father. Mr. MacLayne also plans to accept a post in the governor's office."

Even as he read the details in the broadside, Matthew Campbell could not believe the Mac he knew would ever purposely be so cruel and disloyal as to have sent the article to Laurel, even if he did intend to leave her to marry the woman from his past. "Laurel Grace, please come here and talk with me. None of this makes any sense."

Laurel placed the last potatoes in the third basket, picked it up and carried it to the root cellar to store with the others. "Now that's done." Laurel closed the sturdy door and put the bar through the lock braces.

"Where are you going now, Laurel Grace?"

"Back to the widow's cabin. I've got work to do."

"It'll wait until we can talk this out. This can't be true. Mac would not do this. Read the rest of this article and then tell me if you see these to be the actions of Patrick MacLayne."

"I can't read anymore, Uncle. I've known all these weeks that Mac wouldn't come back. It's my fault. I broke the covenant between us. Mac wanted a business relationship, a marriage of convenience. I was the one who stepped across the boundary. I fell in love with him, and I told him the morning he rode away toward Memphis. It's not his fault. He told me from the start he did not want to love me. He'd never let anyone into his heart again."

"Even more reason to doubt this article. Mac would never go back to a woman who betrayed him."

"You know, Uncle, it's a thin line between love and hate. I don't want to talk about this anymore. I've got things to do at the cabin."

"You can't just turn off how you feel. What are you going to do about this?"

Laurel looked up at her uncle. Silent tears ran down her face. She didn't make a sound, but pain was etched across her face.

"Nothing I can do. It's not Mac's fault. He has done a great deal for me in these past six months. The least I can do for him is to give him his freedom so he can go back to Maryland and start the family he has always wanted. I'll be leaving tomorrow if I can find a freighter going to Bolivar. From there, I'll get passage on a stage to Texas. I haven't seen my brother Daniel in several years. I know I can support myself teaching down there. He's told me in letters they need a teacher in their settlement."

"Laurel Grace, stay here and confront Mac. You deserve an explanation."

"I couldn't do that Uncle Matthew."

"Laurel Grace, how will you survive on your own?"

"Can't you see, Uncle? I'm a whole person. I am bright, worthy, and able. I'll make my own way. The Lord tells us about becoming a new creation in Him. Well, Mac and you and the good people of Shiloh have taught me that."

"I won't let you go, Laurel."

"I am an adult, Uncle Matthew. I don't need your permission, just your prayers. I'll come by your place tomorrow before I go to Greensboro." Laurel mounted Sassy Lady and galloped away back toward the widow's cabin. She needed to pack and finish writing out the lessons for the Sunday school class. She could not stay any longer in Shiloh. If she stayed even a couple of days, she would run the risk of seeing Mac again. Seeing him was one thing she couldn't bear.

The moment she stepped inside her sanctuary at the widow's cabin, the overbearing emotion broke through her reserved façade.

She poured out her grief in deep sobs that tore at her heart. She fell across the beautiful old four-poster and wept. After a while, she slept. When she awoke, the cabin was dark. The sun set, and there was no moon that night. When she was fully awake, she remembered the broadside and wept again. After midnight, Laurel pulled herself together and sternly scolded herself. She knew what she must do. She knelt by the wonderful bed and laid her agony at the foot of the cross. She tried to praise, thanking the Lord for the happy times she'd shared with Mac--brief as they were. She earnestly gave thanks for the strength and confidence she gained during this time. The Lord had made her a better, if not happier, person. When she arose, she wiped her face, lit two lamps, and set about packing, taking little, for she came with little. She took the remainder of her father's dowry to her, just over $200. She packed her own prayer book and her family's Bible, and the green ribbon sash from her wedding. She was ready to leave Shiloh.

The rest of the night she wrote out detailed plans for the Sunday school lessons. She did not fail to write in her promise to them that they would be able to read Scripture at church by New Years. She would make her Uncle Matthew promise to keep the Sunday school open as long as there was a need at Shiloh.

At daybreak, Laurel rose from the table in the little cabin. She climbed to the loft and dressed in her simplest clothes, a black skirt and white lawn blouse. Her eyes were red and swollen behind her oval spectacles. She braided her hair and pulled it into the coronet across the top of her head. Even with all her efforts to hide Laurel MacLayne, very little of the nature of the spinster of Hawthorn came through. Laurel stood tall and confident. She would not let the old nature reclaim her. She was a new creation. She would take what she learned into a new life for herself. She picked up her satchel, mounted Sassy Lady, and rode to her uncle's homestead.

"Laurel Grace, what can I say to change your mind?"

"Uncle Matthew. I am at peace. Mac can't help how he feels. He hurt me, but he didn't intend to do it. I've given it to God, and I'm going to be all right."

"What happened to that shy, backward girl who came to us in April?"

"She grew up is all. She saw the truth for once. Please promise me you and Aunt Ellie will keep the Sunday school opened. Our congregation needs to learn to read. Ann and Elizabeth both can teach. I've written out the lessons plans for you." She handed him several pieces of paper, pages of different colors and sizes. They appeared to be end sheets of books. "I couldn't find much paper, but I think you will see what I am doing."

"Laurel Grace, they need you."

"No, they just need a teacher. Both you and Aunt Ellie read.

"What do you want me to tell Mac when he gets back?"

"Nothing. He will be relieved not to have to deal with me face to face." Laurel turned and hugged her aunt. "I am glad for the chance to know you, Aunt Ellie." She turned and hugged her uncle and kissed his bearded cheek. "You've given me so much. I love you, Uncle Matthew. God bless you and your family and the work you are doing here at Shiloh."

"Laurel…" She stopped him short.

"I need you to see after the homestead until Mac gets back. Here is five dollars to pay John and Roy's pay. They will look after the animals and can start cutting the hay when it's time."

"We'll take care of things for you."

"I've finished all the things Mac wanted me to do. If he sells the homestead, please take all the food I've put in the larder and give it to anyone of our congregation who can use it. I've already bought a hog and paid to have it slaughtered. You can put that to good use among our needy, too. Uncle Matthew, Mac won't want my family things so please store them for me. Someday I'll find a way to get them."

"Laurel Grace, we don't want you leave us."

"His will – not mine." Laurel walked to the door. She remembered the wide gold band Mac placed on her finger in March. For the first time that day, tears fell again. "Uncle Matthew, please return this to Mac. It belonged to his mother. He'll want it back." Laurel handed her uncle the ring, wet with her tears. "But ask him…please…not to give it to her."

"If I can't convince you to stay, Laurel Grace, I'll ride with you to Greensboro."

"Thank you. I was wondering what I'd do with Sassy. She has always been a good horse."

Mid-afternoon, Laurel climbed to the wagon seat next to the local freighter. Her Uncle Matthew warned the freighter, whom he paid well, to look after his niece until she boarded the stage, wherever they were able to catch it. Matthew hugged Laurel one final time, and he too wept.

"Laurel Grace, I'm sorry for the part I played in all this. Please write to us soon as you get to Daniel's and let us know where you've settled in Texas. We love you. God keep you, niece." Laurel waved goodbye as she left Greensboro, thinking she'd never see Greene County again. She would build a new life. *I can do anything with God's help.*

CHAPTER FOURTEEN

*Cast not away therefore your confidence, which
hath great recompense of reward. For ye have
need of patience that, after ye have done the
will of God, ye might receive the promise.*

Hebrews 10:35-36. [KJV c1850.]

M idafternoon, the day after Laurel left Shiloh, Mac rode
into Greensboro. He pushed Midnight faster and farther
in the past two and a half days than he'd ever ridden any horse. He
patted the mane of his reliable mount and whispered an earnest
prayer of thanksgiving that the animal served him well and was
not hurt. Mac tied Midnight on the shady side of the street and
rushed to see Al Stuart. He had failed to take care of too many
things before he left, and he didn't want to face Laurel with news
of a lien on his land for failing to pay the taxes.

"Well, MacLayne. It's good to see you're still alive. We'd about decided the bottoms swallowed you, horse and all."

"Didn't you get my letters? I sent you two, at least."

"Well, I thought I'd get at least one. We get our mail pretty regular here in town. You never been one to let your taxes go unpaid."

"Oh, never mind that now. Did Laurel come and get money to keep the homestead going while I was gone?"

"She never came to me for money. I'd been happy to see her through if I knew she needed any. I just figured you'd given her all she needed."

"You'd a thought I'd be smart enough to do that. Well, let me pay the taxes. I know I always get that done by the end of July."

"No tax due right now. Mrs. MacLayne paid them all on the Saturday after school was out. Paid yours and five years back taxes on Widow Parker's homestead when she recorded the deed."

"Recorded the deed?"

"Yes, she bought that thirty acres when the widow went west with her daughter."

"Where did she get that much... Oh my dear Lord! She used her dowry money. Thanks, Al. I'll be in to talk over all this land business soon. Right now, I must get home, hopefully long before dark." Mac took Midnight to the local livery to board and rented another horse to finish the ride to Shiloh.

The four miles back to his homestead took forever. Mac wanted to see Laurel, to pull her into his arms, to kiss her warm mouth, and to say the words he should have spoken to her in early July. He wanted Laurel to know that he loved her and that he had loved her since that first day they'd walked in the apple orchard in Washington County. The minute she 'told him off,' he lost his heart, but his male pride and stupidity blinded him to the fact until a confrontation in a Maryland stable.

As he rode into the homestead, he was pleased to see the changes that took place in the two months he was gone. He saw the windows reflecting the late afternoon sun, flower beds laid out in front of the porch and lined with natural stone so abundant along the ridge. He also saw late summer flowers blooming. He jumped from the rented horse before it came to a complete stop and ran up the porch stairs calling out, "Laurel, are you here? Laurel, where are you?"

Of course, there was no response. Mac realized that Laurel wouldn't have moved from the widow's until he got back. He'd told her that he would carry her across the threshold of their home. He walked through the nearly furnished cabin. He smiled when he saw Laurel's things had come from Powhatan, and she'd already placed pieces in the rooms where she wanted them. He ran his finger along the lace-edged curtains Laurel hung at the windows in the front room. He went into the bedroom in the second pen. He saw the bureau her father carved long ago and the rocking chair that belonged to her grandmother. Both pieces survived the trip from Washington County no worse for wear. He saw the pretty blue curtains hung at the two windows in the second room. He admired the beautiful walnut plank floors and the polished wax finish that covered the floors throughout the cabin.

As impressed as he was, Mac was most awed by the filled larder in the kitchen. He could hardly believe how much food was preserved and laid aside for the coming winter. Mac was humbled by the tremendous level of commitment that had led to this perfectly complete homestead he came home to. "Lord, thank you. Your plan for me is so much better than anything I ever dreamed. I never deserved such a helpmate. She has my heart, and I am blessed. "

Mac went out to retrieve the horse and ride to Matthew's home. Perhaps he would find Laurel there, but if not, the trip on to the widow's cabin was not much further. As he rode by the barn and garden, he saw cords of wood stacked under the lean-to and a garden plot nearly harvested. He wondered how Laurel accomplished so much, and then he realized she must have kept his helpers working all summer. She must have spent her own money to pay the help. In his mind Mac calculated the expense and realized Laurel spent most of her dowry money to pay for so much. Not only did she pay the hire of the two boys, but she'd paid freight costs for the windows and the cost to deliver her family heirlooms, the cost of the thirty acres and taxes, and all the daily expenses for the two months he was gone. His wife cared about his dream and made a tremendous sacrifice for him. The realization only added to the guilt he felt because he forgot to take the steps to assure her needs would be met while he was away. Another thought dawned on him…perhaps the spinster of Hawthorn didn't need him to take care of her. She seemed quite able to fend for herself. He would beg her forgiveness for the ridiculous oversight and restore her dowry to her as soon as he could.

As Mac rode into the churchyard of Shiloh Church, he saw Matthew's horse tied at the porch rail. He walked into the log sanctuary and saw his friend, kneeling at the altar, earnestly praying. As he approached, Matthew rose and walked toward him.

"Matthew, you are a blessed sight. I am happy to see you and so glad to be back."

"Are you staying long?" Wide eyed and with a dropped jaw, Mac looked at Matthew.

"What do you mean? I'm home. Where is Laurel? Is she staying with you?"

"I'm not a violent man, but I feel like taking you behind the church and beating some sense and compassion into you. Lord help me, I know that is not the way the Lord would handle this."

"Matthew, what's happened? Why didn't y'all answer my letters?"

"You've got a lot to explain. You'd better come home with me."

"I'm riding to the widow's. I can't wait to see Laurel."

"You won't find her there."

"Well, she is not at the homestead. Where is she?"

"Gone."

"Gone? Where has she gone? Why?"

"Come to the cabin with me and explain a few things. If I am satisfied, I'll tell you what I know." The two men rode the final mile to the Campbell homestead in a tense silence. When they arrived, Matthew took both horses and locked them in the corral, without taking a minute to unsaddle them.

Ellie came out on to the porch with a lamp. "You ain't welcome here, Mr. MacLayne. Matthew, how could you bring him home?"

"Mr. MacLayne? Ellie, I've never heard you speak a harsh word as long as I have known you."

"After the cruel way you treated Laurel Grace! I don't want you to come here again."

Matthew approached his wife. "Ellie, go bring me those papers off the table. Get all of them, please. I'll talk out here. Mac has a right to tell me his side of this sad story." Matthew motioned for Mac to sit on the porch in one of the rocking chairs. He paced back and forth across the length of the porch. He spoke a silent prayer. In a short time, Ellie returned with the papers Matthew asked her for. "Thank you, sweetheart. Please leave the lamp and go tend to the kids." Matthew hugged her briefly and gave her a peck on the cheek. "I'll be in soon."

When they were alone, Matthew sat nearby and looked Mac squarely in the face. He didn't speak for a while. One moment he appeared to be praying and another a tear would come to his eye. Matthew Campbell continued to look at the drawn face of his friend.

"Matthew, if you don't tell me where Laurel is, I may lose my mind. I've spent the last six and a half days pushing forward every minute to get back to her."

"Mac, why didn't you write to her? I understand you may have been busy with your mother. But, Laurel must have written you a dozen letters, and she never got any after the one you posted in Memphis."

"Oh, my dear Lord! I was afraid of that. What she must think. I promised to write often – and I did, Matthew. I did. Please believe me, I did write to her and to you and to Al Stuart. I wondered why I never got one letter from anyone here at Shiloh. Not until the week after my mother died. I got that brief note from you asking me to write to Laurel."

"Laurel Grace made lots of excuses for your silence--bad mail routes, your ma's illness, and difficult travel conditions. The last reason she gave me was the hardest to hear. She told me she was to blame that you didn't want to come back. She told me she overstepped the bounds of your marriage commitment when she told you that she loved you. Did she tell you she loved you?"

Mac dropped his head into his hands. All the way back to Arkansas, he'd pictured a happy reunion with Laurel. He'd pictured the life they would share in their home. He'd seen the smile on Laurel's face when he admitted to her that he loved her.

"She did tell me of her feelings that morning, just as I was leaving for Maryland. I have no excuse. I was dumbstruck by what she said. That was the first time she'd ever said anything to make me think...I just couldn't think of a reply. I hugged her a minute and rode toward Greensboro."

"Lord help you for the fool you are. How hard is it to say three words? You could've said...Well, it's not my place to judge."

"Matthew, I never wanted to hurt her. I know I must have."

"That is to say the least. If you wrote all those letters, why didn't none get delivered except the one we got on Monday? That was a cold heartless thing to send."

"What letter? The last one I sent said I'd start home by the 29th at the latest. I actually got to start home on the 24th."

"We didn't get any notice of you heading home."

"I depended on the Goldens to post my letters. That was my fault. They didn't mail any of them, and they kept the letters y'all sent when they picked up our mail at the Baltimore post office.

Marsha was angry with me, but I didn't know she'd keep the mail from me."

"Mac, that poison broadside came in an envelope **you** addressed. When Laurel saw your script, she was so happy for about two minutes. Then she tore the envelope open and found the single sheet newspaper. It was like a knife in her heart."

"Matthew, you know I'd never send anything to hurt Laurel. You know me better than that."

"I didn't think you were capable of such cruelty, but I recognized your hand writing too."

"I never sent any newspaper."

"Can you explain this?" Matthew handed Mac the broadside, and the envelope which was addressed to Laurel in his own handwriting.

"This is my mother's obituary from the Baltimore paper, but I don't know how it got in this broadside. The local paper in Baltimore has four pages of print. It's the major advertiser in the whole area, even the capital."

"That is not the article that Laurel couldn't deal with. Turn the paper over and read the one at the bottom of the page."

Mac read every vile lie that Marsha wrote. "I can't believe this, Matthew...How vicious can she be? Laurel must hate me! Where is she, Matthew?"

"She is not in Shiloh anymore, Mac. She asked me to return this to you." Matthew reached into his pocket and pulled out the wide gold wedding band that Mac placed on Laurel's finger. "Her only request was that you not give it to your new wife. She loves you enough that she wants you to have your freedom to marry the woman you love."

"I am married to the woman I love. I've loved her from the first day I met her. I just wouldn't let myself accept it. Matthew, please tell me where she's gone. I don't want a life without her."

"All she told me is that she is going to Bolivar and find out how to make a connection to the stage line that runs to Little Rock.

From there she plans to book passage to Texas to see her brother Daniel. I don't know where in Texas he settled."

"How long has she been gone?"

"She left Greensboro yesterday about noon."

Mac slammed his fist against the porch rail. He cried out. "Lord, why?" He paced like a caged animal and continued to cry out in his pain. Matthew sat and waited for Mac to control his temper, and he offered a silent prayer for his friend and his niece.

The trip to Bolivar was a long one, not that it was many miles away, but because Laurel's mood was low. Her companion, the freighter Hank Brewer, kept up a continuous conversation, but Laurel heard only noise and made no sense of any of his stories. Her mind was with her heart, and she didn't know where Mac was. Her own musings were frequently distracted with memories of her recent past. After about an hour of sitting on the hard wagon seat, she recalled the long hours she'd spent riding beside Mac on their trip across the state. Her little wagon that brought them and her belongings to the homestead at long last now sat in the new barn at Mac's home. She shook the sad thought away. On the outskirts of the Jonesboro settlement, she saw a tiny cabin that reminded her of the widow's cabin where she spent several happy days with Mac. Behind the cabin, she saw a sun browned woman tending a garden at the height of harvest. She thought of the bountiful garden she just harvested in Greene County. Near Greenfield, another new community, she saw a small clapboard church with a cross attached to the top most part of the porch eaves. She thought how much more beautiful was their log church at Shiloh, and how much bigger. Later in the afternoon, they passed a young couple standing in a small grove of hickory and oak trees. Laurel saw him pick up her hand and bring it to his lips. She looked at her now bare hand and remembered the kiss Mac placed on her hand the day they wed. Just as they stopped at a small homestead where they would board for the night, Laurel smelled the delicious aroma of apples and cinnamon cooking in the kitchen. Too many incidents from her past were brought to her awareness during the day. How could it be a coincidence?

Before Laurel even reached Bolivar, she realized she'd made a bad decision. She acted hastily in her hurt and unhappiness. She didn't take the necessary time to pray or even logically think out what she should do. Why should she give up her home? Mac would leave it all behind anyway when he returned to his father's estate and his new job with the governor of Maryland. He'd always wanted to be involved in politics. He wouldn't bring the woman from his past to live in the Arkansas frontier. In Shiloh, she owned a cabin and barn with thirty acres. She loved her teaching job and her Campbell family. God would provide for her there at Shiloh.

Of course, people would talk about her being deserted and pity her for the poor treatment she'd received. She hated the thought of being the subject of gossip, but she also knew it wasn't her shame. She kept her vows. No! She would not break the vows she'd made. If Mac wanted his freedom, he would also take the responsibility. She would go back home...back to Shiloh.

"Mr. Brewster, is there a boarding house in Bolivar where I can stay until I can manage to find a way back to Greensboro?"

"Why, Missy, we'll be in Francisville by noon tomorrow, right in time to catch the stage to Little Rock. We won't need to stay in Bolivar. Mrs. Granger, here, sets a fine table and although sleeping in the barn ain't as nice as a hotel room, it's warm enough for tonight."

"Mr. Brewer, can I find a place to stay in Bolivar?"

"Yeah, but there ain't no need. That Little Rock stage is due and only runs one time a week. Don't you want to catch the stage?"

"No. Mr. Brewer, I want to buy a horse and return to Shiloh."

"I can't let you go back alone. Brother Campbell will have my hide if anything happens to you."

"I'm a grown woman, Mr. Brewer. I can ride thirty-five miles alone on a good road."

"Ain't the road I'm fretting about. A lone woman just don't travel these parts by herself. If you're so all-fired set on starting back, I'll try to find a reliable person to see you back. Can't say I like it much."

"I will be fine." The next morning, Hank and Laurel completed the trip to Bolivar around noon. Hank took Laurel to the boarding house in the supply hub town. He helped her down from the wagon seat.

"I'll deliver my haul to the mercantile store. When I'm done, I'll go to the livery and see if I can find any trustworthy freighter headed north. I'll come back with news one way or the other."

"I'll be pleased to head home as soon as possible. I'll buy a horse if I must." Laurel went in and paid the landlady one dollar for room and board for the night.

"Well, little lady, who are you?" The sound came from the tiny, wrinkled old woman who did not seem large enough to contain the strong, deep voice.

"My name is…" Laurel hesitated. Today marked a fresh start. Laurel MacLayne was a dream gone. She would not carry the name of a man who replaced her with another. Laurel intended to be independent and self-sufficient, more than able to create a new life, using her own wit, education and faith. She would be her own woman. "I'm Grace Campbell. I need a place to stay tonight before I return to my home."

"I got a nice corner room at the top of the stairs, end of the hall. Supper will be at 6:00. Tonight is ham and beans with cornbread. Got some nice fresh milk, too."

"Sounds very filling. I'd like to clean up and rest a while, Mrs…"

"Everyone here 'bouts calls me Lizzy. Me and Mr. Lee, my husband, run this here boarding house and the general store down the street. Welcome to Bolivar, Grace. Let me take you up. Get you settled for the night."

Laurel bathed as best she could with the water in the wash bowl. She pulled down the shade at the window, and then lay down on the brass bed for a short nap, for she slept little the previous night. She felt more tired than she'd ever felt in her life. Perhaps some sleep would give her energy enough to get through the rest of the day. After a few minutes, she fell asleep, but the sleep was not peaceful or restful. Laurel tossed and turned, the old fears returning. The old nightmares had returned since Mac left for Maryland. There was no one to share them with so they haunted her rest many nights. Just as she saw a vague form reach out to cut her hair, she awoke and bolted from the pillow on her bed. She was trembling, drenched in perspiration.

Laurel took some time to push the dreadful memories away. She wanted to be safe again, but there was no one here to offer her the security she'd known at Shiloh. She arose from the bed, washed away the clammy feeling from her skin and repaired the damage to her braids. She dressed in her gray Sunday dress and then put her glasses on.

Shortly she was seated at the Lee's dinner table with four other boarders. A few minutes into the meal, Hank Brewer came to the table to join them.

"Looks like a fine supper Lizzie. Got a spare room for me to-night and tomorrow?"

"You know I do for you, Hank. I thought you're headed on to Francisville after lunch."

"Change of plans. Can I have a cup of your coffee, please?"

Hank turned to Laurel. "Missy, I worked out a way to get you home, if you still want to go."

"I do, as soon as I can leave."

"I swapped a load with another freighter who was heading north. He wanted to get back to Helena. His wife is due any day.

I'd like to get back with my family at Davidsonville for a couple of days, so we swapped hauls. He already left about 4:30, but my load won't be ready 'til day after tomorrow so if you'll just wait, I know you'll have a safe trip home."

"I don't guess one day more will make any difference to me. Thanks for going to the trouble."

"Was good for me too and Lee Willis. Good things worked out for all of us. The Lord must have His hand in our plans."

"I've found that He has a way of working out His will, whether or not we realize it."

After supper, Laurel took a short walk around the little town of Bolivar. This town was in Poinsett County, just south of Greene. The town was home to a fair-sized population and several buildings lined its streets, although a few were empty. Even in the evening there was activity around the center of the town, as freighters packed loads for an early start or tended their mules, getting them bedded down for the night. The livery stable was the busiest site in town which served as a pick-up point for several freight companies based in St. Louis, Memphis, and Little Rock. These companies shipped large hauls to the hub town where local freighters, like Hank Brewer, would hire on to deliver the goods to dozens of smaller communities all over eastern Arkansas. Nearly all the other businesses already locked their doors, and only a sole clapboard saloon at two intersecting roads seemed as if it were about to come alive with its nightly business.

Laurel sensed an eerie difference here in Bolivar. During her walk, the reason became clear. Although this town was about the same size as Greensboro and less than forty miles from Shiloh, this area was flat, with large expanses of fields being worked by slave labor. As the sun was dipping below the horizon, many of the slaves were leaving the cotton fields carrying their cotton sacks across their shoulders as they made their way back to their quarters. Bolivar was very much a part of the delta. Laurel was glad that Shiloh was on the side of the ridge where hills and valleys made up the landscape. For the most part, the farms were small acreage and worked by their owners. If Shiloh were in the delta, Laurel knew she'd never have felt at home. When the full moon sank below the horizon beyond a large cotton field, she knew it was time to return to the boarding house. The warm September breeze brushed the back of her neck. Laurel reached back to feel her hair, having forgotten her braids did not provide the cover for her back and shoulders that her loose curls did. Strangely, in the short time she'd worn her hair down she became most accustomed to it and for a brief moment she felt strange...not quite herself. She brushed the feeling away. Her mask was back in place to protect her again. Soon, the braided coronet would feel normal again. She knew the role of spinster so well. Perhaps now she would become the Spinster of Shiloh.

CHAPTER FIFTEEN

And this is the confidence that we have in Him, that if
we ask anything according to His will, He heareth us.

1 John 5:14 [KJV c1850].

"Matthew, I'm headed to Bolivar tomorrow. If I ride hard and fast, I can catch Laurel before she reaches the stage to Little Rock.

Matthew clutched Mac's shoulder and turned him around so he could look him squarely in the eye. "Mac, don't go after her unless you plan to make her your true wife. I won't have her hurt again, do you hear me?"

"I thought you understood. The engagement announcement is a fraud. I never spoke to Marsha about anything except Louis's death. She told me what caused my best friend to challenge me in that stupid duel."

"What happened between you and that vicious woman is not my business, but Laurel is family. I need to know that my niece has a chance to be happy and to have a real home. She deserves nothing less."

"Matthew, I promise you that I will do all in my power to make her happy. I am surer than ever, God intended us to build a life together. I love her. I didn't know it was possible."

"Well, God's speed then. Stay with us tonight. You can get a fresh start in the morning, although that horse sure looks tuckered out. Where is Midnight?"

"I left him in Greensboro this afternoon. He earned a rest, after crossing the St. Francis bottom land. I'll get him when I go through Greensboro. I can make much better time with him."

"Well, come on in here and have some supper. You must be hungry after travelling all day."

"No, thanks, Matthew. I can't deal with any more explaining. You can tell Ellie whatever you think is best. I'm going to the widow's cabin to sleep tonight. Maybe I can find some clean clothes, too."

"Mac, don't be upset with Ellie. She was just so heartbroken when Laurel left. She'll be fine when I explain to her what happened to you both. She never denied a hungry traveler his keep."

"Thanks for asking, but I'm not in a civil mood tonight. Pray for me to find her. I'll see you when I get back." Mac walked to the stock pen behind the barn to get his horse, and as he rode past the porch, he stopped to speak with Matthew, "And Matthew, please have John and Roy move everything from the widow's cabin to our new homestead. Maybe some of the women will help put things away. I want to bring my wife to our home. We have kept our lives on hold too long already."

Mac rode to the widow's at a very slow pace. He was in no hurry to get there. Nothing awaited him but an empty cabin. Mac hated to return to the place where he's shared good times with Laurel.

He spent a restless night, and shortly after sun up the following morning, he was at the livery where he left Midnight to rest for the night. He hoped his good mount would travel fast and far enough to get him to the stage stop before Laurel left for Little Rock. He would travel day and night to find her before she was lost to him forever. Daniel Campbell lived in Texas, and Texas was a huge track of land to search. Mac's constant prayer was a simple one... "Lord, let me find her. Let me find her.... Please, Lord, let me find her."

Before noon a heavy rain covered nearly all eastern Arkansas, but Mac did not stop for shelter. The military road between Greensboro and Bolivar was in good condition, having been well traveled by freighters and homesteaders moving west. The longer he rode, the more miserable he felt. Progress slowed considerably as the rain continued. The muddier the road became the slower Midnight could cover the distance. Even in his anxiety, he knew he could not continue at the pace without letting his horse rest frequently. He decided he would rest ten minutes in each hour he was able to ride. He couldn't guess how far he rode, but by the time the sun sank below the horizon, the pragmatic side of Mac's nature forced him to stop for the night. Midnight's pace slowed considerably. He didn't want to maim his animal.

Still, his greater fear was he didn't know the freighter's schedule or when he would arrive at the stage stop in Francisville. The night would be a miserable one, as he found little in the way of shelter. Even a tight grove of trees or an abandoned barn would have been a blessed sight that wet evening. Mac pushed on a bit further, and shortly he made out the shape of a small log building down the road. He identified the structure because it bore a white painted cross on its porch. To the side of the building was a covered area where the congregation held their dinners on the ground and other outside celebrations. Mac assumed the area at some time in the past served as a camp meeting grounds, but tonight it would serve as shelter for himself and Midnight. At least for a few hours, he could get out of the rain and allow his fine horse to rest before they completed the ride into Bolivar.

Prospects for a restful night were nil. Mac was dry under the camp meeting grounds roof, but he brought little to eat and one bedroll blanket to use for a bed. He tied Midnight to one of the posts holding up the roof. He fed the animal a few handfuls of oats he packed and made sure the lead was long enough for the horse to get to grass if he decided to eat. Water was certainly no problem. The steady rainfall of the day filled many low places in the open ground. Midnight would be well supplied with water. Taking his saddle and the horse blanket, Mac made himself a place to sleep in the middle of the roofed structure, hoping to keep most of the rain off. He pulled his blanket over his shoulder and promptly fell asleep.

The next morning, Mac was awakened by Midnight's neighing. He sat up, very stiff and sore from his hard bed, and looked up to see a man standing over him. "Morning, stranger. I see you found some shelter here under our roof. You'd have been a sight more comfortable inside the church there. You'd have been welcomed to use it."

"Morning. I didn't mean to sleep so late. I am on my way to Bolivar. My name's MacLayne."

"I'm Barton Masters. I'm the circuit rider who serves this congregation on the first Sunday of the month. We'd be mighty pleased to have you join us for worship this fine sunny morning."

"Is today Sunday?   I've been traveling for so long, I have lost track of my days. I need to reach Bolivar before..."

"The Lord will bless you, if you give Him his due. "

Mac knew the preacher was right. He'd not been to church since he went to Baltimore to see his mother. As a matter of fact, he had spent too little time in worship since he travelled to Ann Arundel County. All of his prayer time was spent in asking, not praising. "I'll try to clean myself up a bit, and I'll be glad to join your service. Thank you for asking me."

By 8:00, the tiny churchyard was filled with several wagons, horses, and one covered buggy. Mac was glad he stayed, knowing there was no better way to spend the morning than with people who were worshipping and singing praise. Midnight was comfortable near the camp ground shelter, and he had been fed already, so Mac turned his mind to Sunday's purpose. The first hymn they sang was one of his favorites, "When morning gilds the skies, my heart awaking cries, may Jesus Christ be praised…" By the close of the last verse, Mac felt his spirit began to rise. He realized that he'd removed himself from his source of strength by his long absence from worship. He knew joy and endurance came from worship, and he was woefully lacking in those qualities at that moment. After a couple of more songs, the circuit rider rose to the pulpit before the twenty-five or so people who gathered that Sunday morning. He read from the book of 1st Corinthians, chapter thirteen. The familiar words of Paul's statement on love spoke to his heart. He mouthed the words to the last verse as Brother Masters read from the pulpit.

"And now abideth faith, hope and charity, these three; but the greatest of these is charity."

The preacher spoke a powerful message on the importance of human relationship through his explanation of the term charity… the word so misunderstood. Charity means love, opening the heart to a relationship with God and with other people. Toward the end of the sermon, he made a statement that Mac knew came to him as a message from above. Brother Masters said, "When we close the door to any love that has been offered to us, be it our brother, our child, our friend, or our spouse, it's as if we say… 'No thanks, Lord, but I am above that gift.' Pride and fear are powerful demons that kill the very thing we seek. Let yourself have charity…Let yourself love. It's the best way to let God use us for his work. It's the only path to happiness."

Mac felt convicted of his ridiculous pledge to never love again. He spent all those wasted years being both proud and fearful, and those two things nearly cost him a dream of home and a good life at Shiloh. Once again, he silently prayed, "Let me find her, Lord. Let me find her." At the close of the service, Mac stopped the minister to thank him for the message he'd needed to hear. He offered the circuit rider a gold piece to help with his work.

"Thank you, Mr... Sorry, I don't remember what you told me."

"Name is MacLayne. Just Mac to those who know me."

"Are you a believer, son?"

"Thank the Lord, I am. I am a member of the Shiloh congregation over in Greene County."

"You're a long way from home."

"Yes. Do you know how much further the trip to Bolivar is?"

"Near fifteen miles, I'd say. You can get there near dark if you keep a fair pace."

"Well, I need to get on the road then. Do you know if there is a place to stay in that town?"

"The Lee's run a clean, safe boarding house. Right on the main road. You won't miss it."

"Again, thanks for the sermon." Mac went to saddle Midnight and within a very few minutes, he was once again headed south, and as he rode from the camp meeting grounds, the sun shone for the first time since he left Greensboro.

By dark, Mac arrived on the main street of Bolivar, and he stopped in front of the boarding house. In the quiet town, he saw few people out and about, but it was Sunday evening. He entered the boarding house and almost immediately met Mr. Lee, the owner.

"Howdy, stranger. You looking for board tonight?"

"Yes, a room, a bath, and a good hot meal would be a God-send right now, but before I decide to stay the night, I need to find out if my wife is still in town. Have you got a lady here named Laurel MacLayne?"

"Let me see…my wife keeps track of our boarders usually. Let me look at my log here. No, we got no lady here named MacLayne."

"Is there another boarding house, hotel or inn nearby?"

"Nary a one." Mac felt deflated with that news. Laurel must have gone on south already.

"Have you seen a comely woman, long tawny curls near her waist and slim of stature? She was riding with Hank Brewer, a freighter."

"No, but then my wife would know more about goings on here. She'll be back in about an hour. I can serve you up a hot meal. We ate Sunday supper here early, but plenty of vittles are left."

"Yes, I'd like that." Mac slumped in a chair near the window. Shortly Mr. Lee returned with a heaping plate of food. The meal was good, but Mac wouldn't have cared if it were sawdust. He was hungry. The biscuits, gravy, fried potatoes, and ham began to sate his ravenous hunger. He ate slowly and then asked for a second cup of fresh coffee. Mrs. Lee's fine coffee was the first Mac tasted since he left Matthew's house.

"Got some nice apple pie, if you're still hungry."

"Yes, that would go fine with that second cup of coffee." The very first bite of the pie brought back more memories of Laurel. The first meal she put in front of him ended with an apple dessert. Dozens of jars of canned apples sat in the larder of their nearly complete cabin. The first time she told him off was in an apple orchard. When she awoke after the fever brought on by the snake-bite, she'd asked about her orchard cuttings, and he recalled the image of the Spinster of Hawthorn speaking her wedding vows to him holding the tiny bouquet of four apple blossoms tied with a green ribbon. A huge wave of regret and sadness washed over Mac as he sat in the dining room of the Bolivar boarding house. He felt little hope now of finding Laurel. The distance between him and the capital was too far to be covered before Laurel would take the stage to Texas. He may have been able to manage another night of travel, but Midnight couldn't stand up to such a demand. Mac decided to take a room and sleep through the night. He would decide later if he would make the trip south or north.

Mac asked Mr. Lee where he could board his horse for the night. He was relieved that the livery was only about two blocks down the street. Because this livery served as a freighter's hub, the blacksmith was always on site. Mac put Midnight in a stall, brushed him down for a few minutes, and gave him a generous helping of oats and hay. He'd earned the rest. As he walked slowly back to the boarding house, the fatigue took its toll. Not only was he so physically tired he could barely put one foot in front of the other, he felt defeated. He would probably return to Shiloh the next morning.

When Mac entered the boarding house, he paid Mr. Lee for the meal he'd eaten and for a room's rent. "You look like you got the weight of the world on your shoulders, young man."

"I'm tired. It's been a long ride." He carried a burden he could not bear. Why would God not answer his prayers? Was he being punished for the pain he'd caused Laurel? He shook those thoughts away. He knew that was not the nature of his God. He went back into the sitting room and sat by an open window. A small woman came in to pick up a few things left by her boarders, tidying the room.

"Mr. MacLayne, this is my wife, Lizzie. She may be able to answers to your questions."

"Lizzie, this here is Mr. MacLayne. He's boarding with us tonight."

"Welcome. Can I help you?"

"I'm looking for my wife, Laurel."

"We got no one by that name here. We don't get many lone women travelers through here."

"Have you seen a pretty lady with long, curly hair, quite a bit taller than you?" She came through here with a freighter named Hank Brewer."

"Well, we sure know Hank. He's a regular with us. He got here on Friday night, but he brought an unmarried lady with him. Hank usually goes on from here to meet the stage in Francisville or river-boat in Napoleon. He didn't do that this time. He's leaving tomorrow with a haul to Old Davidsonville. He got held up because his haul ain't ready."

"Is Mr. Brewer here?"

"Haven't seen him since supper, but he'll be at breakfast in the morning."

"Mrs. Lee, that woman with Mr. Brewer, did she look at all like the lady I described to you?"

"Goodness, no. Sweet as she is, she's far from pretty. Couldn't tell you much about her hair. She wears it braided tight on her head. Wears glasses...you know those school teacher glasses. Her name's Miss Campbell."

Mac knees buckled. For a brief time, he stood breathless. God heard his plea. "Where is she? Please, Mrs. Lee. I have to talk to her."

"Well, I don't know... She seems shy and nervous like and stays by herself mostly."

"Please tell me, Mrs. Lee. I promise not to frighten her. I have to see her."

"You seem decent enough." Lizzie Lee looked Mac over. She glanced toward her husband. "Seems okay. Should we tell him? Lee nodded. "When I left her, she's at the church, just north of here."

"God bless you, Ma'am. Thank you, Lord!" Mac ran out the door toward the church he passed on the way into town. Within a few minutes, Mac stood on the porch of the white clapboard Lutheran church. He put his hand on the door handle and hesitated to open the door. His heart was racing and perspiration lined his forehead. Again, he prayed for the right words.

When Mac opened the door, he saw little as the small sanctuary was lit by a sole lantern on a shelf mounted on the back wall. He walked a step or two inside, and his eyes adjusted to the dim light. Then he saw her kneeling at the far end of the altar. The words of her prayer were barely audible. Mac, not wanting to intrude, sat on a split log bench at the back of the room, watching. The sight of the Spinster of Hawthorn kneeling, making her plea to God, filled his heart as much as Mrs. Lee's dinner fed his body. He couldn't take his eyes from her. Mac didn't care that Laurel's hair was in braids, she'd gone back to her old clothes, and she'd hidden behind her German silver glasses again. He saw nothing, but the woman he loved kneeling before their Lord.

After several minutes, Laurel rose and turned toward the door. She was startled to see the shadow of a man in the back of the church. Neither spoke for what seemed to be an eternity. Finally, Mac gathered his wits and nerve enough to speak.

"Laurel Grace, will you let me speak with you?"

Only a few syllables passed before Laurel recognized Mac's voice. Her strength left her, and the tiny church spun around her. Her biggest hope and her greatest dread stood in shadow at the back of the tiny Lutheran church. She moved to the front pew and sat down, her composure gone. She needed to remain calm if she were to respond with any degree of dignity.

"Good evening, Mac." For a few seconds, Laurel could think of nothing else to say. She decided to answer the question Mac posed. Laurel was determined no harsh words would pass between them.

She remembered the lesson the Lord taught her when Mac was called to Maryland. She didn't have to be loved to love. "Yes, Mac. I will listen to what you want to say."

An audible sigh of relief came from him. Laurel thought that Mac must have been holding his breath as he waited for her to reply. She heard him whisper, "Thank you, Lord." He rose from the bench and walked toward her. "Laurel, will you let me come sit near you?"

"If that is what you want."

"I have so many things to tell you. I don't quite know where to begin."

"I am sorry for your loss. I know how much you loved your mother."

"She's no longer in pain. We laid her to rest in the family cemetery next to my sister and the memorial to my brother, Sean." Mac approached as he spoke and sat on the same plank bench where Laurel sat. He didn't sit too close to her, nor did he attempt to touch her. Laurel didn't say anything. She could listen to Mac, but she could find no words to speak.

"You did a fine job with the homestead while I was gone. You must have spent hours every day to preserve so much food, to stockpile all those cords of wood, and to have the construction of the cabin completed."

"I tried to do what you wanted done."

"You did more than take care of the homestead. I am very grateful to you."

"You're welcome."

"First, I have to ask your forgiveness…for so many things. I am more than ashamed I went off without leaving money for you to live on. That was thoughtless of me. I didn't remember until I stopped at the Hopefield ferry and found the money pouch I meant to give you. We never really got around to talking about money so I just didn't think about it. Laurel, I promise I will return all your dowry money to you, every cent."

"I'm not concerned about it."

"Actually, that is not the whole truth. I planned to leave you money, but I was at a loss when you told me you loved me. Every word I planned in my farewell to you vanished from my thoughts."

"All is fine. Papa gave me the money to help build a good house. There was plenty to take care of the expenses for those two months. I never felt it was a matter to forgive. You were preoccupied with getting home to your mother. That's no sin." Laurel's reply was hesitant and filled with pauses. She tried with all her being to keep her tone strong, yet warm and kind, but impersonal. She found it very hard to play the part of a sympathetic acquaintance. She would not look at him since her composure would dissolve the minute she did.

"You are too good. I certainly never deserved such an understanding help mate."

"Thank you." Laurel was exhausted, trying to maintain a curt, polite front with Mac, and she was near tears. She wanted to go back to her room and sleep.

"What are your plans, Laurel?"

"Mac, I'm very tired now. I want to return to my room and go to bed. Will you excuse me, please?"

"Will you stay with me tonight? I have so much on my mind."

"No."

"Will you let me walk you back to the Lee's?"

"If you want to."

"Laurel, please promise me you won't run away from me. I will meet you for breakfast tomorrow, and we'll decide what we will do from there."

"I'll pray about it."

"Laurel, if you won't promise, I'll sit outside your door all night if I have to. Please give me your word. We have so much more to talk about. After you've heard me out, if you want to go to Texas to be with Daniel, I'll see you get there safely. Please promise you'll give me the chance to explain."

"I will stay." The MacLaynes walked the short way back to the boarding house. When they entered the parlor, no one was downstairs. Mrs. Lee left a lantern lit on the dining room table.

"Good night, Laurel. I am relieved I found you." Mac picked up her hand and started to kiss her ring as he often did. Of course, her hand was bare. She pulled away and hurried to the stairs.

"Good night, Mac. I will meet you for breakfast in the morning." She used all her composure to make herself walk to her room instead of run.

⊨⊣ ⊢⊨

When Laurel entered the Lee's dining room the next morning, the seats around the table were nearly filled with boarders from the previous night. Mac was at the head of the table with an empty chair to his left. Laurel was the only woman present. The Laurel who entered the room was the very image of the Spinster of Hawthorn again, or nearly so. The clothes, the hair, the glasses, and the brown work shoes were the same, but the dignity and sense of confidence were new. The other men at the table paid little attention to this plain woman who joined them at the table. Two of them didn't even rise when she approached. However, Mac was fascinated by the changes he saw in Laurel. He wished they were alone that morning because he wanted to ask her scores of questions. Of course, a total lack of privacy prevented the asking, so his questions would have to wait.

The mistress of Lee's Boarding House laid a hearty spread for them. She prepared fresh dropped biscuits, eggs, sausage, and oatmeal. She supplied them with apple butter, jelly, and sorghum to sweeten the cereal. She refilled the coffee cups constantly as Lizzie brewed the best coffee around, according to the local freighters. The boast must have been true as Mac found himself downing three cups before he'd finished his breakfast. Laurel picked at her meal, eating only one biscuit and sausage and drinking about half a glass of milk. Mac noticed how little she'd eaten. "Are you well this morning, Laurel?"

"I'm fine, thank you."

"Good. Did you sleep well last night?"

"Yes, quite well." The polite lie kept the conversation impersonal. Neither of them spoke again until the dining room was empty.

"Where would you like to go so we can talk privately?"

"I haven't really thought about it."

"I'd like to walk for a while. Will you walk with me?"

"I have to go to the livery to speak with Hank Brewer. I had planned to leave with him when he finished loading his wagon."

"Mrs. Lee told me Hank is going north today."

"Yes, I know."

"Laurel, Little Rock is southwest."

"I am aware of that."

"I don't understand, Laurel. Were you going home today?"

"I was going back to Shiloh."

"Why?"

"I'm not sure. God put it on my heart before I even reached Bolivar. He made me understand my place is in Shiloh. He reminded me about the vow I'd made. I will not be the one to break it. You will have to bear that responsibility."

Now, Mac couldn't find words. He was elated that Laurel knew Shiloh was her home, but he didn't know what to make of her decision to maintain the vows after she thought he broke his. The Laurel he left behind would have run from that rejection. She would have never willingly faced the gossip the community would share. This new person was so much more attractive, and the attraction had nothing to do with the way she looked. The strength, confidence, and courage she'd gained were at the core of his admiration.

"Excuse me, Mac. I can't keep Mr. Brewer waiting for me."

"Laurel, are you coming back?"

"Yes."

⊷⊹⊶

Twenty minutes later when Laurel returned, she found Mac waiting for her on the porch. She looked at him closely for a minute. She noticed his beard was less kempt than usual, and his clothes were soiled and rumpled. She didn't believe she'd ever seen Mac so poorly dressed and groomed.

"Will you walk out with me now?"

"All right."

They walked down the main street of the community until they reached a more isolated area where they would have the privacy to talk. He pointed to a nice grassy area under some shade trees on a rise that wasn't too wet from the recent rains. The spot he picked was several yards off the road. Laurel sat on his jacket he'd spread for her, and he sat in front of her. Strangely, she felt very calm although she knew she'd never been involved in a more important conversation in her life. When she looked into the face of her husband, he looked none too confident.

"Laurel, will you let me hold your hands while we pray together? I have truly missed our study and prayer time together. I need God's help to be able to say the things that will make you understand all that's happened." Laurel laid her hands in Mac's waiting palms. "Dearest Lord Jesus, please give me the words I need. Give me the grace and courage to say what I have to say. Thank you for letting me find Laurel and her willingness to let me speak my mind to her. I know you have blessed me today. Amen."

Mac gazed up into her gray-green eyes. At a loss for a way to start, he simply said, "You're different, Laurel."

"By the grace of God, I've learned a few things. I've grown up quite a lot in these past two months that we've been apart."

"Your father is proud of you. I have no doubt you have learned your worth and are able to hold your own with anyone."

"I have learned I am my own person now—whole and capable. With my faith always grounded, I can do anything I have to do to make my way in the world."

"I believe you can…. There is so much I want and need to say to you, but I don't know where to start."

"Mac, you may have your freedom. I have only two conditions. You must get the divorce or annulment, if that is what you prefer. In the eyes of the church, there has been no real marriage anyway. No one will blame you when you seek an annulment for a marriage that was never consummated…and I want the piece of land I bought from Widow Parker."

Mac took the small wooden cross from the pocket of his vest. He wore it on his watch fob where he placed it the day Laurel pressed into his palm when he had left for Ann Arundel County. "The day you gave me this, you told me you couldn't let me leave before you told me you loved me."

"Yes, I remember. I apologize for my emotional outburst that morning. I overstepped the boundary you'd set for our relationship. I know I am to blame…" Mac stopped her mid-sentence.

"If you believed I'd never return, why did you do all the work to finish the homestead?"

"To keep my word. I told you I'd have your home finished when you returned to Shiloh. I did the best I was capable of doing."

"Laurel, I told you I'd come back."

"And you did…" In words as sharp as any knife, Laurel spoke, "just as the announcement in the paper said. You have to finalize the sale of your property and take care of some legal matter in Arkansas."

⇒+ +⇐

Those words were as painful for Mac to hear as they were for Laurel to speak. Mac could imagine only one thing worse. He couldn't bear to hear Laurel say she had been mistaken and didn't love him. Yet, he was astonished at Laurel's calm and control as she spoke to him. Mac had seen her in crisis before, but this morning she was not distraught. Laurel could've been made of ice. This behavior brought more fear to him than anything that had happened between them since the day they met. Did the lies Marsha wrote destroy the love she declared to him two months ago? "Laurel, will you read this?" He handed her the broadside Matthew had given him the day he had returned.

"No, thank you. I've already seen it."

"Laurel, will you look at this then?" In his other pocket, he had a much bigger paper with the same name. Thank the Lord, he packed the paper in his saddlebags so he could save the tribute to his mother's passing. The date was one day earlier than the date on the broadside. Laurel took the paper and saw the obituary she'd read in the broadside. When she turned the paper to the other side, she didn't find the betrothal announcement.

"What does this mean?"

"The broadside is a fraud, Laurel. Marsha printed the broadsheet to cause problems for us. She was angry with me and probably even hates me now, but that is another matter. I feel sorry for her, but at the same time, I guess I am grateful to her. During the last argument with her, I knew I never loved her. I lusted after her as all the men in our circle of friends had done. She was beautiful and desirable, but that was all. She pushed me to edge of my tolerance that morning, declaring she'd make me a good wife. I told her I already have a good wife. I told her she could never have been the life mate you are, and that God gave me the only woman I wanted."

Laurel looked at Mac. His too blue eyes were focused on her face. He was watching her every reaction, wanting to see how she would take these words. "Laurel, it was during that fit of anger with Marsha that I knew I spoke the truth – to myself – for the first time. I was haunted by your last words to me my entire trip. When I spoke the words aloud, I knew why." Without taking his eyes from Laurel's face, Mac paused and took a deep breath. "I love you. I have loved you since that afternoon you first jutted out that stubborn chin and told me off in the orchard at your father's homestead."

He stopped and waited for Laurel to respond. He was all too aware she was the one who must take the next step. Like other incidents in their time together, pushing her to do anything only drove her back behind the fortress she'd built to protect herself. Like at their wedding, when he offered his hand, Laurel chose to take it. When they nestled in each other's arms, she initiated that too. She was the first to speak words of love. Now Mac waited to see if she would make the choice to come home with him.

"She must love you very much to go to such measures to drive me away."

"No, I don't believe she ever did. She wanted social standing and wealth, a place with the social and political elite of Maryland. I am sorry she failed to reach the misplaced goals she'd set. She is an unhappy, bitter person, but Laurel, I don't want to talk about her. She is part of my past that I laid at the cross. We can't do anything about what is behind us. I want to know if we have a future together."

"I don't know if we do or not. Mac, I told you nothing would change for me as long as I knew you were coming home. I left Shiloh because I believed you wanted to be free to marry the beautiful woman from your past. Nothing has changed for me. In July, I told you I love you. I still love you, enough to let you go if that is what you want. You see, the thing I learned is loving has nothing to do with being loved. Love must be unconditional, or it isn't love at all. I will not break the vows I made to you last March. Whether we have a future together depends on whether you plan to keep your vows."

"As long as God wills." He took her hand and kissed her bare ring finger. "Did you lose something?"

"No. I gave your mother's ring to my Uncle Matthew to return to you. I knew you'd want it back."

"That's true." Mac drew the wide gold band from his pocket and slipped it back where he placed it on their wedding day. "I want it back where it belongs. Please never take it off again." Mac kissed her ring and pulled Laurel into his arms. She came willingly, welcoming his embrace, his kisses, and his declaration of love. Laurel never expected to know the joy she felt at that moment. Mac revived the hope she'd never totally allowed to die. Was it even possible? The Spinster of Hawthorn was loved.

CHAPTER SIXTEEN

Now faith is the substance of things hoped
for, the evidence of things not seen.

Hebrews 11:1 [KJV c1850].

Mac and Laurel talked the afternoon away. Laurel told him about all the changes at the homestead, including the addition of the thirty acres and the Widow Perkin's cabin.

"Laurel, why did you buy her homestead?"

"I thought you'd be pleased. After all, it borders the north side of your property. It's near the creek where we swim. The widow told me you'd asked to buy it from her a few years ago."

"I am pleased, Wife, but I didn't provide for you, and yet you spent the whole time I was gone working for me."

"I didn't do it just for you. The widow needed the money to help her children move west. She didn't want to be a burden to them, so she took what she wanted from the cabin and sold me what I wanted. Besides, the happiest memories of our life together come from there and the time we spent in that little cabin."

"Well, I am pleased, but I will return your dowry, the tax money, the building costs, and the cost of the land."

"It doesn't matter. I've not been hungry."

"It matters to me."

"Let's not fight about money. It's too petty to argue about. It's time we went back to the Lee's for the night. We'd have been a quarter of the way home if we hadn't spent the whole day talking. Anyway, I'm hungry. We did skip our midday meal."

"We will talk about money soon. I want you to know about our finances. Never again will I fail to provide for you. Of course, you're right. It's near dusk now. Are you ready to go home tomorrow?"

"I'm ready to be back home." Mac helped Laurel to her feet, took her hand, and they walked back toward Bolivar. Shortly, the boarding house became visible.

"Laurel, we need to tell Mrs. Lee that we won't need that second room tonight. Do you want to move, or do you want me to come to you?"

"She'll frown at us spending the night together. I told her my name is Campbell."

"I know. Mr. Lee told me when I checked in that no married woman was staying in their boarding house. I nearly left, but thank the Lord, I was too tired. I rode more than four days with little rest--only about four hours at the widow's...I mean your cabin."

"You must be exhausted. Why did you come after me without any rest?

"I would do whatever I must to find you. After I realized I loved you, every minute I spent away from you was an eternity. Matthew told me you'd only left the day before...well, I was afraid if I didn't find you before you reached Little Rock, I never would. I was afraid. I need you in my world. You are the better half of me." Mac stopped and stared into Laurel's eyes. He stood for several seconds and pulled her close.

He held her until he sensed she was becoming uncomfortable with the public display of affection. "Back to our dilemma. What are you going to tell the innkeepers?"

"Me?"

"I'm teasing, Laurel. I'll just tell her you are a timid bride who ran away from me before our wedding night."

"Mac! You can't embarrass me like that."

"I'm teasing, Laurel. I'll think of something, maybe even tell her the truth. Let's go see if we are too late for supper."

As they entered the dining room, the guests were sitting down to supper. Mac pulled out a chair for Laurel, and he sat next to her. He took her hand as Mr. Lee spoke a simple blessing, and together they ate a filling meal. The four other guests and the Lees provided an entertaining diversion for about forty-five minutes. Laughter and interesting conversation brought both Laurel and Mac into the pleasant company. At least, it was pleasant until a boarder named Forrester began a discussion about the secession talk he'd heard in Little Rock the previous week.

"I just wished the courage of Southern gentlemen would rub off on those lily-livered legislators we got in the capitol. With a smidge of gumption, they'd go ahead and declare Arkansas's stance on this secession business and get this discussion on slavery out in the open. The federal government can't tell people what to do with their property. Don't you agree, MacLayne? Shouldn't we just get a war started so we can show the abolitionists they can't take what's ours?"

"Well, there are a couple problems with your argument. First, the legislature won't meet until November of next year, and no, Mr. Forrester. I want nothing to divide our country. I don't hold your view that people are property."

"You an abolitionist, sir?"

"Frankly, I haven't given it much thought."

"Well, maybe you should. Arkansas will stand with the South when the vote comes."

"Well, let's just hope that vote never happens, then. We have too much to lose."

"Hey, fellows. Don't be a spoiling such a pleasant suppertime talking about politics." Mrs. Lee felt the tension rising in the room. "Could I bring anybody dessert now?"

"Mrs. Lee, I apologize for my part in this discussion. Please forgive my lack of good manners. And yes, I'd love some of that great looking cake and another cup of your fine coffee. Laurel, do you want cake?"

"Laurel? You told me your name's Grace. Grace Campbell."

"I did say that, and it's partly true. My maiden name is Campbell. Mac is my husband, Patrick MacLayne."

"What's the problem here, MacLayne? Got yourself a runaway wife?" Forrester laughed and continued to taunt Mac. "What happened, sweetheart? Couldn't this abolitionist satisfy you? I'm sure you'd have better luck with a true southerner who knows how to treat a lady."

Mac moved across the room and jerked Forrester by the arm. "Forrester, you will apologize to my wife for that crude remark."

"I ain't hearing her complain. After all, you did have to come get her." Mac took the crude man by both sides of his shirt collar and jerked him from the chair. When the man stood, the chair crashed loudly against the floor.

"You men, take your feud outside this instance. I'll have the constable here before I let y'all tear up my place." Lizzie spoke in her deep voice at a level just below a scream.

"Mac, it's all right. I don't want you to get involved in a fist fight. Please just ignore him." Then Laurel turned to address Ben Forrester. "And Mr. Forrester, please never address me again. Next time I'll encourage my husband to teach you courtesy, by force if necessary." Laurel's bold tone showed her resolve. People sitting around the dinner table hid smiles. She'd earned the respect reflected in their eyes, including Mac's.

Mac stood and spoke. "Again, I am sorry for the hubbub, Mrs. Lee. Good night. Laurel and I will be leaving for home in the morning." Mac stopped by his former room to pick up the few items he'd left and then walked down to the end of the hallway to Laurel's room. "Only a little ugly spot on this wonderful day, Wife. I'm sorry I let my temper loose. I just get pulled into political discussions too easily. I planned a very different evening." Mac placed his saddlebags in the chair nearest the window.

"Mac, that was not a political discussion…that man insulted you. How could you not get angry?"

Mac walked back to lock the door, then he turned to Laurel. "I said I wanted something different his evening." He pulled Laurel into his embrace, one she didn't initiate. "Laurel Grace, from this day forward, I will not ask you for your hand when I want to touch you. I have earned my right to be your husband. I've kept the promises I made to your father. You proved that to me just before we came upstairs. My wedding ring on your hand is the outward sign of the inward bond that we have forged together. I love you. You said you love me. You are my wife. God meant for us to be together."

"There is no reason to ask, Patrick. I am proud to be your wife. I do love you, just as I said in July. My ardent hope is that you will be happy with your decision to keep your vows."

"I am happy, and I have been since the moment I gave up that ridiculous vow I made to myself. When God wants a man to fall in love, he just can't refuse."

"I know. Romans 8:28." Mac lowered the wick in the kerosene lamp so only a faint shadow fell across the small, yet neat boarding house room. He walked the few steps from the table back to the window where Laurel stood looking out on the nearly empty street. The open window allowed the late summer breeze to cool the room. The well-worn chintz curtains moved languidly from the occasional wisp of wind. Mac released the ties that held the curtain open. He took his jacket off and hung it on a peg near the washstand. He removed the rawhide lace that held back his chestnut colored hair. With his left hand, he shook his locks and freed the unseen restraint from his shoulder length hair that was the result of his long-held habit of tying his locks back from his face. He walked up behind Laurel and pulled her back into his chest and wrapped his arms around her. He laid his head on her shoulder, his face nestled at her neck. There was no conversation–just an overwhelming sense of wholeness and right. Mac sensed the most intense feelings of intimacy, standing with his wife in his arms. He never felt this emotion before. He knew the feelings of lust because he'd experienced it with the uncounted women. This emotion was not lust. It was not his body who called for his woman. He knew they were one. She was as much a part of him as his arm, his mind, and his heart. "Laurel, I love you. Thank God he meant you for me."

Mac picked Laurel up and went to the arm chair where he earlier placed his saddlebags. He nudged them into the floor and sat with Laurel in his lap. Her arms were around his neck, and she placed her braided head against this shoulder.

Laurel sighed, finding no need to talk. Mac was hers. She felt safety and security she'd never experienced before. Mac was the other half of her. She could not stem the flow of tears fed by joy. Mac bent and kissed her. After a brief time, she returned her head to the warm place on Mac's shoulder. He raised her face so he could see her eyes, and he started to whisper to her…but she put her fingertip to his lips. She smiled and mouthed the words to him…

"I know." For the longest time, Mac covered Laurel's face with tiny kisses. She sighed and giggled and laughed aloud.

Then he stopped. "Those braids…I still hate those blasted braids." He began to pull the pens lose one at a time and throw them out the open window into the street below.

"Mac!"

"Shhhh!" He continued until every last hair pen lay in the main street of Bolivar. With his fingers, Mac drew Laurel's tresses into an array of waves and curls that fell around her face, shoulders and down her back. "Wife, your hair is so beautiful. Please don't hide it from me again." Once more, he captured her mouth in a passionate kiss. In the peaceful comfort of the mutual knowledge they shared, Mac and Laurel slept, tucked together in the tall arm chair.

Near midnight, Mac was awakened by rain dripping from the open windowsill. During their three-hour nap, a thunderstorm moved into the Delta again…another round of the same weather which repeated itself all summer. The weather also turned somewhat cooler as the rain fell. Mac didn't welcome another summer thunderstorm. He wanted to get back to Shiloh. The untimely rain would make passage more difficult on the way home. Laurel still slept in his arms. There was little doubt why she slept so hard. They'd lived with high uncertainty and emotional upheaval, thanks to Marsha Golden. With their misunderstanding cleared and their personal barriers broken down, both slept…after six long months, they slept in peace.

Mac picked up his sleeping wife and gently laid her on the brass bed. He covered her with the threadbare boarding house blanket. Before Mac joined her, he sat on the side of the bed and prayed for some time. His prayer was immense gratitude. At that moment, he needed and wanted for nothing. He believed no other man was ever more blessed than he.

A loud clash of thunder woke both the MacLaynes about the time of sunrise the next morning. The rain which started the previous night increased and continued throughout the night. The room was in shadow because there was no chance of sun shining on them that day.

"Good morning, Laurel. Did you rest well?"

"I did. Do you realize how long we have been asleep? It was barely nine when we sat down in the chair. I can't believe we have slept so long."

"I believe I said good morning, Laurel. Have you no morning greeting for me?"

"Well, I am happy to awaken in your arms this rainy September day." Laurel leaned over to her husband and kissed his cheek quickly.

"Well, that was some better than no greeting, Wife, but I know you are a much better at kissing than you just proved." Mac pulled Laurel across his bare chest and kissed her again. The kiss was tender at first, but grew in strength and passion as it continued. Laurel was a more than willing participant. Their need to please each other led them to continue this romantic interlude for some time. "Whoa, Wife. It must be near 6:30, and we have things to do, unless you want to spend the day here in this boarding house bed."

"I hoped we'd get headed back home today, but the rain…anyway, I don't have a horse with me. I left Sassy Lady with my uncle. With the roads being mired, we can't ride double on Midnight."

"No, I don't think we'd get far riding double…for several reasons… and the muddy road may not be the biggest obstacle to our progress home." Again, he pulled Laurel back down to him and kissed her face, her neck, her shoulders, and her eyes. Laurel loved her husband's touch, and she felt no shyness with him. "My darling bride, there is so much more I want to share with you, to teach you to enjoy, but not here in this dreary boarding house room. Let's make arrangements to leave for home. Laurel Grace, I am more than eager to take you to Shiloh." Mac began a series of fierce, passionate kisses that left Laurel shaken and wanting more…just what she did not know.

Mac rose from the right side of the bed and quickly pulled on his clothes. "Laurel, you need to tie back your hair and dress in those old dungarees and a long-sleeved shirt for today. Please remain here behind this locked door until I get back. I am going to find a way for us to get home." He buttoned his shirt, pulled on his boots, picked up his coat and hat, and left the room.

Laurel snuggled more deeply under the blanket and into the pillow. She felt a shiver run down her back. The blanket's warmth and Mac's scent lulled her back to sleep. Within the hour, Mac was knocking on the door of the room where Laurel slept. She rolled over and stretched from the luxury of her prolonged sleep. She realized Mac was back and ready to leave for home. She rose and opened the door, which she never got up to lock.

"Wife, I can't believe my eyes. You haven't dressed for travel. I thought you wanted to be off as much as I do."

"I'll be dressed before you know. Go get your cup of coffee from Mrs. Lee and get us a couple of her great biscuits and bacon for a quick breakfast. We'll be half way to Shiloh by dark. Tomorrow we will be back at the widow's."

After a short time, Laurel and Mac stood before their transportation home. Mac's beautiful black stallion was hitched to the strangest wagon Laurel ever saw. The bottom was painted bright red, blue and green, much like a traveling circus wagon she'd seen one time in Fayetteville. On the top of the wagon bed was a four by six by eight-foot cube with no paint at all. The box was covered with a tin roof, pitched like a shed. The front of the wagon seat was covered by a two-foot-wide awning, the color of ripe pumpkins ready to harvest.

"Mac, a horse would have been fine...I didn't need a traveling cabin."

"Well, I thought about that, but the blacksmith had only a sole jack to sell. I wouldn't make my wife travel home on the back of a donkey. Seems a stage driver bought his last two horses earlier in the week. He did give me a good deal on the peddler's wagon. He said it was a steal at $12.00, and he'd not let it go at that if he didn't need the space in his livery."

Laurel laughed as Mac finished the tale. He helped her into the seat and put his saddlebags and her two small bags in the back with his saddle. At least all their meager possessions would stay dry beneath the tin roof of the "cabin" for their thirty-nine-mile trip back to Shiloh. He said they'd make the Snoddy settlement or at least Greenfield and stop for the night. It would mean another night camped out, but neither of them were strangers to sleeping on the trail. If they rode into the night, they could reach Shiloh early the next day, but that was not the way he intended to bring Laurel home. He would carry Laurel over the threshold of her new home and give her some of the things she'd missed at their wedding. Their wedding night would be perfect, even if the wedding wasn't. Besides, Midnight didn't need to work so hard. He provided such good service to his master over the four years Mac owned him. That is the story he'd give Laurel if she asked about the leisurely, if wet, trip back home.

All morning, the rain fell in a steady stream, so the bright yellow-orange awning proved to be a great asset. Laurel snuggled closely to Mac, and he laid his arm across her shoulder and enjoyed the nearness. They also enjoyed the conversation. They both missed the talks they'd shared before Mac's trip to Maryland. Regardless of the slow, muddy roads, the miles passed so that by early evening they reached the small village that had grown up around Snoddy's forge and livery. He decided this would provide a good opportunity to tell Laurel of his plans.

"Laurel, Snoddy's place is just a short piece on up the road, but I think we need to find a place to camp near there. The wagon wheel seems loose. It's not riding as smooth as it was." Laurel wondered how he could tell the difference as the wagon bounced and jolted over the wet roads the entire trip from Bolivar. "Besides, Midnight is worn out. He's travelled some rough roads today, and he's not used to pulling a wagon. Maybe we can find some place to get some hot food."

"Don't you think we could finish the trip after we give Midnight a while to rest?"

"That's not wise. We'll travel a bit farther and then, all else failing, we can bed down in our little "traveling cabin." Believe it or not, there is a cot built into that shed. We'll be home tomorrow before noon." Just then the lightning flashed and the rain began to fall in torrents. "See, it's time we stopped." Mac searched the nearby area hoping to find some shelter for them and his horse. The sparsely populated countryside offered no barn, shed, or lean-to to help keep the sheets of water from them. At the curve in the road, he saw a huge old oak tree with large sprawling limbs to protect the stallion. Mac flapped the reins on Midnight's rump to hurry his pace to the oak. When he reached the sheltering branches, Mac jumped down to secure the animal near the tree and behind the wagon, providing as much shelter as he could. Laurel climbed down and found a large rock to scotch the rear wheel before she opened the small door to the cabin on wheels.

Inside, the wagon was very cramped, but because of the tin roof, everything was dry--everything but Laurel. Damp most of the day, now she was drenched. Water ran in streams from her face and clothes. Laurel looked for something to dry herself and found nothing. She took her bag in the corner from under Mac's saddle and pulled her petticoat out to use as a towel. She stripped to her chemise, shook out her loose chignon, and began to dry herself. When Mac entered the tiny wagon, a second puddle of water formed on the floor as the rain fell from the brim of his hat and from the back of his coat. "I'd have come in sooner if I only knew what a wonderful sight waited for me."

"Mac, I am a drowned rat!"

"I only see my wife..." He started to take her in his arms. She pushed him away.

"You'll get me wet again. I couldn't find a towel, so I sacrificed my petticoat to get as dry as I am."

"Think I can share it?"

"Yes, but I don't know what I'll wear tomorrow."

"You look fine to me just as you are."

"Very funny. People may be around when we get back to Shiloh."

"I'm counting on it."

"Who'll be at the widow's?"

"I'll tell you later. I wish I'd planned better. I thought we'd be in the Snoddy settlement so we could find supper."

"We'll be all right. There are a couple of those biscuits left from Mrs. Lee's breakfast. I am sorry there's no coffee, but we aren't at a loss for water." Mac grinned at Laurel's attempt at humor.

"It will be dark soon anyway. We'll just get to bed early and forget we are hungry."

"On that tiny cot? We will have to take turns sleeping there."

"I think not...spooning is fun."

"You'd better get out of those wet clothes. I don't want you to be sick when we get home."

"I don't want that either. Do you mind if I undress?"

"I've seen you in your underclothes on many occasions, husband."

"So you have." Mac removed all his top clothes, boots, and socks. He took Laurel's petticoat and dried himself. He lit the sole lantern, which hung from a hook on the side of the tiny cabin and a faint yellow glow and the scent of kerosene filled the little space. He walked to the tiny bunk built into the front of the wagon, lifted the worn blanket and slid into the cot. Mac sat with his back against the wall and motioned for Laurel to join him. He pulled her against his chest and drew her into an embrace. "Not exactly home, but better than any place I've been in a long time. I'm here with you and we're alone."

"I'm not complaining. We've shared worse beds in the six past months."

"Laurel, I hope we never spend another night truly apart. Since the day we took our vows many things have kept us apart. We have been strangers, there have been great physical distances, we've dealt with tragedies from our pasts, and we've been afraid to trust each other. Thank the Lord, He has helped us put so much of it behind us. Before we get back to Shiloh, let's get all those barriers behind us. When we get home, let's go back as the people we know we can be. I want to tell you about my trip home. I'll tell you everything I believe that has kept me from making a real commitment to you. I hope you will tell me about the things that has kept you apart from me. If we can do this, I know we can find our life in Shiloh and live together. We will be happy in our love for each other. We'll live the life God intended for us when He sent me to Washington County all those months ago. Can you talk to me about the past, Laurel?"

Laurel turned to look in to Mac's face. Her hair tumbled in to her eyes. He brushed the locks back with his fingers and waited for to reply. "Patrick, I want to tell you what you want to know. I will try, but I don't remember everything. I know bits and pieces...the nightmare...I'll answer questions...I do I trust you...I'll try...is it enough?" A tear slipped from the corner of her eye.

With his thumb, Mac wiped it away. "Yes, Wife. Tell me all you can. From this point on, we'll keep no secrets from each other. Nothing needs to become a barrier between you and me." Mac placed a gentle kiss on Laurel's cheek. "I love you."

"I know."

"Do you? Seems strange to say because I never loved any woman before. I thought I did. I said I loved Marsha. I told her I did, but I never knew what it was." Mac looked for a moment into Laurel's upturned face and then he kissed her, slowly and tenderly, savoring the touch he'd missed during their long separation. "I've missed you, Laurel Grace." Another shorter, sweet kiss followed. "I know we talked a long time yesterday, but is there anything else about my encounter with Marsha you want to know? Just ask me..."

"Only one thing, Patrick. You carried those feelings for a very long time, for more than a decade. How do you know that it wasn't love? She's certainly so much more beautiful than I am. Are you certain I'm not an obligation and that your own sense of integrity is not what you're feeling?"

Mac began to laugh aloud, and his laughter filled the tiny cabin on wheels. "You, my dear, are so wonderful. My dearest Lord! How long does it take to build a cabin?"

"What are you laughing at? You said I could ask you anything. I want to know."

"Laurel Grace Campbell MacLayne, I said I love you. I said it yesterday. I said it this morning…more than once. I just told you that I didn't know the meaning of the phrase until about ten days ago. Let me tell you one last story, and if you don't finally understand, I guess I will just have to give up."

Laurel tried to push herself out of Mac's arms to get out of the little cot built into the cabin on wheels. "Well, I'm sorry, I asked."

"No, you don't. Sit still. We don't run away any more. We talk until we clear the air." Mac pulled Laurel back in to his arms. "There I like that." He brushed her hair back from her neck and began to kiss her neck. She squirmed against his soft assault on her senses.

"All right. I'll listen to your story."

"Laurel, I want us to be just like my parents. They were sweethearts until the minute my mother died. I wish I'd taken you so you could've known my mother. She would've loved you." Tears came to Mac's lashes as he spoke of his mother. "It was so hard to sit by her bed and watch her suffer those last few weeks. Cancer is a merciless disease, and the medicine did so little to stem the pain… all it did was rob us of the time left to us."

"How hard it must have been for you, Patrick."

"When my mother was awake, she talked to my father and me, but she made no small talk. She used every minute to say things that she wanted us to know. She spoke about real things. She talked about her feelings and hopes and dreams. She told father when she hurt and how she looked forward to Heaven…being with

Kathleen and Sean again. She said she'd miss him and didn't know how she'd sleep without him being beside her. She told him to find a new wife so he wouldn't be lonely with her being gone. She thanked him for the years they'd worked side by side to build their life. She told him where she kept the keys to the estate and her recipe box."

Laurel was in tears before Mac finished his story. "My father told my mother that he was afraid of life without her. He said he was angry with God for taking her away. He admitted he depended on her more than she knew, and he wasn't sure how to handle some of the things on the estate. They actually talked some business a time or two. One afternoon, he kissed mother a time or two and whispered something about his lifelong lover...I didn't catch all of it, but she blushed and smiled all at the same time."

"They truly did love each other always, didn't they?"

"Yes, and that is exactly what I want for us. We can share our life like that if we decide nothing will come between us."

"Help me get to that place, Patrick. How did they get there? How did you learn?"

"Laurel, you spoke of love before I did. Remember?"

"I guess I did." She turned on the tiny wooden cot. The hard, wooden sides of the cot cut into her hip. She sidled closer to Mac, hoping to relieve the ache. In the glimmer of the kerosene lamp, all she could make out was the too, too blue of his beloved eyes. Laurel moved to kiss her husband, not waiting for him to take the initiative to kiss her.

"I like that. I don't think you've ever done that before. Did I answer your question? Do you believe I love you?"

"I know you do...I don't know why you do. It's enough to know you do."

"Laurel, we will keep learning why as we grow together. I am not that man who said he loved Marsha Golden, and the Good

Lord knows, you aren't the Spinster of Hawthorn. I can't believe you ever were."

A resounding clap of thunder shook the tiny cabin on wheels. Laurel sat bolt, upright, trembling as the rain beat a constant staccato on the tin roof inches above their heads. Mac pulled her back into his arms, and they lay spooned together, but Laurel continued to tremble.

"Why are you afraid, Laurel. You are safe."

"I know."

"I'm not sure you do. Laurel, tell me about the nightmares. Help me understand. I've seen you take on men twice your size, like that Forrester man in Bolivar and those ruffians that attacked us on the trail across the Ozarks. You practically scratched out the eyes of one of them to protect me. You've told me off more than once. I know how courageous you can be, but something about a nightmare terrifies you."

"I don't remember everything about that nightmare. I know some of it. I know I never stand up to people until I get angry though. Or when I feel like I can't control what's about to happen, I will try to put myself back in control. I've done it since…since…I guess all my life."

"Matthew told me you were not defensive as a little girl. He said you were happy, smiling, full of life and very much the life of the family…in the middle of everything. He did say you acted grown up and loved the company of adults, but you were the life of the party, teasing, laughing, and getting in the middle of everyone's conversations. He said you didn't have one shy bone in your body."

"He must have confused me with Susan."

"Susan is his own daughter. I doubt he'd make that mistake."

"Tell me what happened at the harvest party after your family moved to Washington County."

"That was almost two years after my mama died. I asked papa if I could go--all the kids from Hawthorn school were going, so I said I wanted to go. He didn't want me to go, but he said I could if my brother Daniel went. So, we did."

"Wasn't the party much fun?"

"No, I don't guess so. I hardly remember it. Daniel went on a hay ride with the older kids...with his sweetheart. They got married a few years later and moved to Texas. The younger kids built a big fire and roasted some corn and ...oh, I don't remember...In the nightmare I remember the fire and the kids standing around the circle with the glow of the fire on their faces and laughing. I don't think I was laughing, though."

"What about the sheep shears?"

"Sheep shear? I don't know anything about sheep shears."

"Laurel, the night you got lost on Crowley's Ridge, you fell and hit your head. Your hair got matted with blood. When I teased you about cutting your hair with sheep shears to get the matted blood out, you said that it wouldn't be the first time. Don't you remember?"

"I vaguely recall telling you something like that, but for the life of me, I don't know why I said it."

"What happened after the party?"

"Nothing really. I already finished school, pretty much. Pa and I decided I'd stay home and start taking care of the house for him. I wasn't quite fifteen, but I was already way ahead of the other kids at school, and I already finished my common school diploma anyway. I was more use at home." Laurel fidgeted in the cot.

"Do you remember when you started having the nightmares, Laurel?"

"I guess about that time, but I'd never really thought about it."

"Who's in the dream besides you?"

"Just the kids from school...I don't know...some boys and ...I just don't remember."

Mac pulled Laurel next to his chest again. "That's enough for tonight. Listen, the rain's stopped."

Laurel tilted her head and noticed he was right. She then tucked her unruly mane onto his shoulder and spooned against his lean frame. "I'm so tired, Mac. Let's go to sleep."

"Yes, ma'am. Dear Father, As we take our rest tonight, we ask you to keep us safe and bring us home, truly home tomorrow. We give You the praise for the steps we have made today to get to know each other. Lord, we ask you to keep us moving on this onward path toward each other and to You. Amen."

⇒╪ ╪⇐

As the sun passed its zenith the next day, the funny looking peddler's wagon stopped near the porch of Matthew and Ellie Campbell's cabin. "Mac, we could have been at the widow's cabin by now. Why did you take the left fork back there?"

"Told Matthew, I'd let him know when I got back. He's been taking care of the homestead and the animals for me."

"We could've dropped by tomorrow. I look a sight."

"Hey, Matthew. Anyone here?" Within a moment, Matthew, Ellie, and three of their children came out to greet the MacLaynes.

"Laurel Grace, I am happy to have you home. Thank the Lord, Mac found you. Mac, please forgive those last words I spoke to you."

"Just forget it, Ellie."

Matthew helped his niece down from the wagon seat and twirled her around as if she were his daughter Mary. "I'm so grateful the stage lines are not very reliable around here."

"I was headed back anyway, Uncle Matthew. Leaving didn't seem right. Too many things on the trip shouted at me...go home to Shiloh. I listened."

"Come on in and have a bite of lunch. Got plenty of left overs."

"Thanks, Ellie. I'd love some food. We haven't eaten much since yesterday's breakfast." They sat at Matthew's table and ate a fast, filling lunch. They barely cleaned their plates before Mac spoke. "Matthew, can you help me with a couple of things for the next hour or two?"

"Mac, I thought we were going home."

"We'll get there in a little while. I just have a few things that I have to do today before I can call it a day."

"If that is what you want." Laurel's reply was compliant, if not freely made. She wanted a bath, some clean clothes, and a night's rest in the tall bed in the widow's loft.

The men left the cabin.

Laurel shook her head in disbelief. "What got into him? He told me he couldn't wait to get home."

"I don't know, but I am so happy you're back. Come and talk a spell." Ellie replied.

⊷╪ ╪⊷

As the men rode from Matthew's homestead, Matthew turned in his saddle to speak to Mac. "Why are we off in such an all-fired hurry?"

"I've got a lot of things to take care of before I bring Laurel home for the first time."

"We took care of all that last Saturday. The whole community pitched in."

"You don't understand. It's got to be just right. This is Laurel's special homecoming." As they reached the church-yard, Mac stopped and turned. "Did those freighters come from Memphis?"

"Yeah. I said we took all that to your homestead Saturday, and the stuff from the widow's too. Why are you so edgy?"

"Matthew, I just want tonight to be perfect for Laurel. Her homecoming has a lot to make up for. She deserves at least part of a bride's dream."

"Seems like a lot of fuss just to move into your new house. You'd think you'd never spent a night together before." Mac didn't reply. He lowered his head so his hat covered most of his face. Matthew looked at his friend. Silence became awkward between the men. "Not meaning to intrude if it's not wanted. You got something you want to talk about?"

Mac pulled Midnight to a stop at the fork leading to his land. "No. I just want your help in getting everything ready. Laurel deserves so much more than she's ever been given. She lost her youth. Her wedding was thrown together. She wore a dress that didn't fit her. She cooked her own wedding supper. She didn't have a day-after party or special clothes, except the mourning weeds she put on two days after she was wed. She made herself a pretty dress for Easter and gave it to a girl we met on the trip across the state. She told that girl's brother that every girl deserves to feel pretty on her wedding day. I have never lost that vision of her kindness and love. I saw her face when she spoke those words to Lonnie. She didn't feel pretty the day I married her. She felt obliged to make her dying father happy. Thanks to the grace of our Lord, we learned to love each other. Now, I'm bringing her home. Her wedding night has to be special, the best I can make it."

"You've not bedded her yet, have you? I'd thought your reunion in Bolivar would certainly take care of that formality."

"Matthew, the boarding house in Bolivar was run down and seedy-looking. The bed was a creaky old brass bed with worn bed covers…she deserves more."

"All she wants is to be loved by you, Brother."

"I love her. She is the best part of me. That is why at least part of our marriage must be the dream she put behind her when she was fourteen. You know how much she has been hurt by my past, but even then she would not break the vows she made to me. She was on her way back to Shiloh when I found her in Bolivar. She said loving me has nothing to do with me loving her. Matthew, I'm not sure I believed unconditional love existed outside God. She has taught me so much."

"My friend, you are a lucky man. Let's go get your home ready for your bride."

"Matthew, I've waited for this night a long time. We've been married for more than six months. I'm no stranger to the joining of a man and a woman but making love to someone you love…"

"Brother, you're talking to the wrong man for advice. Ellie and I were just kids when we got married, her just sixteen and me nineteen. We bungled our way through, learning as we went, but I do know if you really love each other, as I believe you do, the Lord will bless your union. That is the greatest gift God gave man, except salvation. You're lucky you've found a woman to love. Just be gentle and patient and thank the Lord. That will be special enough for my niece."

CHAPTER SEVENTEEN

My beloved is mine and I am his.

Song of Songs 2:16 [KJV c1850].

J ust before sunset, Mac and Matthew returned to the Campbell homestead. Mac rode to the porch and tied Midnight to the rail. He took the bundle from the back of his horse and walked up to the place Ellie and Laurel sat on the porch, peeling potatoes. Laurel's thoughts constantly returned to the image of spending the night with Mac in the tall bed at the widow's cabin. Her daydreams so consumed her that when he rode into the yard, she did not see him at first. When she realized Mac had returned, she looked at him and thought him the most handsome man she'd ever seen. He wore his Easter shirt, unbuttoned at the neck. His hair was freshly groomed and his beard trimmed. His boots shined, having been recently brushed. He smiled broadly, and his gaze never left his wife. He stepped toward her. He bowed slightly to Laurel and acknowledged Ellie's presence.

"Ellie, my dear friend, will you take these things inside and help my dear life mate make herself beautiful? I will wait here, somewhat impatiently, I might add."

"Mac, what are you doing?" I would like to get back to the widow's so we can be home tonight."

"Being home is exactly my plan, darlin'. Just do as I asked, please."

Ellie drew Laurel into the downstairs bedroom and opened the bundle Mac gave her. Inside, she found the pink party dress that Laurel asked Mrs. Dunn to make for the Fourth of July dance. She also saw her new white shoes, several petticoats, a lacy chemise, and silk stockings. Except for her pink dress and white shoes, Laurel had never seen any of the other things before. A small black box lay at the bottom. Ellie handed it to Laurel, who opened it to find the beautiful gold antique broach with the tiny mother of pearl daisies Mac gave her on the day he left for Maryland. "Ellie, this is nonsense. We will get home just in time to do the evening chores. Why should I change into this dress?"

"Laurel, Mac intends for you to dress for a special evening. That is the reason he took such pains to dress and groom himself before he came back. You'd better do as he wants you to. He didn't seem in the mood to argue about anything. Let me get you some warm water. Here's a brush. Take your braids down while I get some bath water."

"Take my braids down? It'll be time to put them up for bed by the time we get back to the widow's."

"I'm sure Mac's not planning to take the school marm home with him tonight." Laurel caught Ellie's intended meaning, and she blushed a bit. However, she began to take her hair down.

After several minutes, Mac called from the porch. "Hey, Wife. The sun is near set. When'll you be ready to go?"

"Just be patient Mac. She's doing the best she can in such a short time." Ellie put the gown over Laurel's petticoats. She pulled the bodice together in the back and began buttoning the many pearl buttons from her waist up to her mid-back.

"Ellie, I can't wear this dress. My shoulders and half my décolleté are bare. I don't have a shawl to cover myself."

Ellie turned and smoothed the deep collar down over Laurel's shoulders. She then took the black box from Laurel and pinned the lovely daisy broach between the edges of the collar. "You look lovely. I know Mac wants to see you just this way."

Laurel felt beautiful. Her curls fell in abandon down her back. The full skirt of the pretty pink party dress with its hem just brushing the floor swept widely around her. The toes of the new white shoes just peeked out as she took a step. When she saw her reflection in the mirror, she gasped at the image reflected there.

"Ellie..."

"Laurel, Mac is waiting for you. It is time he saw the beautiful woman he married."

Together they walked out to the porch where Mac and Matthew stood, waiting.

"My goodness, niece, what a vision you are! You are certainly the sprite I knew many years ago in North Carolina."

Mac didn't speak. After a moment, he walked to her, picked up her hand, and kissed it. "Madam, your transportation awaits. Let me take you home." He mounted Midnight and then reached down to help Laurel sit in front of him. He pulled the rein, and then he turned his stallion toward the church. The MacLaynes spoke little. When they reached Shiloh church, Mac took the east road toward their homestead.

"Mac, the road to the widow's is there."

"We are going home, Laurel. We will spend our wedding night in our own home."

Laurel was even more confused. She knew many things needed to be done before the cabin would be a comfortable home, but Mac planned her homecoming, so she didn't complain. She moved closer into his arms and rode in a sense of complete happiness. It mattered little where they were headed. The moon was bright, the stars shown above, and the night air was warm and blew gently through her hair. Laurel was at peace, secure in Mac's arms. God was in his Heaven, and all was right with her world.

Mac bent forward and kissed Laurel's bare shoulder. "Laurel Grace, you are beautiful."

"I feel beautiful. It's because I am happy. I didn't know I could be this happy, Mac."

"I know that feeling, too. I am so pleased we are finally going to be home together here at Shiloh."

"Home here at Shiloh. Those are special words." As they approached their cabin, the last rays of the setting sun disappeared below the horizon. Laurel saw dim lights through the windows. She looked at the porch where she saw two cane bottom rocking chairs on either side of a small table. A lantern with a low-trimmed wick was producing a welcome light. Mac brought Midnight to a stop at the steps, where he stepped from the stirrup and landed on the lowest step. He picked Laurel up from the saddle and carried her to the door. He opened it and carried his wife across the threshold of their home. Laurel was quiet. She laid her head on Mac's shoulder and savored the dream coming true. She tried to remain very still, thinking she would awake at any moment, and the happy dream would end. Amazingly, it didn't.

"Laurel, welcome home." Mac put her down, but he did not release her from his embrace.

"How? When I left...You did...."

"Our neighbors and family moved all our things here so we would have a home when we got back. They knew we were coming back because this is where God wanted us to be, the place we will raise our family and build a future together." Laurel looked at him, thanking God He had led her to this place.

"Everything is too perfect. My old family keepsakes, some things from the widow's, and some things I don't recognize at all, but everything seems to belong." Laurel moved from Mac's arms and stepped around the room, touching her mother's rocking chair and the carved side table from the loft at the widow's cabin. On the table lay the Campbell family Bible next to Mac's well-worn scripture book. She turned up the wick of the kerosene lamp, and the light gleamed on the walnut plank floor and on the glass panes of the windows, bordered on either side by her lawn curtains with the lace trim. She ran her foot over the torn-rag rug her mother made for the Campbell homestead so many years earlier. She imagined a cold winter night when she and Mac would sit near the hearth, reading and talking together before a blazing fire. "This is so much more than I've dreamed, I…"

"So small a part of what you deserve. Thank you for being my wife. I love you." Mac pulled Laurel into his arms and in full abandon kissed her. Laurel melted into his arms, fully returning his kiss.

After a few minutes, Mac let Laurel go. "I am pleased you think your home is perfect. I've more to show you. Your dinner awaits, ma'am." Her husband had prepared a grand table, using her mother's pewter candlesticks on either side of a small yellow pitcher overflowing with Shasta daisies he'd picked near the spring house which shaded them from the hot summer sun. He used his green tie he wore on their wedding day to make a bow around the yellow pitcher. Mac led Laurel to the side of the table, pulled out her chair, and waited for her to sit down. In the several hours, he and Matthew were away, the two men prepared a special dinner from the ample stores Laurel stored into the larder. Mac brought warm roasted chicken, baked potatoes, creamed corn, pole beans, a pone, butter, chilled cider, and something that resembled a peach pie. "We'll call this a cobbler. Seems neither your uncle nor I quite got the hang of making a pie crust, but I'll bet with all the butter, molasses and spice we put in it, it'll taste fine."

"Mac, I'm honored you went to so much effort to make this homecoming special. Come, bless this food. I've decided that I'm hungry."

"Lord, I only know one thing tonight. Thank you."

Laurel and Mac spent more than an hour sharing their first meal in the MacLayne cabin. They talked about the trip home, the goodness of the Shiloh community, which brought their home together for them while they were gone, and the excessive effort put into getting their homestead ready for the coming winter. Mac told Laurel about the things that he'd shipped from Maryland: the china and silver his mother had sent to her. He described the ruby red crystal lamp he would someday put on the side table in their sitting room, the antique mantel clock he wanted to set above the fireplace, and the decorative screen that would always have the place of honor in front of the hearth when freighters could bring those precious objects from Memphis. Patrick described in detail the MacLayne family crest brought from Scotland. The crest was the only thing his grandfather owned from his ancestral home, and even that the elder Patrick MacLayne had stolen as he was a fifth son and far down the line of inheritance from the intended head of the MacLayne clan. He hid and protected the crest during his crossing to America. When he married the red-headed lass he'd found in the colonies, he had worked the crest into the intricate wrought iron fire screen that Mac would someday place in his completed cabin.

"Patrick, it's all too wonderful. Our home will be just too fine to believe."

"Laurel, that is the very first time you have ever said 'our home.' *Praise the Lord!* Well, there is one more thing I brought back from Maryland." Mac walked across the room to the desk at the window. "My pa asked me to give this to you. He gave it to my mother for her wedding present, Laurel. If you'll have it, I want to give it to you."

"The chest is beautiful, Mac. We'll use it to keep our family keepsakes, and we'll one day pass it to our own children, like Papa gave me the Campbell family treasure box."

"We'll have to keep everything in the Campbell box, Laurel. This one is already filled." Mac turned the box over and with a small attached key, he wound the box. He turned it over and opened the lid. The music that came from the carved box was a waltz. "May I have this dance, Laurel? I missed the one I was looking forward to on the Fourth of July."

Laurel walked into his arms. Mac and she waltzed around their sitting room until the music stopped playing. Mac wound the box again, and they continued to dance to the music of a Schumann waltz that was his mother's favorite. Nothing existed in their world that night except each other, and the bliss they were experiencing in their own home. When the music ended after their third dance, Mac walked to the armchair and pulled Laurel into his lap. They didn't speak. They sat for some time, just being together. The intimacy they felt sated their needs of the moment. The two had become one. The feelings of emptiness, longing, and hurt from their pasts were gone from their awareness. The silent prayer between them was simple. "Please, Lord, let it never end."

How much time passed, neither of them knew. They were brought into awareness when the mantle clock chimed.

"Laurel, do you know how beautiful you are?"

"Seeing myself through your eyes, Patrick, I can see only what you reflect to me. Thank you for this night. I am blessed to be at home with you beside me."

Mac rose with Laurel in his arms. He carried her into the second pen of their cabin. "I hope you find this room to your liking as well, Wife."

Laurel looked around the room. The tall bed, which once nestled in the loft in the widow's cabin, sat across from the fireplace. Her grandmother's rocking chair, the tall bureau her father built, and two small side tables completed the furnishings in the room. Mac had placed crystal clear oil lamps on the tables. The beautiful double wedding ring quilt covered the tall bed. To the rear of the room was the small cubicle that Laurel believed to be too small for a nursery. Just inside the doorway, she saw a large copper bath tub and a lavatory table, topped with a white porcelain pitcher and large wash bowl. Mac ordered the tub as a surprise when he'd sent for the glass paned windows.

"Mac...such luxury. No one here at Shiloh has a copper bath tub!"

"We do...and I can't wait to enjoy many pleasant baths there, both mine and yours." Laurel's laughter filled the room, for she remembered how shyly she approached Mac the night in Powhatan when they'd shared their first bath experience together. "Now, I'll leave you for a time, so you can change your clothes. I've been told a new bride needs a few minutes of privacy."

"But Mac, I need your help in getting these buttons undone."

"My pleasure." He turned her around and began to undo the buttons on her party dress. With each button loosed, he kissed her back where he'd just moved his hand. Laurel shuddered slightly at the tenderness of each touch. The delicious sensation lasted too short a time. "And when you are finished you'll find your new night dress on the bed. I hate to tell you, but we seem to have lost that "lovely" thing your mother left for you."

Mac left the cabin to put Midnight in the barn for the night.

Laurel looked toward the tall bed and saw a creamy white silk negligée and wrapper lying on the quilt. The bodice of the low-cut gown was attached to a long flowing skirt. The wrapper fell in a wide circle at the hem, and the sleeves flowed from the shoulder to tiny lace cuffs at the wrists. Laurel spoke aloud in the empty room. "This is too beautiful for me to wear. I've never owned anything so elegant."

Within the ten minutes, Mac returned. "Mac, this is too expensive a gift for me."

"Darling, that gift is not for you. It's for me." He closed the door and walked to the foot of the bed where Laurel stood. When he looked at her, he saw his wife, more elegantly beautiful than he'd ever imagined she would be. Without a single word, he reached out and brought her into his arms and kissed her. "I knew I'd found an angel. I want you to know how beautiful you are…not just these clothes, but everything about you, your smile, your demeanor, your eyes…you have enchanted me. Have you bewitched me, Spinster of Hawthorn?"

"Please, sir. Don't call me that name. I am Mrs. Patrick MacLayne."

Again, he captured her lips with his own. He handed her his Bible, picked her up, and carried her to the rocking chair near the fireplace in their bedroom. He sat down with Laurel nestled at his shoulder. "The first night of our married life has been everything I've ever wanted it to be. Let's read God's love song from the Song of Songs. Solomon's praise for the love he found in marriage is recorded there. I doubt if we could find a better example to copy." Mac read the second and fourth chapters of the book to Laurel. She did not understand some of the images she heard, but she did sense the joy, hunger, peace and pleasure the two lovers were experiencing in their marriage relationship."

"I'd never heard those words from the Bible before. Solomon certainly loved his mate and took great pleasure in looking at her and touching her, didn't he?"

"Yes. Just the way God planned. He ordained the marriage relationship to be one of man's and woman's greatest pleasures. Laurel, Solomon's passion and needs are no greater than mine." Mac laid his Bible back in its place and rose to carry his bride to the tall bed. He threw the finely crafted quilt into the floor at the end of the bed. He laid Laurel in her place at the right side of the bed, and in the dimly lit room, he removed his clothes and went to his place on the left side of the bed. He drew Laurel into his arms and gently removed her wrapper. Lying together in this intimate state, Mac offered his evening prayer. "Thank you, Father, for our perfect homecoming. I am awed by the gift of Laurel Grace, my wife and helpmate. I ask you to help us both grow in our love for each other and for you. Be with us always. Amen."

Mac kissed Laurel again. "Laurel, I love you. I need you and I want you."

"I love you, Patrick. Please teach me to be your lover. Show me how to bring you pleasure. I want to be more than a helpmate to you. I want to be your lover, and I want you always to find happiness in my arms."

Mac was overjoyed and humbled at Laurel's request. For the briefest of moments, a dark shadow crossed his awareness. He could not give Laurel his innocence as she just offered hers. He pushed the shadow away and remembered the words Matthew spoke to him earlier. *Be gentle and patient and thank the Lord. That'll be special enough for my niece.* Mac smiled down at Laurel and began covering her face, neck, and shoulders with short, sweet kisses. He pulled her so closely and held her for a short while. He then whispered, "Thank you, Lord." He then patiently and tenderly led his virgin bride into her new role as his lover, his spouse, and his wife.

The MacLaynes lay together for some time in the aftermath of their joining. Laurel was unsure of how she should react. She wondered if she should try to tell him how she felt. "Patrick..." Mac put his finger to her lips, and then he drew her into a strong passionate kiss, the only response he was willing to give her at that moment. He pulled her back against his chest and nestled them both into their pillows and drew a crocheted lace spread his mother sent to Laurel for her wedding bed from the foot of the tall four-poster. No words were spoken. The room was quiet and peace-filled. They slept.

CHAPTER EIGHTEEN

*Husbands, love your wives, even as Christ also
loved the church, and gave himself for it.*

Ephesians 5:25 [KJV c1850].

Long before dawn, Mac was awakened by the sound of distant thunder. Laurel nestled next to him, but he managed to remove himself from the tall bed without waking her. He walked to the curtained window and looked out across the valley below the cabin. Faint lightening flashed in the distance. He hoped this storm would pass them by. His plans for the day didn't include rain. Since their "honeymoon" started in mid-week, Mac arranged for Laurel and himself to spend two more days alone before life called them back into community at Shiloh. Matthew Campbell would put John and Roy to work at his homestead for the rest of the week. Mac planned to share his attention with no one except Laurel.

Mac stood to his full six feet and stretched, trying to push the sleep away. He then walked to the bureau to retrieve work clothes. He pulled on his dungarees and cotton work shirt, picked up his boots and hat, and carried them to the front porch. He'd paid little attention to his animals after he'd brought Laurel home last night, barely taking the time to put Midnight away. He walked toward the barn to assure himself they fared well despite his lack of attention. He pulled open the heavy door and once inside, he lit the lantern. He saw all his stock, safe and peaceful. Midnight and Sassy Lady were in clean stalls, and his two jacks were penned in their place in the back of the barn. The milk cow lay on a bed of fresh straw. Mac realized Matthew did the evening chores before they'd ridden back to the Campbell homestead to retrieve his bride. Mac stopped and looked around. The smell of the fresh spread hay, the soft neighing of his fine horse, the soft light falling across his well-built, sturdy barn were sensations that led him to know there was nothing more in the universe he needed or wanted in that moment. His thoughts went back to the night he'd spent with Laurel in their own home, warm and comfortable. The pleasure he'd experienced with his life mate and the restful night they spent together after their lovemaking sated his every desire. He lowered his head to offer his praise and gratitude for the gift of home he knew he could never deserve, and he prayed he'd never lose.

The overwhelming sensations of peace and completeness were the strongest emotions he'd ever known, feelings so strong that he couldn't put into words his thanksgiving. He felt tears in his lashes. "Lord, such grace you've poured out on me, the worst of sinners. Your grace and Laurel Grace have given me a home. Please show me how I can serve that I may be even a bit worthy of it all. Thank you, Lord." By the time Mac finished his praise, his emotions were again under control. He picked up the pail and milked the cow and gathered the eggs and carried it all the short distance to the back porch. The sky lit up a time or two with flashes of lightening, but the thunder told him the storm was far off and would miss them that day. His plans wouldn't have to change. He pushed open the door and placed his load in the dry sink.

When Mac returned to the bedroom, the horizon showed a slight hint of sunlight. Laurel still slept, and her knees were pulled close to her body and her arms wrapped around them. Mac saw her do this before. She was chilled, so he picked up the double wedding ring quilt he discarded the night before and covered her. He walked to the bathing room to wash up from his chores. Shortly he returned to the tall bed where Laurel greeted him with open arms. "I didn't mean to wake you."

"I'm glad you are back. I missed you being here to keep me warm."

"Well, I'm here now..."

"Are you hungry?   Shall I..."

"Yes, I am." Mac captured Laurel's lips and pulled her next to his bare torso. The MacLaynes made love again and with the first rays of the sun beginning to steam across the ridge, they slept, wrapped in each other's arms.

At mid-morning, Laurel woke Mac with a soft kiss. Mac opened his too blue eyes and blinked. He could not remember a time he'd slept so late. Regardless, he made no move to get up. His memories of the time he'd spent with Laurel since he'd brought her back to their cabin were joy to him. He struggled to accept the reality of the absolute satisfaction and fulfillment he was experiencing. Was it possible to go from the sheer misery and torment he'd felt during his long ride to Bolivar--nearly hopeless, yet praying and not really believing he would find Laurel--to the state of bliss he was living this moment? "Wife, I want you to know, I am the world's most blessed man. Thank you, Lord!"

He rose and pulled the lace coverlet from the bed and pushed back the quilt. "Oh, Mac. Do we have to get up? It's so early."

"Yes, perhaps early afternoon...You can't spend all day in bed. I've plans, Wife."

"What kind of plans?"

"An adventure...a plan to spend the entire day with you, my darlin'. Rise and let's learn to play together." Mac kissed Laurel soundly and dragged her from the tall bed.

"All right, Mac. I am happy to go on an adventure with you where you can teach me to play. Go draw me some water, and I'll fix breakfast for you.

⊨⊨ ⊨⊨

Mac smiled as he left the cabin, singing his own version of *Annie Laurie*. Laurel stoked the fire in the hearth, put on Mac's morning coffee, prepared biscuits to bake and worked up the milk Mac brought in much earlier. She'd ask him to take the sweet milk and the cream to the springhouse before they began their "day of play." Even on days set aside for play there were chores to be completed. Laurel placed the bread she'd prepared into her hearth oven to bake and went back to the second pen to dress for the day.

First, she made up the tousled bed, feeling a slight blush come to her face when she recalled the night before. She covered the lace coverlet with the wedding ring quilt. She'd have to ask Mac about the lace coverlet. When she picked up Mac's pillow, she put it to her face. She could almost feel the warmth where Mac's head lay the night before, and she laughed aloud. Laurel was happy, more than at any other time in her life.

She picked out her gray muslin skirt and pink blouse for her 'first day' clothes. She thought back to the other 'first day' of her marriage when her papa became so ill. "Thank you, Papa, for making me do what was good for me. I do love Mac...I just want you to know."

"I am so happy to hear you say that. I love you, Wife, and Papa Campbell, I just want you to know."

"Oh, you!"

"I've the right to brag a little. I have finally met every promise I made to your father."

"Let's go eat breakfast. I think I can smell biscuits ready to take from the fire."

"I'm hungry, too. When we get finished, will you make us a picnic lunch? We will go exploring for the rest of the day."

"All right, but what are we going to explore?"

"Oh, our property, our pasts, our dreams, each other...We'll make a day of it." Laurel packed an ample lunch, as Mac asked her to do. They were off for the day. They rode away from the barnyard on Midnight and Sassy Lady. Laurel was happy to be riding again. Sassy, too, seemed happy to be out. She took to the path at a trot, prancing about and enjoying the freedom of the trail.

The day was a glorious late summer day. Because of the recent rains, the air was clean and clear. None of the crisp fall temperatures remained though. The day would be warm, and the warm southern breezes were making quick work of drying the wet, muddy paths. Travel would be easy that day.

"Laurel Grace, today we are going to visit our property. We'll make memories of our home. I want you to know all our land, and I know you'll love it as much as I do. We will talk and walk and laugh and rest and ride. Then we'll talk and ride and laugh some more. We have only two short days before we have to return to the world."

"You've given this time a lot of thought, haven't you?"

"I've thought of little else. During those four long days on the train from Baltimore to Memphis, I asked myself again and again, what would make our honeymoon perfect? The only thing I wanted to do was spend every minute with you. Of course, I thought we'd have an entire week, because I didn't know about the little side trip to Bolivar. I don't care about that now because even that time, since we've been together, has been good. In fact, it's all been so fine, I'd like to live it over and over."

"I am happy that you think our time together has been good, but if we only relived these two days again and again, we'd never be able to build new memories. I want to build a lifetime of happy memories with you."

Until mid-afternoon, as they rode together, Mac showed Laurel all he loved about his Shiloh homestead. He pointed out the valleys where he'd graze his future herds. As they rode along the banks of the two streams on their land, Mac explained how their abundant water supply would guarantee a bountiful harvest of whatever crop they decided to plant. He took her into the timbered areas of their acreage she'd never been to before. Mac told her that sometime in the future, their family may decide to harvest some of the hard-woods. This section of their land was ripe for lumbering.

"Laurel, we'll never be hungry here in this good land the Lord has given us." Mac led Laurel to the Southern parts of their land where he and his crew, John and Roy, built fences around a score or more of acres where he would raise cattle next spring. Through Mac's eyes, Laurel could see the vision of a future he wanted and why he loved this land. Opportunity lay everywhere they looked. By mid-afternoon, Mac turned back toward the glade near the creek where they'd swum before he'd gone back to Maryland. "You know, Laurel, this is the place I'd planned to build my cabin. I am glad you didn't let me destroy this natural sanctuary."

"I love this Eden too, Mac. Let's never let anything change this place. We have plenty of other land to work."

"That is an easy pledge to make. This place will always be our private sanctuary. We'll share it, you and me...maybe someday we'll let our children come here, too."

Mac stopped under several large trees, dismounted, and helped Laurel down from her mare and then he unsaddled both horses and tied them near water and good grazing. He took the blanket from the horse and placed it under the largest oak tree in the glade, in a well-shaded area. The afternoon sun made the day very warm, a perfect day for their outdoor adventure.

"This is a fine land, Patrick. All day you've been so excited when you talked of your plans. I'm sure this homestead will make a good living for us with our hard work."

"This is your doing, Laurel. It sickens me to think that back in February, I was about to give all this away."

"You would have changed your mind."

"No. I'd lost the dream. I've owned this land, well most of it, for more than four years. In all that time, I'd done nothing to build a home here. You gave me the reason to make these acres into a real working farm."

"You'd have done it eventually, but I'm glad I can be a part of all this."

"No, I don't believe I'd ever have wanted to stay without you, so I could build a family here at Shiloh. I've never before known anyone strong enough to do what you have done. I believe God destined you from the beginning to be my life mate. He meant us to be together, and I'm very grateful, Laurel. Thank you for walking out in faith with me."

They continued to eat their lunch and talk under the mighty oak in the center of their Eden. They shared stories of their childhood and youth. At a pause in the conversation, Mac looked up into Laurel's eyes. He began to speak in a low, almost despondent tone of voice. "Laurel, I've told you only about parts of my past. I was blessed to grow up in a happy secure home with two parents who doted on me. I never knew much about the hardships a lot of people grow up with. While Pa is not a wealthy man, we have always had ample worth. He educated me, raised me in the social circle of Baltimore society, and supplied my every need and most of my wants. Laurel, I'm trying to say we are not poor people. I can afford to give you a good home."

"You were indeed blessed to have both your parents. I missed my mother when she died so young. Her dying took a toll on my papa, too. He was never quite the same man after she passed."

"Her dying young had its toll on you, too, darlin'." Laurel nodded in response, knowing Mac had seen the shortcomings that had arisen from her not having had her mother's guidance during her youth. "Laurel, I've not told you much about my sordid past life. I didn't want you to know about the ugly wasted times of my twenties. Before I came to know grace, I was a much different person. I don't think you'd have liked that man very much."

"That is impossible to believe, Patrick. You've proven to be everything my papa told me you were. You are exactly the kind of spouse he wanted for me. When I said I'd marry you, I believed you asked me out of respect for a dying man and because of your friendship with my uncle. I never felt worthy of being your wife---even now I'm not sure I measure up, but I'll try. You are so much more than I ever dreamed ...too much above me."

"I know you have learned better now. I've seen you hold your own with everyone, especially me. Laurel, you know you have value. You know how much you mean to me. I want us to keep growing together. I want no secrets between us, so anything you want to know, just ask me, and I will answer truthfully."

"Mac, I don't need to know anything beyond what I have seen. You are a good man, and I am grateful you love me." Mac saw the honesty in her reply, and he kissed her.

"Regardless, I have three things I want to tell you, Laurel. Some of this is way past telling, but I want you to know."

"Very well, Patrick. I'll listen. Here, lie down and put your head in my lap. We've got all afternoon to share."

"First of all, Laurel...I owe you some over $300.00. I still get furious with myself when I remember how I went to Maryland and didn't give you one cent to cover costs at the homestead."

"Mac..."

"No arguments. I am going to repay every last cent. The cost of the freight, wages for the boys, taxes, the widow's property, and just daily living costs…What a fool I was! You worked miracles here for me the whole two months I was away, and you did it spending your money…And you didn't think I was coming home. It's beyond belief."

Mac took a small pouch from his coat pocket and placed it in Laurel's hand. "Laurel, this money went with me to Maryland and back. That morning when you told me you loved me, well, it took me by surprise, to say the least. As often as I'd told you I'd never let myself fall in love again, courageously you spoke the truth to me. Frankly, for twenty-four hours, that was the only thing I thought about. I didn't find that money bag I meant to give you until I got all the way to Hopefield. Of course, then I realize I failed to give you a single cent to care for the homestead or yourself. I won't be in debt to you…not for money."

"I was well taken care of… I didn't go hungry, not one meal was missed, but I thank you for returning Papa's dowry. I'm sure I won't need it, though, for you've taken fine care of me since we met."

"And I plan to take care of you for scores of years to come. I have to tell you about the first moment I knew I loved you. We were together when we shared your telling me that July morning, but you were nearly one thousand miles from me when I first realized I love you."

He stopped the story telling for a few moments. Laurel knew he was choosing the words he would use, so she remained silent. "I rode over to talk with Marsha Golden. I was compelled to confront her about my friend, Lewis Rawlins's death. Even when I knew I felt nothing for her, I couldn't let go of the guilt about the duel. Lewis and I were good friends, especially after my brother went off to fight in the Mexican war. I couldn't understand why he'd pushed me into that duel."

"Those must have been times of great sadness for you, Patrick."

"Yes, those few weeks and the seven-year trip through hell I spent roaming the country in Kentucky and Tennessee. Those are the years I was my worst, Laurel. That man is the Mac I hope you never meet."

"That man died at the cross, Mac. You told me that story already."

"Thank the Lord! Anyway, I got into a heated argument with Marsha. She asked me to take her back. She said she'd be a good wife for me. I told her I was blessed with the good wife I wanted. Like a bolt of lightning, the truth of what I said lit my whole being. At that moment, I knew I loved you and that you are the best part of me."

Laurel lowered her head as Mac's words touched her heart. She could not hold back the tears. He tilted her head up to meet his eyes. "You cast a spell on me that first day we met when you told me off there in the apple orchard. Do you remember that afternoon, Laurel?"

"I remember I wasn't very nice to you, I'm afraid. You scared me, so the only defense I knew was to hide behind my wall of meanness. I've done it all my life."

"I want us to make sure that wall never comes between us again. Knowing you and really talking with you as we've done since I found you in Bolivar only makes me love you more."

Mac was silent for a time. Laurel too found herself at a loss for what to say. Finally, Mac spoke. "Let's go for a swim. It's warm, and I doubt there'll be many more perfect swimming days. Fall will set in before we know."

"Sounds like a wonderful plan." Laurel agreed.

They shed their outer clothes and ran into the cool creek water. For over an hour, they played as two children, swimming, splashing, and dunking each other in the water. They swam down to the bend in the creek in an impromptu race.

Mac caught up with Laurel and pulled her into his arms. "Do you remember when we did this the first time back in late June?"

"I remember you pulled me into the water with my clothes on. I'd have drowned if you'd let me go with all those wet petticoats yanking me down."

"Don't you like swimming this way much better? Anyway, I never intended to let you go."

"I remember you pushed me away, and we got into a spat that afternoon."

"We did that more than once. Every time I let myself get too close to you, when I let my wall down, I found myself too attracted to you. Oh well, I pray those days are gone. Next time I want you, I'll just do this." Mac kissed Laurel again and again, with all abandon, and Laurel responded in kind.

"Let's get out of this water. With the sun going down, it's gotten too cool." They returned to the blanket under the tree. They sat for a while to dry their wet clothes. Laurel leaned against the ancient oak, and Mac lay with his head in her lap once again. In a short time, Mac fell asleep. Laurel sat, holding him. She looked around the beautiful meadow she had named Eden. She was content at that moment. How could she ever be happier? Silent tears of joy streamed down her cheeks as she looked at the sleeping face of Patrick MacLayne, a man so good, so faithful, a God-fearing man who loved her. One of the tears fell onto Mac's cheek and he woke…

"Laurel, what's wrong? Why the tears?"

"I am sorry. I didn't mean to wake you. I was just looking at you, sleeping here, both of us together in our perfect Eden. Joy overwhelmed me."

"Are you sure that's all?"

"Oh, yes, darlin'. I'm beyond happy." Laurel paused for a short time… "Have I made you happy?"

"How can you even ask? You've given me everything I've ever wanted."

"Did I please you…when we made love last night…were you disappointed with my awkward…. Oh, never mind."

Mac turned her to face him and looked deeply into her eyes. "Do you remember I would not let you talk to me afterwards?"

"I guess I was worried...I didn't know what you were thinking."

"That was the third thing I wanted to tell you today. Laurel, I was overwhelmed by your response to me. I told you that I am no stranger to women. I could not come to you as you came to me. With my past, I could hardly believe I'd have a bride like you who wanted me to teach her to be my lover. Laurel, I've taken more women than I want to remember, but I've only made love with you. I've never known the pleasure of a union between a man and a woman who love each other until last night. I had no words I could share with you."

"Then I am happy. I just wanted to know you weren't disappointed with me."

"I am happy. I have never been so happy. And Laurel, we'll learn to give each other even more pleasure. How many men have a mate honest and open enough to talk about her love life? Laurel, you are a wonder."

Mac pulled Laurel into his arms and kissed her with such urgency. "Laurel, I want to make love to you here in Eden." For a moment, Laurel was hesitant, but only briefly. Two images came to her mind. What a priceless memory she'd have...loving the man she belonged to here in their perfect Eden. She would carry that memory to her grave. Secondly, she wanted to celebrate her love for Mac. The picture of a perfect love, like the image of Adam and Eve in their innocence in the Garden of Eden, washed over her. She wanted that experience.

"Mac, I am your wife. You love me beyond any hope I'd ever had. Love me here in our Eden."

Later, as they lay quietly in each other's arms, Mac noticed the sky was now lit with the full moon and innumerable stars. The cool breeze blew across the meadow, and it was not entirely comfortable. Mac pulled Laurel closer. "Are you warm enough, Laurel?"

"I am now."

Shortly he spoke again, in a quiet, tender way. "Do you want to have a family soon, Laurel?"

"As soon as the Lord allows, I want a baby to complete your dream of home and family."

"That would be only more icing on a cake, Laurel Grace. You have already made this land our home, just because we are together." For a time, the MacLaynes were again lost to the world as they shared in each other's embrace. "As much as I hate to end this day, we'd better go back to the cabin. I guess we can't live in Eden always, but I promise we will visit here…often."

The two following days proved to be as memorable as their adventure day. On Thursday, they'd played all day. On Friday and Saturday, they worked, from early in the morning 'til the sun set each night. Because they were together, the work could have been play as much as they knew. They laid out the three outbuildings Mac needed to finish on their homestead, they cared for their animals, and they laid out beds for plantings around their cabin they would use in the spring. In the nights, they continued to build bonds between them, exploring their lives as one. Laurel reveled in Mac's lovemaking, learning that she enjoyed giving as well as receiving pleasure.

Saturday night marked the end of the private time Mac set aside for their honeymoon. They closed the day in their cane-bottom rocking chairs on their front porch. Talk, which once brought tension and arguments, now seemed natural to them both. Mac reached across the short span and took Laurel's hand.

"Laurel, you know we have to go back to the real world tomorrow. I wish we could take more time."

"The time we've taken was blessed. I'll not complain, but if we were sure the rest of our lives would be as perfect, I'd not complain about that either."

"Heaven doesn't happen in this lifetime, Wife. I am certain we'll have trials to face, problems to solve, and disagreements to overcome. Life happens to everyone."

"Strangely, that doesn't scare me anymore. I know we'll face whatever comes our way, and with God's help, we'll come out on the other side stronger and happier."

Mac turned to look into her face. He dared to ask, "Are all your demons gone, Laurel? You haven't awakened with a nightmare since I found you in Bolivar."

"I don't know, Mac…. When you are here with me, I feel safe, and whatever brings those nightmares loses its power to frighten me. Maybe someday, I'll know all the reasons, but for now, I'll rest safely in your arms."

"That's a promise I'll hold you to. I have such fine plans for our life together. Laurel, my dearest life mate, I have such dreams and hopes for this land. Arkansas holds promise and opportunity for us, and anyone who will work hard and give her the direction and respect she deserves. Look at what we've done in only six short months. Someday, maybe not in our lifetime, but someday this good land will be home to thousands of people who were willing to build their hopes and prosperity on the promise of Shiloh."

Mac continued to talk of bringing a herd in the spring and of his desire to serve their community in the state legislature. He shared his plans to add to their holdings and perhaps to bring other families to share their abundance. He told her that he wanted his father to come from Maryland to live near them in Shiloh. "I knew my grandfather, and I want that for our children, too. Pa won't miss my mother quite as much if he has grandchildren to care for and share all his stories with." He became quiet for a time, and then Laurel saw the faint light of the lantern reflected in Mac's storm blue eyes.

"And Laurel, I want a child… soon."

Laurel listened, smiling all the while her husband laid out his heart to her. She knew she'd been blessed beyond measure. The dream she'd given up so many years ago in Hawthorn was now the life she saw in front of her. Shiloh was no longer a dream. Shiloh was home.